W9-AVM-263

THE WINDFALL

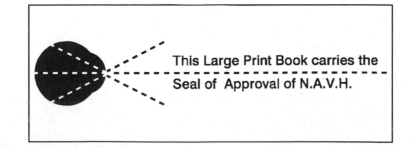

This Large Print Book carries the
Seal of Approval of N.A.V.H.

THE WINDFALL

DIKSHA BASU

THORNDIKE PRESS
A part of Gale, a Cengage Company

Farmington Hills, Mich • San Francisco • New York • Waterville, Maine
Meriden, Conn • Mason, Ohio • Chicago

Copyright © 2017 by Diksha Basu.
Thorndike Press, a part of Gale, a Cengage Company.

ALL RIGHTS RESERVED
Thorndike Press® Large Print Peer Picks.
The text of this Large Print edition is unabridged.
Other aspects of the book may vary from the original edition.
Set in 16 pt. Plantin.

LIBRARY OF CONGRESS CIP DATA ON FILE.
CATALOGUING IN PUBLICATION FOR THIS BOOK
IS AVAILABLE FROM THE LIBRARY OF CONGRESS

ISBN-13: 978-1-4328-5107-1 (hardcover)

Published in 2018 by arrangement with Crown, an imprint of Crown Publishing Group, a division of Penguin Random Publishing Group, LLC

Printed in the United States of America
1 2 3 4 5 6 7 22 21 20 19 18

FOR MY PARENTS
AND THEIR PARENTS

ONE

Mr. Jha had worked hard and he was ready to live well.

"Seeing that all of you are here, we have some news," he said to the neighbors assembled in the small living room of his home in the Mayur Palli Housing Complex in East Delhi. He was nervous, so he looked over at his wife, who was standing in the doorway of the kitchen, and his son, Rupak, who was at home for the summer vacation, sitting on a dining table chair. His wife met his gaze and nodded gently, expectantly, encouraging him to hurry up and share the news. And he knew he had to, before the gossip spread through the housing complex. Tonight they had invited their closest friends — Mr. and Mrs. Gupta, Mr. and Mrs. Patnaik, and Mrs. Ray — to tell them that after about twenty-five years (they had moved in when Mrs. Jha was eight months pregnant) they were moving out, and not just moving out, but moving to Gurgaon, one of the richest new neighborhoods of Delhi.

It would have been easier, in a way, to announce a move to Dubai or Singapore or Hong Kong. Mr. Jha himself had often been part of conversations that criticized families for moving to different Delhi neighborhoods the minute they could afford to. And certainly nobody of his generation had moved out in recent years. He was fifty-two years old, his wife was forty-nine, and their twenty-three-year-old son was in business school in America. The move was going to be seen as an unnecessary display of his newly acquired wealth. And since the money had come from the onetime sale of a website, everyone in Mayur Palli treated it with suspicion. Nobody believed it was hard-earned money. "A lucky windfall," he had heard Mr. Gupta call it. But Mr. Jha knew that it had been anything but luck; it had been hard work.

If an outsider, a stranger, were to see them all gathered here, would he see that Mr. Jha was different, Mr. Jha wondered? He was five foot eight and was neither impressively fit nor impressively fat. The fact that he didn't have the traditional trappings of success worried him these days. He liked fitting in.

The new house in Gurgaon was a two-story bungalow with front and back yards, and they knew nothing at all about the neighbors yet. The house was tucked into a quiet lane away from the traffic and chaos of the rest of Delhi. Unlike in other parts of the city, all the drains were properly sealed and the streets were swept and cleaned on a regular basis. Big, decades-old neem trees lined both sides of their lane, and it was the kind of quiet that made it a place that hawkers and beggars avoided.

It was a much more lavish home and neighborhood than Mr. Jha had ever imagined himself living in. Not only did the doors fit in their frames, but most of the light switches had dimmers. There was a separate servants' quarter at the back, and a wall went around the periphery so nobody could look in or out. Unlike Mayur Palli, and the rest of East Delhi for that matter, the houses in Gurgaon were spaced grandly apart and interactions between the neighbors seemed minimal. Mr. Jha knew he was supposed to want that — that was how rich people's tastes were supposed to be.

Above his head a fat fly thumped repeatedly against the tubelight. The new house had better screens in the windows to stop flies and mosquitoes from invading. Mr. Jha took off his rimless glasses and wiped them with the white handkerchief he always kept in his shirt pocket. He wished he had opted for a short-sleeved shirt today instead of the long-sleeved blue one he had neatly tucked into his khaki slacks.

The Jhas were one of the original residents of Mayur Palli when they moved there in 1991. Mayur Palli meant, literally, the home of the peacock, but Mr. Jha had never seen a peacock anywhere near the area. Four buildings, each five floors high, were built around a dusty courtyard small enough for everyone to be able to peer into their neighbors' windows. Every morning, wet laundry hung from ropes on the balconies, water dripping down to the courtyard. Downstairs, what had once been a space for the children to run and play and ride bicycles was now a clogged parking lot. A parking lot filled with scooters and Marutis and maybe the occasional Honda, bought for aging parents as a gift by adult children living abroad.

But now, on top of the fact that the Jhas were moving, the Mercedes Mr. Jha had ordered had arrived early and, embarrassingly, he had to take possession of it here in the old housing complex. He hadn't wanted the car delivery person to see his current home, or his current neighbors to see his new car. What must the delivery person have thought driving it across the bridge to the wrong side of the Yamuna River? The silver car was big and shiny and completely out of place in the middle-class neighborhood and was nearly impossible to navigate past the cows in the narrow lanes. And clearly the car was annoying others. Just the previous morning, the undersides of the door handles had been covered with toothpaste and Mr. Jha had had a very minty-smelling morning drive. He was grateful it was only toothpaste.

Sometimes Mr. Jha himself couldn't believe how much money his site had made. It had been such an easy idea — www.simply-call.com — that began as an online resource for local Delhi phone numbers and services. Mr. Jha had been trying to call his old friend Partha Sen in Chittaranjan Park to reminisce about their college days but had accidentally called a Partho Sen from the directory. He had chatted with the unknown Partho Sen for a good four minutes before either of them realized it was a wrong number.

Despite others' perception, this was no lucky windfall, Mr. Jha now reminded himself. He had sold the website a little over two years ago, after working on it for five years. And before that he had had several more complicated ventures that had failed completely. But all that was in the past. This was now and he had to break the news.

"You've found a bride for Rupak?" Mr. Gupta said before Mr. Jha could continue. He was leaning back on the sofa and holding a fistful of peanuts in one hand and a glass of whiskey with ice in the other. He wore a crisp white kurta and pajama, his uniform of choice ever since he had become the president of the housing complex, and his feet were bare and resting on top of his sandals. "Is she also living in America? Don't let her family talk you into having a wedding in America."

As the current president of the housing complex, and one of the biggest gossips in the neighborhood, Mr. Gupta was the one who was going to take the news the hardest. He would see the move from Mayur Palli as a betrayal. The Patnaiks, who were a few years younger than the Jhas and were quieter versions of the Guptas, would probably try to move on the Jhas' heels. Mr. Patnaik already dressed similarly to Mr. Jha and had recently bought the exact same pair of glasses but then claimed it was a co-incidence. And if anyone asked Mr. Jha to describe Mrs. Patnaik without looking at her, all he would be able to say was that she had strangely curly hair but no other discernible features.

"That is true," Mrs. Gupta added. She was also eating peanuts, one of which had fallen and was cradled on her glasses, which were hanging off a metal chain around her neck. She wiped her hand against her sari and leaned forward to pick up her glass. "Our nephew got married there and all the Indian weddings end up in the huge halls of the local Hilton or Marriott. You make sure the wedding is in India, in a temple."

"Or outdoors," Mr. Gupta said. "Lots of young people these days want to get married outdoors."

"Personally I don't think that is a good idea. You don't want the flame of the fire to be blown out during the ceremony," Mrs. Gupta said.

"The flame will go out soon enough after marriage," Mr. Gupta said, laughing loudly and tossing the remaining peanuts into his mouth.

"That's not the news," Mr. Jha said.

"Rupak will find a good bride here," Mr. Patnaik said.

His wife nodded and added, "He will. It's best to find someone known. Someone close to the family."

She turned toward Rupak and smiled, but his attention was focused on his phone. Everyone in Mayur Palli knew that the Patnaiks wanted Rupak to marry their daughter, Urmila.

"No," Mr. Jha said. "This isn't about . . ."

"Oh dear. Is Rupak marrying an American girl?" Mrs. Gupta interrupted, twisting around on the sofa to try to look at Rupak.

"This isn't about Rupak," Mr. Jha said. "We have some other news. About us."

He stopped as Reema Ray entered his line of vision, settling into the seat across from him with a glass of white wine. He knew his wife had already told Mrs. Ray about the move but had still insisted on inviting her tonight for support. Mrs. Ray was leaning forward and fixing a strap on her sandal, and the pallu of her chiffon sari slipped off her shoulder. Her blouse was sufficiently low cut for the tops of her heavy breasts to be visible. Her hair, worn loose and messily around her shoulders — unlike any of the other women in the room — fell in front of her and she tossed it back as she leaned forward.

Mr. Jha looked toward Mrs. Jha, still standing near the entrance to the kitchen, wearing a stiff starched pale blue sari that

14

was held up on the shoulder by a safety pin and her hair pulled securely back in a low bun. He knew that his wife would never run the risk of letting her pallu casually drop. And even if it did, her blouse came up to her collarbones so nothing would be visible. And even if anything were visible, Mr. Jha would feel no thrill. Such was the problem with a stable marriage.

Mrs. Ray was sitting upright again, so Mr. Jha continued, "We wanted to invite all of you, our close friends, to dinner tonight, to tell you about our home. Our new home. Our —"

Mrs. Jha sniffed the air. "Oh no. Oh no, oh no, oh no. I've left the stove on. The chicken will be burnt."

She went rushing into the kitchen, irritated with herself. The stress of moving to Gurgaon was really getting to her. She wasn't sure she wanted to leave Mayur Palli. She didn't want to live surrounded by women in designer saris who shopped in malls. She didn't want to use olive oil instead of vegetable oil. She didn't want to understand what interior decoration meant. The point of life was not just to keep moving higher and higher. What happened if you made it to Buckingham Palace?

"Are you okay? Do you need some help in

here?" Mrs. Ray came in after Mrs. Jha. "Your husband has started on what the idea of 'home' represents. He's having a hard time making this announcement, isn't he?"

"The chicken is burnt. Oh, Reema. The chicken is burnt. And the packing isn't finished. I know I should be happy, but I'm exhausted. I don't know why we decided to do this whole move in the middle of summer. The heat is just getting to me."

"Where are your maids? Do you want me to send Ganga over every morning until you leave? She hardly has anything to do for just me these days."

"That's very nice of you, but we still have our maids. But Anil has decided he doesn't want them at home all the time."

Mrs. Jha stirred the pan, scraping the wooden spoon along the bottom, trying to pry free the burnt bits of chicken. The screw holding the red handle in place was coming loose and she still had not ordered new kitchen supplies. This kitchen was made for maids to use; it was small and badly ventilated, and being in here meant being completely separated from the rest of the people in the apartment. The new house had a huge kitchen where a few people could stand around while the host prepared dinner or put together a platter of appetizers.

That kitchen, in fact, was specifically meant for nonmaids. It was a kitchen that was meant to be shown off. It was a kitchen that needed new pots and pans with secure handles.

"Why doesn't he want maids?" Mrs. Ray asked.

"We got this dishwasher installed and Anil wants people to notice it. He's convinced that if there's a maid picking up all the dishes, everyone will just assume she's washing them by hand and won't know that we have an expensive imported dishwasher. I don't know. I don't understand half the things he wants these days," Mrs. Jha said. The kitchen was small and stuffy, but she appreciated Mrs. Ray coming in here with her. On the next stove, the pressure cooker hissed and Mrs. Jha jerked away from its angry sound. Mrs. Ray came to the stove and turned it off.

"Move," Mrs. Ray said. "You relax. Take the raita out of the fridge. I'll handle the stove. You didn't need to invite us all over in the middle of your packing."

Mrs. Jha stepped away and opened the fridge. She could feel the sweat gathering under her arms. She leaned down and allowed the refrigerated air to slip down the front of her blouse. She was gaining weight.

She looked over at Mrs. Ray, who seemed to become younger and more beautiful every day. Granted, at forty-two, Mrs. Ray was seven years younger than Mrs. Jha, but her glow wasn't just about age. She looked younger now than she did when Mr. Ray had died five years ago. Mrs. Ray had been only thirty-seven when her husband died, and at first widowhood had forced her to immediately become older. But Mrs. Jha had noticed Mrs. Ray gradually reversing that trend, and now she looked over at her friend with happiness and a sudden stab of envy. Even her hair seemed to have become thicker.

"Your hair is looking good these days." Mrs. Jha said, and shut the fridge. "Are you using some new hair oil?"

Mrs. Ray turned around from the stove, wiped her hands on the towel that was on the counter, and touched her right hand to her hair.

"It's improved, hasn't it?"

"Share your secret, Reema."

"The usual," Mrs. Ray said. "Lots of leafy green vegetables and coconut oil in the hair overnight once a week."

"We've been doing that for years. It must be something else," Mrs. Jha said.

Mrs. Ray laughed a little and turned back

to the stove to open the pressure cooker.

"What is it?" Mrs. Jha asked. "What secret are you keeping from me?"

Mrs. Ray faced Mrs. Jha.

"Oh, Bindu, it's ridiculous. Prenatal supplements! I'm taking prenatal supplements because I read that it helps the hair, and it's true — my hair has never looked better! Every alternate day I take one pill," Mrs. Ray said. "I feel so crazy when I go to the chemist to buy it; I make up some excuse or the other each time, as if I'm buying it for my niece or for a friend or something. Imagine a childless widow getting prenatal vitamins."

Mrs. Ray spooned the daal into a glass bowl for serving. She shook her hair out and looked over her shoulder at Mrs. Jha, laughed, and said, "Prenatal vitamins for widows! Don't tell anyone."

In a way, being widowed young and childless allowed Mrs. Ray to have a second youth, one unencumbered by family. And as far as young deaths go, Mr. Ray's quick and powerful brain aneurysm five years ago at age forty was as simple as possible. At least he didn't suffer and Mrs. Ray didn't have to deal with the guilt in the aftermath of a loved one's suffering. Mrs. Jha knew it had been difficult for Mrs. Ray — young

19

widows make people nervous. When Mr. Ray died, a lot of the other women in Mayur Palli treated Mrs. Ray like a bad-luck charm or a seductress — but Mrs. Jha looked over at her friend now and saw only vitality and a good head of hair. She immediately felt guilty for envying a widow. *May God always keep my husband safe,* she quickly said to herself.

"Do you know what I had to do this afternoon? I had to unpack all the decorations for the drawing room and put them back up so the guests wouldn't guess as soon as they walked in," Mrs. Jha said.

She took out the bowl of chilled yogurt mixed with onions, cucumbers, tomatoes, and spices, pushed the fridge door closed with her hip, leaned against it, and sighed. Mrs. Ray was now ladling the chicken into a large glass serving bowl, and she laughed.

"You're living the dream, Bindu," Mrs. Ray said. "In any case, you should be glad you're getting out of here. This housing complex is not the same as it used to be."

Mrs. Ray reached over for a napkin to wipe the curry off the rim of the bowl. She turned off the second flame on the stove and said, "Someone stole a pair of my yoga pants from my balcony."

"What?" Mrs. Jha said. "Are you sure?"

"One hundred percent," Mrs. Ray said. "Anyway, it's silly. I didn't even want to mention it, but be glad you're moving. Everybody here interferes too much in each other's lives. You are lucky to be going somewhere where you will have some privacy. Count your blessings."

"Reema, you have to complain about this at the next meeting," Mrs. Jha said.

"And what? Draw more attention to myself? Forget it. It's my fault. I shouldn't be doing yoga on the balcony." Mrs. Ray said. She turned back to the counter and put a large spoon in each serving bowl. "Here, the chicken and the daal are in the bowls. I'll take them out to the dining room. Do you need anything else?"

Mrs. Jha turned to Mrs. Ray and said, "Thank you. Just send my husband in here, please."

Mrs. Jha picked up the pan from the stove and dropped it in the sink. Water splashed out and wet her sari, darkening the blue fabric near her bellybutton.

Mr. Jha came into the kitchen. It was smoky and felt as though the loud exhaust fan above the window was pushing hot air back into the kitchen. It would be nice for his wife to have a new kitchen with a door leading out to the backyard instead of this

21

small space that was the same size as one of the bathrooms in the new house. All the surfaces had become sticky with years of oil splatter. Mr. Jha wanted one of those kitchens he had seen in television cooking shows — all stainless steel with pots and pans hanging off hooks above the stoves. Even though he never cooked and hardly even entered the kitchen, he wanted the spices kept in clear glass bottles in a wooden holder hammered into the wall. He was sick of the salt and sugar being browned by fingertips and clumpy through humidity.

"I think they're ready for the news now," Mr. Jha said. "I tried to get them started on the idea of 'home.' Said it isn't defined by location. I made some quite moving points, I think. I talked about home being where the heart is and all that. No need to mention that home is where the double servants' quarter is."

He paused, then continued, "What are you doing in here? I was just about to announce our plans when you rushed off screaming about the chicken. Would you prefer it if I called people in here? The Guptas have definitely not been over since we got the new dishwasher."

"I am not screaming about anything. I'm just trying to serve our guests a decent dinner. If you had let the maid stay, I would have had the help I needed. I have been spending all day every day packing boxes, going back and forth from Gurgaon in the heat, setting up the water filters, dealing with the air-conditioning installation —"

"It's your fault that you're going back and forth in the heat. I've told you a thousand times to take the car. You act as if you're scared of the car. The car, the new house, a washing machine, everything. Everything, Bindu. You think the new dishwasher will ruin the serrated knives — you're scared of everything."

Rupak entered the kitchen.

"What are you two doing? The guests are getting restless. And, Dad, Reema Aunty wants some more wine. Should I take out another bottle of white from the fridge?"

"Don't call him Dad!" Mrs. Jha said as Mr. Jha returned to the living room. "What's wrong with calling him Papa? You're studying in America, but you aren't an American."

Mrs. Jha didn't want Rupak turning into one of those typical rich kids who assume they'll never have to work hard. For that, she was grateful that they had lived very average lives until recently. But Rupak was changing fast. As soon as they were settled into their new home, it would be time for them to go to the United States to see how he lived.

Rupak ignored his mother and rummaged in the fridge for the wine. His parents had gone from keeping no alcohol at home, to keeping some Kingfisher beer and Old Monk rum, to keeping bottles of white wine that was made in vineyards outside Mumbai, to keeping imported bottles of red and white wine from countries as far as Chile. Rupak closed the fridge and opened the freezer to take an ice tray. It was next to a frosted bottle of Absolut vodka that still had the plastic seal around the neck. So much had changed at home since he had left for the States.

Once the food had been brought to the dining room and the guests had sat down and begun to serve themselves, Mrs. Jha whispered to her husband, "Will you please tell them? Stop avoiding it. I can't organize one more dinner like this."

Across the table, while taking from big bowls of food, Mr. Gupta said quietly to his wife, "I think you've got enough chicken. Leave some for the others. It looks bad."

"The chicken is half burnt. I am doing Mrs. Jha a favor by eating so much of it,"

Mrs. Gupta whispered back, peering into the other bowls to see what else had been cooked. "Otherwise it will all be left and she will have to give it to the maids and she'll be embarrassed. I'm being kind."

"Would you like another drink?" Rupak asked Mrs. Ray on the other side of the table.

Ever since he had gone to America, Rupak had decided he would never date an Indian woman again, but seeing beautiful Mrs. Ray made him aware that there were exceptions to every rule. But Mrs. Ray wasn't that old, he reminded himself. He knew that she was friends with this group only because she had never had children, so now she had more in common with the older women whose children had left home. And glancing to his right and seeing Mrs. Gupta trying to pry a piece of burnt chicken out from her teeth reminded him of the rules.

"Rupak," Mr. Gupta said. "Bring me another whiskey and come and tell me more about America. My wife's niece also studies in America. Sudha, where does that girl study?"

"I can never remember," Mrs. Gupta said. "Perhaps New York? I will find out."

Mr. Gupta wobbled his head and said to

Rupak, "Maybe you know her. We will find out where she is studying."

"I doubt it," Rupak said. He was always amazed by how small some people in Mayur Palli thought America was.

"Urmila is planning a trip to America next year," Mr. Patnaik added. "She should add Ithaca to her list of places to visit."

"You must meet lots of pretty women there," Mr. Gupta continued. "White skin, white hair — those girls are like cotton balls. Do you have a girlfriend?"

"Do it," on the other side of the table Mrs. Jha whispered to her husband. "Tell them now, otherwise I will. You've done well, you've bought a new house — I don't know why you're so ashamed."

"A girlfriend?" Rupak said. Here was his chance to tell them. His parents would have to react calmly to the news of his American girlfriend if all the neighbors were watching. "Well, you know in the U.S. . . ."

"He doesn't have time for girlfriends while he is studying. A wife will come later. He's just like his father. They both want to do well in life," Mrs. Jha said. "Such ambitious men I'm surrounded by. In fact, that's why we called all of you here tonight."

"So that is all," Mr. Jha said. "Nothing too

big to discuss. We are not selling this apartment. We are simply renting it out for now. We have found a lovely young couple from Chennai who are going to move in. They have a young son also. Very decent people. And next time we will have dinner in Gurgaon. Enough about us. Why don't we have some more food?"

"Wait," Mr. Gupta said. "This new house you've bought — is it through the Meritech company? I heard they got in trouble with the government about bribes. Did they accept the full amount in check?"

Mr. Gupta was certain that Mr. Jha was a tax evader. All these new-moneyed people were the same. People acted as though engineers were honest, simple-minded people, but look at Mr. Jha here — he was obviously making lots of money now and had probably paid for his house with mostly black money. But Mr. Gupta knew that just because he himself had been a police officer, the assumption was that he was corrupt. It was unfair. He had never taken a bribe over five thousand rupees. A lot of other policemen had worked their way up financially and drove fancy Hondas and Toyotas, but Mr. Gupta had simply upgraded from a scooter to a Maruti 800 to a Swift. He had been content with his life in

East Delhi. He knew many young couples who used it as a stepping-stone to fancier neighborhoods, but people of his generation stayed put. They no longer got their walls painted after every monsoon, and they no longer complained about the regular electricity outages. Their lives, he thought, had fallen into a nice comforting rhythm. They didn't need to impress their spouses or their neighbors. But now here was Mr. Jha announcing their move to Gurgaon while his pretty wife looked on proudly. Their son was visiting from the United States of America and probably had a white girlfriend by now. Mr. Gupta looked over at his own wife, who was heaping her plate with another helping of chicken curry. Their daughter, married to a chartered accountant and also living in East Delhi, was turning into her mother far too quickly, and Mr. Gupta knew he would never have the luxury of objecting to a white boyfriend.

"I really prefer not to talk about finances like this," Mr. Jha said. "Especially not in front of the ladies. But, you know, India is changing. International business comes with different standards."

Mr. Jha had in fact paid more than the usual amount with taxable money. It had raised the cost of the house considerably,

28

but ever since he sold to a company based in America, he knew that the government was keeping an eye on him.

Mr. Gupta shook his head as he used his thumb to push another bite of chicken and rice into his mouth. These people would never give a straight answer about taxes.

TWO

Mrs. Jha switched off the light in the hallway and walked toward her bedroom door. It was hot in the hallway, the Delhi summer in full swing. There was an air conditioner in each room, jutting out of a window, but they never kept all three of them running at the same time. The electrical circuit would not be able to handle the load. Instead, they cooled only the rooms they were using. The kitchen, the bathrooms, and the hallway remained hot. When they first got an air conditioner installed, it was only in the master bedroom and Rupak would drag a thin mattress in and sleep on their floor.

Mrs. Jha stopped in front of Rupak's bedroom. The air from inside his room trickled out from under the closed door and cooled her feet. She considered knocking, but she thought she heard a muffled voice. Either he was watching something on his laptop or he was on the phone, and she no longer felt comfortable letting herself into his bedroom to have a chat. She pushed her ear against the door, but the white noise of the air conditioner made it impossible to make sense of the voices. That was okay, she didn't need to interfere, she told herself. She just liked knowing he was home and she liked feeling his presence. As much as she swore she never had a preference regarding the sex of her child, she was glad she had a son. A son who, despite quickly adopting some Americanisms she didn't much care for, was soon going to have a master's in business administration from Ithaca College in New York State. It really did give her a sense of security.

She continued to her bedroom and entered as her husband was coming out of the small attached bathroom. The warm smell of sandalwood soap and a hot bath filled the room.

"Did you turn off the geyser?" she asked.

Mr. Jha poked his head back in the bathroom to check the switch and nodded.

"The geysers in the new house are all automatic, which means we can leave them on twenty-four hours a day," Mr. Jha said. "That's twenty-four hours a day of not having to wait for hot water in the taps. In the sink too! Just imagine."

"I know," Mrs. Jha said. "I'm the one who got them all installed. But they say it's best to keep the switches off when they're not in use."

"You know in Korean apartments you can operate all your switches from your phone. Lights, gadgets, everything. You can even draw your curtains with a button on your phone. You can be on the way home and turn all the lights on so you don't have to enter a completely dark house."

"Couldn't you just leave a light on when you go out so it's still on when you come home?" Mrs. Jha asked.

Mr. Jha looked at her, thought for a second, and nodded. "That is another possibility."

A minute later he added, "You could turn the teakettle on so the water would be hot when you got home."

"That was a successful evening," Mrs. Jha said to her husband as he buttoned the top button of the white kurta he wore to sleep every night. For as long as she had known him, he had always worn the exact same outfit to bed. He owned four sets of kurta pajamas and he had asked her to stitch numbers onto each top and each bottom so they would remain sets and, even though they were all identical, he would never wear

32

a number two top with a number three pajama.

"That Mr. Gupta interferes too much," Mr. Jha said, rubbing a small towel through his hair.

"He was just being curious. Don't let it trouble you."

"I just think it's impolite — he wouldn't go asking other rich people how much they've paid in black money," Mr. Jha said.

"They're our friends, Anil. They can ask us such questions. Anyway, I thought you handled the question very gracefully. Now please forget it and come to bed. And don't rub your hair so roughly, it'll damage the roots."

"And why did he say we were too old for change? You heard him — he said at this stage to make a move like this was to become a small fish in a big pond and we'd understand that only after leaving the pond we know. I'm not a fish, Bindu. Is that any way to speak to a friend?"

"Those are his own issues. Forget it," Mrs. Jha said, although she hadn't been able to stop thinking about Mr. Gupta's comment either. How were they meant to start from scratch at this age? Why were they trying to start from scratch? They were happy. How was she supposed to make new friends and adapt to a new world? She was sitting on the edge of the bed rubbing Nivea cold cream into her cracked heels, trying not to let her husband see her concerns. Not tonight. It had been a difficult night for him.

"I read somewhere that fish have very basic nervous systems," Mr. Jha said. "I never get nervous. Except in airplanes, but that's understandable."

He stooped in front of the small mirror that was attached to the dresser in the corner of the room and combed his hair.

"I'm looking forward to having a full-length mirror in the bedroom," he said. "This is like looking into a phone camera, it's so small."

Let Mr. Gupta say what he wanted; he was going to get a full-length mirror in his bedroom. Mr. Jha thought about his mother. She always took such pride in how she dressed, but while she was alive, forget a full-length mirror, they did not even have a dresser. The only mirror she had to use was the small one that hung in the bathroom in a plastic frame above the sink and had become speckled with dried toothpaste over the years. Mr. Jha wished his mother had lived to see him become successful. She would have died a happier woman if she'd had any idea what her son would go on to achieve.

Mr. Jha's father had died when Mr. Jha was eight years old. Before he died, his father was doing well enough, climbing the ranks of an income tax office in the small, dusty, tier-three town of Giridih — which used to be in the state of Bihar but was now part of the new state of Jharkhand and was a town most people in Delhi hadn't even heard of. He wore black slacks and carried a briefcase every day. Once a week, they went out for dinner and Mr. Jha's mother would dress in the latest fashions of the town and push her feet into sandals with high heels and stiff straps that made her ankles bleed and she loved it.

But soon after his father died, Mr. Jha and his mother could no longer afford to live alone. They ran through Mr. Jha Senior's savings in a year, even without going out for dinner, and they had no option but to move from Bihar to the outskirts of New Delhi to move in with Mr. Jha's father's older brother and his wife. Even at that age, Mr. Jha always understood that they were an imposition, an addition. They didn't belong in Delhi. He never felt comfortable lingering in the bathroom, and he noticed that his mother always woke up when it was still dark outside so she could shower and use the bathroom before anyone else was awake. His mother taught him to take his dishes to the kitchen after every meal, wash them, and put them on the rusted metal rack that sat near the sink, even though a cleaning lady would come and wash all the other dishes later.

As a child, he often felt anger toward his mother for making them live their whole lives as guests. As he got older, he felt guilty about that anger and so he worked. He studied and he worked hard to make sure he could give his mother a home that would be her own, and a reason to wear uncomfortable shoes again. And he had mostly succeeded. He had a nice wife, a son, and a stable job that gave him a small but reliable income every month and a domestic holiday every year. For years Mr. Jha had been the manager of a franchise of a Technological Training of India (TTI) center and supplemented his income by teaching specialized computer programming classes there on Saturdays. His mother saw all that, but she died before he managed to give her a full-length mirror to check the pleats of her sari.

"How do you manage to tie your sari so well without a mirror?" Mr. Jha asked.

"When you do it every day, it becomes the same as pulling on a pair of pants," Mrs.

Jha said.

"But it'll be better for you to have a full-length mirror, right?"

"I suppose so, yes," Mrs. Jha said. She knew what was going through her husband's mind. "Are you thinking about Ma-ji?"

"She would have enjoyed tonight's dinner," Mr. Jha said. He sat down at the edge of the bed, tired after the evening and the adrenaline and the performance of hosting a dinner party. He took his glasses off and placed them on his side table. This bedroom was less than half the size of the master bedroom in Gurgaon. In here, there was room only for the bed, the attached wooden side tables, and two metal cupboards in which they kept all their clothes. One of the metal cupboards had a small built-in safe that was big enough to hold all their valuables. In Gurgaon, he had had a safe the size of one of their cupboards built into the wall of the master bedroom, and he was determined to own enough valuables to fill the whole thing. He rubbed his eyes. "She would have really enjoyed the new house. Forget traveling outside India, she died without even seeing the fancy side of Delhi."

"A lot of people do," Mrs. Jha said. "That's not something you need to feel guilty about. You gave her a very good life."

Mr. Jha pulled the sheet aside and got in under the covers. The Usha fan creaked overhead on every turn. Mrs. Jha reached across her pillow and placed her hand gently on his shoulder.

"It was a good night, Anil," she said.

Mr. Jha nodded.

"I'm glad Rupak was here," he added after a brief silence. "America is suiting him. Just imagine if he gets a job with a big multinational after finishing his MBA. I'll throw a party for the whole city when he gets a job — all our friends from here, and our new neighbors from Gurgaon."

"We must book our tickets," Mrs. Jha said. She had to go and see her son in America soon. She worried every day about how he survived on his own. He needed someone to take care of him while he studied. He had to do his own laundry, make his own food, even change his own bedsheets. She wanted him to come home after his degree so she could fuss over him for a little while. What was so bad about working in Delhi?

"Right after we are settled in, we will go," Mr. Jha said. "In business class, Bindu. We will lie flat on our backs while flying through the skies."

"Don't be crazy!" Mrs. Jha said. She gently slapped her husband's shoulder.

"Business class tickets are ten times the price of economy! For what? Hardly twenty hours. We're getting carried away."

Mrs. Jha laughed, turned off the small lamp near the bed, and pulled the white sheet up to her shoulders. She ran her large toe against her husband's ankle and said, "Good night."

Mr. Jha rested his hand against her thigh.

"Why are you whispering?" Elizabeth said on the phone.

"My parents are still awake," Rupak said, and regretted it immediately.

"And you haven't told them about me yet."

He had promised Elizabeth that he would tell his parents about her this summer, and now the summer was almost over and he had still not told them. He also had not told them that he was starting his second year on academic probation because of his shockingly low grade point average the previous semester. They would both be so disappointed. He knew how proud they were that he was studying in America and seemed poised on the brink of a bright future. He had decided it was best not to tell them; he would work to get his grades back up this semester and they would never have to know.

It was all his own fault, Rupak knew. He got to America soon after his parents became wealthy, and he immediately fell in love — not with Elizabeth, but with the whole country, and with the bank account that his father kept replenishing. He found himself falling into a version of what he thought life in America was meant to be. He signed up for sailing lessons on Cayuga Lake and golfing lessons at the Robert Trent Jones Golf Course. But he didn't end up going for the golf classes, and now a thousand-dollar golf club set sat unused in his apartment. He bought an iPhone and an iPad and a GoPro camera. He downloaded Final Cut Pro and spent his time filming his life in America and creating his own mini film versions of the shows and movies he had grown up watching.

His parents were under the impression that after his MBA, he would find a job with a big bank or consulting firm and then they would find him a suitable Bihari match. When Mr. and Mrs. Jha were introduced in 1989 through Mrs. Jha's uncle's friend who was the head of the Bihari Ladies' Club of East Delhi, Mr. Jha was finishing a master's in electrical engineering and Mrs. Jha had recently finished a bachelor's in social work and was working with a local organization to help collect and distribute free school supplies for slum children in the area. From what Rupak had heard, his parents had been allowed to meet alone once before they decided to get married. They were going to push for a contemporary equivalent for Rupak. He would be given at least a few months to get to know the woman and would technically have the right to refuse. Even though the word *dating* would never be used, they would be allowed to go out for dinners and movies alone and the final decision would be theirs to make, but Rupak wanted to do it his own way. However, he still had not managed to say anything to his parents, and he knew that was going to upset Elizabeth.

"What are you doing all day?" Rupak said to change the topic. She was spending the summer doing an internship in the finance department of Doctors Without Borders in New York, but he pictured her lying in her bedroom in Florida, her dog on the floor beside the bed. He sometimes thought he was more fascinated by her life in Florida than she was by his life in India.

"Working. And my mother's visiting so I'll take her out for dinner tonight. She says she wants sushi, but her idea of sushi is only shrimp tempura rolls," Elizabeth said. "How was your day?"

"Fine. Good. All my parents' friends were over for dinner just now. I grew up around these people but I feel so detached from them now. It's strange."

Rupak tried to picture Elizabeth being a part of tonight's dinner party. His parents would have no idea how to react to her and her snug jeans and T-shirts. They would all assume they knew everything about her based on what she looked like. She was about his height, and blond, and had visible collarbones, and Rupak himself found it difficult to see past her looks. She wore no jewelry and, as far as he could tell, hardly ever used makeup. She took her contacts out and wore glasses in the evening, before bed, but he preferred her in her contacts so he could look at her face uninterrupted. How would Mrs. Gupta talk to her, he wondered? How would he explain her to them and them to her?

His father, always aspiring, had sent Rupak to an elite private school in central Delhi, and the world of his rich classmates, the world his parents were about to have in Delhi, was so much simpler to explain in America. In his classmates' homes, in leafy lanes in central Delhi where it always felt five degrees cooler than it did in East Delhi and where cars honked much less often and you could hear brief stretches of actual silence, at four p.m., trolleys with cheese toast and slices of Black Forest cake from Khan Market and bottles of Coca-Cola would be wheeled into the air-conditioned room where the children played. In his home, maids grumpily offered oily samosas from the local market and glasses of pink, syrupy Rooh Afza. When he was young, they had no air conditioner, only a loud cooler that sat outside the main window in the living room and did little to actually cool down the apartment. Their television had no remote. His India was neither rich nor poor. There were no huge homes and elaborate weddings, nor were there slums and water shortages and child laborers. The middle ground was too confusing to explain to an outsider. It was neither exotic enough nor familiar enough.

"Hang on. My mom's calling for me," Elizabeth said. And then Rupak heard her shout out, "I'm leaving in half an hour. I'm on the phone with Rupak," and return to the phone and say, "My mom says hi."

"Hi," Rupak said.

"I miss you," Elizabeth said.

Rupak turned to his side and looked at

his bedside table. On the top right corner were the remnants of a sticker of the Indian cricket team from 1996. He had tried, over the years, to scratch it off, so you couldn't make out the faces of any of the players anymore but you could see the blue uniforms.

He couldn't help but think about what Mrs. Gupta had said tonight after his father told them about the move and after her husband was done trying to ask how much they had paid in black money. Mrs. Gupta, with a mouthful of chicken and rice, had simply said, "Why?"

Rupak had been wanting to ask his parents that himself, but he hadn't, and seeing them stumble to find an answer made him glad he hadn't asked. "Why not?" his father had said, and his mother had just gotten up and started taking dishes back to the kitchen.

"Escaping the minute you can?" Mr. Gupta had said with a laugh.

"Hardly," Mrs. Jha had said from near the kitchen entrance. "This will always also be home. We raised our family here."

"But it will no longer be your home," Mr. Gupta had said, and Mrs. Jha had ignored him and walked into the kitchen.

And he was right, Rupak thought. This was no longer going to be home.

"It's nice being home with my parents," he said to Elizabeth. "Of course, I miss you too, though."

"Tell them to come visit soon," Elizabeth said. "Or I'll come to India with you next time."

Rupak scratched at the sticker of the cricket team again. A few small pieces came off under his fingernail, but the rest remained stubborn. He gave up and fell back against his pillow. Even though he was twenty-three, when he was at home with his parents, he immediately returned to feeling like he was fourteen. For the last two weeks, his mother had been reminding him every morning to pack up his room so everything could be moved to Gurgaon, and Rupak still hadn't because he didn't quite believe that they were actually moving homes. Had the money come just five years ago, he would have been part of the transition, but now, like the neighbors of Mayur Palli, he felt like an observer. The money had made his parents more youthful, less parentlike. Under normal circumstances he would get a good job after his MBA and then buy a Mercedes and show it off to his parents, who would look on proudly. Instead, yesterday, his father had taken him out for a ride in the new car and insisted on heating the car seats despite the summer temperatures.

Rupak suspected that if his father had waited, he could probably have sold his website for much more than he did, but when he sold it, the twenty million U.S. dollars that was offered felt like more money than there was in the whole world. Another small startup, www.justcall.com, bought the site and used the technology and was now worth close to two hundred million U.S. dollars. He wondered if his father ever felt angry about how little he had made compared to how much the site was now worth, but he realized, as he got older, that it was such an outrageous amount for his father that he could not actually understand the difference between twenty million and two hundred million dollars.

Mr. Jha had grown up with very little and, until the sale, earned the equivalent of two hundred dollars a month. Rupak thought now about how he had spent that amount on a pair of shoes recently.

"I think I would like India. Bring me back some books by Indian writers," Elizabeth continued.

Rupak hardly read. He didn't even know the names of the current Indian writers.

"Done. And you bring me books by writers from Pensacola."

"There's no such thing," Elizabeth said with a small laugh. Rupak heard her let out a small moan as she stretched her body in bed. "I should get to work."

"I really do miss you," Rupak said.

"Send me more pictures. I like being able to see what you're seeing. Your pictures make India seem not so far away."

"What else should I get you from here?" Rupak asked.

"I don't need anything else," Elizabeth said. "Except knowing that your parents know about us. See if you can get me that."

Rupak wanted to get her that. He pictured her languorously getting out of bed and stretching her arms up over her head, a sliver of her stomach exposed, and he wanted to get her anything she wanted.

THREE

On Sunday evening, in the small multipurpose room on the first floor of A block in Mayur Palli, the monthly meeting for the residents was coming to a close. On the last Sunday of every month, the Ping-Pong tables were pushed aside, the young boys and girls who used that space to play games and flirt with each other were sent home, and the board members and any residents who had grievances to share would settle into old plastic chairs for two hours. Four tubelights along the edges of the room gave a cold, clinical quality to the light, and two old metal standing fans creaked noisily in opposite corners, forcing everyone to speak loudly. Every meeting ended with a discussion about having ceiling fans installed in the multipurpose room.

Many residents had grievances to share on these Sunday evenings. Tonight, there had already been the following — on the main billboard, Mrs. Patnaik had glued a notice to sell stuffed teddy bears over Mr. Prasad's notice that he was looking for a new mechanic. How long should notices be allowed to stay up uncovered? Mr. Ruddra was cutting his toenails off the edge of his balcony and the half-moon clippings were falling into Mrs. Kulkarni's potted plants on the balcony below. Could he please be asked to stop? Mr. Ghosh should have warned the B block residents that his furniture was being delivered at night. Mr. Baggaria had confused the sound and rumbling of the cupboards being taken up the stairs for an earthquake and gone running down the stairs in a state of panic in his pajamas. Mr. Rastogi suspected that Mr. Sen was stealing his newspaper in the morning, completing the crossword puzzle, and then replacing it.

The last order of business had been Mr. Jha letting everyone know about their new tenants — the Ramaswamys, a young couple from Chennai. They were not officially required to get approval for their tenants, but now that they had told all their neighbors that they were moving, Mrs. Jha had insisted that it was in good form to go to the meeting and tell the board about the Ramaswamys.

"You know how people here can be," she said. "We don't want the tenants to feel unwelcome from the minute they come in."

"I'm looking forward to having neighbors who interfere less," Mr. Jha had said.

He was pleased that he had more money, and he wanted to travel more and spend more freely. He wanted the new car, the home with a driveway, crystal chandeliers, sparkling water, better shower heads, and softer shoes. He wanted to be a member of a private club. He wanted to get a bidet installed in the master bathroom. And he knew that if he did any of that while still living in Mayur Palli, he could face criticism and judgment. He did not think life needed to be a lengthy experiment in sacrifice.

"Mr. Jha, what work do they do, the Ramaswamys?" Mr. Gupta, presiding over the meeting, asked. He had been the president for the last six years because the only other person who had run against him was Mrs. Ghosh, and Mr. Gupta had found it easy to convince everyone that the idea of a woman being the president was preposterous. As a compromise, he made Mrs. Ghosh the "head of communications," which meant that she was responsible for writing a newsletter after the meetings and leaving copies in everyone's mailboxes. Mrs. Ghosh would sometimes attach her favorite recipes along with the newsletter — she had dreams of putting together a cookbook. The neighbors suspected her dreams would go unrealized because in her last recipe for fish with mustard curry, the first paragraph called for a large chopped onion, only for the onions never to be used.

"The husband will be working for Standard Chartered Bank, and the wife — also an IIT graduate, I'm told — teaches bharatanatyam dance classes in Chennai and may start a class for some of the young girls around here."

"Dance classes become fronts for brothels too easily," Mr. Ruddra objected.

"That is a very good point," Mr. Prasad said. "Dance classes cannot be allowed."

"I'm sure Mr. Gupta will make sure nothing untoward goes on," Mr. Jha said. He wanted to go home. Mr. Ruddra thought everything was a front for a brothel. When the new air-conditioned coffee shop opened across from the gates, he spent hours monitoring the young women who went in and out. One of the women finally complained to the manager and Mr. Ruddra was told that he could not sit there without making a purchase.

51

Mr. Gupta leaned back in his chair, pushed his fingers together like a steeple, and nodded.

"Interesting. Mr. Ruddra does bring up a good point. Mr. Jha, you will have to ask Mr. Ramaswamy to come and see me before his wife starts running a business from their home."

"Of course," Mr. Jha said. "I will make sure of that. Is that it for today, then?"

"Mr. Jha," Mr. Ruddra added. "Would you mind telling us why you are renting out this apartment? Surely you don't need the money?"

"Maybe they're getting carpets made of gold thread," Mrs. Sen said.

"Or lightbulbs with diamonds," Mr. Prasad added.

"Or a twelve-foot-high fence to keep the commoners out," Mr. Madhavan said.

A small laugh went through the crowd.

"Don't be silly," Mr. Jha said, eager to end this meeting. The fence that was in place was sufficient and, frankly, lightbulbs with diamonds was not a terrible idea and if he wanted to get that done, he should have the freedom to get it done. But he said none of that. "We don't want to leave this lovely apartment empty. It'll be nice for another family to enjoy it for now and who knows what we may do in the future, or where we may live."

"You mean you may move back here?" Mr. Gupta said.

"Perhaps," Mr. Jha said. He had no intention of moving back to Mayur Palli after living in Gurgaon, but he also did not want his neighbors and friends to dislike him. They were, after all, their closest friends in Delhi, and what if making new friends in Gurgaon was not as easy?

"Oh, that will be just lovely," Mrs. Patnaik said from the back. "This will always be your home."

"You may return here to the masses someday?" Mr. Gupta said. "That will require lots of adjusting."

"Yes, it will. And so will moving to Gurgaon in the first place. All of this will require adjusting, and my wife and I are doing exactly that. We are not building carpets of gold and our lightbulbs will . . . probably . . . not have any diamonds on them, but we are moving. And we will have full-length mirrors in our home. Mr. Gupta, this is the life that my family has chosen, and I assure you, we will adjust. I have always adjusted. Are we finished here?"

"That is all for this evening, yes," Mr. Gupta said. "Thank you to everyone who attended. Frankly not enough members of this housing complex take these meetings seriously. I am considering imposing a fee on residents who do not send at least one member of the household to the meetings."

A faint murmur of approval went through the twenty or so people who came to the meeting every week, and then the sound of scattered conversations picked up. Shatrugan came in and turned the fans off. Someone said, "Mr. Gupta, please see to those overhead fans," and others agreed.

"I have one more thing," Mrs. Ray said from the back row, raising her hand. Why did she raise her hand? She wasn't a schoolgirl. And why had she waited until the fans had been turned off? Now the silence was like a spotlight on her. She sat up straight, cleared her throat, and repeated, "I have one more thing to discuss."

Mrs. Ray knew it was her last chance to bring up the stolen yoga pants. She was fairly certain she knew who the culprit was, and her accusation was nothing more shocking than what had already been discussed, so there was really no reason for her to avoid it any longer.

But the difference between her complaint and the rest was that she was a widow. And not a widow like old Mrs. Chabbra, who hardly left her home and walked only slowly, bent over a walker, and had a few stiff white hairs that sprouted on her upper lip. Widows of that genre were the norm. But nobody knew what to do with widows like Mrs. Ray.

Not too happily married when she was nineteen years old, Mrs. Ray had never known the feeling of young flirtation, new romance, and endless possibility. She had gone from her father's home straight to her husband's home, and there had been minimal fun along the way. Her husband wasn't bad — he didn't drink, never hit her, and, as far as she knew, had never had an affair — but he had also never caused her stomach to flutter with excitement. Even at the start of their marriage, they never went dancing, they hardly ever went to watch movies, and they certainly never flirted with each other. Her marriage, and her life in general, had always felt like a transaction — she was handed certain items, and she paid in kind. She went to college until her parents found her a suitable match, and the price for that was to stop going to college. She moved to Delhi because her husband's work needed him there, and she put Mumbai behind her and set about building a new life. They didn't manage to have children, so she befriended the older ladies in the neighbor-hood and accepted a life without little toes. Her husband didn't want her to work and she liked her husband, so she didn't work. She followed all the rules and did everything that was expected of her and still her husband died when she was thirty-seven years old. How was that fair?

The rules had failed her, so in widowhood she decided she was not going to play the role of a widow. She liked sheets with higher thread counts than she'd ever had before, and she paid extra to buy a cream that was meant to be used only on the feet when regular Nivea cold cream would obviously work just as well. She liked the occasional cigarette and she liked to play her music on speakers even if the neighbors could hear the widow next door enjoying music. She didn't want or need a man, but she did want to live well, even on her own. Especially on her own.

After Mr. Ray's death, Mrs. Ray felt like a television character who moves to a big city to make it all by herself. She did indeed break her bangles and remove the vermillion from her hair when Mr. Ray died, but instead of plain white saris and daily prayers, she changed into tight gym clothes, got a yoga instructor, dyed the few gray hairs that had started to come in, and started taking prenatal vitamins. You were supposed to live for yourself, all the American afternoon talk shows always told her. So she tried. It was difficult in this housing complex where everyone watched and discussed her every move and she came home every evening to a dark and empty home that she shared with only her maid. She knew that everyone thought that her living well meant she didn't miss her husband. But she did. She missed him almost every day, but she also wanted to install shower heads that had a massage setting.

She wished she had some company tonight. She shouldn't have given Ganga the night off to visit her relatives in Kalkaji. The room settled into silence again as everyone turned to look at Mrs. Ray. She adjusted the dupatta that was draped around her shoulders and stood up to face everyone.

"Mr. De has stolen my yoga pants," she said, and pointed over her shoulder in the direction of Mr. De, who was snoozing in the back row with his chin against his chest. His bald head was reflecting the tubelight above him and the second button on his shirt had come unbuttoned and wispy gray chest hairs were visible. As the newly appointed treasurer, Mr. De was required to attend these meetings.

The few people who had started to leave the room all came back in and took their seats again.

"Reema, what are you saying?" Mr. De said, spluttering awake.

"Please call me Mrs. Ray. And it is because I have been doing yoga," Mrs. Ray said.

"You don't need yoga pants to do yoga, you know," Mrs. Kulkarni said. "Those tight, tight pants are not in our culture. You can do yoga just as well in a salwar kameez."

Mrs. Baggaria, who was sitting next to Mrs. Kulkarni, wobbled her head in agreement.

Mrs. Ray inhaled, wishing again that she had had another glass of wine before coming to the meeting, and said, "Mrs. Kulkarni, that is hardly the point."

"That is true," Mr. Gupta said. "All foreigners are even teaching yoga these days. And you see our young Indians suddenly excited about yoga because the Americans are doing it. Bikram yoga — have you heard of it? Who needs a heated room? You can just do yoga outdoors in the summer in Delhi. And that Bikram has gone and made millions and millions of dollars."

"I hear he has relations with plenty of American women," someone added.

"That is exactly what yoga has become," someone else said.

"Because of the clothes," Mrs. Kulkarni said, and looked toward Mrs. Ray.

"Mr. Gupta, this is not about yoga. Or about what clothes to wear while doing yoga. This is about my yoga pants that have been stolen and I have every reason to believe it was Mr. De who stole them," Mrs. Ray said.

She was certain it was him. The Des' balcony was the only one from which you could reach Mrs. Ray's balcony, where Ganga put out all her clothes to dry, including her yoga pants. In the past, Mrs. Ray had caught Mr. De watching her doing yoga and even though she could not imagine why he would steal her yoga pants, she was certain he had. And watching him now taking off his glasses and wiping the sweat off his face, she was even more certain he was guilty.

"Mrs. Ray, Mrs. Ray, Mrs. Ray," Mr. De said. "What would your husband say if he were still with us? May he rest in peace. Am I right?"

Mrs. Ray looked at Mr. De looking around shiftily, laughing, trying to get the support of the others in the room.

"Besides," he continued. "The ladies are

correct — you can do yoga just as well in a salwar kameez. Probably even better. Mrs. Kulkarni, you are always wise. And Mrs. Baggaria, that is a lovely sari you are wearing today."

They all agreed with each other, and Mrs. Ray wanted nothing more than to also move away from Mayur Palli. But where would she go? She looked toward Mr. Jha to see if perhaps he would defend her, but he was busy staring down at his shoes. She had hoped Mrs. Jha would be there tonight, but Rupak was due to leave this week so she was at home.

"You know what? It's fine," Mrs. Ray said. "It's okay. I just wanted to mention the yoga pants, and I am glad I did. I trust that I will be left in peace now."

She looked over at Mr. De, who was just shaking his head and whispering to Mr. Patnaik next to him, and Mrs. Ray regretted not just having mentioned her stolen yoga pants, but having worn them in the first place. She walked out of the meeting room and hurried home before anyone else could catch up with her.

Back in her empty apartment, she poured herself a glass of cold white wine. What else was there to do except wait until Ganga came home and told her about her relatives and the prices they paid for fish and why their fishseller was robbing them blind? Ganga was always full of stories and Mrs. Ray admired her for that.

Ganga had been a widow ever since Mrs. Ray knew her. Ganga's aunt was Mr. Ray's parents' maid in Mumbai, and when Mr. and Mrs. Ray got married and moved to Delhi, Ganga's aunt told his parents that she had a perfect maid for them — her niece in Calcutta who had recently been widowed and was looking for full-time work and would be happy to move to Delhi. Mr. Ray was thrilled at the thought of having a maid who could cook authentic Bengali prawns in mustard curry and agreed to hire her immediately. In her white widow's sari, Ganga showed up in Delhi only six months after the Rays had moved to Mayur Palli, and Mrs. Ray had hardly known life in Delhi without her.

Ganga made herself at home in the new city faster than Mrs. Ray had. Within a week, she had walked the entire market area outside Mayur Palli and made friends with the fishseller, the vegetable seller, the cobbler, and the local electrician. Ganga had the luxury of not feeling shame or shyness. It was a perk of being poor. In a city in which all the men stare and many of them touch, Mrs. Ray always noticed how poor women marched around without a care in the world, widowed or not. How was she supposed to continue living here? Now everyone knew about her accusation and once the Jhas moved, she would be left with no friends in the neighborhood. But she had nowhere else to go. She would not know how to sell this apartment and, even if she did, all she would be able to afford with that money would be another similar apartment in a similar housing complex in a similar part of the city with people who would look at her the same way. There was no way to start over.

The doorbell. Mrs. Ray opened it thinking it was Ganga, but it was a man with a big jute bag offering to sell eggs and pav bread.

"This late on a Sunday night?" Mrs. Ray asked him. "You can't go around ringing bells this late at night."

"But you will need this for breakfast," he said.

"No, thank you. And please don't come so late at night again," she said, and went to shut the door, but he held it open. He looked small and Mrs. Ray was feeling warmed by the wine, which meant she felt invincible despite the events of the day. But now that he was standing closer, she could tell that he was warmed by something as well. She could smell it on his breath and it was foul.

"But you will need this for breakfast," he repeated. "Just one egg and one pav, right? Just one?"

Mrs. Ray pushed the door. He pushed back. She thought about screaming, but after the night she had already had, she did not want the neighbors to have the satisfaction of hearing her scream. She considered buying the egg and bread in case that would just get him out, but something about his dry hand pushing against the door told her that he wouldn't go away after making a sale.

"Stop pushing my door. Go. Get out. Get out or I'll scream."

He sucked his teeth.

"Don't get so upset," he said, smiling at her. "I'm just trying to take care of you. You must keep your body healthy."

Mrs. Ray heard metal clanging coming up the stairs. Ganga kept her keys tied to the end of her sari. Through heavy breathing, she heard Ganga say, "Is someone there?"

The man dropped his hand from the door and said, "I'll check in again some other evening. To see if you need anything."

Ganga reached the floor. "What are you doing?"

Today, like every day that Mrs. Ray had known Ganga, she was wearing the widow's uniform of a white sari with a white blouse. Ganga had beautiful dark skin that shone and showed no signs of age. She was short and round and walked with a slight limp.

"Just selling eggs and pav, but madam says she doesn't need any," he said, moving past Ganga and down the stairs.

"Fool," Ganga called out after him. "Don't come knocking again so late at night. That useless Shatrugan — fast asleep at the gate downstairs."

Ganga pushed past Mrs. Ray into the apartment, muttering about Shatrugan, and Mrs. Ray wanted to agree with her, wanted to agree with all that Ganga was saying. She wanted to tell Ganga that she was happy to have her home, how were her relatives, what did she eat, did she know that she'd come back at exactly the right moment, but she did not say any of that.

Mrs. Ray wondered if Ganga was also lonely. She used to think Ganga was too busy being worried about being poor to be lonely. Like all the homeless people you see everywhere — they couldn't possibly have time to be sad. But you couldn't say that to anyone. Of late she wished she and Ganga could talk about their sadness, their loneliness, their widowhood. But they couldn't. Instead Mrs. Ray poured herself another glass of wine.

"You don't need anything more to drink." Ganga reappeared from her bedroom without her bags. "Let me make you a cup of tea instead."

She stood in the doorway of the kitchen. Ganga was like a ghost sometimes. She seemed to appear just at the moment you were thinking of her. Mrs. Ray had a dream a few months ago in which Ganga was dead but the doorbell rang and Mrs. Ray knew it was her. In the dream, she opened the door and dead Ganga was standing there in the same white widow's sari. She looked just like living Ganga except one of her legs was a wooden peg. Mrs. Ray must have screamed when she woke up because Ganga came running to her room. Of course that just terrified her more. But both of her legs were intact, thank God.

"What do you do in that room of yours after dinner in the evenings?" Mrs. Ray said.

Ganga turned the gas stove on and poured water into a metal pan. On the counter near the stove, she placed a large cup and brass tea strainer filled with a few pinches of black tea leaves.

"You finished that new bottle of whiskey last night," Ganga said. "You don't need more alcohol today."

Ganga stood watching the water. Mrs. Ray left her in the kitchen and walked out to the balcony and lit a cigarette. At least at night she could smoke in peace without all the neighbors peering in.

"Tell me something," Mrs. Ray said, when Ganga brought her steaming cup of tea out to the balcony. "Which one of us do you think will die first? I've been doing yoga almost every day, you know. Doesn't it trouble you not to know how old you are? I don't understand how you villagers just approximate your age. How will you know when you might die?"

Ganga placed the cup of tea on the small wooden table by Mrs. Ray's feet.

"It's good that you're doing yoga. Now you need to drink and smoke less," Ganga said. "You know how it affects your mood."

"Don't lecture me with your mouth full of chewing tobacco. How did you get to and from Kalkaji tonight anyway?"

"I took the train. It's as modern as the radio says. You should try it sometime. There are different compartments for ladies and everyone behaves very well."

Mrs. Ray had not yet taken the new train in Delhi, and it felt like a lifetime since she had last taken a local train in Mumbai by herself. She was eighteen then, and studying commerce at St. Andrews College, and every weekday morning she boarded the regular compartment of the 9:14 a.m. Churchgate local. That day a middle-aged worker fell out of the compartment and onto the tracks, his head smashed open. She was late for class and took only the bus from then on.

"What were you doing with your cousins this late? It sounds rather suspicious, you know. Do you have a man in your life? We're too old for all that now, Ganga. It's done for us."

"I've told you a dozen times," Ganga said. "I was talking to them about returning to Siliguri. You never listen. Now stop all this self-pitying and come inside and get ready for bed. The neighbors can see you when you smoke out here."

"You will never leave," Mrs. Ray said. Rupak left, the Jhas were leaving, Ganga couldn't leave. Mrs. Ray wanted to again thank Ganga for never leaving, for being Mrs. Ray's family, but instead, as always, she said nothing.

FOUR

"I can't carry chicken curry all the way back to New York, Mom," Rupak said to his mother on the morning of his departure. "Ma."

Mrs. Jha ignored him and his use of the word *Mom* and kept stirring. The onions sizzled in the hot oil, the garlic jumped, and the smell of fenugreek rose up from the pan. Her mother had taught her how to make this chicken curry and it had always been Rupak's favorite. She hoped Rupak's wife would someday learn how to make it. Wait, no — she was supposed to say she hoped Rupak himself would someday learn how to make it. She sometimes forgot to be a feminist. But she felt this dish needed a woman's touch. She dropped the pieces of chicken — on the bone, always on the bone — into the pan and used the wooden spoon to push them around and coat them with the gravy. Even before her husband had

68

developed his crazy ideas about not having maids around, this was one dish she always made herself. She tried teaching one of the maids, but it wasn't the same. Mrs. Jha was never the type of woman to express her emotions through food. She was perfectly happy being at work helping rural weavers package their work for urban markets all day and making a quick call around three p.m. to tell the maid which vegetables to cook for dinner. But her methi chicken curry was hers alone, and if she had to let her son go across the world all by himself tonight, the least she could do was pack him a proper hot meal. She lowered the heat on the stove, covered the pan, and turned to the fridge to take out a bottle of coconut water. Coconut water came in bottles these days. She poured two glasses and handed one to her son.

"That smells good," Rupak said.

"You should learn how to make it so you don't go hungry in America."

"I hardly starve there, Ma. And I doubt I'd get half the ingredients for it in America. I don't even know what the English word for *methi* is," Rupak said.

"Fenugreek," Mrs. Jha said. "And maybe it's best you don't learn so you keep coming back to me for the chicken curry."

Mrs. Jha used to cook it on Sundays, the one day of the week when the three of them would sit down for a proper lunch together. They would all wake up late and have a lazy morning. Mrs. Jha would often drop by the Rays' home for a cup of tea. Mr. Jha would go downstairs for a walk and chat with some of the other husbands in the neighborhood. Or he would go to the barber for a head massage and shave. Rupak watched television or, if the weather permitted, went downstairs for a few rounds of cricket with his friends. Mrs. Jha would return home before the men and cook methi chicken or prawns with mustard — it was always one of those two dishes for the main course on Sundays. The maids would make rice, daal, and a vegetable dish, but Mrs. Jha took charge of the main dish. While she was cooking, Mr. Jha and Rupak would come home and take turns having hot showers, and the same smell of the sandalwood soap that Mr. Jha had been using since 1983 would mix with the food and fill the rooms. It was the one day of the week when they listened to music loudly — Mr. Jha would put in old Geeta Dutt cassettes, and in the kitchen Mrs. Jha would sing along to the high-pitched songs while the curry simmered on the stove. She hoped Rupak remembered those afternoons. Everything was changing so quickly now. Taking the chicken all the way to Ithaca and reheating it in a microwave was not the same as eating it hot from the kitchen on a lazy Sunday afternoon. But it was something.

She would put it carefully in many plastic bags and pack it in his check-in bag. It was a twenty-four-hour journey and airports and airplanes were always cold; the chicken would be fine.

"Ma, seriously. I'll eat it before leaving for the airport tonight."

Rupak did love the methi chicken curry she made and missed it often in Ithaca, but even if it survived the journey, which he doubted it would, Elizabeth was going to pick him up from the airport in Syracuse in her open-top Jeep Wrangler, and she probably wouldn't appreciate it smelling of methi chicken curry, even if you called it fenugreek.

Even though he had never met Elizabeth's family, Rupak felt he could picture them perfectly. They lived in a house near the beach and donated a percentage of their income to the church. He didn't know much else about her life and childhood, but in the same way that Rupak thought he knew America, he thought he also knew

71

Elizabeth from *Saved by the Bell* or *The Wonder Years* or an Archie comic strip. But Elizabeth said she had never even read Archie comics. He had grown up reading the comics and watching those shows on hot, sticky afternoons in Delhi.

As a child, Rupak was one of the few students who took a bus home after school and one of the even fewer ones who returned all the way to East Delhi. The bus would be all but empty by the time it reached his stop. He would have to get off at the bridge and then walk the last dusty kilometer home. When he got home, Rupak would tear off his sweaty blue uniform and take a cool wash, pouring mugfuls of water from a bucket over his body. Then he would change into shorts and a T-shirt and the maid would put together cucumber and mint chutney sandwiches. Rupak would sit on the cane chairs in the living room and watch television until the sun had gone down, the heat had become slightly less oppressive, and it was time to go downstairs to play cricket with the other boys.

In Delhi, most of his wealthy classmates regularly went abroad for holidays, so they would all carry fashionable JanSports and flashy pencil boxes with Michael Jackson and Whitney Houston on them. But Rupak had only a metal Camlin geometry set. He used to keep his Apsara pencils, small white eraser, and one ink pen in a wooden pencil box with golden stars and moons carved into it that his mother had bought for him at the Thursday market. Two small hinges that had started off golden but quickly turned to rust that powdered at the touch held the lid in place. He thought now that a box like that would be something Elizabeth would love. Elizabeth liked to smoke pot and those little wooden pencil boxes would be the perfect place for her to store the paraphernalia.

"Ma, do you have any of those old wooden pencil boxes?"

Rupak saw his mother's face relax into a smile as she looked up from the hot pan on the stove. He was still her little boy from Delhi, Mrs. Jha thought. She remembered what joy she would feel when she came home from work in the evening, in through the main gate of Mayur Palli, and saw Rupak in the small field right near the gate with his cricket bat and group of friends. The grass was patchy and it was often hot and dusty, but in her mind she could see a montage of Rupak on that field getting taller and broader and older and manlier.

The field had a few metal seats fixed into

the ground around the edges, and the older residents of Mayur Palli would sit there at the end of their evening walks and catch up on gossip and watch the young children play. Whenever Mrs. Jha stood there after work, she had assumed that was how they would live out their old age. Buying bhelpuri from the vendor outside the gate and, who knows, maybe watching a grandson play cricket in the same spot where their son had played. If Rupak remembered the wooden pencil boxes, maybe there was still hope for it all.

"The type you used to take to school?"

Rupak nodded.

"They may sell them at Cottage Emporium for tourists. Nobody uses pencil boxes anymore."

"I thought it might make a good gift. It's no big deal, though."

Mrs. Jha stirred some more mustard oil into the chicken and tried to sound casual. "Who would you like to give it to?"

Rupak wondered if it would be easier to tell his mother about Elizabeth first. And then let her tell his father while he was safely on a flight back to America. It wasn't that his father would not approve or would forbid it. They would both simply fidget and not quite know how to respond, and that would be worse than any explicit lecturing.

Elizabeth had been engaged once, to a man she met during her undergraduate years, but that engagement broke off after six months and she hardly ever talked about it. For some reason Rupak was always intrigued by how her ex had proposed, but Elizabeth never offered any details. All he knew for sure was that the ex's mother had called Elizabeth after the breakup to ask for the ring back. "That sums up the kind of guy he was," Elizabeth said. Now she was in no rush to get engaged again or married. But she still wanted his parents to know about her.

This was the moment to confess, he decided. He had set it all up. It was going to be easy. But instead he found himself saying, "Gaurav. He's an Indian guy on campus who hasn't been back to visit in years, and he mentioned the wooden pencil boxes. But it isn't worth going all the way to Cottage Emporium."

"Do you want me to pack some rice with the chicken? That way you'll have a full meal as soon as you arrive. I've also put in a bottle of tamarind chutney. Don't worry, I've taped the lid down carefully and put it in three plastic bags — there's no chance it will leak. I can pack some extra for Gaurav as well. I didn't know you had an Indian friend there."

This was her chance to get closer to her son, Mrs. Jha thought. She knew very little about his life there. Was he lonely? Was he eating properly? Was he drinking too much? Was he carrying on with women? White women? Black women? Was there even a Gaurav? His changing body made her nervous. He had been a skinny boy who needed glasses at an early age, but now he wore contacts and his arms and chest looked broader than she would ever have expected. He looked like a man but not the type of man Mr. Jha was. He was starting to look like the type of man who bought drinks for women at bars and allowed them to do things to him in the bedroom. Did he know about the risks and the diseases out in the world? They never talked about those things and the Indian school system certainly didn't provide classes on the dangers of sex, so she just had to hope that he had good sense and would not be led astray by a woman.

"Do you want me to tell your father to stop at Cottage Emporium and try to pick up a pencil box? Where is Gaurav's family from?"

"Who?" Rupak said, his mind on Elizabeth.

"Gaurav. Your friend."

"Right. Bombay. He's from Bombay."

"Is he also doing his MBA? What do his parents do?" Mrs. Jha asked.

Rupak was always amazed by how much his mother cared about people she didn't know and would probably never meet. She'd become much worse ever since she stopped working. When she first quit, it was in order to handle the new money from the sale, and that made sense to Rupak. His mother had thrown herself into finding a suitable house for them to buy. She must have seen nearly fifty properties, and it would have been difficult for her to also be working while trying to buy and set up a new home. But then they bought the home and her time freed up but she never returned to work; these days she hardly even mentioned it. She had a Facebook account now. But she didn't quite know what to do with it yet. Whenever anybody posted anything, she would comment, *Seen, thanks.*

When he was growing up, she had never been one of those mothers who sat and fussed over him all afternoon. She did not obsess over his homework and interfere in his life. Unlike a lot of mothers, his mother had never abandoned her own life for his sake, and he appreciated that about her.

She used to work for a nonprofit organization that helped rural weavers and craftsmen get their goods to shops in Delhi and Mumbai and get paid. He never really knew the details about her work, but he knew that she was passionate about it and often talked about fair wages for the craftsmen who did all the work and about not wanting them — or was it the shops? — someone, not wanting someone to get exploited. There was more to her work, he was sure, but his father's work always took the main stage so he really didn't know details.

"I'm not sure. But don't worry about the pencil box. It isn't that important."

"Please, can I just take a taxi?" Rupak asked his parents. They were getting ready to drive him to the airport, and something about saying good-bye in the midst of the chaos of the Delhi airport always made him sad.

"No," Mrs. Jha said.

Mr. Jha brought the scale from the bathroom out to the middle of the living room and stood on it. He noted his weight, got off, picked up Rupak's suitcase, and got back on the scale.

"It's one kilo overweight," he said. "I'm

78

sure they won't create a hassle about that."

"If they do," Mrs. Jha added, "just take some books out and put them in your hand bag. Don't pay for excess luggage. Or leave some things behind and we can bring them to you when we come."

"Do you know when you're coming yet?" Rupak asked, trying to calculate how much time he had to make his life in Ithaca seem like the kind of life they would want him to have.

"As soon as we're settled in Gurgaon," Mrs. Jha said. She was tying a piece of red string around the handles of Rupak's two suitcases. "I don't know why you insist on carrying black suitcases. You won't be able to identify yours. Here. Is this red string enough or do you want me to tie another one?"

"One red string is enough. I know what my suitcases look like," Rupak said.

"I wish you were going to be here for the move," Mrs. Jha said.

"Rupak," Mr. Jha said. "I want you to study hard. Make friends and have fun as well. I want you to be well rounded. But don't forget to study. It's important. Take it from me, son. Success makes you happy. There's simply no argument about that. I became successful late in life and I wish my mother had been alive to see it. You have opportunities I never had. Take advantage. Each generation should do better than the previous one, they say. Find a good job in America."

"Or India. There are plenty of good opportunities in India now," Mrs. Jha added.

Rupak was sitting on the couch checking his passport and ticket printouts while his father spoke. His father never spoke so explicitly. Did he somehow know that Rupak was already on academic probation after his first year of the program?

"Anyway, you're an adult now," he continued. "You know all this. But sometimes it is good to say these things. You know I admire that about American families — you see it on all the movies and television shows — they have very serious conversations with each other."

"I think it's too formal," Mrs. Jha said. "Next we'll have to start charging him rent."

"Or letting him 'borrow' money from us that he has to pay back," Mr. Jha said.

Rupak watched his parents laugh. Despite his own concerns and despite some of the tension surrounding the move, it must be fun for them, he thought. Few adults got the chance to start over.

"But your father is right, Rupak. Study

hard. And make sure you can take some time off when we come to visit you."

"Enough now," Mr. Jha said. "Come on, come on. Let's get in the car. I don't want you to miss your flight."

As Rupak was about to zip up his backpack, Mrs. Jha said, "Wait. Don't close that yet. I have one more thing."

She reached into her purse and handed him a wooden pencil box with golden stars and moons embossed onto the cover.

"For Gaurav," Mrs. Jha said.

"Ma, how did you get this?" Rupak asked.

"Friends, Rupak. We have friends. If you live in one place for long enough, you make friends who will help you find an old wooden pencil box that is no longer manufactured. You give it to Gaurav and tell him we want to meet him when we come to visit."

Rupak held the box in his hand and looked around the living room. He suddenly realized his parents were moving and that the only home he had ever known was no longer going to be his home. He looked at his mother picking up her purse from the dining table, and a blurred memory flashed through his mind. He remembered falling on the living room floor and splitting his lip right before his fifth or sixth birthday party.

His father had gone out to pick up the cake, he remembered now, and his mother had seen him on the ground, with blood gushing from his mouth, and quietly picked up her purse, picked him up in her arms, and rushed him out the door to a taxi to the local clinic. She just held him in the taxi with a towel pressed against his mouth and said nothing. He was fine — the doctor said he wouldn't need stitches and would just have a bit of a swollen mouth for a while — and when they left the doctor's office and got back in a taxi, Mrs. Jha had burst into tears. At the time Rupak had rolled his eyes and been impatient to get home to his party, but now, thinking of her face in the evening light in that taxi, he wanted to tell her he was sorry he had ever caused her fear.

"Ma, will you be happy in Gurgaon?" he asked.

Mrs. Jha looked at her son sitting on the sofa. She wanted to tell him that she hoped so. She wanted to thank him for asking and tell him she was confident that she'd be happy anywhere as long as Mr. Jha and Rupak were happy, but she was interrupted.

"Bindu! Hurry up," Mr. Jha shouted from near the elevator. "There's going to be traffic. But you can see how lovely the new car is even when standing still in exhaust fumes from other cars."

At the airport, Rupak waited until the car was out of sight and pushed his cart across the road, opened his suitcase, took out the metal box filled with chicken curry and rice and the thrice-wrapped bottle of tamarind chutney that his mother had spent all that morning making and handed it all to two young men who were sitting on the sidewalk with small pull-along suitcases next to them, looking lost.

"Where are you traveling to?" Rupak asked.

They both looked up at him, suspiciously. They were about his age but looked older because of how skinny they were. They were wearing slightly loose slacks and tucked-in shirts with short sleeves. They had cheap black sandals on their feet and their hair was oiled back neatly. Rupak knew they were day laborers heading to somewhere in the Middle East. All the flights leaving for the Middle East always had the worst departure times, and security would only let these men into the airport three hours before their scheduled departure time. They would have to sit and wait and hope it didn't rain before then. That was their life, and handing over home-cooked food before heading back to America was his.

"Qatar," one of them said. "Is the plane going on time?"

"I don't know. I hope so," Rupak said. "While you're here, would you like some dinner? I have some food and I can't take it on the plane with me."

The two men looked at each other, then accepted the food, and then the same one who had spoken said, "I also have a bottle of chutney in my suitcase. My mother gave it to me before I left. Can I take that on the plane?"

"Make sure you check it in," Rupak said.

The man stared at him.

"Just put it in the bag you give to the agent at the counter."

They looked even more confused. There was little Rupak could do.

"You'll see when you get inside," he said. "Have a good trip."

FIVE

Mr. Dinesh Chopra from Block C, Sector 12A of the Delhi suburb of Gurgaon was not afraid of much. He could count on one hand the number of things that frightened him — stray dogs, rusted edges on cans, bearded men on airplanes, and young women in two-piece bathing suits. But the thing that frightened him most was poverty.

And he understood far too well that poverty, like all tragedy, was largely relative, and the Mukherjees next door had recently sold their house in Gurgaon and moved to London. Not Houndslow, either. Kensington. This had been particularly humiliating for Mr. Chopra because he had spent a considerable amount of money and two months having the dome of the Sistine Chapel re-created on the ceiling in his foyer.

"It is a small investment," he told Mr. Mukherjee one afternoon. "But I am a big fan of art. I would be happy to give you the

85

number for the painters. They can re-create anything. Even Bollywood posters."

"I am sure it will turn out beautifully. I just don't think it is worth spending so much right now," Mr. Mukherjee had replied.

"It is quite an indulgence, yes," Mr. Chopra had said. "This market has spared no one, but one must spoil oneself."

At the time, he had walked away feeling smug about his wealth, but looking back at it, now that the Mukherjees had sold their house and disappeared to London — Kensington — he felt humiliated. And nervous. If the Mukherjees had managed to make the move to London — that too without telling the whole neighborhood about it — they were clearly making a significant amount of money. That meant that relative to the Mukherjees, the Chopras were becoming poor. And not just relative to the Mukherjees; relative also to the family that had bought the Mukherjees' house. Mr. Chopra knew that house was not cheap. It was a bungalow with front and back yards. The driveway was comfortably fifteen yards long and the Mukherjees had planted trees so carefully along the fence around the perimeter that you couldn't see any of the barbed wire that ran above the fence. So thick was the greenery that over the last five years, two thieves had injured themselves on the barbed wire while trying to climb into the Mukherjees' property. Not a single thief had tried coming into the Chopras' property. It was worrying. To experiment, Mr. Chopra had the glass shards that lined the top of his fence removed one day. He then sat in his yard at night and monitored those sections, waiting for a thief to intrude. None did. A lone monkey climbed through around eleven p.m., which caused Mr. Chopra to go rushing back into the house and have the glass shards put back in place the next day.

The Chopras were stagnant. The other piece of residential property they owned was a bungalow in Goa with only three floors that wasn't even close enough to the beach for them to be able to rent it out to white travelers at a good markup. And the down payment they had made on a Dubai flat was held up because the builders were under scrutiny for violating local building regulations.

"Why aren't you working?" Mrs. Chopra asked her husband's back from the sofa. He was standing and gazing out the window into the front yard. "And where is Johnny? I haven't seen him all day."

"I don't think he came home last night," Mr. Chopra said, laughing a little. His son, at age twenty-eight, still showed no ambition or signs of having a real career. Mr. Chopra supported him financially and everyone knew that. Johnny went to all the best restaurants in town, regularly traveled abroad with his friends, and wore flashy designer jeans, and Mr. Chopra paid for everything, which made it clear that Mr. Chopra earned enough not just for himself and his wife but also for his son to live a lavish lifestyle. Clearly he was earning the equivalent of at least three high incomes. He often wished they'd had another child, but really only so everyone at the club would know that he was earning enough for four. Shashi Jhunjhunwala, who had made his money exporting slightly subpar medical supplies to hospitals in the Middle East, had four children, all of whom drove BMWs and none of whom had ever held a job.

Mr. Chopra continued to stare out the window.

"The bushes need to be tended. You can't even tell the one on the left is supposed to be a swan. Don't give the gardener's wife any more old saris until the bush looks perfectly like a swan. And I think it may be time to install a swimming pool."

"Everything grows too fast this time of year. The house is fine for now. Only thing I want is to get the Mona Lisa, Bollywood style, with a bindi on her forehead, painted on the wall in the master bathroom. Why are you standing and staring out the window?"

Mr. Chopra turned around to face his wife. She was sitting cross-legged in her nightgown on the large white L-shaped leather sofa that went along the wall of the living room. In front of her, a wooden box sat open with her jewelry spilling out. A gold bangle had fallen on the carpet in front of her. Not many homes in Delhi had full carpeting, but theirs did. On the low glass coffee table, Mrs. Chopra's iPad was open with the current Bollywood hits playing with a tinny sound.

"I'm standing here because I want to meet the neighbors. It is only polite to say hello. And then I'm going to the club. Why is your jewelry box out?"

"I'm looking through my jewelry because I need to buy some new gold. How do you know the neighbors are coming today? You're wasting time. If you want something to do, check on all the arrangements for Upen. That brother of yours is getting too demanding with old age. You tell him if he plans to eat vegetarian food only, he can make his own arrangements. And I don't want to hear one word about carbon footprints while he's here. After his divorce, he's hardly one to go around talking about the environment."

"They are coming to get some work done. The gas installation men are waiting outside the gate for them. It doesn't look nice not to at least say hello and ask them a little bit about themselves. Upen doesn't need arrangements; he just needs a break from Chandigarh."

"I don't know why you are in such a state. Go do some work and once they have settled in, we will call them over for a drink," Mrs. Chopra said.

"It is not that simple," Mr. Chopra said. "It's almost noon. Please go and put a sari on. Wear that new Manish Malhotra one you just bought."

"That one is too nice to wear around the house. This is fine for now. I've got Sunita coming over to give me a pedicure later anyway."

"Why can't you get a pedicure while wearing the new sari?"

"I also want a full massage. My back has been hurting lately from all this weight I've gained," Mrs. Chopra said, and rubbed her back and laughed.

Mr. Chopra went back to staring out the window. Ladies were changing these days, but his wife refused to. Just look at Upen's ex-wife. She had had an actual affair. Not that Mr. Chopra wanted his wife to have an affair, but she could at least try losing a bit of weight.

"Why don't you go to a proper beauty parlor instead of having Sunita come home?" Mr. Chopra said. "And please get your upper lip threaded as well."

Mrs. Chopra ran her finger across her upper lip and said, "No need yet. I'll give it another week."

Mr. Chopra heard a car coming down the road. Sunita took a bus from wherever it was that she lived and then walked in from the main road, so it had to be the new neighbors.

"They're here. They're here," he said. "I must go and say hello. It is time, Geeta. Keep your fingers crossed that they have come back from London."

Mr. Chopra looked over at his wife, now focused on Bollywood music videos and thoughtlessly fingering the six-lakh diamond necklace around her neck while a gold bangle still lay on the floor. Mrs. Chopra, originally Ms. Khanna, came from wealth;

she came from a family of farm owners in Ferozepur, and she didn't have the same relationship with money that he did. Since before independence, her family had endless acres of farms. Her brothers were all politicians in Ferozepur with mistresses in Chandigarh. When the British army showed up in their village on the morning of August 14, 1947, to draw a border and create India and Pakistan, the Khannas on the other side of the border merely got up, walked across to the Indian side, and immediately started work on claiming new land to make up for what they had lost to the other side. They did not complain about the British — and how could they? Before independence, most of their closest friends were British, and Mrs. Chopra's parents firmly believed Indian independence was to be a temporary misfortune. They died waiting for the British to come back. They did not dramatize the separation of the countries, and they did not worry about the massacre that followed. They were very aware of what they could and could not control, so they quietly set about re-creating whatever they had lost, through whatever means needed. And this was the attitude with which Mrs. Chopra lived every day.

Mr. Chopra's parents, on the other hand,

made their money in the construction business in Chandigarh after independence, and it did not come easily. There were financial ups, and there were downs and more downs, and it took quite a while for it to become largely ups. They had gained membership to the local club and then lost it because of an inability to pay the annual dues. They then managed to get in again, but it was never quite the same. He was aware of what his parents had been through, and that always made him nervous about his own money, even though his father had bought him the mica mine when he was eighteen and he had never actually experienced any difficulty. His older brother, Upen, had never been afraid. He had taken over their parents' construction business right in Chandigarh and never cared much about money. He was more interested in trying to convert people to using solar power than making money for himself. That was probably why his wife had an affair and eventually left him to move to Hong Kong with a hedge fund manager. Not that Upen's life seemed to have been destroyed by any of this. He looked fitter and younger than Mr. Chopra even though, at sixty-three, he was four years older. What, he wondered, was the secret to his brother's youth? He didn't even eat meat.

Mr. Chopra himself had worked extremely hard in the beginning. And it paid off. Now he only went to the mine two or three days a month, and he usually chartered a helicopter to get there. The mine was in the Bhilwara district in Rajasthan, which was close enough to do in a day but far enough to justify spending a night if he needed a night away from his wife's nagging. The rest of the time he did the minimal work required to manage the mine from his home office.

Mr. Chopra made his way down the driveway toward the gate. He saw Balwinder, the security guard, snoozing.

"Balwinder! Do we pay you so much just to sleep all day?" he said. "Get up. And how many times have I told you to wear your hat even if we aren't expecting visitors?"

Balwinder lazily picked up his hat, brushed off the dust, and placed it on his head. He liked working for the Chopras. There was hardly anything for him to do. On days when Mr. Chopra went to Bhilwara, he opened the gate once in the morning to let Mr. Chopra's Jaguar out and once in the evening to let Mr. Chopra's Jaguar back in. Other than that, he only had to open the gate a few times a week to let Mrs. Chopra's BMW in and out as she headed to the mall or her ladies' lunch parties.

The Chopras were good employers. They made him sleep out near the gate only on nights when they were having parties. Other than that, he went to his quarter at the back at ten p.m. and anybody who needed to be let in or out buzzed the bell at the gate that rang in his room. The only one who went in or out after ten p.m. was Johnny, and Johnny always had pretty young girls in flimsy clothing with him. Just last Sunday he had seen Johnny and a girl stumble out of a taxi and down the driveway. About halfway there, Johnny had pushed the girl against the compound wall and slipped his hand down the front of her tight jeans. The girl tilted her head back and moaned, and the image kept Balwinder warm through the night.

Mr. Chopra peered over the gate and saw Mrs. Jha step out of a taxi.

"Sir, would you like me to open the gate? Or call for the car?" Balwinder said.

Mr. Chopra ducked down and said through clenched teeth, "Be quiet, you good-for-nothing. I am trying to see the new neighbors. And put your hat on properly."

Mr. Chopra waited a few seconds and then went back on his toes to look through the protective barbed wire on the top of the gate. It was a regular black-and-yellow taxi. Not air-conditioned. The woman inside was wearing a simple pale pink sari, heavily starched, with a dark pink blouse, and Mr. Chopra's first thought was that the new neighbors had fancier maids than he did. Perhaps it was time to put his staff in uniforms.

Mrs. Jha could feel sweat dripping along her spine and wished she had opted for a lighter cotton sari. She didn't want to give in to the pressure of this new neighborhood, yet she had worn one of her nicer hand-loomed saris today. But the houses here were so spaced apart that it was unlikely that she would encounter anyone. The only sign she had seen of people on this road was a passing blue Aston Martin with such darkly tinted windows there was no way of knowing if there was a dog driving the car. A year ago she wouldn't even have known what an Aston Martin was.

Suddenly, Mrs. Jha heard voices. She looked up toward the closed gate to her right just in time to see a balding head vanish from above the gate.

"All the staff needs to wear uniforms. Not

just the guard and driver." Mr. Chopra burst into his living room. His wife had applied a mud pack to her face and looked like she had leaned into a pile of cow dung as she settled back peacefully on the brown leather sofa. The news was playing on television, but on the couch Mrs. Chopra was ignoring it and watching a YouTube video of a little child sitting on the ground shrieking with laughter every time his father tore a piece of paper.

"My weekly inspections are thorough," she said. "They look just fine. Have you seen the remote control? I can't find it and the television is too loud."

"I'm worried that the new neighbors are from London. What if this is just a holiday home for them? We need to put more pressure on the builders in Dubai or put an offer on another property. Have you spoken to the real estate agent? Maybe we can also consider something in Singapore."

"They have returned from London? How nice. I miss Harrods. Is it a family?" Mrs. Chopra said, and lifted her fingertips to gently feel the mask on her face. It was almost dry.

"What are you going on about Harrods for?" Mr. Chopra said. "You handle the staff uniforms and call the real estate agent tomorrow, and I will see about getting a swimming pool put in."

"We are not getting a swimming pool. And where is Johnny? When are you planning to speak to him? He does nothing all day every day," Mrs. Chopra said, allowing her mask to crumble.

"He's fine. He has a tennis coach now. He's improving."

"He's twenty-eight. He is not going to become a tennis star. Coach or no coach, I've seen him play — he has no talent. You promised you would talk to him about getting a job."

"Shh," Mr. Chopra said. "Your mask is cracking. I'm going to the club. After you are done with the uniforms, order one of those little round vacuum cleaners that goes around the house by itself cleaning everything. It looks better than having a maid pushing a huge vacuum cleaner around every morning."

The Gurgaon Select Luxury Recreation Club (the LRC, as everyone called it) was barely a ten-minute drive from the Chopras' home, and it had an eighteen-hole golf course, a driving range, an indoor swimming pool, an outdoor swimming pool, a full gym, tennis courts, table tennis tables, a

98

bar, a formal dining hall with Chinese food, one with Indian food, and an outdoor casual restaurant with the best club sandwiches in all of Delhi. There was also a small Hollywood-themed mini-golf course, but that was used only by children and some of the women. There had been talk about installing an ice-skating rink.

As usual, Mr. Chopra felt himself relax as he pulled up to the gates of the LRC. The sounds of traffic were distant and workers with large pails were busy watering the plants that lined the driveway. They watered everything three times a day to keep the dust settled within the LRC. Becoming a member was no easy or affordable task, and it was unlikely that the new neighbors had a membership yet — you had to have a Gurgaon address, be recommended by someone who had been a member of the club for at least one year, and have another Gurgaon reference on file. Applications were only accepted twice a year, in January and July. Then, if your application made it through the first round, you had an interview with the board. And, if all that was approved, you had to pay a twelve lakh rupee initiation fee plus an annual eight lakh rupee. Even if the new neighbors were earning in dollars, nearly thirty thousand dollars was not cheap.

Mr. Chopra noticed Johnny walking down the long driveway chatting with Vivek, who doubled as a personal trainer at the gym and a golf caddie. As usual Johnny was wearing jeans that were so tight, they looked like they belonged on a girl. He was wearing one of his many collared shirts with the collar unfolded upward. And as Johnny walked next to Vivek, Mr. Chopra could clearly see how short Johnny was. Mr. Chopra knew he himself was not a tall man, but he always wished Johnny would grow taller. For men, it was one thing being short if you were successful. If you were short and unsuccessful, it was just embarrassing.

"Stop, stop, stop," Mr. Chopra said to Nimesh. "What is Johnny doing walking along the driveway like some laborer? Stop the car."

Once the car pulled alongside Johnny, Mr. Chopra said out the window, "What are you doing walking? Why didn't you take the car? And push the hair out of your face. I swear you spend more time at the beauty parlor than your mother."

Johnny looked surprised to see his father. "I was out, so I took a taxi. I don't know why they don't allow taxis into the LRC. This driveway is really long. Did you know they make all the workers park their cars and bikes next door and then walk in? Seems silly when this parking lot is usually half empty. Vivek is caddying for you today."

Vivek looked over at Mr. Chopra and waved.

"Good evening, sir. Nice weather tonight. It's easier to play when it's a bit cooler."

"It is indeed. I'll see you on the course, Vivek. Johnny, get in the car. Where are you going?"

"The bar," Johnny said, opening the door and getting into the front seat of the car.

"Get in the back," Mr. Chopra said. "I need to speak with you."

"I like the front. I don't know why you don't drive this car. It is so smooth. Nimesh knows." Johnny patted Nimesh on his shoulder and smiled.

"Johnny, you are the only member of the club who walks in. It doesn't look right."

"It's fine. Kunal will drop me home after."

They had just about reached the main entrance to the clubhouse. Johnny's best friend, Kunal Jhunjhunwala, son of Shashi Jhunjhunwala, was pulling up in a shiny new Lexus at the same time.

"He's got a Lexus now?" Mr. Chopra said. "What happened to the BMW?"

"His father bought him the Lexus for his

birthday last month," Johnny said.

It was practically impossible to get a Lexus in India, everyone knew that. And Shashi Jhunjhunwala kept beating Mr. Chopra at golf. To have his son pull up in a taxi and walk to the bar while Kunal arrived in his Lexus was adding insult to injury, and he had had enough. He would buy his son a car, Mr. Chopra decided. Johnny had been asking for one, but Mrs. Chopra refused to allow him to get one until he had a job, which didn't look likely to happen anytime soon. He spent his days either playing tennis, flitting around with his pretty little girlfriends, or writing poetry. They had sent him to the United Kingdom to study, but he came back with a degree in English literature and no earning potential.

Johnny got out of the car and slapped hands with Kunal Jhunjhunwala. Kunal came over to Mr. Chopra and said, "Hi, Uncle. How are you? I hear you are having a golfing tournament next week. I should start playing more often. We can have a father-son competition. Johnny?"

"Not for me. I'm not any good at golf. I'll play you in tennis," Johnny said. "Bye, Papa. Kunal will drop me home later."

"I can play on your father's team and you can play on my father's team to balance out the skills," Kunal said. "Bye, Uncle."

That little brat, Mr. Chopra thought. The teams would not need balancing out.

SIX

"Now that the new car is here, will you take it the next time you go to Gurgaon?" Mr. Jha asked his wife over breakfast the next morning. He felt bad when he saw her return the previous evening sweating, with her sari crumpled and hair escaping from the tight low bun she always wore it in.

"I'm not comfortable driving it," Mrs. Jha said. "Besides, we need to get the car blessed before we use it."

Mrs. Jha was sick of being nervous. She double-locked all the doors and windows before bed every night. She checked the vault at the bank at least once a month, and she had even joined a ladies' investment club and taken their advice and put a significant amount of money into gold bricks. The wealth was exciting but it also made her nervous. And now with this flashy car and big move to Gurgaon, she was having sleepless nights. They needed God on their side now more than ever, she thought.

"Don't be silly," Mr. Jha said, pouring hot milk on his bowl of oats. "Such a shiny Mercedes is already blessed. I'm not wasting time taking it to the temple for the pujari to bless it. Did you happen to see the neighbors yesterday?"

"No. I didn't see anyone. Sometimes I wonder if all the houses in Gurgaon are abandoned. But listen, I'm telling you we're attracting the evil eye. It'll take less than an hour. We have to do this. Bad luck is coming."

Mrs. Jha hardly went to the temple these days herself. Last time she went, about three months ago, there was a hand-painted sign that advertised, *Rupees 25 for special exam time prayer.* Sometimes God's home resembled the local shop that sold rice and flour by the kilo. As much as she loved the feel of the temple, lately she always left thinking it made religion feel too much like a transaction. She still tried to go every few months, for the well-being of her family, even though Mr. Jha and Rupak never accompanied her.

"Do you think the neighbors might be foreigners?" Mr. Jha asked. "I've heard that some of the multinationals own houses in Gurgaon and their international workers come and stay for long stretches of time.

Imagine if we move in next to an expat from America. I've always wanted to organize a Fourth of July party."

"How come Americans get called expats but if we move to America, we're called immigrants?" Mrs. Jha asked.

"To-may-to, to-mah-to. No need to find reason to be sensitive about everything."

"Anil, you turn everything into a joke, but I'm not comfortable with all this change. If we offer just a bit extra, I'm sure the pujari will be more than happy to bless the car. I'll pick up the coconut on the way myself."

"Are you mad? I will not drive the car through these wretched narrow lanes, and I absolutely will not have the pujari's filthy hands touching vermillion to the car. And the coconut — yuck — who knows what it will do to the paint job. Not a chance. The car stays in the garage," Mr. Jha said. "End of discussion."

"No, it isn't the end of the discussion," Mrs. Jha said, standing up and collecting her empty bowl and glass. She picked up her husband's bowl while he was still holding the last spoonful up to his mouth. "Forget the car. We'll take the keys and get them blessed."

Mr. Jha ate his last bite and put down his newspaper. He looked at his wife. Stubborn woman. Fine, it had been what had attracted him to her in the first place. The first time he had met her, with his mother and aunt with him, and her parents with her, at the end of the meeting, she had said, "I'd like to meet him alone next time, please." Mr. Jha still remembered how the older generation had gone silent in response to her request. "There's nothing you can't say in front of us," her mother had said to her then. "That is true," his mother had added. "A marriage is a marriage of the families."

"But it's really a marriage between us, and I'd like to meet with him alone next time, please," Mrs. Jha had repeated calmly. Mr. Jha himself had laughed and said, "I'd like that too," and their parents had had no option but to agree. The following week Mr. Jha met Mrs. Jha for ice cream sundaes at the Nirulas in Connaught Place. Her father dropped her off and browsed in the shops downstairs for an hour exactly. Mr. Jha had ordered chocolate sauce drizzled on his sundae and Mrs. Jha hadn't, so he offered her a taste of his. She said no at first but then leaned in and had a spoonful when the hour was almost over, so Mr. Jha was not surprised when his mother came to him the next afternoon and said, "The girl has said yes."

This impending move to Gurgaon had not been easy on her, Mr. Jha knew. Getting the car blessed was the least he could do.

"The spare keys only," he said. "And we won't spend more than half an hour there. The incense makes my eyes burn."

"Answer me one thing, Bindu," Mr. Jha said, bending down to untie his laces, outside the main entrance of the temple. "How come even as Hindus with all our gods, we say we believe in God singular?"

He took off both his shoes and held them out to Mrs. Jha.

"And here, I don't trust all these godly types — put my shoes in your purse," he said.

"Just leave them here. Nobody is going to steal your shoes."

"These are from Woodlands. Look at how nice the leather is. Some beggar will steal them and won't even know what they're worth," Mr. Jha said. "Gods or God, Bindu? Which one is the right term?"

"I don't know, Anil. I suppose it's the collective idea of God in many different representations and forms, so you can say either. And if you're so worried about your shoes, don't leave them out here, go and deposit them — they have a shoe check-in. You would know if you came a bit more often," Mrs. Jha said, dropping a ten-rupee note into a small metal can belonging to a man with leprosy, who was sitting in his wheelchair at the entrance to the temple.

"Ten rupees?" Mr. Jha said. "That's what beggars get these days? While the world is in recession. Absurd."

He wandered off to find the shoe deposit. The summer heat was getting on his nerves. The heat in Delhi summers did not just come from the air; it radiated up from the ground and came off the walls of the buildings and pushed you from every direction, making it difficult to move. What was the point of all this new money if he couldn't escape the blistering midday temperatures? It should be possible, Mr. Jha thought, to have a small portable air-conditioned Plexiglas cubicle built to walk around in. After all, he had had a shower installed in the Gurgaon bathrooms so he would no longer have to use a bucket filled with water and a mug to pour it over his body. So maybe he could have a similar contraption — completely sealed and cooled — to take everywhere with him. It would make life a lot more pleasant. Maybe something with wheels. But then that would just be a car.

"Sir, twenty rupees for the bin and fifty rupees for the individual," the bare-chested man with a red tika was saying to him. The shoe handler, who was sitting behind a counter, with burning incense and loud ragas, looked like God's own guard.

"Fifty rupees to store my shoes for twenty minutes?"

Mr. Jha walked away. He hadn't made his money by being cheated out of small amounts. He saw his wife standing near the entrance with her fair feet naked against the hot, dirty asphalt.

"They're robbing people blind with the shoe check-in," he said. "I'll leave one shoe outside the temple and keep one in my back pocket — nobody will steal a single shoe."

"You can't carry a leather shoe into the temple, Anil," Mrs. Jha said.

"Why not? You're carrying a leather purse."

They entered the main foyer of the temple, and the sudden oasis of peace and quiet silenced them both. It was built in a way to maximize the cross-breeze, and the air smelled of incense. Templegoers all chimed the large bell that hung on the main door to announce their arrival to the gods. A few priests sat scattered on the ground around the periphery, wearing white dhotis with the Brahmin thread crossing against their bare chests. Everyone was barefoot and quiet.

"Where is the temple in Gurgaon?" Mr. Jha whispered. He realized that he had never seen one there. Did rich people not need temples anymore? Or maybe it was more fashionable to go to church these days.

"I'm not sure," Mrs. Jha said. "But more and more people have prayer rooms in their own homes. And you can all a pujari home, depending on what you're praying for. I was reading about how some of these rich industrialists have puja parties in their homes that would put the biggest temples to shame. With gold-embossed invitations and return gifts for a Ganesh Puja. Just imagine."

"Interesting," Mr. Jha said. "Maybe we should do that."

"Don't be ridiculous. You don't even like coming to the temple," Mrs. Jha said. "We don't need to copy everything other people in Gurgaon do."

Mr. Jha had never heard of a puja party, but now he was intrigued. You could probably be as lavish and show off as much as you wanted if you used God as an excuse. He followed his wife in toward the sanctum sanctorum.

"It's so nice and cool in here," Mrs. Jha said. "Even without air-conditioning."

She was relieved to feel the cool clean temple floor that felt like silk beneath her feet.

"Doesn't look like God is doing any of these people much good. Any of the gods," Mr. Jha whispered to his wife as a man with a white bandage covering one eye walked past them.

"Well, you don't know what state he'd be in if he didn't come to the temple," Mrs. Jha said.

Maybe she was right, Mr. Jha thought. He had been very fortunate so far; it was risky to offend the gods. Maybe he should have left the shoes with the Brahmin shoe attendant after all. He certainly shouldn't have a leather shoe in his back pocket right now. He would put some extra money into the donation bowl when his wife wasn't looking. When nobody was looking — the gods would notice that he hadn't done it for any kind of human credit and would be particularly appreciative.

The silence seemed to get louder as they got closer to Lord Krishna's shrine. You could tell this was the main god because the blue idol was nearly six feet tall and stood gracefully in his signature pose with one foot bent in front of the other and his flute raised to his lips. His pedestal was a deep red, and the yellow of his dhoti matched the yellow of the flute. It was the busiest part of the temple but also the most peaceful. The priest's assistant was carrying the lit diya through the crowd of believers, all of whom were passing their hands over the flame and then over their own heads to receive God's light. Mr. Jha waited his turn. He wanted God's light, but because he hadn't done this in years, he moved his hand too close to the flame and then screamed in pain as the flame licked his hand. Everyone turned to look.

"Why must you always make a scene? You don't take anything seriously," Mrs. Jha said, smiling. Her husband was a self-made man. Relying on God was a comfort, not a career. She put her hands together, closed her eyes, bowed her head, and thanked God for finding her a good husband.

At the same time, Mr. Jha, with his hands pressed together, eyes closed and head bowed, was also thanking God for finding him a good spouse. He rarely visited temples, he never followed rituals, he had a leather shoe in his back pocket, and he regularly ate beef — although, in his defense, he'd heard that the beef in India was actually buffalo and those aren't sacred — but thanks to having a wife who truly believed and prayed for him, he had managed to find success. Maybe it hadn't all been just a result of hard work and good luck; maybe it had been because of his wife's prayers.

"Do we ask the pujari to bless the keys here?" Mr. Jha whispered.

"I'm not too sure. Maybe you can just take the keys and hold them up to your head near the main shrine? I'm not sure if we should disturb him," Mrs. Jha said. The priest was standing just a few feet away and looked about as trustworthy as their real estate agent and better fed than any of the gods here. It wasn't easy to trust someone with visible gold caps on his teeth and rings on most of his fingers, and seeing him now she was reminded again of why she came to the temple less and less these days.

"Now that we've come all the way here, may as well get the pujari to actually bless the keys," Mr. Jha said. "I don't want to go home without doing it and then have you blaming me and saying I'm impatient and whatnot."

"I'm just happy you agreed to come. I'm sure God will also be happy," Mrs. Jha said.

"Let's just give a small donation and go home."

"You are giving a donation for a blessing?" the priest walked over to the Jhas to ask. "What would you like to have blessed? You know, with the moon in the fifth quarter, it's an auspicious day today."

He had been listening. He was always listening for the word *donation.* If this couple handed him the donation, he would be able to pocket it, but if they put it in the donation box, it would go directly to the temple's main management. Unfortunately priests didn't work on commission.

"Our new car," Mr. Jha said.

"Oh, nothing," Mrs. Jha quickly added.

"A new car?" the priest said. "A new car must be blessed. You have done well, praise God. People these days come to me only with misfortune upon misfortune. God has been kind to you. It was good of you to come to me. Where is the car? Have you brought a coconut or should I get one?"

"No need, no need," Mrs. Jha said. "We just came to pay our respects to God. Thank you for taking the time to speak to us. That is more than enough."

"But, Bindu, we've come all this way and he is being so generous," Mr. Jha said. "Let us at least get the keys blessed. We couldn't

115

bring the car, but we brought the keys."

"Well," said the priest, eyeing the unfinished peace sign symbol of the Mercedes car keys in Mr. Jha's hands. "I can bless the keys here, but if you would like, for just a small amount — a donation — I can come to your home and do a prayer for the actual car."

"Just the keys will do," Mrs. Jha said.

The priest took the keys and said he would take them to the back directly near the idol and sprinkle them with holy water and have them blessed.

"Right here is fine," Mrs. Jha added. "The evening prayer rush will start soon and I don't want to delay you."

Mrs. Jha did not want him taking the keys out of their sight. She had been hearing about a series of crimes in Delhi lately in which thieves apparently took quick imprints of keys in bars of soap and then created copies of the keys and stole things effortlessly. She wasn't going to fall victim to a key-copying priest.

"Bindu," Mr. Jha whispered. "Now why are you causing a scene? This is why we came. Let's get the keys blessed."

"We are getting the keys blessed. Here in front of us, right now," Mrs. Jha said.

"But if the keys can get closer to God, we

should let them."

"You be quiet," Mrs. Jha said. "You have a leather shoe in your pocket. Now let's just finish up here."

Mr. Jha took out a hundred rupee note from his wallet, but before he could place it in the priest's donation bowl, his wife snatched it out of his hand and walked toward the locked wooden donation box near the idol.

"I'll just put it in directly," she said to the priest. "Why increase your work?"

She looked over her shoulder, saw her husband busy talking to the priest, put the hundred rupee bill in her wallet, took out a fifty rupee bill, and slipped it into the slot of the locked donation box. Fifty was a lot, but at least now it was going directly to the temple management.

Outside the temple, back in the hot sun, on the dirty asphalt, Mr. Jha felt rejuvenated. He had gotten the priest's cell phone number and would find out more about a prayer room in Gurgaon. He took his right shoe out of his back pocket, put it on, and limped over to find his left shoe. Mr. Jha picked it up, placed his left foot gingerly in it, flexed his toes against the soft leather, and stood up satisfied. God would protect them.

Behind him, Mrs. Jha also slipped her feet into her sandals, which were hot from the sun, and felt relieved that they had come to the temple. Even if parts of the temple were getting more and more commercial lately, it was still the home of the gods and it was wise to hedge their bets. They would be safer now and, despite not paying extra for the exam time prayers, she was certain that God would look after her son, across the world in America.

In Ithaca, Elizabeth walked into Rupak's living room, where he was sitting on the floor with his management textbooks spread out around him, all closed, while he flipped through the manual for the new camera flash that had arrived in the mail the previous day. Elizabeth was wearing jeans and a plain white T-shirt, and she held a bottle of water in one hand and her iPad in the other.

"There's an a cappella concert on the quad. Do you want to go?"

"I should study," Rupak said.

Elizabeth sat on his lap, straddled him, and kissed his neck.

"If I don't, how will you marry a rich Indian investment banker? You go. I'll be more fun after I finish this problem set," he said.

"You won't ever marry a white girl anyway," Elizabeth said, laughing.

"What? That's not true."

"Yes, it is. I'm a stopover for you. It's okay."

"Hold on," Rupak said, lifting Elizabeth off his lap.

"I was just joking. Relax," she said, pinching a section of his neck between her front teeth.

Rupak felt the comfortable stir in his pants. His penis reacted immediately to Elizabeth's touch, and he sat back and allowed it. He had avoided the relationship conversation with Elizabeth since he'd been back. It was easy to avoid the topic when the sun was shining and they were both busy trying to make the most of the fall. It was even easier since Rupak had hinted that he had told his parents and then quickly changed the topic. He was good at changing the topic.

"How do you find time to study?" he asked Elizabeth now. "I'm struggling to pass and the semester has only just started."

Elizabeth shrugged her shoulders and got up and walked to Rupak's kitchen.

"You just do. We're here to study, right? So that's what you do. You don't say you're studying while playing with your new camera flash."

"You make it sound easy," Rupak said, putting the manual aside and picking up a textbook.

"It isn't hard. It isn't easy but it isn't hard. We aren't in high school being forced to take these classes," she said, opening his fridge and looking in. "I wish you knew how to cook Indian food."

Rupak thought back to the chicken curry he had left with the men at the airport and felt guilty. He would call his mother more often, he promised himself. And he would not fail the semester.

"I just can't seem to focus," Rupak said, putting the textbook down on the floor and leaning his head back against the sofa.

"That's because you should be studying film, not business," Elizabeth said, returning to the living room with a handful of grapes. She sat down on the sofa behind Rupak and ran her fingers through his hair.

"Please don't say that," he said. "You know I can't study film."

"You can, though. You're an adult — your parents aren't going to disown you for choosing to study something you like studying. I bet they'd respect you for doing something you really enjoy."

"I don't even know if I really enjoy filmmaking. I can't give everything up for what's basically a hobby. You don't know what it's like to have Indian parents," Rupak said.

"You're right, I don't. But I think you underestimate them. From what you've told me, they sound pretty nice. You were so nervous about telling them about me and that worked out fine."

"What time is the concert?" Rupak asked, reaching for his phone, which was on the coffee table.

"Now. In ten minutes," Elizabeth said. She kissed Rupak's head and got up from the sofa. "I should leave."

Rupak grabbed her ankle and looked up at her.

"Don't go," he said. And he meant it. He wanted her to stay. And he wanted to have the courage to tell his parents about her and he wanted to have the courage to quit his MBA and study film.

"If you hadn't spent all day playing with your new camera, you could have come too," Elizabeth said. "Focus, put your phone away. Call me if you get done and we'll have dinner."

Rupak watched her leave the apartment. He opened his e-mail and saw one from Serena Berry, with the subject line *Delhi Connection.*

Dear Rupak,

My aunt, Mrs. Gupta, from Mayur Palli, gave me your e-mail address. She said you're studying at Cornell? I just started my master's here and apparently my uncle was very keen that I meet you. Do you want to have a cup of coffee in Collegetown this weekend?

Best,
Serena

Under other circumstances, he would have ignored an e-mail like this, but he didn't want his mother to hear he had been rude. But there was no such thing as just a neighbor's niece anymore — and it was quite a coincidence that Mrs. Gupta's niece was studying in Ithaca after all. Serena probably knew all about the Jhas' new money. Her aunt and uncle had probably told her that they were moving to a bungalow in Gurgaon and had an unmarried son in the United States. Over the last year, Rupak had often been introduced to the daughters, nieces, and granddaughters of neighbors, friends, and acquaintances, and not one of them held his interest. Most of them already resembled their overweight mothers. His parents might have bought a new home and ordered a new car, but they didn't yet have new friends. They were outsiders in both places at the moment.

Over the summer, the Patnaiks, who lived in D block and hardly ever socialized, bumped into him repeatedly at the new Café Coffee Day and insisted on paying for his coffee and chatting with him. Their daughter, Urmila, with her frizzy hair and visible stretch marks on her upper arms, sat with them quietly, smiling coyly in his direction, not saying a word while her mother told him how good she was at cooking.

"Not just cooking," her father added. "She is a modern lady. She also takes dance classes and is thinking of joining a course for hairstyling."

After that, Rupak stopped going to Café Coffee Day in the mornings.

So he didn't expect the Guptas to have a particularly exciting niece and was already plotting a way to avoid spending more than fifteen minutes with Serena. And he didn't want her to think he was too available, so he replied saying yes, they could meet at Stella's at six next Friday for a quick drink. And then he would report to his mother and then, definitely then, he would also tell her about Elizabeth. Much to his surprise, Serena's reply didn't sound particularly keen on more than a quick drink either. In fact, she specified that it would be a cup of coffee.

SEVEN

The following week, on an unusually over-cast September day, Mr. Jha pulled into the quiet lane of his new Gurgaon home. He had never been here by himself, he realized. Mrs. Jha was usually with him, and this summer Rupak had come with them a few times, and there were all the contractors and painters and builders buzzing around, working. He had never really appreciated the silence and the greenery before. Gurgaon felt still while the rest of Delhi throbbed.

The air was heavy with heat and the promise of rain. On the radio, a Bon Jovi song played. "It's been raining since you left me," the lyrics said. How funny, Mr. Jha thought. An Indian song would have to say, "It hasn't rained since you left me." Unless, of course, you were happy that they left you.

An electronic shoe-polishing machine in a large box was on the passenger seat of his

Mercedes. He had strapped it in with the seat belt. It was beautiful. And it was expensive. It was not a planned purchase. This morning he had a breakfast meeting with two young men who were launching a website that would help people find handymen around Delhi, and they asked him to join their team as a consultant. He declined. He did not have time to take on any new work until they were done moving homes. And then they had to visit Rupak, so he was not going to have any free time until November or December. And then it would be the holiday season, so really it was best if he took the rest of the year off.

The meeting was over breakfast at the luxurious Teresa's Hotel in Connaught Place in central Delhi, and after filling himself up with mini croissants, fruit tarts, sliced cheeses, salami, coffee, and orange juice, Mr. Jha went for a stroll through the lobby and the other restaurants in the hotel. All the five-star hotels in the center of town were little oases of calm and cool. Mr. Jha was walking by the large windows that overlooked the swimming pool that was for guests only when he thought he would book a two-night stay here. He knew his wife loved the indulgence of nice hotels and he had recently read about what youngsters were calling a staycation — a vacation where you don't leave the city or the home you usually live in, but you give yourself a few days to take a holiday. Of course, since he didn't work much anymore, most days, weeks, months were a staycation, but how wonderful it would be to check into a hotel and have a lazy few days. Having room service — or, like they were called at Teresa's, butlers — was a different sort of pleasure than having servants bringing you food and cleaning your home. Butlers showed that you had made the progression from servants to expensive appliances to uniformed men who ran the expensive appliances.

He was about to go to the front desk to inquire about rates for the following week when he saw an electronic shoe polisher on the floor. He had not used one of those in ages. Mr. Jha placed his right foot in between the motion-sensor bristles, which promptly started whirring around his shoe. He did his left foot as well and then looked down happily to see how shiny his shoes were. They hadn't looked this good since the day he bought them, so he changed his mind and decided that an electronic shoe polisher was a much better use of money than a staycation. They had just bought an expensive new house, after all, and thinking of a stay in a hotel as an "escape" was offensive to the new home. But the one thing missing in their hotel-like home was an electronic shoe polisher.

So instead of making a reservation for the following week, Mr. Jha asked the pretty woman at the front desk where they bought the electronic shoe polishers. She had no idea, so she had to call the manager while he waited. A shop in INA Market, she said, and wrote down the name on a small yellow sticky paper.

Mr. Jha left Teresa's and went straight to the market, found exactly what he was looking for — more than what he was looking for — the newest model of the polisher had arrived recently, so Mr. Jha bought that one — and was now arriving in Gurgaon with the box safely belted on the front seat where there were front and side air bags for safety. He did not want to take the box back home to Mayur Palli, because he got the feeling his wife would not like it quite as much as she would have liked a staycation, so it would be best if she saw it later, when they were settled in and happy and excited about their new lives.

Mr. Jha reached the big metal gate of their new home in Gurgaon and was about to step out of the car to push it open — they would have to hire a guard soon — when the gate next door opened and a man walked out followed by what looked like a guard wearing a white uniform. Mr. Jha pressed the button to roll his window down. Had he remembered to show Rupak the power windows?

"Look at the chair," the first man said to the guard. He pointed at what Mr. Jha assumed was the guard's chair placed right outside the gate. It was plastic, with a dirty-looking brown cushion on it. A stack of newspapers lay under it. "This reflects on the house, Balwinder. I can't keep repeating myself. Get the cushion cover washed, and throw away all the papers. What will people think?"

"Yes, sir. Sorry, sir," Balwinder said, while looking at the idle car parked near the next gate. The new neighbors, he realized! The ones Mr. Chopra was waiting to meet. "Sir," Balwinder whispered, pointing toward Mr. Jha's car. "Sir, look behind you."

"Balwinder, focus. I'm late for golf already. Clean this up and take the contractor to the backyard when he comes," Mr. Chopra continued. "If my wife is going to keep objecting to a swimming pool, we're just going to have to have the contractor take measurements when she's out shopping."

"Sir, madam told me this morning not to let the pool contractor in when she goes shopping. I think she knows," Balwinder said.

"How does that woman know everything I'm doing? Before I've even done it. Never get married, Balwinder."

Mr. Jha stepped out of his car and said, "Good morning! Hello!"

Mr. Chopra spun around. He was wearing khaki pants with a single crisp crease running down each leg. Mr. Jha would have to tell his wife to get their clothes ironed more carefully. He looked down at his pants, which were crushed along the upper thighs, and tried quickly flattening them with his palms. Mr. Chopra was wearing a white long-sleeved shirt on top that stretched taut over his belly that looked hard like a well-tuned drum. He had a white baseball cap on his head. He might not be a foreigner, Mr. Jha thought, but he certainly looked fashionable.

"Good morning, good morning, good morning. Lovely day. Are you our new neighbor? Chopra. I am Mr. Dinesh Chopra. Welcome. Welcome to the neighborhood."

"Anil Kumar Jha," Mr. Jha said, extending his hand. "A pleasure. We are not shifting in yet — just dropping some things off, and getting the place cleaned and some work done."

Mr. Chopra's cell phone rang. He took it out of his pocket, looked at it, motioned to Mr. Jha to please excuse him for one moment, answered, and said, "I will be there in under ten minutes. I am just leaving now. Seven. Seven minutes. I will be on the course in nine minutes." He hung up and shouted, "Balwinder! Tell Nimesh to hurry up and get the car out."

"Course?" Mr. Jha said.

"Golf. My golfing partner at the club is waiting for me. Do you golf? Where are you from? Delhi? London?"

"I haven't golfed in a long time," Mr. Jha said, which was technically true. His lifetime was a long time and he hadn't ever golfed during it.

"Once you have settled in, we must play," Mr. Chopra said. "What do you do? Oh, I want to know all about you."

"We must, we must," Mr. Jha said. "I work in technology. Computers. And you? We must have a meal and get to know each other."

Computers. Maybe they had moved from San Francisco, then. Mr. Chopra looked into the window of the Mercedes. An image of the shoe-polishing machine was clearly printed on the box in the front seat.

"Oh good, are you throwing away Mr. Mukherjee's shoe polisher? Thank goodness. Who gets shoes polished these days? Am I right? It is so much easier to buy new ones. I'm glad we will have neighbors with better taste now!" Mr. Chopra said.

His car came out of his driveway right as his phone rang again.

"So sorry," Mr. Chopra said again to Mr. Jha. His phone kept ringing. "Oh dear. I simply have to run. But will you be here soon? We must chat. I don't even know where you're moving from. But I am in the process of getting a swimming pool put in, so maybe we'll make it a pool party once you're settled. I know your house does not have a pool."

He opened the back door of his car, and the air-conditioned air spilled out and cooled Mr. Jha. He would have to learn golf and he would have to hire a driver who would quietly pull up in the car and wait patiently while Mr. Jha wore a baseball cap and pants with crisp creases in them. But first, he had to see if the shop in INA Market would allow him to return the shoe-polishing machine.

"We will be fully moved in soon," Mr. Jha said. "But it is so nice to have already met a neighbor. It will make my wife happy to know there are friendly people in the area."

"Wonderful. I'll be off then, Mr. Jha. Here's to our friendship!"

"Please call me Anil," Mr. Jha said as Mr. Chopra's car door slammed shut and the car pulled away down the lane.

At home in Mayur Palli, in the bottom drawer of her husband's desk, Mrs. Jha found Rupak's birth certificate. She put it on the pile of papers on the floor beside her and took a sip of her tea. Dust particles floated in the late-afternoon sunlight that was coming in through the window.

She ran her finger over the back edge of Mr. Jha's desk and looked at the light gray and black dust that collected on her fingertip. Was it possible that one of the particles was from Rupak's tenth birthday? Could there be one from the day he had come home in the evening with his lip cut open from a playground brawl? Perhaps one of the dust particles was from the afternoon when Rupak, seven, maybe eight years old, had fallen asleep on the school bus and not come home at the usual time. The maid had called her at the office to tell her that Rupak was gone and Mrs. Jha had rushed home in a taxi, crying and scared, only to find Rupak coming in the front gate, holding the bus driver's hand, an hour after he should have returned. Mrs. Jha blew the dust off her finger, wiped it on the rag that she was using to clean up, and picked up the birth certificate again.

She was so scared when Rupak was born. Mr. Jha's mother, Janaki, had died just eight days before Mrs. Jha went into labor, and the entire time she was giving birth, she prayed it would be a boy so she would not have to name the child Janaki. If it had been a girl, Mr. Jha would have insisted on naming her in his mother's memory, and nobody named for her mother-in-law could be a happy person. Of that much Mrs. Jha was certain.

Janaki wasn't so bad at first. She wore the most beautiful white widow's saris. For many years, even after everything was arranged and they were married, Mrs. Jha always remembered that boy from Goa that she had kissed once on holiday with her friends from college and never saw again. That was part of why she agreed to marry Mr. Jha in the first place — to undo the guilt of having kissed a strange boy in Goa. Her parents never said anything about what happened in Goa, but she knew she had returned to Delhi slightly altered. Her parents must have also noticed, because the next week they set up the first meeting with a boy and his family. The first one — she didn't remember his name now — sat in between his parents on the sofa, and she knew immediately that he wouldn't work for her. To test him, she had said that she'd like to meet him alone before deciding anything. His father had said that wouldn't be possible and he had simply stared down at his feet. Mr. Jha was different — even though the families discouraged them from meeting alone, he agreed with her and made it happen. They went out to the Nirulas in Connaught Place for ice cream sundaes and Mr. Jha offered her a taste of his sundae, and it reminded her of the boy in Goa who offered her a taste of his bibimca, saying it was a sin to not have ever tried the Goan dessert. That was when she knew she would marry Mr. Jha. At first, every time Mr. Jha would touch her at night, she would shut her eyes tightly and think about that boy and her body would relax.

Mrs. Jha put Rupak's birth certificate carefully back in a folder and placed the folder in the box. It had been so easy to conceive Rupak. The first two years of their

marriage, they were not financially comfortable enough to have a child, so they had
always timed their intercourse. When,
however, it started becoming clear that
computers were not going to vanish anytime
soon, within a month, Mrs. Jha was pregnant. She always wanted another child but
no matter how hard they tried, she never
again managed to get pregnant. And Mr.
Jha always refused to go to a doctor about
it. "That's too indulgent," he would say if
she ever brought it up. "These things should
happen naturally."

Every year, even now, Rupak's birthday
celebration was always muted because Mr.
Jha was still mourning his mother. The night
before she died, Mr. and Mrs. Jha had just
come home from dinner and Mrs. Jha was
heavily pregnant. She had dressed up that
night because, in one of his few romantic
moments, Mr. Jha had suggested they go
out for dinner, since they would never be
just the two of them again. When they came
home, Janaki looked at the sari Mrs. Jha
was wearing and said, "Are the rest of your
clothes with the washerwoman?" The next
morning when they woke up, Janaki was
dead; those were the last words she ever said
to Mrs. Jha. Now that she was long dead,
Mrs. Jha could be more generous. It must

have been difficult for her mother-in-law to have spent a much larger part of her life as a widow than as a wife.

What would Mrs. Jha do, she wondered, if Mr. Jha died? Would she focus all her love and attention on poor Rupak and make life miserable for his wife? Mrs. Jha worried that Rupak had figured out that an American girlfriend would be a good way for him to avoid responsibility. She watched enough American television shows to understand that it would not be an easy choice for Rupak to return to India. Everyone in India was going on and on about the country changing and, yes, there were malls with high ceilings and better roads and more freedom for young people, but India was not America.

Of course, more and more Americans were coming to India for holidays, but within a few months, once they had done yoga and tried half heartedly to teach English to prostitutes' children, they got on planes back to their homes in Michigan or Texas. Mrs. Jha saw these young white people in Connaught Place and Janpath with their Fabindia kurtas, looking like they were the latest Mother Teresa. They laughed with the slum children and pretended not to mind touching their filthy hands. Of course they didn't mind. It would be easy to touch those children if you knew you were leaving and next week you would be back at home, drinking tea in your nice big kitchen telling people how those children laugh and smile even though their lives are so difficult.

"Are shoe polishers silly?" Mr. Jha came into the room where Mrs. Jha was packing.

"Like the cobbler downstairs? Why would he be silly?" Mrs. Jha said.

"No, no. Not like the cobbler. Shoe-polishing machines. Like they have in hotels. You know — where you put your foot in and the shoe gets polished."

"I don't know if *silly* is the right word. Where have you been all day?"

"Why are you sitting on the ground packing things so slowly?" Mr. Jha said. "I told you, you don't need to do that. The movers will take care of everything."

"I don't want the movers touching your papers. They smoke bidis all day. I'd rather put the important things in boxes myself so they don't touch anything," Mrs. Jha said. "But I was thinking — why don't we go out for dinner tonight? Just the two of us."

"Bindu, do you know how much this move is costing me? We can't go out for dinners all the time. Can you just make something quick? And where is Rupak? He hasn't called in almost a week. Frankly I am getting a bit worried about how useless he is. It will be embarrassing if he has to come back and find some midlevel job here."

"What's wrong with working here? You work here, lots of good companies and intelligent people work here. I think it would be good for him to come back," Mrs. Jha said. "It will be different for him than it was for us."

"He's probably fallen in love with some American girl already," Mr. Jha said.

EIGHT

At six p.m. the next Friday, Rupak got a surprise. Sitting at the bar at Stella's was a woman not anything like what he had expected. Serena was slim and wearing tight black capris and a dark red silk shirt with thin straps that showed off a set of darker red bra straps. Her black hair hit at her prominent collarbones. She was fiddling with her phone, her face lit up by the blue light, when Rupak entered.

"Serena?" he asked, worried that she'd say no.

But it was her. And she looked up at him and smiled and stood and leaned forward and gently touched her cheek to his and said, "Rupak, it's nice to meet you."

She smelled nice and her voice was deep, like a smoker's. He sat down next to her and looked down at his own cargo shorts and T-shirt and flip-flops and quickly motioned the waiter over to order drinks to settle his nerves. He asked for a beer and turned to Serena.

"I'll just have a cappuccino, please. With skim milk."

"Are you sure?" Rupak said. "It's a Friday night, after all."

"Thanks," Serena said. "But I have to get to a dinner after this."

Rupak already didn't want her to leave.

"So you're doing your MBA at Cornell?" Serena said once they were settled in with their drinks in front of them.

He had been rejected from Cornell. The first year that he applied, he had been rejected from all the Ivy League universities, and MIT and the University of Chicago. When he applied again the following year, he changed his approach and applied to NYU, Boston University, University of Michigan, and, what he thought would be just a safety school, Ithaca College.

So Ithaca College it was. With no fellowship money even though, from what he heard, almost all graduate students got at least some fellowship money. Rupak knew it wasn't the most prestigious of universities, but by that point, he really just wanted a way out of India, so he didn't care about the brand-name universities.

"I'm doing my MBA but I've always had

a real interest in film. What are you studying?"

No part of that sentence was a lie.

"I'm doing my master's in performing arts. I just finished class across the street at the Schwartz Center. Have you been to any shows there?" Serena asked.

Rupak motioned for another beer before he had finished his first one.

"Not yet. First year was really busy."

Still no lies. He continued, "I write a little bit but I would love to move into directing. Does performing arts mean you're an actress?"

Was that too obviously flirtatious? You could only ask pretty women if they acted, everyone knew that. But Serena laughed and said, "No, I don't act. I tried for a while but it didn't go anywhere." She smiled.

They waited in silence while the bartender brought Rupak's second beer over and poured it into the glass.

"Do you think you're going back to India after this?" Serena continued. "I hear your parents are shifting to Gurgaon."

Despite seeming uninterested, she seemed to be investigating his future plans, Rupak thought. It was a good sign. It was probably best to downplay his interest in film.

"I doubt it. I'll probably get a job in New

York. Maybe L.A. Investment banking. I'm also looking at consulting jobs. What do you want to do?"

"I'm going to go back to Delhi," Serena said. "I produced a small play there this summer and it did pretty well. My sister and I want to set up a theater company. I really feel there aren't enough non-Bollywood voices there."

Rupak was worried she was going to fire back more questions about his professional plans, and he had no professional plans, so he pressed her to tell him more about her theater company. She had moved into the production side of theater after trying her hand at acting. It was hard, she said, doing theater in Delhi, in the shadow of Bollywood, but she didn't expect to make massive amounts of money out of it. She and her sister were living at home with their parents — "My father isn't doing too well at the moment so I think it's nice for them to have us at home."

"How did you first start acting?" he asked. "Did you also model?"

He noticed a message flash on the screen of her phone. Serena glanced down at the phone, smiled, pressed the button on the top right to darken the screen, and looked up at him distracted and said, "Sorry, what did you say?"

"How did you start acting? Did you also model?"

Suddenly an image of Mrs. Gupta passed through his mind. Had she also once been young and beautiful, sitting with a man, drinking a cup of coffee? Was Serena related to Mrs. Gupta through her mother? Were those her genes? No. He shook the image out of his head. There was no reason to ruin his evening.

"I did not model, no. Modeling and acting are not interchangeable, even though everyone in India seems to think that. I always liked the stage — even in school, I always auditioned for the plays. I never got the lead roles. I should have taken that as a sign."

Serena laughed and Rupak used that laugh as encouragement to ask, "Are you sure you won't have a drink?"

Serena looked into her coffee cup and tilted it toward her as if, perhaps, the answer lay beneath all the foam. She checked her watch, bit her lower lip, and said, "Sure. I think I can fit in a quick one. I'll just have a glass of pinot grigio."

Rupak's phone flashed then, and it was his turn to look down and check his screen. There was a message from Elizabeth.

Drinks at Benchwarmers tonight. Come after your romantic date. See you there.

It hadn't occurred to him that he might have needed to lie to Elizabeth about where he was going tonight.

Elizabeth always woke up early on Sundays, even if, like the previous night, they had been up late drinking.

"Sundays make me think of death anyway," she would say. "If I slept for half the day, I'd go crazy."

When he first heard her say that, he was intrigued but too hungover to ask more, so he had just rolled over and gone back to sleep while she sat near the window in the living room with a cup of coffee and a book. And it wasn't just the hangover; in the image he had of her, there was no space for being anxious about mortality. Like so much else, it didn't fit so he didn't ask.

Rupak had been thinking about Serena all of Saturday and still couldn't quite get her out of his mind this morning. She had stayed for another glass of wine on Friday, and they had discovered that they had both grown up going to the Delhi Book Fair in Pragati Maidan every year — he only went to buy comic books but he didn't tell her that — and they also both discovered how nice it was to talk to someone who remembered what Pragati Maidan used to be. Speaking to her that night, he had felt a fleeting moment of nostalgia for Delhi, despite the fact that her version of the city was quite different.

But even though she had been on his mind since Friday night, there was a deep pleasure he felt when he was around Elizabeth. This Sunday morning he could hear her in the living room, on the phone with her parents. He heard, through the door that was pulled shut but not fully, the sizzle of bacon hitting a hot pan. The smells of Sunday morning breakfast in America crept in and he looked around her bedroom. On the wall above the bed was a framed print of the painting of the American flag by Jasper Johns. He hadn't heard of Jasper Johns until he had met her and when he first saw that flag he thought, yes, she was as American as he had hoped. But it turned out that the flag was actually considered a piece of art, not a symbol of patriotism. If he was outside this room and had to describe it, he would have reached into his American sitcoms and filled this room with posters of Marilyn Monroe and maybe one of Van Gogh's *Starry Night,* but that wasn't what the room was at all.

Elizabeth was never turning out to be

146

what he expected. He thought back to their first meeting. It was after the first-year orientation, where they had briefly locked eyes. Later that afternoon, he was waiting at the bus stop to go to the grocery store and she had driven past in her Jeep. She stopped at the bus stop and shouted out to him, "Hey!"

He looked around, uncertain that this beautiful blond woman would be shouting out to him, but the only other person at the stop was an older Chinese woman who was knitting while waiting and did not even look up.

"You were at orientation this morning, right? Are you waiting for the bus? Do you need a ride somewhere?" Elizabeth said.

"I'm going to get groceries," he said.

"Me too," Elizabeth said. "Get in. It'll be easier to bring stuff back in the car."

It worked out well because he bought much healthier food than he would have if there hadn't been a beautiful woman in line with him at the store. They had then gone back to her apartment for dinner and wine and stayed up talking until two a.m., and Rupak was mesmerized. He remembered asking her if she had been a cheerleader in school or undergraduate, but now he didn't remember her answer.

He stretched and stepped out of bed. He walked out of the bedroom and saw Elizabeth, no longer on the phone, in her shorts and black tank top, hair loose, standing in the kitchen while bacon and eggs cooked on the stove. Would his parents' new life ever look like this, he wondered? He loved this. He loved the smells and the sights and, yes, in Delhi they could now buy bacon and fancy coffee, but the *feel,* the feel of this room and this space with Elizabeth in it was not something money could buy.

"Look how nice it is outside," Elizabeth said to him. "We have to go do something. I was thinking we have breakfast and then go to Beebe Lake, maybe go for a run and have a picnic?"

"How are you not tired? We drank so much beer last night," Rupak said, kissing the top of her shoulder and reaching over her to break off a piece of bacon that was on a paper napkin on a plate on the counter. "Were you a cheerleader in high school?"

"What? No. You ask me that so often and I always say no," Elizabeth said. "Come on. Let's go sweat it out, you'll feel better. And we can take a bottle of wine for a picnic to help us through the hangover. Do you want a cup of coffee? Oh, that reminds me — next time you go to India, I want you to bring me back some South Indian coffee. I read an article about it last week and I want to try it."

"Sure," Rupak said, pouring milk into his cup.

"Or I could just come with you next time you go to India," Elizabeth said. "I was thinking we could move there after graduation even. So many of the Indian companies recruit in America. It could be more interesting than just moving to New York like everyone else."

"You would never move there," Rupak said. "You would hate it there."

"Why do you always say that? I think I'd actually love it there. I'm being serious about this."

"It's completely different there. You wouldn't . . . I don't know . . . you wouldn't get it," Rupak said.

"You moved here from India. That's the same change as moving to India from here. You know you find my life in Florida as exotic as I find yours."

"That's different. Everyone knows what America is, no matter where they've grown up. It's not unknown. All the world's images are America, you know. It's hardly a culture shock."

"I just think it's something to think about.

From both a work perspective and a personal perspective, it's an interesting idea."

"Sure." Rupak slipped his arms around her waist and leaned his chin against the back of her head. He was too sleepy to have this conversation right now. He couldn't even bring himself to tell his parents about her; he would never be able to bring her to India. "Here, let me finish making breakfast. I'll bring it to you in bed."

"How romantic," Elizabeth said with a laugh. "But I'm almost done. And I don't want to go back to bed. We're going out."

"How can anyone say no to you?" Rupak said.

NINE

Balwinder was sitting near the Chopras' gate reading the gossip section of the Hindi newspaper he had borrowed from the guard two bungalows away when he saw the same Mercedes from earlier turn onto their small road. The new neighbors again! Mr. Chopra had told Balwinder to keep an eye on the driveway next door and report to him about everything he saw.

"If they have other cars, I want you to check what kind. If there is luggage being delivered, I want you to find out where it is coming from. If you can get close enough to tell me the brand of his watch, I'll consider giving you a raise. If his wife comes, I want to know what she is wearing. Everything, Balwinder," Mr. Chopra had said. "And if I'm at home when they come, you call me immediately."

During the day, unlike a lot of other homeowners in the neighborhood, the

Chopras did not require Balwinder to sit in the booth outside the gate. He usually spent the morning in the shade under the big banyan tree across the gate and napped in his room in the afternoon. Today the Chopras had taken Mr. Chopra's brother, Upen, who had arrived the previous night, to the LRC for lunch, and Balwinder was waiting for them to return when the Mercedes drove down the lane. The Mukherjees had driven the Chopras mad with their quiet wealth, and he was curious to see what this family would cause. And he wouldn't mind wooing the pretty maid in the starched sari despite the fact that she looked a lot older than him. Paying for sex — even though Sugandha had breasts that would make the sultriest Bollywood stars jealous — was starting to feel insufficient. He would see Johnny and his friends, all with pretty girls on their arms, coming home night after night and wonder why he didn't have the right to that. He was young, he was handsome, and he was definitely more intelligent than Johnny. Why was he stuck scrambling out of bed and opening the gate for them instead of slipping his hand up the shirt of a pretty young girl? The girls did not even look at him. Occasionally a nice one would mutter a thank-you, but mostly they just flicked their cigarette ash and walked past him without a care in the world. He had wanted, a few times, to grab the bottom of one of these passing beauties. When they came in late at night, with their eyes glazed and the boys' hands all over them, they were unlikely to notice.

The Mercedes pulled up and Balwinder saw the same pretty maid get out and push open the heavy metal gate. They would need to get that gate replaced, he thought. It was about nine feet high and the sections in between the iron slats were covered with some sort of Plexiglas. The Mukherjees had been scared of having their home robbed again, so they had slowly built themselves a completely private fortress. Balwinder much preferred the Chopras' gate. It was taller — about twelve feet high — and Mr. Chopra had had bird shapes bent into the wrought-iron rods. The gate next door was heavy and rusted in parts and looked bulky.

The driver's-side window rolled down and Mr. Jha looked out toward Balwinder. Balwinder got up and rushed over, hoping he would be able to catch a glimpse of his watch.

"Namaste," Mr. Jha said. "Is Mr. Chopra at home?"

"Good afternoon, sir," Balwinder said.

"Sir and madam have gone to the LRC."

"The what?" Mr. Jha said.

"The LRC, sir. The club. But they should be home soon. What time is it, sir?" Balwinder said and moved closer to the car window to try to see Mr. Jha's watch.

"Well, hopefully we'll see him later this afternoon," Mr. Jha said, and put his window back up and pulled into the driveway.

Not, however, before Balwinder looked into the car and saw the woman — he assumed the wife — sitting in the backseat, wearing big sunglasses that covered most of her face. Her hair was loose over her shoulders and she looked like she was wearing Western clothes. It was strange that the lady of the house sat in the backseat while the maid sat in the front when the husband was driving — it was usually the other way around. Or, if there was a driver, the maid sat at the front, and the man and woman of the house sat at the back. He would have to remember to tell Mr. Chopra this detail.

When they pulled into the driveway and Mrs. Jha had pushed the gate shut behind them, Mrs. Ray stepped out of the backseat of the car. She was glad Mrs. Jha had invited her along to see the house today. After the fiasco with the stolen yoga pants (which had shown up one morning, bundled and

154

thrown into a corner of her balcony), she needed a break.

"Oh, this is just lovely," Mrs. Ray said. "Look at all the greenery. Who would even know you're in Delhi? This is beautiful."

"It's silly," Mrs. Jha said. "It seems a shame to push the city away so much, doesn't it?"

"Not at all. The only way to survive in Delhi is to push it away," Mrs. Ray said.

She looked around the lawns feeling a hint of envy. Her husband had died leaving her with enough money to get by every month, but she had no way of making her way out of Mayur Palli. Here were the Jhas, Mr. Jha ten years older than her, getting a fresh start, with a new home and new neighbors and friends. It wasn't even a question of dashed dreams for her; she realized now that she simply had no more dreams. At some point, she had become aware that the number of days she had ahead of her were probably fewer than those behind her. She could dress youthfully, do yoga, and paint her walls red all she wanted, but was there anything left for a childless widow her age to look forward to? She looked down at her flared jeans that were so tight she had a hard time sitting comfortably in them. Her nails were painted pink, but did the girls at the beauty parlor laugh behind her back after she got her pedicures?

"It's an oasis of calm," she said.

"This is nothing," Mrs. Jha said. "You should see some of the other houses around here. I peeked in through the gates when I was here last week — the first house on the road has a small racing track built into the front lawn for their children. And one of the houses near the main road is built like a miniature version of the Taj Mahal."

Mrs. Jha was glad Mrs. Ray was the first person from Mayur Palli to be seeing it — she hoped it didn't look too ostentatious. But she also hoped it looked impressive. Seeing it with a friend from Mayur Palli for the first time, she looked up at the home and realized it looked quite regal.

"Who built a house like the Taj?" Mr. Jha asked. He hoped Mrs. Ray didn't think the new home looked run down. They just hadn't yet had the chance to get everything done properly. He would have to remember to get a gardener in soon. He would have to buy some wrought-iron-and-glass furniture, and maybe have some exotic plants flown in from Indonesia. He wanted his guests to forget they were in Delhi. They couldn't live in a neighborhood like this and not keep up with the neighbors.

■ ■ ■ ■

"Sir, sir, the neighbors are here again," Balwinder said when Mr. Chopra's Jaguar pulled up to the gate almost two hours later. But Mr. and Mrs. Chopra were not in the car. It was only Upen. Balwinder opened the gate to allow the car in.

"Sir, please call Mr. Chopra-sir and let him know that the neighbors are here. I could not quite see what kind of watch Mr. Jha was wearing, but his wife was wearing big sunglasses."

"What are you talking about, Balwinder?" Upen said, walking toward the front door of the house. At nearly six feet, Upen was taller than his brother and many men in Delhi. And he was slim. His hair was gray and still thick — it was said about men that if they were lucky and their hair started graying before it started falling, it would remain thick as it grayed. Upen was lucky. He had a neatly trimmed salt-and-pepper beard to match his hair, and he had inherited their mother's light brown eyes that made him look like a North Indian warrior who had descended from the mountains and, if anyone were to see Mr. Chopra and his brother side by side, they would find it impossible to believe that the two were related and that Upen was the elder one. Today he was wearing dark jeans and a plain long-sleeved black T-shirt. "Don't shut the gate. Nimesh just came to drop me home. He has to go and pick up Dinesh and Geeta from the mall."

Balwinder followed Upen to the front door.

"Sir, please call Mr. Chopra and tell him to hurry home."

"Balwinder, you're a stubborn fellow," Upen said. "My brother doesn't know how good you are. I should offer you more money and take you to Chandigarh."

Upen dialed his brother on the phone.

"Dinesh, this guard of yours wants me to tell you that the new neighbors are here. And something about a watch and the wife's sunglasses."

"They're there now?" Mr. Chopra said. He was at the DLF Mall waiting in line for a scoop of Mövenpick ice cream while his wife collected a stone figurine of pugs in a basket that they had ordered from a home décor shop. "How long have they been there? Have you sent the car back? I hope we get back in time to speak to them properly. Hold on." Mr. Chopra was at the head of the line. "Two scoops of chocolate swirl caramel. I want it with a wafer cone but keep the cone separate. Put the ice cream in a cup and hand me a cone. Otherwise it gets too soggy and you can't properly enjoy the cone. Give me two cones. My wife will also like one. But no ice cream; she is gaining weight." He returned his attention to his brother and said, "I hope they're foreigners. Then our property value will go up. Upen, why don't you make yourself useful and see what you can find out about the neighbors before we get home?"

"I'm not going to pester your poor neighbors. I'm going for a run and if I see them when I'm out, I will be polite, but I'm not going to go cross-examining them about their income. And buy your wife some ice cream. You've gained more weight than her."

"You look like a fool when you go running through the roads here," Mr. Chopra said. "People will get nervous thinking you are being chased. Nobody runs here. If you insist on exercising, I've told you a thousand times to use the gym at the LRC. It has a wonderful sauna."

"You know I don't like running indoors. And all the ladies at the LRC make me nervous, the way they look at me. I don't know why you tell everyone I'm widowed."

"Widowed is much easier to explain than

divorced. Very few of the men at the LRC are widowed; all the widowed women are looking to see if you're interesting. And most of the other women know that with their husbands' eating habits, they will also soon be widowed. But nobody wants a divorcé. That is exactly why you should go to the LRC. I don't know how you can handle being all alone in Chandigarh. Are you putting up with some young college student again?"

"You go eat your ice cream and do your shopping. I will get changed and go for my run."

Upen put the phone down and went upstairs to the guest room to get changed. He had to admit he was also slightly curious about these new neighbors. Maybe they really would be foreigners. He would not usually have cared much, but the truth was that he had recently had a brief affair with Sue, a young American filmmaker who was directing a film in Chandigarh and was using his marble-and-tile warehouse to shoot. The young woman, "a bisexual" she had freely said about herself, was half Irish, half Indian, and was making a feature film about farmers in Punjab. Upen met her the first day she arrived at his factory and spent the next three weeks sleeping with her when

160

she wasn't filming. After that, she packed her equipment and her actors and headed to Sri Lanka for the next segment of their filming schedule without even pretending she might be interested in seeing him again.

Maybe his brother was right about using the gym at the LRC. Part of the reason for coming to Delhi was to meet some new people, after all. Chandigarh got boring day in and day out with its neatly laid-out streets and small-town mentality. He would go for a run outside today and try the gym at the LRC tomorrow. Upen sat and tied his laces on the large wooden swing that Mr. Chopra had installed on the front porch. He could hear voices and activity from the front yard next door.

Mr. and Mrs. Jha were having an argument about the bathrooms in the house while workers stood in the driveway holding materials for the showers that were going to be installed.

Mrs. Ray, who was sitting on one of the discarded plastic chairs in the front lawn listening to the Jhas argue over a bathtub, knew she was about to be asked to pick a side, so she stood up and walked toward the gate.

"I'm just going to walk down the lane and take a look at the other homes," she said as she opened the gate.

"A bathtub is terrible for the environment, Anil. Even a shower is much worse than a bucket and mug, but I've agreed to that," Mrs. Jha said.

"Bindu," Mr. Jha said. "Why leave a carbon fingerprint when you can leave a carbon footprint?"

Mrs. Ray pulled the gate shut. Outside, under the banyan tree, Balwinder was snoozing when he was woken up by the creak of the Jhas' gate. He got up in a rush and brushed off the dirt and grass that was sticking to his pants. Although Balwinder was hoping for another sighting of the pretty maid, he was happy to see the glamorous woman next door come out. He was about to say hello when Upen pulled the Chopras' gate open and stepped out, and the woman next door looked only at Upen.

Balwinder was used to this. He was mostly invisible on this street. He didn't blame anyone. When he went to Sugandha's neighborhood, he was the wealthy one and he had the luxury of ignoring the poorer, dirtier men who hung around in the narrow alleys around her building. And being invisible here made it easier for him to observe others. The woman next door, in her tight jeans and short red kurta, was beautiful, and Balwinder noticed Upen also taking her in.

"Good afternoon," Upen said, bowing his head toward the woman who had just pulled the gate shut next door. Upen had not expected someone so beautiful to step out of that driveway.

"Good afternoon," Mrs. Ray said, feeling incapable of saying more. The Jhas had a handsome new neighbor. Handsome in the way none of the men in her world were. Did people in Gurgaon look different from people in the rest of Delhi, she wondered.

"Lovely day," Upen said. "You can feel winter around the corner."

"Thank goodness. It's been a hot summer," Mrs. Ray said, reaching instinctively to stroke her neck. She had meant to stroke it to imply that the summer had been sweaty, but she realized now that her gesture was far too sexual for a woman her age.

Upen was going to ask her more, for his brother's sake, when he found his eyes lingering on the spot on her neck that she had just touched. A thin gold chain vanished into the neckline of her kurta and Upen was too distracted to say more.

"Well, I must be off then," he said, and walked briskly away in the direction of the main road. He was not used to finding women over the age of thirty-five attractive.

Mrs. Ray watched him turn and walk away. She wanted to continue the conversation; she wanted to know more about him, but she had lost her window. In any case, his wife was probably somewhere inside their home, and she knew that women rarely appreciated it when their husbands spoke to her.

"Good afternoon, madam," Balwinder said from behind her, now that Upen had left. "You have just shifted in, madam?" he asked her in Hindi.

"My friends. Not me. I have just come with them to see the house today," Mrs. Ray said. "You work here?"

"Yes, madam," Balwinder said. So she wasn't the lady of the house then, he thought. That means the woman in the tidy matching saris and blouses who sometimes came by taxi and opened the gate herself was the lady of the house. How strange. "I work for Mr. and Mrs. Chopra, and their son, Johnny. Madam, they will be staying here from tonight onward?"

"No, not yet. They're just getting some work done today — getting showers fitted, air conditioners, dishwasher, and so on. I think they will be shifting in a few days."

Mrs. Ray smiled and nodded good-bye

and walked along the lane. It was quiet and one side was lined with trees. She couldn't see into any of the houses because they all had high fences and gates with guards outside them. Some of the guards had big mustaches and bigger guns, and they ignored her completely. Some of the less imposing ones watched her as she walked past. As lovely as these homes were, she would be lonely living in one of them, she realized. All the lives here were so private. Did more money mean more secrets? If she had more money, she would have entertained the idea of moving to Europe, at least for a little while, after her husband died. Instead she had just worked to continue living the exact life she had been living before his death, with nicer bedsheets and peppermint foot cream. She had never even bought a new bed. She probably wouldn't actually have traveled the world, but if she had money, she would at least have allowed herself to think about it. She would have imagined walking the streets of Paris or Amsterdam or Lisbon and taking dance classes and reading books while sitting near lakes and ponds and rivers. She would have planned to return to India eventually because she could not bear the thought of dying anywhere but here, but she could have imagined sampling a different life. Only the rich claim that money can't buy happiness.

Mrs. Ray continued walking toward the end of the Jhas' lane and turned left at the end of the street, toward the main road. There were hardly any people anywhere. Unlike the lanes around Mayur Palli, here there were no hawkers on the road selling cigarettes or tiffin boxes or bindis. There were no groups of maids sitting around having lunch and gossiping. There were no stray dogs or cows. It was all empty and quiet and neat and tidy. Even the drains that ran along the side of the road were covered. Who could blame the Jhas for moving when even the government seemed to prefer this part of town? Not just compared to the slums where people lived on top of each other in rooms the size of cupboards, but compared to East Delhi where people like her lived. There was no visible stagnant water anywhere in Gurgaon.

Near the gate of a house at the corner, Mrs. Ray saw a white BMW stopped but running, with two women standing and talking near it. They both looked, at first glance, like she did — one was wearing jeans and a kurta and the other was wearing black yoga pants and a red jacket. They were probably in their late forties, just a few years

166

older than Mrs. Ray. Or, more likely, they were a full decade older but were better preserved through lotions and potions and less exposure to the polluted Delhi air. Both had sunglasses propped up on their heads. Unlike her, though, diamonds flashed from their wrists, their ears, their fingers, and their noses, and their hair looked professionally blow-dried. They were both wearing makeup that had caked itself into the creases near their eyes. Mrs. Ray heard snippets of their conversation as she walked past.

". . . salwar kameez to yoga class. Just imagine . . ."

". . . just not the same anymore . . ."

". . . the new people . . ."

". . . Upen was at the LRC, I heard . . ."

She smiled at the women as she walked past. Both of them went silent, smiled weakly back, and watched her walk away. She wondered what they thought of her. Did she look obviously like an outsider? A poor wolf in sheep's clothing. Mrs. Ray made her way to the main road, where it felt more like the Delhi she was used to. She could hear traffic rumbling by, and there was a man pushing a cart full of guavas for sale. Mrs. Ray waved him over and picked a ripe guava and asked him to cut it in fours and powder it with the spicy

167

orange masala they all carried in little plastic bags near the fruit. The man did as he was told, displaying no interest in her, asking no questions. Even the street vendors here were different from the ones in the lanes around Mayur Palli. Here, they were not interested in her or her life. There, they wanted to know everything, and every interaction quickly turned into a conversation.

"It's a good time of year for guavas," Upen said. He had seen the woman next door from down the street and had composed himself enough to redirect his run her way, anxious to be able to speak to her without trying to see where her necklace fell. He had been caught off guard, yes, but being nervous around women was simply not his style. And, despite his age, he thought he looked quite good out for a jog.

"It is, yes," Mrs. Ray said, surprised to see him again. Had he come toward her deliberately? What were the rules of this world? She wondered what the two women around the corner would do in her situation. Would they, like young women in films, toss their hair back casually, make a joke, touch his arm, and laugh? Or was one of them Mrs. Chopra, who would come charging around the corner in a rage?

"Would you like one?" Mrs. Ray asked, feeling her stomach tighten into a ball.

Upen smiled and picked a guava and handed it to the vendor to cut.

"No masala," he added. "It looks suspiciously orange, doesn't it?"

Mrs. Ray looked down at the quarter of the guava covered in orange masala that she was holding and wished she had also asked for it without the added spice.

"But I'm sure it's delicious," Upen added, now having noticed that this woman was eating the quarter of her guava covered with the spice and realizing that he sounded like someone with a weak stomach. He did not want her thinking he might have to run to the toilet after eating this.

"Sorry, I have not introduced myself. I'm Upen Chopra. I don't believe I've seen you around before."

"Reema. I'm Reema Ray. It is very nice to meet you," Mrs. Ray said, extending her hand to shake his.

"Well, Mrs. Ray, it's a pleasure to meet you."

"Please call me Reema," Mrs. Ray said. She wanted to say, *It's Miss, not Mrs.,* but that was too obvious. And how did it work for widows? She wasn't sure. She still used her late husband's name, but as a widow, did you get to go back to *Miss* at some point? Mrs. Ray had never even thought about this. Regardless, the guard had said that there was a Mrs. Chopra and a son named Johnny, so it did not really matter. In fact, this whole interaction did not really matter, and Mrs. Ray was worried she was going to make a fool of herself. She needed to get back to the Jhas' home.

"Do you live here? With your family?" Upen said. He wanted to keep her here and talk to her more.

The white BMW that Mrs. Ray had passed pulled up next to them near the guava stand, and the dark window of the backseat went down. The woman in the yoga pants put her head out the window and said, "Upen, darling, how nice to see you. It's been ages."

"Sheila. It has indeed. How are you? You look lovely, of course."

"All for you. What are you doing walking the streets? Come. Come along to the LRC with me."

"I would love to, but I was just having a chat with Reema here . . ."

"It's quite all right. I must be going anyway," Mrs. Ray said quickly, and walked away from the guava cart and the white BMW and the handsome man. She could never call him *darling* and invite him into her car. She quickly glanced over her shoulder and saw Upen still standing near the car, his hand resting on top of it, talking into the window. He looked up and saw her looking at him while walking away and he smiled. She smiled back quickly and turned away.

Mrs. Ray walked into the Jhas' house and went to the kitchen, which was at the back of the ground floor with a door leading out to the small backyard and servants' quarter. In Mayur Palli, she had no privacy from Ganga, and Ganga had none from her. Ganga's "servants' quarter" was just the side room that was used for storage and happened to have a small bathroom attached to it, with an Indian-style squatting toilet. Ganga kept a thin rolled-up mattress to sleep on, and all her belongings fit in a metal trunk that doubled as a table and shrine for her various gods.

"Some tea? How is the rest of the lane?" Mrs. Jha asked, turning off the gas and pouring hot tea, catching the tea leaves in the brass strainer that she held over each cup.

Mrs. Ray nodded.

"So peaceful and quiet. You are lucky to

be living here. I think I met the man who lives next door and he was very friendly. And some of the ladies who live around the corner as well."

"You did? Oh, thank God. I haven't seen anyone yet. Did you talk to them?"

"No, not really. Just a smile and a hello. They were busy chatting. But they seemed friendly."

"Oh, Reema," Mrs. Jha said. "How does one start from scratch at this age? How do I make friends here all over again?"

"The man next door, Upen Chopra, was very friendly. I'm sure his wife will also be wonderful," Mrs. Ray said.

"Or maybe there's no wife and you will fall in love with him and move in next door and then I'll have my friend," Mrs. Jha said.

"He was quite a handsome neighbor, I must say. But there is a wife. And a son. I don't think I'll be shifting in."

Mr. Jha came into the kitchen.

"The showers look so lovely, I want to jump in right away and take a long, hot shower. Bindu, are the towels here yet?" he said.

"I'm using the towels to pack the dishes. They'll come with the movers. Are the workers done? Let's finish the tea and get going now. I want to avoid rush hour."

"We have a six-CD changer in the car, Bindu. Rush hour is no longer a problem."

"But we don't have six CDs in the car," Mrs. Jha said. "You lock up upstairs and bring the car. Reema and I will walk ahead; I want to see the lane. And you can pick us up near the main road."

On his way back home, Mr. Chopra dropped his wife off at the tailor because she needed to get some of her blouses loosened, so it was just him and the driver in the car when he saw Mrs. Ray and Mrs. Jha standing near the main road, looking around at the new neighborhood and chatting.

"Nimesh," Mr. Chopra whispered. "That's her. That must be her. The new woman of the house — in the jeans and red kurta. I have told my wife a thousand times to lose weight and instead now she is getting her blouses loosened. She ate more than half of my ice cream at the mall just now. Speed up, speed up. If they are still here, maybe Mr. Jha is at the home."

"Sir, would you like me to stop near the ladies?"

"No, you fool. You can't just pull up next to ladies in Delhi and stick your head out the window and say hello. They'll call the police."

Mr. Chopra's Jaguar reached his gate right as Mr. Jha's Mercedes was reversing out of the next driveway.

"Mr. Jha!" Mr. Chopra said, getting out of the car.

"Oh, hello, hello, Dinesh. Please, call me Anil," Mr. Jha said. He put his car into park and got out to shake hands with Mr. Chopra and push the big gate closed.

"You'll have to hire a guard soon, Anil," Mr. Chopra said.

"Yes, we must. As soon as we are settled in," Mr. Jha said. He knew that Mrs. Jha thought it was unnecessary for a guard to be there all day just to open the gate a few times. Most of the guards weren't there for actual security purposes anyway. What would these skinny men with no training do if there was an actual break-in? Nothing. Run and hide, probably.

"How is the move coming along? Please do let me know if I can be of any help."

"How kind of you. I will certainly let you know. And we must raise a toast. But right now, alas, my wife has walked ahead to the main road to explore the area and I must pick her up. But we will be making the final move next week!"

"I think I drove past her while turning in from the main road. Will it be just the two of you?"

"It will be mostly just the two of us. We have a son, but he is in business school in America at the moment."

"Wonderful. We also have a son. He lives at home. You will meet him. And my brother Upen is also visiting from Chandigarh. God knows why he insists on living in Chandigarh when there's no family holding him back. In any case, you must come over and meet everyone next time."

Mr. Jha wondered how this man could have a son young enough to still live at home.

"Yes, that would be lovely. We will come over as soon as we are settled in," Mr. Jha said.

"Good, good. And in the meanwhile, let me just give you our phone number in case you need anything at all. Please, take my card. Take two, one for your wife also."

"That is so kind of you," Mr. Jha said. "I will tell her. I would like her to speak to some of the ladies in this neighborhood. She is considering going back to work after we settle in, but let's see."

"Oh dear," Mr. Chopra said. "Well, these are the times we live in, Mr. Jha. Life is expensive; many people need to have a double income at home."

"What?" Mr. Jha said.

"No harm, no shame. It is perfectly acceptable for women to work these days. I wish my wife would do more than shop all day! I've spoiled her," Mr. Chopra said with a laugh and a shake of his head. "Anyway, don't keep your wife waiting. But please do give us a call. We look forward to having you next door."

When Mrs. Ray and Mrs. Jha got in the car, Mr. Jha said, "Bindu. Will you please look into hiring a guard immediately? It is important."

Mr. Jha was learning that in this neighborhood, your guard was a direct representation of how much was worth guarding in your home. Guards with guns meant bricks of gold somewhere in the house. Maybe he would also get a guard with a gun, Mr. Jha thought; it would be cheaper than buying bricks of gold.

"I met Mr. Dinesh Chopra just now as I was pulling out of the driveway. Our new neighbor," Mr. Jha said.

"You mean Upen Chopra?" Mrs. Ray said.

"Who is Upen Chopra? You mean Upen Patel, that actor?" Mr. Jha said.

"No, Upen Chopra. The neighbor. I also

met him when I went for a walk," Mrs. Ray said.

"No, Dinesh Chopra. Oh yes, he mentioned Upen. That is the brother who is visiting from Chandigarh. Mr. Chopra said Upen does not have a family, so he doesn't understand why he doesn't move to Delhi. Isn't Chandigarh the city that is known for its grid system of roads? Like New York City — I like that kind of order. I would also not mind living there," Mr. Jha said. "Anyway, Dinesh has given his phone number and invited us to dinner once we are settled, Bindu."

Mr. Jha passed Mr. Chopra's business card to his wife, who looked at it and then passed it to Mrs. Ray in the backseat with a smile.

"There's a brother," Mrs. Jha said. "With no family."

"Chandigarh," Mr. Jha continued. "I wonder if we should buy a summer home there — what do they call it? Something French. A pedicure? A pediterre? Bindu, what's the term I'm looking for?"

"A pied-à-terre," Mrs. Jha said. "And no, we don't need one in Chandigarh."

In the backseat, Mrs. Ray looked at the business card. Was Mrs. Jha trying to set her up? She was not twenty. She was not

177

going to call a strange man and introduce herself. She reached the card back to the front seat toward Mrs. Jha, who swatted her away gently.

"Why don't we stop at Khan Market for a pastry on the way home?" Mrs. Jha said. "That way we'll also avoid rush hour."

In Khan Market, the three of them went to Big Chill, the café in the back lane, and requested a table. After ordering some cake and tea, Mrs. Ray excused herself, saying she needed to quickly pick up a book and would be back by the time the food arrived.

"Excuse me," a young white woman wearing a salwar kameez and a backpack said to them, touching Mrs. Ray's chair. "Is this seat taken?"

"No. Yes," Mr. Jha said, "It will be. Mrs. Ray . . ."

"No problem," the woman said, smiling, and moved along to the next table to look for a chair. Mr. Jha was not used to seeing so many foreigners in Delhi. You certainly never saw foreigners around Mayur Palli. The Ghoshes' daughter had married a Canadian who had visited once, but with his short height, round face, and glasses, he looked more like a Bengali than most Bengalis so Mr. Jha never considered him a foreigner. But these days, they were everywhere. He saw the white woman find a chair and pull it up to join a mixed group of friends at a table nearby. He heard her also ask for a glass of water in English. That was how much Delhi had changed now. Earlier, the white people who visited would learn basic Hindi words to use while interacting with waiters or drivers or shopkeepers. Now, in these parts of town, they no longer had to do that. They assumed everyone understood basic English, and they were right. Even the taxi drivers in these parts of Delhi could converse in English.

"Do you think Mr. Chopra's brother is single?" Mrs. Jha asked. "Because if so, we should introduce him to Mrs. Ray."

"What for?" Mr. Jha said. He was still looking over at the white woman. "There are so many foreigners in Delhi these days."

"Maybe it will make Rupak want to come back here," Mrs. Jha said. "It says a lot about a city as it gets diverse."

Mr. Jha wondered what it would be like if Rupak married a white woman. He had thought about this since Rupak had left for America. His son was becoming handsome of late, he knew that. He had never considered it before, but maybe it would be fun if he ended up married to a beautiful blue-eyed woman. Maybe they would even come and spend some time with them in Gurgaon. It would be nice to take her out to dinner or to take her to the Chopras' house for a drink. She'd make an effort, wearing a sari but more seductively than was appropriate, with her blond hair in loose curls tumbling down her back. She would stand next to Mr. Jha and when his glass was empty, she would say, "Dad, do you want another drink?" Even though his wife wanted Rupak to marry an Indian woman, Mr. Jha was open to the idea of a white daughter-in-law, as long as she was beautiful. Like one of those *Baywatch* women.

"We should buy swimming costumes," Mr. Jha said to his wife. "Do you think I should go and have a look while we wait for our food? I earlier heard Mr. Chopra was considering getting a pool — I could speak to his builders."

"Anil, you don't even know how to swim."

"If Rupak brings friends to visit from America, it would be nice to have a swimming pool. We'll wear bathing suits, lounge by the pool, drink . . . what is that drink? Pomm's? Pimm's? That's what they drink in England."

"We don't live in England."

"Imagine telling Mr. Chopra to come over

for a glass of Pimm's near the pool. Do you drink Pimm's in a glass? Or would it be a cup of Pimm's? There is so much left to learn in life," Mr. Jha said.

Meanwhile, Mrs. Ray had left the Jhas at Big Chill and was walking quickly toward the liquor store in the adjoining market across the parking lot behind Khan Market. She always preferred buying her whiskey away from the gossiping world of Mayur Palli, where nothing at all was private. And it was not simply a question of privacy. The fact was that in East Delhi, a woman — a widow, no less — buying a bottle of whiskey was something that people felt the need to talk about. What harm was there in her enjoying an occasional drink? No harm. But if she went to the liquor shop across from the Mayur Palli gates, someone would spot her and then the whole housing complex would talk about her drinking. And if she did what she did two weeks ago, and took a cycle rickshaw all the way over to the next market to get it, her own neighbors might not see, but the boys who worked at the liquor store there would look at her lecherously and pass comments.

When she went last time — not to be secretive, really — she had gone to pick up some sari blouses that she had given for stitching and her favorite tailor happened to sit right near the liquor store, so she just thought it would be best to kill two birds with one stone. Like most of the liquor stores in the area, there was no browsing; you had to go up to a counter and ask the men — boys, really — to give you a bottle of what you wanted. There were always red-faced men jostling for space at the counter. At least she didn't have to go to the separate window for the really poor drunks who were looking to buy unmarked locally brewed liquor — the kind that was often laced with pesticides and resulted in death or serious illness.

Mrs. Ray hated walking up to this counter of men and pretending she was there to buy something for her husband. The men at the counter would inevitably get surprised to see her and would push back and make space for her to approach. They would do this under the guise of respect, but Mrs. Ray didn't miss their leers and comments and laughs as she stood there asking, as confidently as she could, for a bottle of Black Label. She did not want to care what these men thought. Let them stare, she would tell herself. But when she got there, she mumbled, "Black Label is all my hus-band will drink. It's just too expensive, but what to do?"

But last time the man who was working there wrapped his fingers around hers while passing the bottle. He pulled away immediately, of course, but not before he bit his lower lip and made leering eye contact.

But in Khan Market, the man working behind the counter spoke to her in English and told her about an Indian brand of whiskey that had recently been launched that he recommended she try.

"Next time," she said, smiling, without feeling the need to mumble anything about a husband.

Mrs. Ray put the bottle into her purse and walked back toward Big Chill for cake and tea, comforted by the thoughts of a strange man from Chandigarh and a new bottle of whiskey in her purse.

When she got back Mr. Jha was trying unsuccessfully to cut his lemon tart with a knife and fork.

"What book did you buy?" Mrs. Jha asked.

"Mr. Jha, wouldn't it be much easier to pick it up and take a bite? They didn't have what I was looking for," Mrs. Ray said. As close as she and Mrs. Jha were, she was never comfortable admitting to enjoying the occasional drink by herself.

"Can we stop by the liquor store on the

way out for a bottle of Pimm's?" Mr. Jha said, the crust of his lemon tart breaking into crumbs on his plate, leaving him to mix it up with the yellow jelly and scoop it into his mouth like rice and curry.

"They won't have anything so fancy here," Mrs. Ray said, nervous that they would have to walk to the liquor store after this and the salesman would recognize her from hardly half an hour ago. "Pimm's will be more appropriate to drink to celebrate once you finish your move."

"I was thinking we should give the Chopras a call," Mrs. Jha said. "Since they were so warm. It will be nice to get to know them. Maybe they'll have a daughter for Rupak."

"They only have a son," Mr. Jha said. "In any case, maybe Rupak will meet someone himself in America."

TEN

Rupak got a C on his first prelim. He also got a C on the first two problem sets for his accounting class, along with a note from the teaching assistant that said, "Please come and see me during office hours. I'm worried you may need extra tutoring."

He hadn't bothered to see the teaching assistant yet because she was a young Indian woman who was doing a PhD in economics and it was embarrassing. She reminded him of Serena.

His parents would not be pleased if he had to retake classes over the summer before Ithaca College would give him his MBA, and since that was looking likely, having an Indian girlfriend would really help smooth things out at home. And his parents were now planning a visit to America, which meant that he had to start arranging his life accordingly.

Even though he certainly was not ready to

let Elizabeth go, maybe it was best to see how things went with Serena. After all, he had never technically discussed exclusivity with Elizabeth. If anything, she was putting too much pressure on him by repeatedly asking him to tell his family about her. Maybe it wasn't cowardice. Maybe he just wasn't ready. That's what he would tell her.

He had been exchanging text messages with Serena since he saw her and they were easy and fun and familiar. This morning she had texted him,

Have you seen all the places in College-town charging $5 or more for turmeric milk? Good old haldi doodh that our mothers make every day. Forget banking, that should be your next big business idea — something from our childhood at marked-up prices. I'm thinking Maggi Ramen. Wait, that might actually be a good idea.

He found himself missing a Delhi he never thought he liked. So now on Friday night, when Elizabeth was in Minnesota visiting her old college roommate, he texted Serena again to invite her out. Rupak wanted to suggest something unusual and, he hoped, interesting, so he asked her to join him for

186

a walk around Beebe Lake the next morning.

"Did you have pets growing up?" Rupak asked as they strolled down the wooded path.

"In Delhi?" Serena said. And that was all she needed to say. Of course she did not have pets growing up in Delhi. Like him, she had also grown up in a crowded apartment complex with little room for extravagances like pets. He learned that she had lived in a more fashionable part of Delhi than him. Her parents were both political activists and instructors at Jawaharlal Nehru University. She came from a world in which money was never too little nor too much to be an issue. He could sense a slight anger toward money, though. When he mentioned the school he had attended, full of Delhi's financial elite, she shook her head and said, "Was that difficult? I've heard all the big business families manage to get their kids in there even if they fail the entrance exam just by paying a huge amount."

"It was pretty bad," Rupak said.

He didn't tell her that, yes, even though it was known that his school put more emphasis on "donations" than entrance exams, and he had originally probably been accepted to fulfill a quota of nondonation students, he still hadn't graduated anywhere near the top of his class. He didn't tell her that he envied his classmates and their foreign summer vacations and private tennis coaches. He didn't tell her about his friend Apoorv's twelfth birthday party for which his parents had rented an elephant to give guests rides in the front yard of their large home on Shah Jahan Road. He didn't tell her that he could hardly sleep that night out of envy and excitement. He didn't tell her that in their new home they could easily fit pets. And not just fish, or birds, or maybe a cat. In Gurgaon they could have Alsatians, and golden retrievers, and Dalmatians.

"I envy the people out there in a way," Serena said when they walked over the bridge where other students jumped confidently into the water. "But I envy them in a strange way," she continued. "It's not that I envy that they're in the water right now and I'm not. I have no desire to be. I envy the fact that they really want to be in the water and so they're in the water. Does that make sense?"

It did. And it was comforting. Boring, but comforting. He had jumped only once, with Elizabeth, even though he didn't have his bathing suit on that day and had jumped in his boxers. At least he had had the sense to switch to wearing boxers as soon as he came to America, before the first time that Elizabeth reached into his pants. His whole life in India, he had worn and liked only what Americans called "tighty-whities."

Rupak wondered how tastes in underwear changed. In Mayur Palli, where everyone's underwear dried on ropes on balconies, people wore underwear that was gray or white or brown or beige. He had sometimes wondered why some of the older women bothered with bras that did nothing to actually support their breasts.

Gurgaon would be different. The wives of the neighbors there probably bought their underwear from La Senza in the big DLF malls, or from Victoria's Secret on trips abroad. In Mayur Palli, the women bought their underwear from the traveling salesmen who came to the neighborhood every Thursday evening with the weekly market. It was such a public way for women to buy such personal items. The undergarments would be stacked unceremoniously under naked lightbulbs, next to fake plastic flowers and metal tiffin carriers. Women, including his mother, would stand at the stalls holding up the underpants and bras, testing the elastic-ity of the straps or the metal hooks of the bras.

"I like that you suggested Beebe Lake," Serena said. "That's unusual."

"It's nice out here, isn't it? Next time we should go down to Cayuga Lake. You can rent Jet-Skis there," Rupak said. He knew this only because he had gone Jet-Skiing with Elizabeth in May to celebrate the end of the last academic year. He loved the way the water moved like glass in the middle of the lake.

"I don't even know how to swim," Serena said with a laugh. "How did you become such a water baby, growing up in Delhi?"

"You don't need to know how to swim. They give you life jackets. And the first time, you can just ride on the back of my Jet-Ski and then you'll get the hang of it." That was exactly what he had done with Elizabeth at first — sat on the back while she drove.

"I like the idea of doing stuff like that; I just never have," Serena said.

"We aren't in Delhi anymore," Rupak said. "We should take advantage."

He smiled at her. Unlike Elizabeth, she would fit in more in Mayur Palli than in Gurgaon, he thought. But he wasn't completely convinced that was a good thing.

■ ■ ■ ■

Their last weekend in Mayur Palli, Mr. Jha went to the market to get a shave and a head massage because he probably would not be able to get one, at only a hundred rupees no less, in Gurgaon. There, he assumed, people got a barber to come home and provide the services, or went to one of the posh salons in the five-star hotels. He would have to remember to ask Mr. Chopra.

The local market in Gurgaon was smaller and better kept than the one they were used to. The one in Gurgaon had a shop that sold the basics — milk, daal, rice, nail cutters, soap, butter, oil, ghee, cigarettes. There was an auto repair shop that had big signs boasting that it was a licensed mechanic for BMW, Mercedes, and Audi. There was one fruit seller who set up below a big banyan tree and one vegetable seller with a pushcart filled with brightly colored vegetables. And there was a small coffee shop that had big glass containers filled with coffee beans from different parts of the world that you could buy by weight. For everything else, you had to drive to one of the big new malls in the area.

The market outside Mayur Palli was

completely different: scattered and dusty and crisscrossed with residential buildings and the local school. There were cycle rickshaws pulled by shirtless men in dirty dhotis to help you get from place to place. There were local tailors — some of whom sat with their sewing machines on the street to watch the people go past while they made a woman's blouse or altered a pair of pants for a man who had gained weight recently.

On the corner near the barber there stood a large, open Anand Sweet Shop. Outside, on huge big metal platters, potato patties hissed as they fried. The cook used a large ladle to toss the ready patties onto bowls made from banana leaves. Another cook crushed the patties, covered them with spiced yogurt, drizzled tamarind chutney, sprinkled chili powder, covered the dish with coriander, and passed it to the men waiting. Big heaps of garbage overflowed from the small blue garbage bin that sat on the side, and a cow grazed through the empty banana leaf plates. Nearby a dog lounged in the sun, and two small puppies were jumping and falling over themselves near the big dog. A driver had abandoned his rickshaw to play with the puppies. Mr. Jha dropped a two-rupee coin in a beggar's bowl as he walked toward his barber.

With Mr. Jha gone to the market, Mrs. Jha found Mr. Chopra's business card and dialed the landline number and asked to speak to Upen Chopra.

"Hello?" Upen Chopra said when he came on the line.

"Hello? Mr. Chopra? Upen Chopra? This is Mrs. Jha calling. My husband and I are in the process of moving into the house next to your brother's in Gurgaon. My husband met your brother just a few days ago. And I believe you met my friend, Reema Ray?"

"Yes, yes, of course. I did. I think you must be looking for my brother — Dinesh? Why don't you hold on and I'll see if he's home; I'm afraid you may have just missed him."

"No, no, I am calling to speak to you. My husband mentioned that you are visiting from Chandigarh, is that correct? You and your family live in Chandigarh?" Mrs. Jha said.

"I live in Chandigarh, yes," Upen said.

Mrs. Jha appreciated the clarification. So her husband had been right — there was no family. That was the likely situation, of course. Family men didn't come to visit their brothers without the rest of the family.

"Well, my friend, Reema . . . she has been wanting to visit Chandigarh for some time now. She is very interested in the Rock Garden there, but she doesn't know much about the city and I'm afraid I'm of no help either — I have never been there. Perhaps you could give her some advice? It isn't easy to travel in India as a single woman, so as her friend, I would feel much better knowing that a neighbor is helping her," Mrs. Jha said.

"Of course. It would be my pleasure. Chandigarh is indeed a great city. It was designed by Le Corbusier, did you know that?"

"Oh yes, I'm sure it's lovely," Mrs. Jha said. "But no need to tell me all about it. Why don't you give Reema a call instead?"

Mrs. Jha gave him Mrs. Ray's phone number and felt an odd thrill. Surely they were too old for such behavior. This was what the young girls did — calling boys and telling them to call their friends. This was not what her generation did. In her generation, parents called other parents and talked about their children, who then met and got married. She was a little envious, she admitted to herself. After all, it was Mrs. Ray who was now going to get the phone call and whatever else followed. But probably nothing else would follow, Mrs. Jha reasoned. They were all too old now.

Mrs. Jha was in the bedroom closing the last two suitcases when she heard Mr. Jha come in the front door from his haircut.

"Bindu!" he shouted. "The sofa has arrived. They brought it to the Gurgaon house but I did not want them to leave it there unattended so I told them to bring it here. We'll take it with us when we go on Monday."

"How is the sofa here early? Anil, there's no space for it. And now we'll have to pay again to move it to the new house. Why did you get it sent here? I thought you were out getting a haircut."

"I was. You know, in America, they call a haircut lowering the ears," Mr. Jha said while behind him three men carried in the large black sofa with Swarovski crystals embedded into the stitching that Mr. Jha had had custom-designed and ordered from Japan. "See? Because the tops of the ears are more visible after a haircut."

"Anil, why did you tell them to bring it here?"

"Bindu, they called from Gurgaon and there was nobody there to accept it. This is exactly why we need to hire a guard. The

Japanese are too efficient is the problem. I wonder if the new neighbors will like this sofa. Just look at how the crystals catch the light."

"What do the neighbors have to do with it?" Mrs. Jha asked.

"They just seem like they have good taste," Mr. Jha said. "It doesn't make sense to live in a new neighborhood and stick to all our old ways."

"What are you talking about?" Mrs. Jha said.

"Nothing in particular. Just that the same way Mayur Palli has its norms and customs, so does Gurgaon. You asked for Mrs. Ray's opinion before we bought our new fridge, didn't you?"

"Anil, just please don't let them remove all the packaging. I don't want to have to repack the whole thing in two days."

The men put the sofa down in the middle of the living room, waited for their tip, and left. The sofa was not made for their small Mayur Palli living room, and between the old furniture, the packed boxes and suit-cases, and now the new sofa with the glint-ing crystals, you could no longer see the floor. Perhaps it was better this way, Mrs. Jha thought; perhaps it was better to spend this last weekend surrounded by chaos and furniture so that when they did finally get to Gurgaon with all their things and all the excess space and silence and greenery, she would feel a sense of relief that would overpower her sense of sadness.

ELEVEN

On Monday morning, Shatrugan opened the gates to allow the Reading Moving Company van into the Mayur Palli compound. Nobody had moved in or out of this building in years. Some of the older couples had gone abroad to spend months at a time with their children, but no family had fully packed up and left in at least the last ten years. It was only the younger generation that left — to go to colleges or to their husbands' homes in other parts of Delhi or the world. When the younger ones left, it never felt permanent. Their moves did not involve vans and sweaty men. Their departures were not talked about for weeks in advance and for weeks to follow. Their moves were done by their parents, in their cars, with suitcases and bags. The only other departures that took place were by hearse or ambulance, and those were a different breed of good-byes entirely.

Most people, Shatrugan found, did not die at home. People would get sick and go to the doctor or to the hospital and not survive, but there had only been two deaths in the actual compound. The bodies of those who died at hospitals were usually brought back to Mayur Palli for the neighbors to pay their last respects and because the soul can be freed more easily if the body is brought home before it is cremated.

Mr. Jha's mother was one of the two who died at home. Shatrugan heard rumors from the maids that she had a heart attack on the toilet in the morning. He had never liked Mrs. Jha Senior, but that was an undignified death for anyone. All the rites were performed quickly. She had no other children and her husband had died years before, so they did not have to wait for anyone else to come to town for the cremation. They did not even need to put the body on ice. She was dead in the morning and her body was reduced to ashes by sundown.

But then there was the young Patel boy who died when he was only sixteen years old in an accident in South Delhi on a Saturday night. He had been riding on the back of a friend's motorcycle without a helmet, Shatrugan heard. It was after dark and a car door swung open. The motorcycle had swerved to avoid the door and the young boy had been tossed from the bike into the middle of the road and a truck went over him before anyone had a chance to react. Shatrugan wasn't on duty the night that the police came to Mayur Palli to tell the Patels the news, but he was there forty-eight hours later when the boy's body had been sent back on ice so that his soul could be freed. Shatrugan had opened the gates for the hearse and he saw the boy lying in the back. His whole body was covered with a sheet, even his face, because the damage was so severe.

All the ladies, in their white mourning kurtas and saris, had held Mrs. Patel upright while she just stood screaming. As the hearse pulled away that day, Mrs. Patel vomited directly on Mrs. Jha's sari. Mrs. Jha and Mrs. Patel weren't even close friends. Mrs. Jha simply covered the area where Mrs. Patel had vomited and helped to take her home while her husband and the other men took the boy to the crematorium. Two years later, when the Patels finally cleared out their son's room, they gave Shatrugan his transistor radio. Shatrugan thanked them and then threw it away.

By the time he had helped the moving van park in the middle of the courtyard, Mr.

Gupta appeared on the scene.

"This van is going to get in the way of the cars."

"It's only blocking Mr. Patnaik's and Mr. Jha's parking spots," Shatrugan said. "And Mr. Jha spoke to Mr. Patnaik already."

"Mr. Patnaik agreed? He yelled at everyone when the milk boy's bicycle was parked in front of his garage. What if there is an emergency? Did Mr. Jha pay Mr. Patnaik for this? I will not have Mayur Palli become a commercial center," Mr. Gupta said.

He went up in the elevator and rang Mr. Jha's doorbell. Mr. Gupta wondered if the Patnaiks actually had given permission to block their car in. As if allowing them to block their car would get them the Jhas' son's hand in marriage. Everyone wanted to set Rupak up with their daughters or nieces. His own wife wanted to set up Serena, her niece in America, with Rupak, but Mr. Gupta did not want his wife's brother's family getting their hands on the Jhas' wealth, so he had discouraged that.

Mrs. Jha opened the front door. She was wearing a starched green sari. Her glasses hung on a gold chain around her neck and her hair was pulled into a bun but parts of it — especially the grays that framed her face — had escaped.

"Oh, Mr. Gupta, good morning. It is a bit chaotic — the movers are arriving just now," Mrs. Jha said.

"Yes. Shatrugan has helped them park the van downstairs. Mrs. Jha, is your husband at home?"

"He is in the shower. Is there anything I can help with?"

Mr. Gupta peered over Mrs. Jha's shoulder into the living room. There was a black sofa that he had never noticed before. It looked soft and plush and there were what looked like diamonds studded into the intersections of the seams.

"I'll tell my husband to come and find you as soon as he's ready. Be careful in here — all the dust has been churned up while packing. I don't want you to start wheezing," Mrs. Jha said while starting to inch the door closed.

"Not a problem. My asthma has been cured. I found an excellent ayurvedic doctor in Defence Colony. I can inhale all the dust in the world. I'll wait for your husband," Mr. Gupta said, pushing the door open. "I haven't seen that sofa before. Diamonds?"

"Oh no, no. Diamonds would be crazy. Only crystals," Mrs. Jha said.

The doorbell rang once again and as Mrs.

Jha went to open the door, Mr. Gupta tapped on one of the crystals with his fingernail.

"I see the movers have arrived," Mr. Patnaik said to Mrs. Jha when she opened the door. "I picked up a papaya for you while I was out. Something sweet for this auspicious day."

"Mr. Patnaik, is that you?" Mr. Gupta said.

Mr. Patnaik looked past Mrs. Jha's shoulder.

"Good morning, Mr. Gupta. It's a big day at Mayur Palli. Would you like some papaya?"

"No, I would not like any papaya. I am waiting for Mr. Jha."

Mr. Patnaik entered the Jhas' living room. Mrs. Jha gave up. There was nothing she could do today. Now there would be no way of avoiding the whole housing complex knowing about the new sofa.

"Is this a new sofa?" Mr. Patnaik asked.

"With crystals," Mr. Gupta said.

"It's quite lovely," Mr. Patnaik said.

"Are the crystals comfortable to sit on?" Mr. Gupta asked.

Before Mrs. Jha could encourage them to leave, the doorbell rang again and as she walked to answer it, both men settled down on the sofa. Shatrugan was at the door with three skinny men in white undershirts and dirty slacks standing behind him.

"Madam, the movers are here. The van is parked where sir told me to."

"Ah, yes, Mr. Patnaik," Mr. Gupta said. "The van is blocking your car. Before they start loading it, you should see that it gets moved."

"It's no hassle at all. It's the least one can do for the neighbors," Mr. Patnaik said. "Mrs. Jha, this sofa is wonderful. Where did you buy it?"

"My husband ordered it from Japan. Shatrugan, thank you for bringing the movers up," Mrs. Jha said.

Mr. Jha came into the living room, fresh from the shower, his damp hair neatly parted to the left, as usual. He was wearing a short-sleeved checkered blue shirt and jeans. When had he started wearing jeans?

"Ah, our good-bye party is assembling. Good morning, good morning. Shatrugan, the movers have parked where we said?"

"Yes, sir. Sir, it is an exciting day for you today. You must be wishing Rupak were also here," Shatrugan said.

"This will always be home for Rupak," Mr. Patnaik said. "You may be moving to another part of Delhi, but you will always belong here."

"Rupak does not even live in Delhi anymore, let alone Mayur Palli, Mr. Patnaik," Mr. Gupta said. "He has moved on. He probably has an American girlfriend by now."

"I'm sure he won't forget where he's from," Mr. Patnaik said. "Are you looking at girls for him yet?"

"Not yet. Let him finish his studies," Mr. Jha said.

"Yes, even Urmila would like to finish studying first," Mr. Patnaik said.

"Really?" Mr. Gupta said. "My wife heard your wife telling the ladies in the library that she wanted to find a match for your daughter as soon as possible."

"Mr. Jha, this is a lovely sofa. Your wife tells me it was made in Japan," Mr. Patnaik said.

"Yes. Those are Swarovski crystals," Mr. Jha said. "They shine like diamonds."

"But not quite diamonds," Mr. Gupta said.

"No, certainly not. A sofa is no place for diamonds," Mr. Jha said.

Shatrugan, still standing near the door, laughed.

"Shatrugan, please go downstairs and stay near the truck. Watch that they load everything carefully," Mrs. Jha said.

She tried making eyes at her husband to get everyone out of the house. Instead he said, "Bindu, perhaps you should put the kettle on for tea? People will be dropping in all day, I'm sure."

Downstairs, in the courtyard, others from the housing complex had gathered around the pieces of furniture, wrapped in old sheets and blankets and covered in tape, that lay around the big truck. Most people of their generation were retired and had nowhere else to be on a Monday morning. When Mr. and Mrs. Jha came down following the last of the boxes, Mrs. Kulkarni came forward to hand them a small box of laddoos, again, something sweet. Mr. and Mrs. Baggaria gave them a box with "basic daal, rice, and vegetables so you have some home-cooked food when you get there." Mrs. Jain came to Mrs. Jha with a small bouquet of flowers. "I went for a walk this morning to see if I could pluck some from the lawn downstairs so you would have something from Mayur Palli to take with you, but there are just no flowers anywhere around here. I had never even noticed. Anyway, I bought these from the market."

Mrs. Jha was about to turn to Mr. Jha and

tell him it was too much, look at all this kindness, how could this possibly compare to pulling up in front of an empty huge bungalow with nobody but the neighbor's guard to say hello to them, when Mrs. Ray came up to her with a small bar of Cadbury's chocolate and a box full of chappatis that her maid had made for them.

"Quite a day," Mrs. Ray said. "Do you need anything else? These chappatis Ganga made can be put in the fridge so you can eat them over the next few days. Do you want her to pack a full meal?"

"Oh, Reema," Mrs. Jha said. "I'm so happy to see you. You are too kind. Mrs. Baggaria already gave us food, but I'm so happy you are here. I'm so happy everyone is here. And I feel terrible about all the times the neighbors have annoyed me. I can't believe it's actually happening. Time just goes so fast, doesn't it?"

Mrs. Ray nodded. "It does. But don't talk as if you are leaving the country. You are still going to be in Delhi. And I will come to visit. It will be good to get out of Mayur Palli every so often."

"Our lives are here. What an age to start again. New starts are for youngsters, not for us," Mrs. Jha said. "I shouldn't say that. Maybe you might find a reason to visit Gurgaon more often? It isn't just us who will be there."

"Don't get ahead of yourself," Mrs. Ray said with a laugh. "But I did get an interesting call from someone in Gurgaon last week. I assume I have you to thank for that?"

Mrs. Jha smiled and used the corner of her pallu to wipe the sweat off her forehead. "It might be nice for you to have some new friends. Outside Mayur Palli. What did he say?"

"It took a while for either of us to say anything because I thought it was the dry cleaner who has not yet finished cleaning two saris I gave him almost two weeks back. Upen introduced himself as Mr. Chopra, not Upen, and that's what that dry cleaner in the market calls himself. So I immediately started scolding him for having taken so long. I said, 'I've been calling and calling and you haven't answered or called back.' Poor Upen seemed quite shocked and said he didn't know I had been calling, what number had I been calling on? And it went on like this for a while until I realized what had happened. It was embarrassing, Bindu."

"But you're smiling," Mrs. Jha said.

"Perhaps. But enough about that — today is about you. Who says only young people should have fun? They don't even appreciate their own youth. I think your move is quite exciting. And it will be good."

"You come and spend full weekends with us, okay? We have too many bedrooms," Mrs. Jha said, glancing up at the Des' balcony to see if they were watching.

"Small, idle minds here. But it provides entertainment, doesn't it? Some days it's fun, some days it's silly, but that's life," Mrs. Ray said. She had noticed Mrs. Jha looking up toward the Des' balcony and she did not want to discuss her stolen yoga pants today.

"Mrs. Ray," Mr. Gupta said. "Did you find your yoga pants yet?"

"They were stolen," Mrs. Jha said. "You don't *find* stolen items."

"Well, we have no proof that they were stolen," Mrs. Kulkarni said.

"Nobody has ever had anything stolen here," Mrs. Baggaria added. "But hopefully you have discovered that yoga works best in salwar kameez."

"Idle minds," Mrs. Jha whispered to her friend. "Ignore them."

Mrs. Jha put her purse into the front seat of the car and turned to Mrs. Ray.

"You really will visit?" she asked. "For me, even if not for anyone else in our neighborhood."

"Of course. As soon as you're settled in, you will invite me over for dinner. Or as soon as you return from New York. And you will keep coming back to Mayur Palli. You can move elsewhere, but you will always belong here. It took a whole housing complex to raise that fine son of yours. We aren't going to let you all disappear," Mrs. Ray said. "You must be wishing he were here today."

"We are finalizing our dates to visit him. You know my husband — he always books tickets at the last minute. But I worry about how Rupak manages in America all by himself. Our Indian boys always need women to take care of them, don't they? Mothers or sisters or wives or daughters," Mrs. Jha said.

"Or maids," Mrs. Ray added.

"Careful, careful. I told you to wrap the sofa with extra sheets. I don't want a single diamond to fall off." Mr. Jha was following behind the movers as three of them carried the sofa.

"There are diamonds on the sofa?" Mrs. Ray asked.

"Oh no, no. Not at all. Just a few small crystals. He doesn't even know the difference. It's nothing," Mrs. Jha said.

"Put the sofa in absolutely last," Mr. Jha said.

Mr. Gupta and Mr. Patnaik came downstairs and joined the group, and Mr. Patnaik noticed a big brown box on his Honda. Not only was his car blocked in, but they were actually storing things on his car. After all this, Rupak had better not return to India with an American wife. If he did, Mr. Patnaik would make Mr. Jha pay for his car to get repolished. Mr. Gupta also noticed the brown box and thought it served Mr. Patnaik right for trying to brown-nose his way into Mr. Jha's new money. He hoped one of the crystals would scratch Mr. Patnaik's car while they were at it.

"Well, everything is fully packed," Mr. Jha said. "Bindu, you're ready?"

Mrs. Jha nodded but did not move. Behind her, Shatrugan had joined the group. He wished he could reach over and touch Mrs. Jha's shoulder and tell her he would miss having her here, but he knew he could never touch any of them. Instead he had to walk to the gate and open it so the Mercedes could pull out with the big truck clattering behind it. At the gate, Mrs. Jha put the window down and handed Shatrugan a bag.

"You take care, Shatrugan," she said.

"Here are some things that may be useful for you. Rupak's old CD player is in there also — he specifically said to give that to you. We'll see you soon."

Shatrugan wouldn't throw that away, he decided. Because Rupak wasn't dead; he was in America. But Shatrugan knew that one CD would cost him at least a full day's income, so it wouldn't be of much real use.

"To Gurgaon, Bindu," Mr. Jha said while closing the windows. "Our new lives await. And for the ride, six CDs in our CD player await. Put some Kenny G on."

TWELVE

The next weekend, after life had resumed its usual rhythm in Mayur Palli, Mrs. Ray was trying to muster up some curiosity about Chandigarh before going to meet Upen. She called for a four-hour taxi from the local taxi stand. It was worth splurging tonight. And in Delhi, it was much safer than relying on public transport anyway. She had not been out late for a dinner ("and drinks," Upen had added on the phone) outside East Delhi in ages, and she was no longer sure how the city functioned at night, especially for a single woman. The only problem was, like with everything else in Mayur Palli, the taxi stand was part of the world and the gossip. The same old sardarji man and his son had been running this taxi stand for the past two decades, and it serviced everyone in Mayur Palli and the neighboring housing societies. Over the years, the sardarji had upgraded the cars from Fiats to Ambassadors to Maruti vans, and he now even had two Innovas in his fleet, but everything else remained the same. The stand was located right outside the main gates of Mayur Palli, near the fish-seller, and everyone knew when anyone else hired a taxi. They all knew when someone went to the airport, they all heard if one of the young boys in the neighborhood had been carted home drunk, and they all knew if someone had been shopping and stopped at Chittaranjan Park to buy better fish than the one their local fishseller brought. So naturally Mrs. Ray was not too keen on taking a taxi from here, but the safety was worth it. And the neighbors talked about her anyway. That wasn't going to change.

"Ganga," she called. "Bring out my red sandals from the front cupboard and dust them off."

Ganga came into Mrs. Ray's bedroom in her white widow's sari and stood in the doorway watching Mrs. Ray powder her face. Mrs. Ray noticed her and put her compact down on her dresser. She pulled out her small black purse from the top shelf of her closet.

"You haven't used that purse in a while," Ganga said.

Mrs. Ray turned the purse over in her

hands as if searching for the date it was last used.

"Really? God knows. Anyway, the red sandals, please. And bring me a glass of water as well."

Ganga didn't move.

"The ones with the heels that you haven't used in years?" Ganga said.

"I don't keep track of exactly when I've used what, Ganga," Mrs. Ray said, and then turned her face into her cupboard to hide her smile. It was true. Everything Ganga was noticing was true. She had not used the red sandals or the small black purse in ages. Where would she use those items? The weekly meetings in Mayur Palli? Give the neighbors even more to gossip about? She had bought both the sandals and the purse on a trip to Hong Kong with her husband ten years ago, and they were understated and elegant and obviously meant for a night out. Mrs. Ray had considered giving them away after Mr. Ray's death, but a small part of her hoped she would find another reason to wear them someday and tonight was reason enough.

Last week on the phone, once Mrs. Ray had figured out that Upen was not the dry cleaner, the conversation had still been a little odd, but pleasantly so.

215

"Mrs. Jha mentioned that you may be planning a trip to Chandigarh?" Upen said.

Mrs. Ray was not yet too old to assume a man she had only met once was calling to discuss Chandigarh, so she decided to be a little confident and accept Mrs. Jha's attempted setup.

"Yes, perhaps," she said. "My husband — my late husband — was an environmental engineer and he always talked about how impressive the city planning was in Chandigarh."

He had, once, Mrs. Ray reasoned. She wasn't lying about her dead husband in order to meet a new man.

"You must come visit," Upen said. "I would suggest around November for the best temperatures. And I can help you draw up your whole itinerary. There's the Rock Garden, of course."

He paused. There was only the Rock Garden and he knew it and she probably knew it too, he worried.

"There's so much more," he continued. "I don't want to list all the places on the phone. Why don't we meet some evening? Maybe next weekend? That would be easier. I'm in Delhi for a while longer — I have no real reason to rush back to Chandigarh so I make these trips nice and long."

"Yes," Mrs. Ray said. "Yes, that would be easier. I'll bring a notebook and we can have a cup of coffee."

"How about dinner?" Upen said.

Mrs. Ray had lain down on her bed holding the phone when he said that. She closed her eyes, smiled, and shook her head. She was like a scene from an American movie about high school cheerleaders who get asked on dates. For hardly a second, though, because then Ganga had come into the room asking what kind of fish she should buy for dinner that night. Mrs. Ray waved her away, sat up, and said to Upen, "Dinner. Yes, dinner."

"And drinks," Upen had said.

And when Mrs. Ray hung up, Ganga was standing there looking at her with curiosity, and Mrs. Ray had looked away to hide her smile. And Ganga was standing there again now, holding her red heels and looking at her with the same look and once again, Mrs. Ray looked away, still smiling, and said, "Ganga, please go to the dry cleaner tomorrow morning and check on my saris. It's been almost three weeks."

Mrs. Ray arrived early to the Lodhi Restaurant, beautifully nestled into the greenery and surroundings of Lodhi Gardens. They had said they would meet at eight for dinner, but the evening temperature was starting to drop so she was worried that her nose would run or her eyes would water, so it was best to get there first, settle in, and check her compact before Upen arrived. What trivial, wonderful concerns, she thought.

Mrs. Ray loved autumn in Delhi. At this time every year she forgot just how brutal the cold would get by the beginning of January, especially with no central heating. But every October and November felt so lovely when the cool air descended across the city after a hot and humid summer. The smell of wood burning filled the air, and scarves and sweaters and closed-toed shoes came out. People would leave their doors and windows open instead of sitting closed up in air-conditioned rooms. Winter in Delhi had the same effect that spring did in books and movies set in the Western world. The start of winter here brought with it the hope for newness.

As she sat down at the corner table, she looked around nervously. A young couple — an Indian woman and a white man — sat at the table next to her. Mrs. Ray felt happy for the woman, not envious. She looked like she was about thirty and was

218

wearing black pants and a black shirt, with rust-colored high-heeled boots. On the table between them sat an open bottle of white wine in a metal box filled with ice. They looked so at ease — with each other, with the dim lighting, with the white tablecloths and the wineglasses.

Mrs. Ray quickly scanned the rest of the room. You never knew who you would run into in Delhi, but there was nobody here who looked familiar. Still, as a precaution, she had taken the seat that left her back facing the restaurant. This meant, of course, that she would not see Upen arriving, but it also meant that the harsh overhead light was not above her head. She was too old for overhead lighting. In any case, if she focused, she would probably be able to see Upen's reflection as he approached the table. She knew she was being silly. She knew nothing about this man. They were meeting only to discuss her alleged interest in Chandigarh. Yes, it was strange that he had suggested doing that over dinner and drinks at one of Delhi's most romantic restaurants, but maybe that was standard for him. He had dropped enough hints that Mrs. Ray was confident that he did not have a wife, but for all she knew, he had a girlfriend in Chandigarh. And even if he didn't, it did not mean that he was interested in her. She was too old for games like these. It was just that she had never had the luxury of games like these.

She had loved Mr. Ray — she still did — and she enjoyed glimpses of longing and desire and a crush early in their marriage, but there were no games, there were no unanswered questions. The moment she remembered most fondly from their early years was one morning in the first month, when they still lived in Mr. Ray's family house in Mumbai, and he had woken up next to her, leaned over, put his mouth against the small black mole she had behind her right ear and said, "This is mine."

She didn't think he had even noticed it. Then he got up and started his day, but she remained in bed a little bit longer, happy. That happiness had carried her through her marriage. She raised her right hand to her ear and touched the tip of a finger to the mole and wondered when Upen would notice it.

She saw, in the window she was facing, the short waitress leading the tall Upen Chopra over toward her table. Before she could respond — before she could even decide how to respond — she felt his warm hand on her shoulder, a sliver of his finger directly against a sliver of her bare neck, as he came around from behind her to her side.

"Should we start with an order of the fennel salad?" Upen asked. "And what will you have to drink? Some wine, perhaps? Or whiskey? I'm a whiskey drinker myself, but I'm happy to share a bottle of wine."

"No whiskey for me, thank you," Mrs. Ray said. "Maybe just a glass of wine. White wine."

She never drank whiskey in front of others. She had, once, when her husband was alive, and Mrs. De had said, "Whiskey. Oh my. Aren't you a modern woman?" with such poison in her voice that she now stuck to only white wine in public, sometimes with soda added in to make it even daintier.

"In that case, I'll have a whiskey," Upen said, and waved the waitress over and ordered their drinks and the salad. She was going to order a glass of the local white wine that tasted awful and was made in a vineyard outside Mumbai, but Upen said, "She'll have a glass of the sauvignon blanc from New Zealand. You'll like it. I went to New Zealand about four years ago and now that's the only white wine I drink."

Mrs. Ray liked his authoritative way even though she had noticed that the foreign wine cost three times the price of the domestic one and she was not sure how the bill was going to be split tonight. She shook that thought out of her head and committed to trying to enjoy herself. She hardly spent money on anything these days; a glass of imported wine would not cause her to go bankrupt.

"I've heard New Zealand is beautiful," she said.

"Oh, you'd love it. It's as if God — if you believe in God — was particularly kind to that whole country," Upen said, and then continued talking about his holiday there through the appetizers. Mrs. Ray had stopped listening after he said she would love it, because the way he phrased it made it sound as though they would perhaps go there together someday, and even though that was an absurd thought to have barely half an hour after sitting down to dinner with this man, it was a thought that made her feel warm inside.

Through the main course — a rather bland grilled sea bass with vegetables for her, and a vegetable korma with rice for him — and her second glass of wine and his second large pour of whiskey on the rocks — they continued to talk about cities and countries far away from where they were as if they both understood that to talk about anything closer would be dangerous tonight. They asked each other almost no questions about their lives. They both knew that by this age, there was too much that was too difficult to speak about and you never knew which question would unravel a carefully crafted conversation. Upen smiled and tilted his empty whiskey glass toward himself. "Another glass of wine for you?"

Mrs. Ray wanted to say yes. She wanted another glass of wine, maybe even a whiskey. She wanted to stay here talking to him and hearing about the world for many more hours, but she was nervous. She was getting to the point where she wanted to know less about the biodiversity of New Zealand and much more about who was with him on his trip, who it was that stood by his side on the viewing deck of the Sky Tower in Auckland, who walked through the dark caves of Waitomo with him to see the glowworms, who tried a bite of the best rack of lamb he'd ever tasted. So instead she declined the offer for more alcohol, but he insisted on dessert and she didn't refuse.

"I'm so happy to hear you're interested in visiting Chandigarh," Upen said as their plates were cleared away. "Did your husband spend a lot of time there?"

"Oh no, he just spoke about it," Mrs. Ray said. "But he always wanted to go."

"It's nice of you to consider making the trip for him," Upen said.

Mrs. Ray felt guilty about using her husband this way, so she simply said, "He was a good man."

Upen nodded.

"My wife was a good woman," he said.

"When did she pass?" Mrs. Ray said.

"What? Oh, my wife. Right. About seven years ago. I've been on my own for the past seven years."

"My husband died five years ago," Mrs. Ray said.

"I'm sure wherever they are now, they want to see us happy. If you had died first, would you want your husband to remarry?"

Mrs. Ray was silent for a moment.

"I've never really thought about that. I know I should say yes, yes, of course, but I don't know. Is that an awful thing to admit?"

"I think it's a very brave thing to admit," Upen said.

"It would have been easier for him to have been the one left behind. The world is more forgiving for male widows. He wouldn't have everyone peering into his windows to see exactly how he was living his life. Male widows are lucky."

Upen said nothing.

"Oh God, I'm so sorry," Mrs. Ray said. "That's not how I meant it. No widows are lucky. Male ones are simply less unlucky than female ones."

Upen laughed and said, "No, no. You have a point. It's definitely easier for male widows, except men don't know how to make dinner."

"They can hire maids," Mrs. Ray said, grateful that Upen had laughed, grateful that the topic of widowhood didn't have to be shrouded in whispers and sadness and guilt.

"We should start a matchmaking agency for the widowed," Upen said. "Men need women who know how to make them dinner."

"Or we could start a cooking class for male widows," Mrs. Ray said.

By the time the New York–style cheesecake with raspberry coulis and trio of macaroons were served, Upen had started talking about Chandigarh again, and Mrs. Ray had come to the conclusion that it was a dreadfully boring city but Upen was wonderful company.

"There's so much more to tell you about Chandigarh. I know it's getting late now, but perhaps we could meet again some night?" Upen said when the check was brought to the table.

Mrs. Ray tried to calculate how much her share was going to be — it was not a cheap restaurant, and there was the international wine order. And the dessert — those three tiny macaroons cost more than a full meal would at the South Indian restaurant in the market outside Mayur Palli. When the high of this evening wore off, she was going to feel terrible. Mrs. Ray was about to reach into her purse when Upen placed his big hand on the little black folder that held the check and pulled it toward himself. She wondered what it would feel like if his hands were ever on her body. They were not a young person's hands, but they were hands that looked confident and firm. Mrs. Ray owed Mrs. Jha a thank-you — for calling Upen Chopra on her behalf. And for moving to Gurgaon.

THIRTEEN

"You might even know some of the people here tonight. Delhi is a small social circle," Serena said to Rupak as they walked through Collegetown on Saturday night.

"Correction: the Delhi you come from is a small social circle. I grew up in a different world in East Delhi. Our worlds don't collide," Rupak said.

As they walked along in silence, Rupak worried that his comment had sounded too rude. Either rude or insecure and he really didn't want to be either.

"Hey, thanks for inviting me tonight," he said.

Serena stopped walking as they approached the apartment block and turned to him.

"Thanks for agreeing to come. I like hanging out with you. It's funny, we grew up probably within — what? — fifteen miles of each other and then we both ended up in

227

this small town in upstate New York, but we're so different, aren't we? It's fun."

"So different?" Rupak said. "I thought the opposite — we have so much in common."

"We have logistical stuff in common, sure — I guess in that we're both from Delhi. But that's about it, I'd say. I don't really cavort with the obscenely wealthy usually."

Rupak laughed at the term *obscenely wealthy,* but he noticed Serena did not.

"But I like hanging out with you. And your texts are pretty funny," she said, and she kept walking and he didn't want to sound petty, so he walked along with her.

The nights in Ithaca were starting to get cold and the trees were almost bare already. The winter was much more of a proper winter here than it was in Delhi. In Delhi, even though the temperature dropped, the days did not shorten as noticeably and the leaves on the trees never changed color.

Groups of undergraduate girls in short dresses and bare legs rushed down the sidewalk huddled together, talking and laughing about the promise of the night ahead. Despite the cold, Collegetown on a Saturday night felt electric with life and energy. Walking down this stretch with Serena felt very different than doing so with Elizabeth. Serena didn't seem to notice the buzz all around them, let alone have a desire to participate. Elizabeth, on the other hand, *was* the buzz. It emanated from her. Rupak felt a pang of guilt about having left her behind in her apartment tonight. He had technically not lied. He had told her he was meeting a family friend from Delhi who went to Cornell. Okay, perhaps he had lied slightly: he had said the friend did not speak fluent English so it would be boring for Elizabeth to come along. Fortunately, she was not the kind to cross-examine him or care. She was perfectly happy going out with her own friends and living her own life. It was another one of the things Rupak loved about Elizabeth — her independence. Although, he thought, maybe it wasn't independence. Maybe she didn't care because she thought he was incapable of looking at another woman. Maybe Elizabeth thought she had Rupak in the palm of her hand and would never have reason to worry. Maybe she thought he wasn't man enough to ever cheat on her.

"Where'd you go?" Serena said. "You went silent."

"Sorry, nothing. I like hanging out with you too. Your friends — are they all studying theater?" Rupak asked.

"No. I'm the only one foolish enough to

do that. There are a few business and law school people. Suresh is here doing his PhD in math and a few are doing their master's in international relations. And one of the women, Pallavi, is doing a PhD in comparative literature. I don't know her too well, though — she's older. Her younger brother was my boyfriend in school," Serena said.

She knocked on the door. Rupak could smell the marijuana smoke seeping out from behind the door and muffled conversation and laughter on the other side. All these people from Delhi with whom he had nothing in common except for a city. It was like an exclusive club and he was not sure he knew how to talk to people studying comparative literature and math. He would have to find the business students and stick with them.

Rupak was welcomed into a room filled with smoke and soft music he did not recognize. This was not at all the kind of gathering he had been expecting — he was prepared for either loud Bollywood music or contemporary American hip-hop. Those were the two brands of Indians he was used to — the ones trying hard to assert their Indianness, and the ones trying hard to assert their Americanness. But Rupak instead found himself standing in the middle of a

room filled with neither. He followed Serena into the kitchen and poured himself a
strong vodka tonic. She stood next to him
while a man passed her a joint. Rupak was
curious to see what she was going to do with
it. He had not expected to see her like this.
She was wearing jeans, the ends of which
were folded up to expose a sliver of skin
and gray ankle boots with short heels. On
top she was wearing a bulky white sweater
and her hair was loose and a little messy.
She tucked some of the hair behind her ear
and took the joint and brought it to her lips.
She inhaled, looked up toward the ceiling,
and exhaled slowly. Rupak and the man who
had passed her the joint just watched. Serena let out a small cough, smiled, passed
the joint to Rupak and said, "Rupak, this is
Ashish. He's doing his MBA. Ashish, this is
Rupak. He's from Delhi and he's doing his
MBA at Ithaca College. But he's also really
interested in film."

While leaving Beebe Lake, Rupak had told
Serena that he was studying at Ithaca College. He made it sound casual, as if there
were no reason why she should have assumed he was studying at Cornell, and she
had accepted it equally casually, as if she
hadn't assumed he was studying at Cornell.
And then they hadn't spoken about it. He

got the sense that Serena thought it was interesting in its strangeness — her less-successful rich friend who preferred Beebe Lake over books. She didn't ask him much about his life, and Ithaca College quickly got tucked away with Gurgaon. Until she just mentioned it, he wasn't even sure she had registered it.

Ashish said, "Hey," and Rupak nodded at him, inhaling deeply from the joint.

"Did you study at SPV too?" Kunal asked.

"No. I know Rupak through my aunt," Serena answered. She picked up her vodka tonic and slipped out of the kitchen, leaving Rupak alone with Ashish. They both looked at each other and sipped and smoked for some time, Rupak wondering if Ashish had ever slept with Serena. Ashish asked Rupak a few questions about his classes, and Rupak answered and did the same.

"Are you looking at jobs in New York next year?" Rupak asked.

"No, I'm going to head to Bombay. I interned at Mahindra after undergrad and I want to work for them full time. My girl-friend lives in Delhi, so that'll be a lot easier. Are you planning to move to New York?"

"I think so," Rupak said. "I hope so. I want to go into investment banking, so it makes sense."

"I would think Bombay or Hong Kong makes more sense. Does Serena know your plans?" Ashish asked.

"Oh no," Rupak said. "We aren't, she isn't . . . we're just friends."

Ashish nodded.

Rupak thought about how easy it would be to date Serena — how comfortably she would fit in his life. Despite what she said, he thought they had a lot in common and his parents would certainly approve of that. But he didn't think Serena thought of him as more than a friend. Seeing her here in this world, he realized she had an ease around her male friends that made it impossible for him to read her. Was she hoping he would kiss her at the end of the night? He wanted to want to. He found her beautiful and appealing, but the word *appealing* wasn't exactly making him excited. He never thought about Elizabeth that way. With Elizabeth, there was a physical hunger — he had never wondered whether to kiss her; he just had to kiss her.

Rupak took back the joint and had another drag. He had to be careful to smoke just enough to feel relaxed but not so much that he started feeling fidgety. He was already feeling more like an outsider than he had in recent years.

"What does your girlfriend do?" he asked Ashish.

"She's a costume designer for films. I'm trying to convince her to move to Bombay with me, but she loves Delhi. I can't deal with Delhi and the whole who's-who of it all. Serena said you make films, right? You should move to Bombay too. Have you spent any time there?"

Rupak shook his head.

"Where did you do film, then? You won't even think of moving to New York once you've spent some time in Bombay. You really feel part of things there, you know — the movement." Ashish stopped. "Did I just say 'the movement'? I've smoked too much. Here, finish the joint. I'm going to go sit down for a bit."

He walked out of the kitchen and Rupak stood there holding the joint and finished his vodka tonic with two large sips. Serena came back in the kitchen with another beautiful Indian woman. Serena took the joint from his fingers, picked up a lighter from the sticky kitchen counter, and used it to relight the end while introducing him to Pallavi.

"She's the one doing a PhD in comparative literature."

"Nice to meet you," Rupak said. "You're

also from Delhi?"

"I went to school there but then I left. I haven't lived in Delhi for years now," Pallavi said, pouring herself a drink. Over her shoulder, Rupak made eye contact with Serena, who was standing in the doorway of the cramped kitchen, smiling in his direction, the vodka already making her eyes sparkle.

"Where do you live now?" Rupak asked.

"I've already been in Ithaca for three years, I guess. My God, it's been too long. But I was living in Goa before this. You're from Delhi, right?"

Rupak nodded and asked, "What was in Goa?"

"I ran a bookshop. And surfed," she said, laughing. "That sounds so ridiculous now. But I got it in my head that I wanted to be a surfer, so I moved to Goa after college."

"And you fell in love," Serena added.

"And I fell in love," Pallavi nodded, "With an Israeli hippie, no less. Don't ask. Anyone need a refill?"

Rupak and Serena declined, and Pallavi took her drink and went back into the living room. Serena stepped closer to Rupak and whispered, "Are you okay here? You're just hiding in the kitchen."

"I've been talking to people. I like it. I like

them. I don't know people like this from Delhi. How did she meet an Israeli hippie?"

"In Goa. Haven't you spent any time in Goa?"

"I went one winter with my parents, but I don't remember seeing any Israeli hippies," Rupak said.

"Goa with your parents is very different. You should go for New Year's Eve sometime. That's the Goa my friends and I go to. We started going right after we finished school. Pallavi had just moved there, so the first time I went was with her brother."

"The one you dated?" Rupak asked.

"The one I dated," Serena said.

"I talked to Ashish for a while. He seems nice."

"He is. He has an identical twin. I can never tell them apart. Fortunately, the twin lives in London now."

"Did you ever date Ashish?"

"No. Why?"

"I don't know," Rupak said. "Sorry."

"Jealous?" Serena said, looking closely into his eyes. "Come on. Come to the living room. I'll introduce you to the others." She took his hand and led him toward the rest of her friends from Delhi.

The party continued in a haze of marijuana and stiff drinks, and Rupak felt his voice slipping back into his comfortable Indian accent and bits of Hindi creeping into his sentences. Serena sat by his side and he rested his hand on her thigh and thought of Elizabeth. By now he wanted to kiss Serena, but he also wanted to go over to find Elizabeth and breathe in the smell of her tousled blond hair and hear what she had been doing all evening. He wanted to hear her talk about her home, her one home. The marijuana and the alcohol and the Indians were making his head spin and he wanted desperately to cling to something stable.

FOURTEEN

In Gurgaon, it was finally the day Mr. Chopra had been planning for. It was time to sit down and get to know the new neighbors.

"Is Johnny going to be home this evening?" Mr. Chopra asked his wife. "And did you have pastries picked up from the club?"

"Who knows when Johnny will come home? Who told you to buy him a new car? Now he will be even more useless," Mrs. Chopra said.

She went back to playing Angry Birds on her iPad. She wasn't as excited about the new neighbors as her husband was, but she was looking forward to having new friends. She went to the LRC on occasion, but those evenings were just an opportunity for their friends and neighbors to get drunk and flirt with each other. She had heard whispers of a few couples trading partners, and it sounded mad to her. Most of them were nearing sixty — they were trading partners for what? Rubbing Icy Hot on each other's backs at the end of the day? All those women huffing and puffing on the treadmills, trying to be young women in old women's bodies. After the gym, they would stop by the bar to see their husbands and have a drink, and they would laugh and shake their ponytails around like the young girls Johnny chased after. She was glad her husband had lost interest in those women with age. At least that was one thing he was sensible about.

"Have you checked the maids' uniforms? And told them to put out the crystal glasses?" Mr. Chopra asked his wife.

"I'm sure it's all fine. Why are you creating such a fuss? It's a weeknight. They won't stay that long. Will Upen be joining us?"

"No, he's gone out for dinner with some college friends. Geeta, do you ever worry about the future?" Mr. Chopra asked.

"About getting old?" Mrs. Chopra asked.

"Worse — getting poor," Mr. Chopra said.

"No, I don't waste time thinking about that. And neither should you. Things are good."

"For now. But what happens if the mine crumbles? Or I lose control of the management?"

Mrs. Chopra put her iPad down.

"That is why we bought property and jewelry and gold. What is wrong with you today?"

"What if everyone else in Delhi becomes rich and the people who are poor now move in next door and suddenly we are one of the poor. What then?"

"Then nothing," Mrs. Chopra said. She knew her husband was impossible to talk to when he got in one of these moods. "You think about it all too much. We will be fine. Things don't just fall apart all the time and economies don't change overnight. Because of your hard work, Johnny will also always live well. Look at him, driving around all day, getting better and better at tennis. Not all fathers can provide that for their sons. Didn't you say the next-door boy is studying in America? Poor fellow."

"That is true. At least Johnny will not have to go in for postgraduate studies, thank God," Mr. Chopra said. "I'll go take a quick shower before the neighbors come."

Next door, Mr. Jha was also taking a shower before their evening out with the neighbors. His wife was probably being stubborn as usual and sitting crouched on her haunches over a bucket of water, with a mug. Mr. Jha did not even like having an overturned bucket in the bathroom with him when he was showering. He liked to have the floor space open to move around freely, so in Gurgaon he installed a section under the sink with a drain where Mrs. Jha could store her bucket and mug after she was done bathing.

She also insisted on keeping a mug in the downstairs bathroom near the toilet. He had started noticing that fewer and fewer Indian homes kept mugs near the toilet these days. Almost all kept toilet paper, and most had traded in the mug for a water gun attached to the wall. Mr. Jha was getting used to those — it was like having a handheld bidet for easy aiming — and he had water guns installed in all the bathrooms, but even here, Mrs. Jha preferred using a mug and would often leave one near the toilet in the downstairs bathroom. He had repeatedly told her to hide the mug when it was not in use, but she always forgot. He would have to use the bathroom at the Chopras' home to see how they had it set up.

They had been in Gurgaon for over a week now and had hardly seen their neighbors. Mr. Jha had left a note with the Chopras' guard suggesting they get together for a drink. Of course they had not yet hired a guard themselves, so, in response, the

Chopras had to throw a piece of paper over their gate inviting them for an after-dinner drink tonight. (A digestif, the note had said, and Mr. Jha had been using the term ever since.)

In the bedroom, Mrs. Jha took her gold chain out of the safe and put it around her neck. She usually only wore it to weddings or other fancy events, but maybe it was time to start using it more often. She smoothed down the front of her sari. She had changed into a starched yellow sari with a dark yellow blouse. An embroiderer in Jodhpur had worked on it. The pallu over her shoulder was covered with delicate patterns of birds and lilies in the same dark yellow as the blouse. She had ordered twelve of this design and color to be sold at the National Crafts Museum.

Mrs. Jha was one of the few women of her generation who had carried on a full career after getting married and even after having a child. Maybe it was time to consider going back to it now. The house was settled; there was not too much else for her to do all day, every day. And it was so quiet and lonely here. It had been over a week that they had been living here and they had not even met the neighbors yet. In Mayur Palli, even when she did not work, life felt hectic, but here it was too quiet. She could hear her own thoughts too loudly. And she could never be one of those women who spent her days at beauty parlors or out for endless lunches with friends. She did not have to work in quite the same way she used to. She could, perhaps, get a car and driver, for instance. And maybe she could even hire an assistant — a young graduate from the National Institute of Design, maybe, who would be the one to actually go to the villages and find the craftsmen. And Mrs. Jha could handle more of the business side of it.

She looked in the mirror to line her eyes with black kohl, and deep down she knew she no longer wanted to spend hours in the heat and dust of villages. Working with local craftsmen around Rajasthan had been fine, and even rewarding, when she was young and had the energy to drive and spend all day outdoors, using the villagers' bathrooms and drinking questionable water. Not that she needed this big luxurious house and lifestyle in Gurgaon now, but she was tired of working. There were too many days when it felt hopeless.

So many of the craftsmen she worked with no longer wanted to do what they were doing, and how could she convince them that they should keep embroidering saris by hand in the heat when a machine could do it many times faster? And machines rarely made mistakes and the saris made by the machines cost much less. Most of the craftsmen she worked with lived in villages, but even the smallest villages now had cybercafés and the villagers were all aware that the world was changing in a way it never had before. Some of the craftsmen in Jaipur had heard about her husband's sale, and they had started pestering her to find jobs in Delhi for their children. One of the women even got angry with Mrs. Jha for being from the big city and not helping to guarantee her children's future. Why couldn't she see how much Mrs. Jha was already doing for them? They didn't understand that she could stay at home in comfort all day long. She did not have to try to help them. She did not have to go back and forth between shops in Delhi and the hot, dirty villages without proper plumbing. She did not have to help them get bank accounts and transport their creations back to Delhi. She did not have to do any of that. And so she just stopped doing it. She told herself it was because of the new house and the big move that was going to require a lot of her attention, but now that was all done and she was just another rich housewife.

Next door, Mrs. Chopra could not find one of her solitaire diamond earrings. It was only a one-carat one, but this was the second time in the past two months that she had misplaced a single earring. The last one, she was fairly certain, had been pulled out of her ear when she was changing and then had probably been thrown into the wash and there was no hope of finding it again. Now where had this one gone? Were the maids stealing? But then why would they steal a single earring? They could easily steal a pair. In fact, they probably had stolen many pairs — Mrs. Chopra never kept track of her jewelry and now that she was looking in her jewelry box, her collection did seem smaller than usual. Maybe she ought to start keeping the more precious pieces under lock and key. But she believed precious things should be treated the same way as nonprecious things. Placing too much value on anything was the simplest way to lose the possible pleasure to be derived from that thing. Still, her husband probably wouldn't be thrilled that she had lost another earring. It was best not to mention it for now. She put on a pair of earrings that had an oval jade stone set in the center, surrounded by a frame of small diamonds. She fixed the pallu on her new sari — it was a dark blue chiffon sari with red vertical patterns from Rita Bahl's new collection. Small pieces of onyx were stitched into the hemline, and the pallu was covered with silver zari work. It was quite a heavy sari, but Mrs. Chopra was looking for an excuse to wear it and she did not have to do much other than sit this evening. She checked her reflection in the mirror. She sparkled. She knocked on the bathroom door, told her husband to hurry up, and went downstairs to find her iPad and play some more Angry Birds while waiting for the neighbors.

Mrs. Chopra heard the next-door gate creak open.

"We should get someone in to oil these hinges," Mrs. Jha said to her husband.

"Once we get a guard, he can probably do it himself," Mr. Jha said.

Mrs. Jha ignored him. It was so quiet and dark out here. You could barely hear any traffic sounds, let alone hear the neighbors talking. The only sound was the occasional jackhammer at work on a construction site nearby; most construction in Delhi happened under the cover of night, and sometimes all of Gurgaon still felt under construction. What did all these people do in their big houses by themselves, Mrs. Jha wondered? There were four lights on the road and, as they walked the few feet between their gate and the Chopras' gate, she was grateful for the eight other guards on the street. But she still didn't think they needed one of their own.

Balwinder saw the Jhas approaching and pushed the gate open for them. He had not had much chance to interact with Mr. Jha, but Mrs. Jha was friendly and comfortable with him — two things that Mrs. Chopra certainly never was.

A few days ago, a taxi had stopped outside the gate and Mrs. Jha had stepped out with bags full of vegetables. Balwinder had walked over to help her open the gate and carry everything all the way in to her house. It was decorated quite differently from the Chopras' house. The living room, which was all he saw, had minimal furniture — there was a black sofa with jewels on it that stood out — and two big bookshelves along the walls. Balwinder had only studied until seventh grade, so he did not get much pleasure out of reading, but he had always liked the sight of books. And Mrs. Jha was so kind to him. She offered him water and asked him questions about how long he had been working next door and where he was from.

Balwinder's own mother had left him with an uncle in Ludhiana when he was two years old, and he had never heard from her again. He didn't miss her because he had never known her. He heard rumors that she had an affair with the man she used to work for — she was a cook — and he had moved her to Dubai when his wife found out. Whenever his uncle got annoyed with him, he would tell Balwinder his mother had left him in order to become a prostitute. Now, in Delhi, Balwinder did not mind the thought of that so much. Sugandha was a prostitute but she brought him such joy. What harm was there that he left some money for her every time? That did not make her a bad person. Even on days when he only sat and chatted with Sugandha, he would leave money for her. She always made him get up and leave in exactly two hours, but he thought of her as a companion of sorts. If that was in fact what his mother was doing, Balwinder felt no shame about it. But his uncle would say it to him in such an unpleasant way that Balwinder left Ludhiana when he was thirteen. He stole whatever money he could from his uncle and made his way to Patiala and eventually to Delhi, where he worked as a tea boy for a few years before joining a security guard agency through the recommendation of an electrician who used to come to the tea shack every evening and had a cousin who worked as a guard in Hauz Khas. Balwinder had always gone through life alone and he was not used to people asking him much about himself, so he was glad Mrs. Jha had moved in next door.

"Good evening, madam. Good evening, sir," Balwinder said as he opened the gate.

"Good evening, good evening. Tell me, young man," Mr. Jha said to him. "Do you know any other guards? Maybe some friends of yours who are looking for work?"

"Sir, the agency will certainly have many people. I can give you their contact. Chopra-sir will also have it."

"Agency? Okay, then. Thank you," Mr. Jha said as they entered the Chopras' driveway. "The guards come from agencies here?" he asked his wife in a lowered voice. "What kind of agency do they come from? He's not a model, for God's sake, he is just a guard."

"I've heard about this. Even all the maids these days come from agencies. In fact, I want to get information for a maid's agency from the Chopras as well. Only for the cooking and cleaning, don't worry. It's a good system. I'm sure they will be more trustworthy if they are with an agency. Maybe they do background checks. And it probably also gives the maids more rights. Some people treat maids so badly."

"I've told you so many times that now you can get a full-time maid if you want. Here we have a servants' quarter, so a maid won't constantly be hanging around looking shabby. We can even get a couple and the man can be the guard and the woman can help around the house. Do some research and see if you can find that at an agency."

Walking down the driveway of their neighbors' home, Mrs. Jha could see the moon and even a star or two. She had been so nervous about this move, this neighborhood, and the new money, but seeing the small lights shaped like birds that lined the driveway, and the wrought-iron chairs and tables in the Chopras' front yard, made her feel peaceful. One of the hedges was cut in the shape of a deer. What nice attention to detail. She had never imagined this would someday be her life.

She looked over at her husband. He was a self-made man and she was proud. She vowed to make this home a happy place. She had complained enough about the

move to Gurgaon. It was time to stop worrying.

"Maybe we can also get some of our
hedges shaped," Mrs. Jha said, and pointed
toward the deer hedge.

As they approached the Chopras' door,
Mrs. Jha smoothed down the front of her
sari and fingered the gold necklace around
her neck. She hoped it would not look
excessive.

"I left the bottle of wine on the table,"
Mr. Jha said. "You go and ring the bell, I'll
rush and get it and come."

Mrs. Jha rang the bell. Mr. Chopra answered. He wondered why the neighbors
had sent the maid ahead.

"Will sir and madam be joining us?" Mr.
Chopra asked in Hindi.

Confused, Mrs. Jha said, "Good evening.
My husband is just coming."

She was standing in a foyer with a domed
ceiling above her head on which, if she
wasn't mistaken, was a reproduction of the
Sistine Chapel. Except in this production,
Adam — it was Adam, wasn't it? — was
wearing a pair of black shorts.

"Of course, of course. Mrs. Jha. You are
Mrs. Jha. Of course. Good evening. So
wonderful to meet you. Welcome to Gurgaon. So nice to have new neighbors. Please

come in. Come and sit. My wife is just getting ready. My brother is also in town but he has gone out. As has my son. Hopefully they will both join us later. Is your sister joining us? I thought I saw her the other day, so I was a bit confused, you see. But never mind. Please come in, come in. What can I get you to drink? A whiskey soda?"

"Oh no, not for me, thank you. Just a club soda will do. I'm not much of a drinker," Mrs. Jha said. "I think maybe you are talking about my friend who was here with me last time? She's an old friend."

She followed Mr. Chopra into the living room. There was a thick beige carpet on the floor, and the doorway that they had entered through was flanked on both sides by two large marble swan figurines. Heavy vermillion curtains covered the windows and made the room feel like a Chinese restaurant in Defence Colony. The sofas were all various shades of brown and white, and in a corner, on a table, was a massive Buddha bust lit up from inside and at the base of the table was a sculpture of a basketful of little dogs. A chandelier hung in the middle of the room. They were not going to find any fluorescent tubelights here, Mrs. Jha thought, except maybe in the servants' quarter out back.

A woman in a sari similar to hers, but purple, came out holding a tray of beautiful crystal glasses. For a moment, Mrs. Jha thought she had managed to wear the right clothes. She thought she looked the part. And then she realized that the woman holding the tray was the maid, and Mayur Palli felt like a different country that they had left behind and here, in this new country, Mrs. Jha did not know the language.

"The other day you mentioned that you had a son, Mr. Jha," Mr. Chopra said. He knew he had been asking questions since they sat down, but now that he knew they had moved from East Delhi, he had to know everything else.

"Anil. Please call me Anil. And yes, our son, Rupak, is in New York right now," Mr. Jha said. He could not take his eyes off Mrs. Chopra. Over the past weeks, ever since he first met Mr. Chopra on the road, he had built up a visual of Mrs. Chopra as some young Kareena Kapoor type who would be wearing jeans and maybe a sleeveless top. He pictured her wearing wedge sandals and having her hair loose. Her fingernails would be long, painted a light pink, and the type that made clickety-clackety sounds against surfaces. But Mrs. Chopra looked like someone had taken Mrs. Gupta from Mayur Palli, coated her in honey, and dipped her in a luxury mall. The real Mrs. Chopra was about five feet tall, fat, wearing an expensive-looking sari and earrings that probably cost more than the Jhas' Mayur Palli apartment had cost when they bought it. Her hair, dyed unnaturally black, was pulled into a bun and her fingernails were short and the nails on her right hand were tinged yellow from years of eating turmeric-infused food with her fingers. Mr. Jha could see that she was wearing makeup under her eyes, but her skin was not very supple and the makeup was caked into the cracks, making her look older than she probably had to. Her fingers were covered in rings of all sorts and, for reasons he could not quite understand, Mr. Jha found himself nervous in her presence.

"Ah, New York," Mr. Chopra said. "The city that never sleeps. The Windy City. The Sunshine State. What a wonderful little town. One never tires of Times Square. Does your son live close to there?"

"No, no. He is in upstate New York. Ithaca. You know — where Cornell University is," Mr. Jha said.

"Ithaca. That is a town in Italy if I am not mistaken," Mr. Chopra said. He did not want Mr. Jha thinking they were the only international family on the street. "I am a big fan of Michelangelo."

"He is just finishing his MBA," Mrs. Jha added. "Let's see what he does after this."

"Excellent," Mr. Chopra said. "He will have good career prospects. I have heard Cornell University is one of the best places in the world. Good. Very good for him."

"Well, he's not studying at —" Mrs. Jha said.

"That is what we are hoping, yes," Mr. Jha interrupted.

"Is he married?" Mrs. Chopra asked.

"Oh no. Not yet," Mrs. Jha answered.

Fine, let her husband keep up the pretense that Rupak was studying at Cornell. Mrs. Jha was enjoying the evening, as long as one of the maids wasn't in the room. Contrary to her expectations, the Chopras did not talk constantly about business or jewelry or obscure luxury resorts in distant parts of the world. They had clearly been around money for long enough to not get too excited by it. Mrs. Jha hoped that seeing them would make her husband calm down. It was true that she had pulled out her gold necklace for tonight, but he was taking things too far. He had even insisted on hiding the mug downstairs and having toilet paper placed in every bathroom. Mrs. Jha did not consider toilet paper sufficiently hygienic. There was no way it cleaned better than water. At least he had agreed to have water guns installed near the toilets. Her reverie on the toilets of Gurgaon was broken by the same maid in the purple sari coming into the room again.

"Drinks. What can I get everyone to drink? Mrs. Jha, are you still insisting on sticking to the club soda? How about soda with a splash of wine in it? We can open the bottle you brought or try one of ours? Geeta loves her white wine spritzers. It's quite a ladies' drink, isn't it?"

So that's what a white wine spritzer is, Mrs. Jha thought.

"I'm fine with soda, thank you," she said. She had never really cared for the taste of alcohol.

"Soda for you. Rekha, *ek soda,*" Mr. Chopra said to the maid. Mrs. Jha smiled at the maid. The maid did not smile back. Mrs. Jha decided not to ask about the agency where she was from because there was no way she would feel comfortable with such a fancy maid. She would have to clean the house before the maid cleaned the house.

"And for you, Anil-ji?" Mr. Chopra said

256

to Mr. Jha.

"I'll have an Old Monk, please. With —" Mr. Jha was going to ask for the familiar Indian dark rum, with a splash of water to release the flavors, but before he could complete his request, Mr. Chopra had started laughing.

"Ah, Old Monk. Oh, that's a good one, Anil. Old Monk. How did we ever drink that in college? Am I right? Will Black Label do? Rekha, *ek soda aur Black Label ka bottle le aao.* And the ice bucket also. Mr. Jha, do you take soda or water with your whiskey?"

"Water. Just a splash of water," Mr. Jha said.

"Perfect," Mr. Chopra said. "Exactly how I take it this time of year. In summer, with two cubes of ice, rest of the year with a splash of water. Have you seen those giant ice cubes they have in restaurants these days? I don't care for those. They get in the way of the whiskey and hit against my teeth. Regular ice cubes are just fine."

Over drinks and galouti kebabs, Mr. Chopra started to create a profile of the Jhas in his mind. Yes, they had bought the house but they had no guard, only one car, and a son trying to work in finance, which all meant that no matter how much money Mr. Jha had, it was not enough to support his son. Even his poor wife used to work.

"Mrs. Jha, I must say. I admire that you were a career lady. Everything is changing these days," Mr. Chopra said.

"Well, I hope that isn't in the past tense," Mrs. Jha said. "Now that we're settled in, I want to see if I can go back to work. I don't know if my husband told you, but I used to work with rural craftsmen and weavers to help them bring their goods to —"

"Oh, how nice," Mr. Chopra said. "Aren't these kebabs just so soft? But Mrs. Jha, I think it is very admirable of you. I was telling your husband the other day that with the way the economy is now, many households need a double income."

"Well, my work isn't the most financially rewarding, but it's certainly emotionally rewarding," Mrs. Jha said, with a small laugh.

"Opposite of financially rewarding," Mr. Jha said with a louder laugh. "Financially draining. When the saris or the carpets don't get sold to the shops, half the time Bindu buys them with our own money."

"Sometimes. I don't want the craftsmen to lose hope. In any case, their work makes wonderful gifts," Mrs. Jha said. She considered offering to bring a hand-embroidered sari to Mrs. Chopra, but she noticed the expensive, and, she thought, rather ugly, designer sari Mrs. Chopra was wearing and realized her sari would likely be given to one of the maids.

"A double-income home." Mr. Jha laughed again. This time, Mr. Chopra joined in and they clinked glasses and said, "Cheers."

"Geeta, you see? Not all women spend their days shopping," Mr. Chopra said. "Can you imagine if we needed another income? My wife here certainly would not be of help."

Mrs. Chopra shook her head and laughed at the absurd thought of having a job and continued sipping her white wine spritzer.

Mr. Chopra looked at Mrs. Jha, sitting at the edge of the sofa, drinking her soda. She took up so much less physical space than his own wife. And not just because his own wife was fat. Mrs. Chopra took up space in every sense of the word — her jewelry sparkled, her voice was loud, her clothes were bright, and she wore her self-confidence around her like a halo. Mrs. Jha was undoubtedly more beautiful than Mrs. Chopra, and he would have expected a woman like her to carry herself with that same confidence, but she didn't.

Mrs. Jha was annoyed that she was getting distracted every time the maid went in or out of the room. Yes, perhaps she and the maid were wearing similar saris, but that hardly mattered. That was nothing to be embarrassed about. Mrs. Jha had spent her life working toward helping the less fortunate. She knew that the sari she was wearing was more valuable than some silly overpriced designer sari. The exploitation of the craftsmen by these designers was, after all, exactly what she was trying to work against. Just because the Chopras were more used to money did not mean she was any less than them. Her husband had worked hard and now her son was working hard and she used to work hard, and would again. Mrs. Chopra did not add much to the conversation, and Mrs. Jha couldn't imagine her doing anything interesting. No, she was being unfair. She did not have to counter her own insecurities by being nasty about Mrs. Chopra.

"*Indian Idol* will be on soon," Mrs. Chopra said. "Have you been following this season? It's becoming quite heated."

"Oh, I don't watch much television," Mrs. Jha said. "But we should be heading home in any case. This has been such a wonderful evening."

Of course Mrs. Jha didn't watch *Indian Idol,* Mrs. Chopra thought. Mrs. Jha probably never did anything enjoyable. Everything probably had to become an issue with her. She did not like the way Mrs. Jha was sitting upright in her simple sari and gold chain looking around the Chopras' house. Mrs. Chopra knew the type — the so-called intellectual ones who come into money and then buy up homes in the fancy neighborhoods but think they're too good for the others. They think there's some moral code to how you spend your money. Mrs. Jha was just this type. She would be the kind to put her arm around a homeless person to make a whole production out of it and then look down her nose at Mrs. Chopra simply because Mrs. Chopra had no desire to get lice herself.

As the Chopras were standing at the door saying good night to the Jhas, Johnny pulled into the driveway in his new Honda Civic. He stepped out, beeped the car doors locked, and walked over to the house.

Mr. Chopra looked at the silver car and worried for a moment that he had given in to his wife too easily. Perhaps he should have ignored her and splurged and bought his son a Lexus. It wasn't just his wife's fault, though; he himself couldn't justify the cost given the import taxes. It would have felt wasteful.

"Johnny, young man," Mr. Chopra said. "Where have you been? Come meet our new neighbors. These are the Jhas. They have just moved in next door. This is Johnny, our son."

Johnny said hello and walked straight past them to the coffee table to pour himself a whiskey on the rocks.

"Like father, like son," Mr. Chopra said, laughing. "Johnny, no drinking and driving. At least not when your mother sees. He's just got a new car and now his mother is forever nervous. You know how it is."

Mr. and Mrs. Jha smiled at Mr. Chopra.

"And what do you do, Johnny? Are you studying?" Mrs. Jha asked.

"Studying!" Mr. Chopra said. "Oh, that's rich. Tell them, Johnny. Tell them what you do."

"I'm a poet. Well, I want to be," Johnny said.

"Oh, how nice," Mrs. Jha said. "A poet. That's lovely."

"Lovely for him that I can support him," Mr. Chopra said. "Johnny, you should learn from their son. He is studying in America, doing his MBA. From Cornell University, no less. It is a top university."

"They will meet soon. Rupak will be back for his winter break," Mrs. Jha said.

"Not Cornell University," Mr. Jha said. "Ithaca College. Near Cornell University. It isn't very good. But so expensive! I don't know how most people can afford sending their children. We are lucky. Anyway, let's see what he does next. If anything."

Mrs. Jha looked over at her husband. What was he doing? He was the one who had always whispered the word *near* when saying Cornell University. Maybe he had had too much to drink. He wasn't used to drinking whiskey.

"It's a good university," Mrs. Jha said. "It's a lot of hard work."

"Hardly working is more like it," Mr. Jha added with a laugh.

"Well, Johnny, hopefully you will see him and learn that some young people have to work," Mr. Chopra said, shaking his head toward the Jhas and laughing. "*Chalo* then, we will see you again soon."

263

FIFTEEN

Despite it being a Friday, Rupak had been studying at the library until nearly midnight, ignoring text messages from both Serena and Elizabeth. His parents had booked their tickets to New York, and he was supposed to book their bus tickets to Ithaca. He was at risk of failing two classes already, and that, combined with his academic probation from the previous year, meant he was at risk of not getting his degree. He had to focus. He was not the kind of student who started excelling in any one subject. There were no professors who wanted to take him under their wing. Some of his classmates had become friends with the professors. The young professors were practically the same age as the students themselves, but Rupak felt embarrassed to befriend any of them. He thought it was because he was fully dependent on his parents for money. He wished, in a way, that he could be like his

American counterparts and work a part-time job as a bartender or a barista to make money, but, first of all, his parents would not want him having a job like that and, second of all, he would have to work far too many hours to make an amount that his father could easily transfer to him. But maybe he would have worked harder if he had to pay for it, or if he knew his parents were struggling to pay for it. No, of course not. How did that make any sense? If he were working part-time to make money, he'd have even less time to study. He just had no explanation.

Rupak left the library and decided to return Elizabeth's text message first. He was beginning to feel guilty about keeping the relationship with her going when he knew it was not a reasonable option at the moment, at least not until after his parents' visit. And he needed to talk to her honestly about it. Which he could do tomorrow morning after he spent the night with her, because he just wanted to relax tonight. He did not want to talk about India, or Delhi, or his parents. He did not want to have to think more about how to face them and how to tell them about his life. They knew almost nothing about his life in Ithaca and he preferred it that way. But now they had booked their tickets. Rupak was going to go to New York to spend two nights with them and then they would all come to Ithaca for three nights. He had not told Elizabeth they were coming but was keen, instead, on convincing Serena to come to dinner with them. It was all exhausting and he knew he had to be more honest with Elizabeth, but first he wanted just one night to relax.

So at around midnight, he left the library and went to Elizabeth's apartment and when she opened the door, the familiar, comfortable smell of her lotion and her skin and her life drifted out from behind her and absorbed all his other problems. He dropped his bag on the floor and pressed his cold face into her warm neck.

"Your nose is freezing!" Elizabeth said.

"It's really cold already," Rupak said.

"How was the library? Did you get everything done?"

"Stop. Please stop. I don't want to talk about work. I don't want to talk about the library. Do you have anything to drink?"

Rupak sat down on Elizabeth's sofa while she went to the kitchen to get beer for them both.

"Why are you in such a mood?" Elizabeth asked.

"What did you do tonight?" he asked.

266

"I went riding at the equestrian center. I told you. You should come with me some time. You'd enjoy it. You seem tense. Do you want to smoke?"

Rupak nodded, and Elizabeth pulled out the wooden pencil box from the drawer of her bedside table. She sat down cross-legged on the brown threadbare carpet of her apartment and opened the box in front of her.

"This is such a useful box. How would your mother react if she knew we used it for pot?" Elizabeth asked, laughing, dropping a small marijuana bud into her open palm.

"Maybe you should go back to using the old Altoid tin," Rupak said.

"Why? I love this box."

She shut the box, placed it on the floor near the coffee table, and licked the edge of the rolling paper.

"I was thinking," she said. "Do you want to come to Pensacola with me for Thanksgiving? My parents would love to meet you, and I think you'd like it there."

Rupak did want to go to Pensacola with her. He wanted to be part of a traditional American Thanksgiving with turkey and stuffing and whatever else Thanksgiving included. He wanted to be on the receiving end of jokes about an Indian coming to

Thanksgiving. He wanted to eat oysters and drink wine on the beach with Elizabeth and go sailing with her friends. He wanted to know who her parents were who tithed ten percent of their income to the church. He wanted to see how he would react to staying in a house with a dog. But he knew it was not fair to his parents. They would be here in less than two weeks, and he had to sacrifice this beautiful blond woman sitting in front of him. And he had to do it now. It wasn't fair to her to wait until morning.

"I don't think that would be such a great idea, Lizzy. I've actually been thinking about it and I think I need to focus more on my work, you know. I'm not doing that well," Rupak said. He thought he was going to say they should end the relationship because there was no chance of a future, they were from different worlds, and there was no point. But instead he found himself giving this excuse that left a window open for them to get back together if he managed to get his grades up and keep his parents happy.

"You aren't going to just study over Thanksgiving break. You should come. It gets really lonely in Ithaca when everyone leaves."

"I'll be fine."

"You can study in Florida. I'll tell my family that you're coming with work. They would love it. My mother rented a Bollywood film from Netflix last week."

"Why?"

"What do you mean, why?"

"Nothing, sorry. I just mean . . . do they . . . how much have you told your parents about us?"

"Just that I'm dating a guy from India. And they've seen a few pictures of you. That's all. Why, what did you tell your parents?"

"The same. That I'm dating a girl from Florida. That's all. Anyway, Lizzy, that's not the point. The point is that I need to focus more on my work. Not just over Thanksgiving, but in general. And I don't want to drag you into my boring life with me, you know."

"I'm studying too. I hardly get in the way of your work. I'm doing fine in school," Elizabeth said. She leaned up from the couch where she had been reclining against Rupak and reached for her beer, which was on a coaster on the coffee table. It was easier to speak to the back of her head, Rupak thought.

"Well, good for you. But I'm not. And I need to focus on my work. I can't spend all my time hanging out with you."

"What are you saying?" Elizabeth looked back at him over her shoulder.

Rupak was trying to say absolutely nothing more. This was exactly the conversation he had been hoping to avoid tonight.

"Oh my God," Elizabeth said, standing up and moving across the room. "You didn't tell your parents about me, did you?"

"What? What do my parents have to do with this?"

Rupak wanted to stand up and be at the same height as her, but he knew that to do that now would seem confrontational. He had to stay seated and stay looking casual.

"You are so pathetic, Rupak. You're a kid. You're a confused little kid. I have never met someone over the age of sixteen who is as confused about themselves as you are."

"Okay, you know what, that's really offensive. And you keep so much from me. Why won't you tell me how Andrew proposed?"

"What?"

"You keep that whole part of your life so hidden," Rupak said. He knew he was flailing, but now he was in too deep. "What, the Indian guy can't know about your past? You think I can't handle the fact that you've had other men in your life? You see me as some conservative stopover before you end up

with someone like Andrew who was probably born knowing how to set up a tent. I'm
just exotic to you. Like some zoo animal."

"What the fuck are you talking about? I
just invited you to Pensacola, into my family and my life. Stop trying to turn this
around. God, take some responsibility. You
can't even figure out that you're failing
because you don't study. That's it. It's
simple. You're just a confused child. Stop
blaming everything else — stop blaming
your parents, stop blaming India, stop blaming America. Figure out who you are and
just be that person. Forget Thanksgiving."

"Fine," Rupak said. "And forget meeting
my parents when they come to visit."

"When are they coming to visit?"

"It doesn't matter," Rupak said.

"They're coming? They're coming. Oh
wow, they're coming. Your parents are coming to visit. And you can't be man enough
to introduce me. I don't even think I'm that
upset because you saved me from continu-
ing to date a child. And you're right —
Andrew does know how to set up a tent,
and it's sexy. I . . . No, I don't have words.
You don't deserve words. But you know
what? You do deserve pity and I pity you,
Rupak. I really pity you. You can leave,
please."

Elizabeth kicked aside the pencil box and went into the bathroom. Rupak heard the shower turn on. She was right. He was a coward who was terrified about what other people thought about him. And he was failing.

Sixteen

"Why don't I meet you out somewhere?" Mrs. Ray said. She did not want to care what anybody thought, but she also was not ready to invite Upen to Mayur Palli. For starters, someone or the other was bound to see and gossip. And, if he came home, then what? Sex, or something resembling sex, would be in the air and she did not know how that worked at their age. Her skin sagged in places, her breasts no longer stayed where they should, and what about him? Was he still capable of getting hard? As for her — frankly, she had never experienced an orgasm. She had had, and enjoyed, sex enough in her lifetime, but it was hard to desire what she did not know. She had read about orgasms — these days, of course, the headlines of magazines screamed about the powerful experience on the covers and it was hard to avoid reading about it or seeing it everywhere, but she had never felt it.

From what she gathered, it felt like a particularly pleasurable sneeze. But her vagina embarrassed her and she could not imagine a man prodding around down there. Mrs. Ray had once looked at porn on her computer. She did not know quite how to do it so she simply went to porn.com. It was horrifying. There were women — mostly hairless down there — sitting freely on men's faces while the men did God only knows what. Was that sex these days? It was best to suggest another meeting out somewhere with Upen.

"We could meet at Dilli Haat for a walk and maybe have lunch sitting out in the sun?" she said.

"We could, but then we'd just both have to travel. I can just as easily come to East Delhi. I've never even been to that part of town," Upen said.

"Well, you really are not missing much. Let's stick to Dilli Haat at one p.m. We can meet outside, near the ticketing desk. I have so many more questions about Chandigarh."

She wished she had not brought up the idea of Chandigarh again, but she did not know how to suggest meeting simply because she felt like meeting, with no other excuses to hide behind. And Dilli Haat

274

would be a good place to do that. The outdoor market had stalls from different parts of India selling local goods — shawls from Kashmir, jewelry from Rajasthan, saris from West Bengal, pottery from Gujarat. Toward the back, there were food stalls that sold food from different parts of the country. Dilli Haat always amazed Mrs. Ray. There was so much about India that she did not know.

While she was still standing near the phone, she remembered that she should call Ganga and check that she had reached her son's home safely. Ganga had left the previous week and Mrs. Ray got the feeling she was not going to return soon. She always went with a one-way ticket and assessed what all was going on at home before calling Mrs. Ray and telling her when she would return. Getting to her son's home was quite a trek, and it would make no sense for her to go all the way for less than a few months. Mrs. Ray offered to buy her a plane ticket to Calcutta to make the trip easier, and to make sure she came back soon, but Ganga refused. She did not want to accept anything other than her income, and she had never really trusted airplanes. Her reasoning was different than most, though. It was not a plane crash she was worried about so much as having her luggage disappear.

"I've heard they take your bag away from you before you get on the plane," Ganga had told Mrs. Ray. "I refuse to fall victim to that. I like trains where I can sleep with my feet on the bag. I'm no fool."

Mrs. Ray dialed the number for the local shop in Ganga's son's village. When she got through, she told the shopkeeper to go and tell Ganga to come to the shop and she would try calling again in half an hour. This was the only way to reach Ganga. She had also refused Mrs. Ray's offers of a cell phone.

Half an hour later, when Mrs. Ray called again, Ganga informed her that she had spent the morning sitting in the local pond cooling herself and getting caught up on all the news from the other villagers. She sounded happy to be back even though she said, "There's still no plumbing here. I have to take my things and walk all the way into the woods just to use the bathroom. That is the one thing you city people have figured out better than us. But the rest is better here."

"Will you be okay by yourself?" Ganga then asked, making no mention of her return ticket. Mrs. Ray said yes, she would be, of course, and Ganga just said, "Good. In that case I'll stay for a little longer this time. I'll let you know in a few weeks how things are looking."

Maybe it wasn't fair to keep her in Delhi, Mrs. Ray thought, while listening to Ganga go on and on about her village and who had gotten married, who was pregnant, who had died, and who was taking English lessons and wearing lipstick. Ganga was so much more than a maid in her village. Of course Mrs. Ray had never visited Ganga there, nor did she plan to — she liked toilets that were indoors — but from everything Ganga described, that was her real home. Mrs. Ray told her she could stay for as long as she needed. She could not ask her to come back simply because she was lonely. In any case, it was a lot easier to get dressed for an afternoon with Upen without Ganga pottering around asking questions.

Mrs. Ray arrived at Dilli Haat before Upen. She had rented another four-hour taxi from the local stand and, again, she didn't want the driver to see that she was meeting a man.

"Madam, I will park across the street. Here you have to pay for parking. Just give me a missed call when you are finished and I will come and collect you from this same spot," the driver said.

All the drivers always communicated through missed calls on their cell phones. He didn't want to waste his precious mobile minutes on a ten-second conversation in which Mrs. Ray would tell him to bring the car to the main entrance to pick her up, so instead she would let it ring twice and then hang up and, since they had already discussed it, he would see the missed call and know that meant Mrs. Ray was ready to be picked up at the main entrance. Mrs. Ray once tried texting one of the drivers that she was ready to be collected, but later he laughed and told her, "Madam, I cannot read any English."

Mrs. Ray bought two entry tickets for Dilli Haat and waited for Upen outside the gate. How nice it felt, she thought, to ask for two tickets instead of her usual one. Or three, if Mr. and Mrs. Jha were with her.

There were some women squatting on the ground outside the market, selling pillowcases and bedsheets. Mrs. Ray thought it might be a nice idea to send a set of pillowcases to New York for Rupak. And it would give her something to do when Upen approached, instead of just standing on the side looking eager. She squatted down next to the one closest to her.

"Madam, this is finest handmade pillowcase directly from Rajasthan. Very modern style, for very modern lady," the pillowcase saleswoman said to her in broken English, because Mrs. Ray was wearing jeans. "You must buy this set. I will give good deal for whole set."

"Yes, yes, I know. It's lovely," Mrs. Ray said in Hindi while trying to look over her shoulder for Upen.

"Madam, how you speak so good Hindi?" the pushy saleswoman said, clapping her hands.

"Oh, stop it," Mrs. Ray said. "You know perfectly well I'm Indian. Flattering me will not get you a sale."

Upen approached from behind her and placed his hand on her shoulder. Mrs. Ray looked up at him and pushed her sunglasses up on top of her head.

"You're here," she said with a smile.

Upen gave her his hand as she stood and she was grateful because, despite the yoga, her right knee always protested slightly when she got up from the ground.

"You made me take out all of them and you won't buy even one?" the saleswoman said. "All you people are the same."

Once they were inside the main market,

Mrs. Ray stopped at a stall selling silk saris from Tamil Nadu in order to give herself something to do.

"Do you wear saris often?" Upen asked.

"Sometimes. I like saris but they aren't very practical."

"You would look nice in a sari. Not that you don't look lovely in your jeans. You do. It suits you. But a sari would also suit you," Upen said.

"Madam, this color will be very good for your skin color," the man selling the saris said to her.

"Thank you, I'm just looking," Mrs. Ray said.

She touched another silk sari, deep red with gold threads embroidered throughout.

"Saab, your wife has very good taste," the man said to Upen.

"Oh, I'm not. No," Mrs. Ray said. "Come on. Let's go. I have enough saris."

"She does have good taste," Upen said, laughing.

Mrs. Ray rushed ahead away from the stall. She had not heard the word *wife* used in so many years that she had forgotten how it felt. In fact, it had never felt the way it had just felt. It felt thrilling when she heard it just now. She liked the idea of ownership it conveyed. She liked the idea that she belonged to Upen.

Mrs. Ray tried to remember if she had found the word exciting when she first got married. If anything, back then it felt like a burden. And then it went from being a burden to simply being a reality. She was a daughter, a sister, and then a wife. But now her parents were dead — did that make her an orphan? Certainly not. Was there a specific age, she wondered, old enough, after which you were not considered an orphan if your parents died? Eighteen perhaps. And then her husband died — so she was a widow. But was there a certain age, young enough, that if you lost your husband you did not have to be called a widow? If a young childless woman lost her husband tragically when she was only twenty-five — or even thirty-seven, like Mrs. Ray had been — it felt unfair to burden her with the label of *widow* for the rest of her life. And Mrs. Ray certainly did not feel like a widow, even though she was reminded that she was one nearly every day in Mayur Palli.

Upen caught up with her and said, "Are you sure you didn't want that red and gold sari? It was lovely."

"It's too bright for me at this age," Mrs. Ray said. "Do you have children?"

"One daughter. She lives in Liverpool with her husband. They recently had a child, a daughter. They've named her Maya like every single Indian living abroad names their daughters," he laughed. "But she's a sweet girl. Just like her mother. Do you have children?"

Mrs. Ray shook her head. He was a grandfather. She was trying so hard not to feel old, not to feel absurd being on a date at her age, and she was mostly succeeding so she just had to put the term *grandfather* out of her head. In any case, he could easily have had his daughter when he was young and then she could well have had her daughter when she was young. *Grandfather* did not have to mean errant ear and nose hairs. She looked over at Upen. He was wearing sunglasses and looked dashing. Mrs. Ray tried to walk them toward a reflective surface so she could catch a glimpse of how they looked together. Some of the Kashmiri shawl sellers were sure to have mirrors set up outside their stalls. As she led him in that direction, she asked about his late wife. She felt she ought to. One must respect the dead.

"Did your wife get to meet her granddaughter?"

"No," Upen said. "Sadly no."

"I'm sorry to hear that. It must have been very difficult for all of you. Was it sudden?"

"Was it sudden? No. Not too sudden." Upen looked away. Had she pushed too much? She would not have minded being asked about Mr. Ray's death. There was no reason for them to hide what they had been through.

"Oh, Reema, I can't," Upen said, stopping and letting his shoulders drop. He pushed his sunglasses onto his head and looked above her into the distance.

"I'm so sorry. I did not mean to ask too much."

"No, that's not it. I meant, I can't lie to you. My wife isn't dead. She's very much alive. She left me. She had an affair and she left me and it's so embarrassing. I find it easier to tell people she's dead. But that's so dreadful, isn't it? I don't want you to think poorly of me. Let's go sit in the sun and have a cup of tea and I'll tell you everything. I want you to know. Come. Let's go sit."

Mrs. Ray laughed. She laughed loudly and without bothering to cover her mouth like she had always been taught. She was charmed by Upen's story about his wife's affair. She thought it made him sound rather exciting and worldly. Everyone in her world was always so busy covering up the slightest indiscretions and living by such strict social laws that Upen's experience made him unusual.

"Well, that's a nice reaction," Upen said. "She's much happier now. I don't speak to her much. I get her updates from my daughter for the most part. But I'm glad to hear she found what she wanted. It suits me more too. They say a marriage is only as happy as the unhappiest partner, and it's true. It is very hard to be happy around someone who isn't happy themselves, and when we were married, she wasn't."

Mrs. Ray nodded. She had always been content. Not happy, not unhappy. Content. But sitting here in the sun, on an autumn afternoon, with a hot cup of tea, talking to Upen, she was more than content. And how wonderful that was.

"Anyway, it all worked out for the best, didn't it?" Upen asked, and Mrs. Ray smiled and looked away, overcome by a sudden shyness. "Do you mind if I ask about your husband?"

"What do you want to know?" Mrs. Ray said.

"How did he pass away?"

"Aneurysm. It was quick. I was in the bathroom," Mrs. Ray said. She had never talked about this with anyone except Mrs. Jha — how strange the words sounded now, years later.

"I'm sorry. Please don't answer anything you don't want to answer," Upen said.

"No, no. Nobody ever asks. Everyone is too scared. I don't blame them — hearing about a forty-year-old otherwise healthy man dying can make you feel very vulnerable, I suppose. But it's nice to be asked — it's nice not to have to pretend death doesn't exist. But really it wasn't as traumatic as people assume. I came out of the bathroom and he was lying in bed, one foot still on the floor, and he was dead. That was it. He was in his office clothes and was going to leave for work so there was no reason for him to be lying down — he must have known something was wrong. He must have felt different."

"And you found him?"

Mrs. Ray nodded, and continued, "The maid was at the market. I didn't scream or cry or shout or anything. It was strange — it was like I knew exactly what had happened and I knew that it had to happen. I'm not a religious person — I think I believe in God but I certainly don't practice anything — but seeing him there was so peaceful. For a little while I lay down next to him, with my hand against his chest. I don't remember now for how long I did that, but I remember a calmness. I had thought about his death before — I don't think you can share a home and a life with someone and not think about their death. But I had always assumed it would be somehow more violent. Not the death itself necessarily, but I assumed my reaction would be violent. I always imagined I'd throw up or scream or run out of the house shouting and lose my mind, but it was none of that. I don't know how to explain it."

She stopped. She had never even told Mrs. Jha about the moments after this death. She had never told anyone.

"I don't quite remember the days following that, so I suppose that's the violence. My mind doesn't remember it."

She looked over at Upen, who was listening and didn't seem scared. But still she smiled to offer him a possible reaction — as wonderful as he was being so far, she knew it was impossible to know how to react to this story.

"Thank you for asking. Honestly," she said. "I think it honors his memory to talk about it. He was a very logical man — about life, death, and everything in between. He wouldn't want his own death to be shrouded in silence."

"He sounds wonderful," Upen said. "It seems like it was a good marriage."

"It was," Mrs. Ray said. "It wasn't exciting, but it was good. It was very good."

"Excitement doesn't last," Upen said. "A good spouse is someone with whom you can successfully run a boring nonprofit organization. Don't you think? Most things fade. But you need to find someone you can do the boring things with. See, that's why the whole arranged-marriage idea worked for so many generations. The expectations were more realistic; divorce rates were lower. Marriage isn't the same as courtship. Marriage is companionship. And that online dating that all the young people do these days is basically what our parents and grandparents were doing for us for years — using a formula to work out compatibility."

"That's a bleak way of looking at it," Mrs. Ray said. "What about romance?"

"That's exactly it, though. That's the romance!" Upen said. "You can't have a lifetime of flowers and holidays. The romance comes from finding the boring stuff fun — like this. Like walking around Dilli Haat. And you can usually guess when that will be there — like with you and me — we're both in the same place in our lives, we're both looking for companionship, we both get along, have similar ideals and views. I'm telling you — if our parents were alive, they'd arrange our marriage."

Mrs. Ray laughed.

"And you'd come with your family to meet me and I'd make tea and bake a cake and sit across from you looking coy?"

"Exactly," Upen said. "And your mother would tell us how good you are at cooking and maintaining a home. And educated — they'd tell us you're educated because clearly we're a modern family."

"Not too educated, though," Mrs. Ray said.

"No. Certainly not too educated. Nothing that would threaten me," Upen said, also laughing. "And then I'd go home and tell my parents you were wonderful and wasn't the cake delicious and sure, I could see myself spending the rest of my life with you."

"Romance," Mrs. Ray said with a smile.

"Romance."

A group of school students, still in their uniforms, sat down at the table next to them and called loudly for a waiter. Mrs. Ray heard them order plates of steamed vegetarian momos, chicken chow mein, and cups of tea. They had personalized their school uniforms — crisp white collared shirts with blue pleated skirts for the girls and blue slacks for the boys — with scarves and jewelry and fluorescent bras that were ever so slightly visible. One of the boys was wearing a necklace. Mrs. Ray looked at them with admiration. Surely the young girls in this group, with their skirts rolled up at the waist to show more leg, and buttons undone to show hints of their young breasts, would not grow up and turn into Mrs. De or Mrs. Gupta. Surely these girls would let each other live in peace no matter what the future held for them. One of the girls and one of the boys were the couple in the group. Mrs. Ray noticed their knees touching under the table and the ease with which they shared a fork. Emboldened by their romance, she allowed her own knee to relax against Upen's. Two of the boys threw a tennis ball back and forth and all of them chattered loudly, mixing English and Hindi. The tennis ball rolled away from them and landed at Upen's feet. One of the boys jumped up and came over to retrieve it.

"Sorry, Uncle. Sorry, Aunty," he said politely and returned to his group. There it was again, Mrs. Ray thought. The world seeing her once again as one half of a couple. And that half felt so much bigger than the one ever had.

"Perhaps next time you can come over for dinner," Mrs. Ray said. Let the world know, she decided.

SEVENTEEN

Mr. Jha was going to the DLF Emporio Mall to buy a set of branded matching luggage for their upcoming trip to New York. This was the first international trip for which he had booked business class tickets for his wife and himself, and he wanted their luggage to fit their surroundings. Mrs. Jha, of course, had said that it was unnecessary — who was going to see their luggage once it was checked in? — but he was not going to stand in the queue outside the airport, or at the check-in counter, with mismatched suitcases, so when she went to take a shower, he quickly left the house to go shopping. He reversed the car out of the driveway and got out to pull the gate shut because, of course, they had not hired a gatekeeper yet. At the same time, Mr. Chopra's Jaguar pulled out of the driveway next door while Balwinder pushed their gate shut.

Mr. Jha had not seen Mr. Chopra since the evening at their home, nearly a week ago. It was difficult to keep up with the neighbors when there was no way to know what the neighbors were doing.

Mr. Chopra's Jaguar came to a stop near Mr. Jha. Mr. Chopra lowered his window and said, "Good morning, good morning. How have you been? Mr. Jha, would you like me to tell Balwinder to shut your gate for you? He won't mind. He hardly has any work to do here anyway. God only knows what we pay him for."

"Oh no, no," Mr. Jha said. Despite the slightly cooler October temperatures, he was already sweating and now this. "Not a problem. We will have our guard here soon. We have just been so busy, you know, with all this settling in and planning our travel. Did I mention that we are off to New York for a holiday? We are leaving in a few days, at the end of this week. And we've been so busy, we booked our tickets at the last minute as usual, so you can imagine the cost. Air travel is just so expensive. But it's time to take a bite of the Big Apple. Have you been?"

Mr. Chopra had not. New York just never interested him. Now Las Vegas — that was a good travel destination. New York was too dangerous. But he had no desire to admit to that.

"Ah yes, to visit your brilliant son. We are looking forward to meeting him. You tell him to study hard and come when he can take a break. And good thing it isn't peak season — tickets are relatively cheaper this time of year."

"Oh, who knows if he is even studying? He tells us he's studying, but I have my doubts. I've spoiled him too much," Mr. Jha said. He was standing now next to Mr. Chopra's car window. "And oh, how I wish tickets were cheaper this time of year. But I don't think there's ever a cheap season to go to New York! And not to mention the amount of shopping my wife will probably do — you should count your blessings that you have not been there."

Mr. Jha laughed loudly but he was sweating, from the bright sun that was beating down on his head and the stress of coming up with ways to show how expensive this trip was going to be — and he realized now that it was going to be difficult to let Mr. Chopra know that they were traveling in business class without saying it explicitly. Unless, he thought, he left the priority luggage tags on the suitcases when they returned to Gurgaon and made sure Mr.

Chopra came to visit while the bags were still lying in plain view. He felt sweat drip down along the side of his face.

Mr. Chopra reached behind his seat, pulled out a tissue from the box on the back window, and handed it to Mr. Jha.

"It's still hot, isn't it? Please tell Balwinder to shut your gate tomorrow. Starting the day already sweating is no fun. Well, I'll be off. Have a good day. And do let me know when we can take you to the club for dinner. You must become members."

Mr. Jha knew his wife would never agree to joining the LRC.

"Yes, yes, it sounds interesting. But let's see — the lady of the house is wanting to spend more and more time in New York. All the shopping in that city drives women mad. But at least then I can justify buying whatever I want at the Apple Store, isn't that right? Have a wonderful day, Dinesh."

Mr. Jha walked back to his car, got in, and drove off. At least not having a driver meant he could leave when he wanted to. Now he would get his matching luggage set from Burberry, pack, and head to New York City to his son. He sat in his car and watched the Jaguar drive down the road. Poor children around Delhi made a sport out of stealing the decals off expensive cars —

many fancy cars were missing the classic symbol of the Mercedes, the BMW, the Audi — and Mr. Jha was forever nervous that he would find his half-finished peace sign gone one day, but Mr. Chopra's Jaguar still boasted the slender animal on the front hood. The car would look so much less impressive without that, he thought. Or with a scratch along the polished, perfect surface. How satisfying it would feel to scratch a key along the shiny body of that car. He shook his head; he mustn't think such thoughts. Mr. Chopra had been nothing but nice. There was no reason to scratch his car. Letting him know they were traveling business class was sufficient.

When Mr. Jha got back from the mall he noticed a black Swift parked outside their gate. It looked familiar and Mr. Jha tried to remember if they had workers coming in today. He didn't think so. Unless his wife was surprising him with a swimming pool installation while he was out. That would be nice of her, he thought. But completely unlike her, he corrected. He parked his car, opened the trunk, and pulled out the new matching sets of Burberry suitcases — two large ones, and two carry-ons with the matching logos. Frankly they looked quite ugly, but without the logo on them, how would anyone know they were Burberry? And, strangely enough, the ones without the logos were more expensive than the ones with logos. That was certainly counter-intuitive, Mr. Jha thought.

He pushed two of the bags to the front door and was reaching around in his pocket for the keys when Mr. Gupta opened the front door.

"Welcome home," Mr. Gupta said cheer-fully. He laughed loudly and said, "Now I know what it feels like to throw open the doors to a big Gurgaon bungalow. Come in, come in. We've just dropped in to say hello."

Of course that Swift looked out of place in Gurgaon, Mr. Jha thought. What were the Guptas doing here?

"Anil, you're home," Mrs. Jha said as he walked in the door with the luggage. She was sitting on the sofa next to Mrs. Gupta and they both had cups of tea in their hands. "Where were you? The Guptas called because they were in the area, so I invited them over for tea."

"I was out buying luggage for our trip," Mr. Jha said, still adjusting to the sight of his old neighbors in his new house. They looked smaller here than they did in Mayur Palli.

"But we already have enough suitcases," Mrs. Jha said.

"Not fancy branded ones," Mr. Gupta said, twirling one of the suitcases behind Mr. Jha.

Mr. Jha turned around and took the suitcase from him and put them both in the dining room, got himself a glass of water, and returned to the living room.

"The branded ones are the most reasonably priced," Mr. Jha said. "No need for anything flashier."

As annoyed as he was to see Mr. Gupta here, he did not want to give him more reason to make jokes.

"The sofa certainly looks better here," Mr. Gupta said.

"How is everything in Mayur Palli?" Mr. Jha asked. "I got an e-mail from our tenants that they're settling in well."

"They are quite lovely," Mrs. Gupta said. "The wife has started her dance classes, and she may do one for the older ladies as well. I am very tempted to join."

"Oh, how nice," Mrs. Jha said.

"Have you made friends with other ladies in this neighborhood?" Mrs. Gupta asked.

"Not really yet," Mrs. Jha said. "I do miss

Mayur Palli. But let's see — I'm thinking of going back to work soon."

"Is that a dimmer on your light switch?" Mr. Gupta said. He got up and walked to the switch on the wall and pushed it up and down, making the lights in the living room dim on and off.

"Dimmers are better for the environment," Mr. Jha said. "And they lessen the electricity bill in the long run."

Mr. Gupta left the lights on and sat back down.

"My wife is right," he said. "Your new tenants are wonderful and we are all happy to have them living in Mayur Palli. They have both been attending all the meetings. Lovely couple. With that cute little son."

"Well, let's see how long they stay there for," Mr. Jha added, for no reason. The Ramaswamys had agreed to stay for at least two years and had said that it was likely that they would stay on longer, but Mr. Jha hadn't expected Mayur Palli to have replaced them so easily.

"Well, I hope they stay. They're like a younger version of your family," Mrs. Gupta added. "From when Rupak was a little boy."

"But they're South Indian," Mr. Jha said.

"Yes, it's nice to have more diversity," Mr. Gupta said. "That Mr. Ramaswamy loves crossword puzzles — now even I've started doing them every Sunday."

"You're sure that dance class isn't turning into anything more . . . sinister?" Mr. Jha said.

Mr. Gupta laughed.

"Oh no, no, no. Absolutely not. That Mr. Ruddra always thinks everything is a brothel. No chance with the Ramaswamys — they are outstanding people. They even go to the temple every weekend. And Mr. Ramaswamy works for Standard Chartered Bank, which is such a reliable job with a steady income every month. Having a reliable job like that is a stamp of approval in many ways, I think."

Mr. Gupta looked directly at Mr. Jha and then tipped his teacup toward himself, saw that it was empty, and placed it down on the coffee table.

"Well, we should be going," he said. "We only wanted to come and say a quick hello and see how you're settling in here."

"We're very happy here," Mrs. Jha said. "It's such a lovely neighborhood. Quiet, peaceful, calm."

Mr. Jha smiled at his wife and added, "A real oasis in the middle of the chaos of the rest of Delhi. So wonderful of you to have stopped by."

"Yes, yes," Mr. Gupta said. "It's very nice. Very different from those old expensive bungalows around Aurungzeb Road. Now those are truly unaffordable. It's nice that they're making more reasonable neighborhoods like Gurgaon."

"Well, those big central Delhi bungalows are never for sale," Mr. Jha said.

"Everything is on sale for a certain price," Mr. Gupta said.

The Jhas walked the Guptas down the driveway out of the gate and toward their Swift.

"Do come again sometime," Mrs. Jha said politely.

As the Guptas were about to get into their car, Mr. Chopra's Jaguar turned onto the lane and stopped right near them. Mr. Chopra put his window down and stuck his head out.

"Friends visiting?" he asked.

"Old friends," Mr. Jha said. "This is Mr. and Mrs. Gupta."

"Old neighbors," Mr. Gupta said. "Come to see their new life."

"Nice to meet you," Mr. Chopra said. "I am Dinesh Chopra, the new neighbor. Is that a Swift? Do they still make that car?"

"Evidently so," Mr. Jha said with a smile. "Nice to see you again, Dinesh. Twice in one day! Golf soon. We must join the LRC."

"You are joining?" Mr. Chopra asked. "But New York . . ."

"Lovely seeing you!" Mr. Jha said, and quickly turned his back.

Mr. Chopra waved and put his window back up, and the Jaguar pulled noiselessly into his driveway, and Balwinder pulled the gate shut behind them.

"Lovely neighbors," Mr. Jha said. "We've already become so close. There's a country club here, which we will be joining. There's a full golf course."

"Mr. Ramaswamy is keen for his wife to start a morning yoga class in Mayur Palli," Mr. Gupta said. "There has been lots of positive response for such a venture. Times are changing. Do come visit."

With that, Mr. Gupta got in the car and leaned over and unlocked his wife's door.

EIGHTEEN

"The airport is more like a train station these days. Too many people get to travel. How do more planes not crash into each other?" Mr. Jha said, as their taxi pulled up to the terminal.

"We've already survived the most dangerous part of the journey," Mrs. Jha said. She knew her husband was going to keep talking to keep his nerves about flying at bay.

"But once something happens, there is zero chance of surviving in an airplane. I've heard that they've reduced the amount of time between takeoffs to less than sixty seconds. That means we can easily bump into the plane ahead of us now. Stop here. Just here is fine. This is the terminal," Mr. Jha said to the driver.

It went completely against nature to lurch up into the sky and over the seas in a heavy metal tube. But he certainly did admire that Richard Branson fellow. He had heard stories about Branson flirting with young journalists and he was always photographed in white linen clothes looking sun-kissed and youthful. Mr. Jha was getting there, he thought — today he had traded his usual slacks and button-down shirt for a navy blue tracksuit and new white sneakers. Maybe he would buy some nice linen clothes in New York City. He would try to convince his wife to also buy some more fashionable clothes. How would she possibly travel comfortably in the sari that she was wearing? He looked over at her in her matching sari and blouse with her brown jacket on, and darker brown shawl draped on her arm. She looked older than she needed to.

Mrs. Jha tidied the pleats of her sari while the driver went to get a trolley for their luggage. She looked over at her husband in his matching tracksuit and new sneakers and wanted to protect him — from his own fears, from Gurgaon, from New York City, and now from the policeman who was blowing his whistle in Mr. Jha's face and rapping on the Innova with his wooden stick.

"Move this car along," the policeman said to Mr. Jha. "Come on. Move it along. Is this your car?"

Mrs. Jha was worried that the policeman would think Mr. Jha was the driver, and she wanted to protect Mr. Jha from that as well. She did not want him to know that his outfit made him look stiff and uncomfortable, the exact opposite of the effect he was hoping it would have. She rushed over to his side and said to the policeman, "The driver is just getting the trolley. He'll move the car as soon as we have our luggage."

With their luggage piled up, Mr. Jha pushed the trolley through the crowds toward the main entrance.

"There should really be a separate entrance altogether for business class travelers. What is the point of paying so much extra if we have to wait in line like this?" he said.

"But then you can say they should have a separate lane for cars of business class travelers, then you will say a separate road leading to the terminal, then a separate highway leading out of Delhi. Where will it end? We can't just separate ourselves endlessly."

"Bindu, this is not the time or place for your communism. Our tickets are nearly three times the price of economy and this is what we have to deal with," Mr. Jha said, standing now behind a young family of four and all their bags and chaos. One short curly-haired toddler stared up at him with a finger up her nose.

As soon as the plane touched down on the tarmac at John F. Kennedy Airport in New York City, Mr. Jha unbuckled his seat belt and jumped up from his seat, feeling as though he had just survived an eighteen-hour brush with death.

"Sir, please remain seated until the plane has come to a complete halt and the captain has turned off the *fasten seat belt* sign," the flight attendant called out to him from her seat at the front of the cabin.

"Not a problem," Mr. Jha said to her. "Small bumps don't worry me."

He opened the overhead compartment as the plane raced down the tarmac.

"Sir! Please close that and sit down and buckle your seat belt," the flight attendant repeated, looking toward the other flight attendant strapped into her seat across the aisle.

"Just getting our bags," Mr. Jha said. "Bindu, get your things together. The sooner we get off, the faster we will get through the line for immigration."

Mr. Jha managed to get a grasp on the handle of his pull-along right as the plane came to a sharp halt at the end of the tarmac and sent Mr. Jha tumbling to the ground. The bag, fortunately, remained in the overhead compartment. The two flight attendants looked at each other across the aisle and shared a small satisfied smile before the first one said, "Sir, are you okay? This is why we ask passengers to remain seated until the *fasten seat belt* sign has been turned off. It's for your own safety."

She looked across the aisle and smirked again at the other flight attendant, who was still peering over and smiling. Indian passengers never listened. They were always the ones who stood up the minute the plane touched down, and the flight attendants always found it satisfying to watch one of them tumble. Mrs. Jha noticed their smiles and reached her hand across to her husband and said, "Are you okay? Come sit."

Mr. Jha stood up, zipped up his track jacket, and remained standing, this time holding the top of his seat for balance and not reaching up for the suitcase. Mrs. Jha was grateful for his defiance in the face of the laughing flight attendants. She smiled up at her husband. They could sit in their tight skirts and pantyhose and lipstick and mock him all they wanted but he had come from nothing, absolutely nothing, and could now fly them both across the world on seats that converted into full beds just by pressing a few buttons. This trip signified the start of their new lives — the move was done, they were settled, and it was now time to try and relax into these roles.

Mrs. Jha had never been to New York City before, but she had read books and seen movies and had imagined herself standing at the crossroads of Times Square looking up at the electronic billboards and ads that spanned the width of full buildings. Sitting on the tarmac of JFK, looking at her husband standing near his seat, Mrs. Jha felt as though she were about to step into a movie.

NINETEEN

"I hardly wear jewelry," Mrs. Jha said, standing in front of Tiffany's on the corner of Fifth Avenue and Fifty-Seventh Street, with the autumn sun bright in the sky and New York City bustling and sparkling around them. "Let's keep walking. I've heard this place is very expensive."

Mr. Jha felt the weight of the Apple bag in his hand.

"Let's just have a look," he said. "You love the movie. We can't come to New York City and not get at least something from here."

Mrs. Jha did love the movie. She sometimes pretended to be Audrey Hepburn when she browsed the sterling silver jewelry shops in Khan Market. It didn't have quite the same effect — she was too old, too Indian, and too bland. Standing here, on Fifth Avenue, looking at all the beautiful people of New York City, she knew that more than ever.

"Fine, let's go in," Mrs. Jha said. "Maybe just something small."

He would buy her something expensive, Mr. Jha decided. She had been through a lot lately with the move to Gurgaon and she had been kind to him, patient. He knew it had not been easy and he felt bad. Plus he had just spent far more than he should have at the Apple Store, so if he bought his wife a piece of jewelry, he would feel better. And it would be worth it because the Chopras would understand the value of a ring from Tiffany's. Mrs. Chopra looked so fancy in her expensive diamonds worn casually.

Tiffany's was depressing. Mrs. Jha looked around. There were just young girls in tight jeans clinging to the arms of their boyfriends, who were wearing baggy jeans and baseball caps. This was not Audrey Hepburn's Tiffany's. Tacky necklaces and purses dangled messily from velvet rods — Tiffany's wasn't supposed to sell purses. Where were the rude staff members and glass boxes filled with shiny diamonds? There was a table that sold brooches — butterflies, elephants, beetles, roses — these things looked worse than the stuff peddled by roadside sellers in Sarojini Nagar. This was certainly not the Tiffany's of her dreams.

"Look at that lovely hat shaped like a cat," Mr. Jha said. "Would you like that? It reminds me of the painting in the Chopras' house."

"It's a purse. And it's not really that nice. Let's leave," Mrs. Jha said. "This is not what I was expecting. Let's take one of those horse carriage rides before it gets dark."

"May I help you?" said a wealthy-looking older white man in a perfectly fitted three-piece suit.

"No, no," Mrs. Jha said quickly. "We're so sorry. We are just leaving. So sorry."

"What are you apologizing for?" Mr. Jha said. He then turned to the man, who he thought was dressed like a fancy magician, and said, "We're looking for rings actually. Nice ones. Where are they kept?"

"Rings?" the man asked.

"Yes. With diamonds."

The man looked at Mrs. Jha and smiled.

"Congratulations," he said. "You're a lucky girl."

Mrs. Jha was horrified. Who was this strange man and why was he referring to her as a girl?

"Our rings are upstairs. You can take the elevator to the right, go to the second floor, and someone will be happy to help you. I'll let them know you're headed up," the man said. He wanted to pass this couple off to the salespeople on the second floor as fast as possible. Indians made him nervous these days. They didn't look obviously wealthy but they spent money so casually. Just last week an Indian man had come in and sat with him to look at diamond earrings on the second level. He was wearing faded jeans, a tucked-in brown T-shirt, and clean white sneakers — not the traditional look of wealth that the second floor of Tiffany's was used to, so he had not bothered being particularly nice. It was a mistake. The Indian man got annoyed and asked for another salesperson, and he had seen, from a distance, the man buying several pairs of several-thousand-dollar earrings and casually dropping the blue Tiffany's bag into an old black JanSport and walking back out to Fifth Avenue. Not, however, before filling out a feedback form that had resulted in the original salesperson being demoted to the ground floor for the next month.

As the Jhas stepped out of the elevator, a man who looked exactly like the man downstairs greeted them and said, "Welcome. You're looking for rings. Well, you've come to the right place."

Even Mr. Jha had to admit he was confused. Did the man from downstairs manage to get up to this level faster than them? There must be some secret faster elevator at the back. These suited, well-dressed men worked like a fancy army.

"We aren't sure yet if we're going to buy," Mr. Jha said. It was best not to express interest so that you had the upper hand if the time came to bargain, he reasoned.

"No harm in looking. I'm Willing, and let's have a seat, relax, and see if we can find something we like today."

He bowed gently and pointed the Jhas toward two soft velvet chairs. Mrs. Jha liked him instantly. How nice of him to say he was willing to help them so much. She liked the ease with which he used the word *we* as if he were also a part of their family. And this was the Tiffany's she had been looking for. It was quieter up here with just some soft gentle instrumental music playing.

"We aren't looking for anything too fancy," Mrs. Jha said. "A simple ring. Or some small earrings. Nothing too flashy."

Willing remembered the Indian man from last week. He had also come in looking for "nothing too flashy" for his wife, daughters, and daughter-in-law and had left after spending more than Willing earned in a year. But then there had also been the Indian couple the month before who had

312

spent hours looking at everything, talking about money, converting all the prices to rupees, drinking lots of free champagne, taking pictures of themselves wearing the jewelry, and then leaving without spending a single penny. You could never tell with Indians these days.

"Why don't we have some champagne first?" Willing said. "And I'll bring out some of the earrings." He turned to find his assistant.

"Champagne?" Mrs. Jha whispered to her husband. "I don't want to waste money. Tell him no champagne. Maybe just a glass of water. Or a fresh lime soda. But champagne? This is how these shops make money."

"Don't be silly," Mr. Jha said. "I'm sure it's complimentary. Champagne breakfast at Tiffany's."

Mr. Jha laughed. This was all going to his head. They were sitting at Tiffany's on Fifth Avenue with an old white man bringing them champagne. Had he ever been served anything by a white man before? He must remember all the details to tell the Chopras.

"Just a pair of small solitaires for me," Mrs. Jha said. "I don't feel comfortable wearing expensive jewelry."

She took a sip of her champagne. The

fizziness went up her nose and made her want to sneeze, but she didn't want the kind old man to think she had never had champagne before, so she swallowed even though her eyes teared up. She didn't like it but she could not waste. She didn't even know if they were being charged for it.

"Some cake with that champagne?" Willing said as his assistant popped up behind him with a silver tray full of little light blue cakes that looked like gifts wrapped in white bows. Mrs. Jha looked at her husband. Would they be charged for this as well? It didn't matter. She couldn't resist Western sweets. She took two and placed them on her napkin. Even if they charged them, it would be worth it. She had to keep remembering that they were wealthy now. They could eat small cakes and learn to enjoy the carbonated wine. They were in New York City, on Fifth Avenue, at Audrey Hepburn's shop, and they had every right to be here.

Mrs. Jha took another, smaller sip of her champagne and then bravely put her hand on her husband's forearm. He looked momentarily alarmed by her physical display of affection. But he had already emptied his glass of champagne, so he placed his free hand on top of his wife's.

"Let's see a slightly larger pair," he said.

"It will look nice. And do you think we should pick up a small gift for the neighbors here?"

Mrs. Jha took her hand back. The neighbors. Again. She did not understand why they mattered so much. As far as she could tell, Mrs. Chopra was about as dull as the long summer afternoons in Delhi. Mr. Chopra wasn't so bad, she'd admit, but she didn't understand why her husband was so determined to impress him all the time.

"No. I'll just get the small set for myself and let's go."

Rupak's Greyhound bus from Ithaca arrived at Port Authority in the midafternoon, and he got into a taxi to take him to his parents' hotel on the Lower East Side. They were staying at the Holiday Inn on Ludlow Street. He did not understand his parents. Why couldn't they be like normal rich parents and stay at the Four Seasons or the W? They would probably try to go for dinner to one of the dosa places in the West Village. His mother always searched for Indian restaurants when she traveled abroad. No, he told himself, he must not start getting annoyed with them before even seeing them. He wanted to get along with them on this trip — he wanted them to see

315

his independent life in Ithaca and see him as more of an adult.

He had convinced Serena to join them for dinner in Ithaca on Monday night, and he was going to tell his parents about her today. They would love her and since they were all Indian, he would just say he was bringing a "friend" with a mild emphasis on the word, and the fact that the "friend" was female would provide enough clues to his parents that she could be more than a friend. Which, in fact, she wasn't. Even though Rupak had seen her a handful of times since her friends' party, they had not actually kissed and had in fact settled into a friendship and he had been enjoying it. Having her around made him miss Elizabeth less, even though he still missed her a lot. But it would have been so difficult to have her around while his parents were visiting. Elizabeth would probably have tried to reach out and hold his hand while walking to the restaurant and if he avoided that, she would never understand why and it would become a source of tension. The current situation was simply much easier for now.

He got a text from his father saying,

We are going for a walk to see the famous

Katz's Deli. Meet us at that corner instead of the hotel.

There was no way his parents knew why Katz's Deli was famous.

Rupak stepped out of the taxi on the corner of Houston and Ludlow and looked around for his parents. He looked down at his cargo pants and black T-shirt. Maybe he should have dressed a bit better for tonight. He couldn't blame them for treating him like a child.

He didn't see his parents. They were unlikely to actually be inside Katz's, because all the meat would make his mother feel ill and they would probably have seen the publicity in the window mentioning the famous orgasm scene and quickly, awkwardly walked away.

In America, there was so much awareness and talk of women's pleasure, but did the older generation of women in India know what that felt like, he wondered? Maybe Mrs. Ray, but she was different. She would probably have the confidence to guide a man's head between her legs, but his own father's head had definitely never traveled down.

His own father's head was, however, at that moment, peering into an American Apparel shop with what appeared to be a yarmulke on his head. Next to him, his mother was standing in a pair of pleated brown pants with a yellow Fabindia kurta and oversized green jacket. Rupak checked for traffic and rushed across the street to where his parents stood. It was hard to not feel annoyance when his father was walking around the Lower East Side wearing a yarmulke.

"There he is!" Mrs. Jha said, and nudged her husband. Mr. Jha stopped looking at the poster of the young girl in a tight black T-shirt that showed off her nipples and turned to face his son.

"Dad! Why do you have a yarmulke on your head?" Rupak said before saying anything else.

"A Rosh Hashanah, you mean?" Mr. Jha said, adjusting the small circular cap on the top of his head.

"That's a holiday," Rupak said.

"Today is a holiday?" Mr. Jha said.

"No," Rupak said. "Rosh Hashanah is a holiday. You're wearing a yarmulke. What are you doing? That's offensive. You can't do that in New York."

"Don't shout at your father," Mrs. Jha said. "We haven't seen you in months. Have the decency to say hello nicely."

"Mom, I'm sorry. But how can you let him wear that?" Rupak said, and then added in a whisper, "Especially in this neighborhood. It's not appropriate."

Mrs. Jha stopped listening after she heard the word *Mom.* She didn't recognize this boy in the cargo pants and T-shirt, with stubble on his cheeks, who spoke with an American lilt and called her Mom. This was not the same boy who was so shy he would wrap himself up in her pallu whenever they went to a party.

"It's colder than I expected," Mr. Jha said. "And I've been losing hair on the top of my head. It makes me feel very vulnerable, but this is just the perfect size and shape to keep my bald spot warm. You know how much I hate hats — makes me feel sleepy, as if there's a pillow against my head — but this yarmulke is perfect. I bought two."

"Dad, you cannot wear that. It's offensive," Rupak said.

"Son, you worry too much about being offensive. America has ruined you. I am wearing this out of a deep appreciation and people can see that. The man who sold them to me was very friendly. Most people are friendly if you stop being so nervous all the time. Now come along. Let us have a cup of coffee."

"There was a McDonald's the way we walked earlier," Mrs. Jha said. "We can have coffee there and make our plans."

"There's a show called *Cats* that I've bought tickets to for tonight," Mr. Jha said. "Humans dress up as cats and sing and dance — what madness. Our seats are in the second row. They were so expensive. I'll have to make sure I get a picture that shows how close to the stage we are."

After the cup of coffee during which the yarmulke was not mentioned, Mr. Jha suggested they stop by the hotel to freshen up for a night out.

Rupak had walked past the Holiday Inn on Ludlow on earlier trips to NYC, and the sight of it always depressed him, but entering with his parents today was different. The Bangladeshi staff at the front desk jumped up and buzzed around his parents chattering away and Rupak noticed his parents come alive.

"Rupak, meet Shonjoy and Ali, they run this place. And they are our Muslim brothers from the East."

Rupak tensed up the minute he heard his father describe them that way. Did his father have no sense? But Shonjoy and Ali both laughed and extended their hands for Rupak to shake. Maybe his father was right.

Maybe he had become too nervous about offending people. Rupak would never dream of using the word *Muslim* to loudly describe someone, but here was his father, Hindu, in his yarmulke, speaking happily to his Muslim brothers from Bangladesh who looked equally happy about the whole situation.

Back in the room, Mr. Jha took off the yarmulke, wrapped it carefully in tissue paper, and placed it on the shelf near the television. It had served him well today but he could see that it was making his son tense, so he decided it would be best to leave it in the room when they went for dinner. Mr. Jha put on his nicest black button-down shirt and took out a fashionable gray tie he had bought from Banana Republic earlier in the day. It was what the salesman had called a skinny tie and was, allegedly, the only way to go these days.

"Rupak," Mr. Jha said. "Are you going to get changed? And when was the last time you shaved? Now hurry up, you two. Bindu, wear the earrings we got today. And please change out of those horrid pants. Don't you have something more feminine? Maybe a skirt?"

"Papa, could I borrow a shirt?"

Mrs. Jha was so happy to hear her son say "Papa" that she didn't bother getting offended by her husband's suggestion that she wear a skirt. She was enjoying herself today. Americans hadn't been so frightening. From the man at Tiffany's to the black man who had helped them get train tickets, people had been friendly. She took the diamond earrings from earlier in the day out of the small blue box that looked like the cake.

Mr. Jha watched his wife put on the diamond earrings and felt happy. They suited her. He was in a hotel room — a bit on the small side but nobody knew them here so it was okay — in New York City with a wife who was not aging too badly, wearing diamond earrings from Tiffany's, and their son studying in America, about to go see humans dressed as cats. How could he be so fortunate? In some past life, somewhere, he must have done something good. Silently, he thanked God.

Mr. Jha loved *Cats*, even though the usher had scolded him loudly for taking a flash photo. It was worth the mild public humiliation to be able to show the Chopras where they were sitting. Since he had had to quickly move the phone down, the picture was mostly of the wooden stage, but explaining that would make it easy to say where their seats were.

When they got back to the hotel that night, Mr. Jha was happy. On the single bed that Ali had set up near the window, his son was happy. Mrs. Jha, however, was nervous. Things were going too well for them, she worried. Maybe another visit to the Mayur Palli temple was due. She hadn't even set up a small temple in the Gurgaon house, she reminded herself. She would do that as soon as they returned to Delhi, and she would donate money to the temple in Mayur Palli. The old neighbors would appreciate that.

The next morning, the sun was shining and New York City glistened in the way only New York City does. The sun reflected off the buildings to make the city twice as bright as the rest of the world.

"We should buy property here," Mr. Jha said. "Maybe just a small one- or two-bedroom. Rupak, maybe you will get a job in New York after you graduate."

"But would New York be a good place to raise a family?" Mrs. Jha said.

"It can't be much worse than Delhi," Mr. Jha said.

"You know, Rupak," Mrs. Jha said. "We were in Khan Market recently and there are so many foreigners working and living there now. Maybe you should come back and work in India for some time."

"What nonsense, Bindu," Mr. Jha said. "We didn't send him to America to study just so he could come rushing back."

"It's just something to consider. It'll be nice for you to have some time at home — have home-cooked food, clean bedsheets, everything."

"I have clean bedsheets in Ithaca, Ma. You'll see. I do okay on my own," Rupak said. "But I'm not completely against the idea of coming back to India either. I know things are changing there."

And he wasn't sure he was going to get a job that would sponsor a visa here anyway, so it was best to start preparing his parents to think he was choosing to come back on his own.

TWENTY

When they arrived at his apartment in Ithaca, Rupak let his mother step out first so he could help his father with the luggage.

"Ma, take a left and it's the door right at the end of the hallway," he said while pulling out one of the large Burberry suitcases. He dragged it down the hallway behind her, his father behind him, and over his mother's shoulder he could see, as they approached the door, the small wooden pencil box lying on the ground on his welcome mat with a yellow sticky paper attached to it. Rupak left the suitcase, pushed past his mother saying he would unlock the door, and quickly picked up the pencil box. The note said:

I'm sure your mother wouldn't want me to have this. — E

Rupak held the box against his stomach as he unlocked the door.

"Is that the pencil box I got for your friend?" Mrs. Jha said. "Why is it lying on the floor in the hallway?"

"It's a long story," Rupak said. "I'll explain in a minute. Here, just come in and have some water and sit down and I'll go get the rest of the bags."

Rupak went into his bedroom and dumped the pencil box into a desk drawer, annoyed with Elizabeth, and went back out to the hallway.

"Did you and Gaurav have a fight?" Mrs. Jha asked.

"Ma, please just sit and settle in and let me get all the bags. That was a tiring bus ride," Rupak said.

Mr. Jha entered then with two of the suitcases and said, "Look at this place. It's like a real American home. I bet you don't even have bottles of spicy achaar tucked away somewhere. Good. When in Rome, Bindu, when in Rome."

Mrs. Jha followed her husband into the kitchen and opened the fridge. It was completely empty except for a bottle of ketchup and three cans of beer. This was exactly what she had been worried about.

"Rupak, what do you eat?" she said.

"Why have you opened my fridge as soon as you came in? Can you please not peer into everything?"

"Privacy," Mrs. Jha said to her husband. "Everything in America is about privacy."

The visit was not off to a good start, so Rupak decided to tell them about Serena right away in order to shift focus.

"Here, why don't you both sit and I'll make some tea," Rupak said, coming into the kitchen and directing his parents back out to the living room, where he had hidden all traces of Elizabeth, marijuana, pornography, and even hard liquor.

"Do that and then why don't we go get some groceries and I can cook dinner? I can make methi chicken," Mrs. Jha said. "Actually I can cook a handful of dishes in bulk and portion them and put them in the freezer."

"No, Ma, don't do that here. The smell of Indian cooking stays in the curtains and carpets for days and gets in clothes and stuff. You can even smell it out in the hallway."

Mrs. Jha looked over at her son. "You don't like the smell of the food we cook? Our house in Delhi smells bad?"

"No," Rupak said quickly. "Our house in Delhi smells fine and I love your food. But the homes in America aren't as ventilated as India and the smell sticks to everything. I wasn't making a comment about your food. In Delhi everything is always open — all our doors and windows. And there aren't heavy curtains and carpets. That's all I meant. I love your food. You know that. And actually it isn't even that. I was going to bring a . . . friend . . . along to dinner tonight, if that's okay with you. I think you'd like . . . her."

"Oh?" Mrs. Jha said, willing to forget his comments about her cooking. "Is she in your class?"

"No, she's doing her master's in theater at Cornell," Rupak said.

"Oh, that's a good university. A master's in theater, though? Interesting," Mrs. Jha said. Americans really allow their children to study whatever they want, she thought.

"She's talented," Rupak said.

"Well, I'm looking forward to meeting your . . . friend," Mrs. Jha said.

"Serena. Her name is Serena," Rupak said.

Serena didn't have to be an American name, Mrs. Jha thought, hoping against hope, because, of course, someone named Serena who was studying theater was going to be American.

An American, Mr. Jha thought! And one studying theater, no less. He must remember to take a picture to show Mr. Chopra.

"Well, then let's make a reservation somewhere fancy," Mr. Jha said.

"We don't need to make a reservation in Ithaca," Rupak said.

"Let me get my iPad and find the best place in the area." Mr. Jha got up and wandered off to find his luggage. He wanted to go somewhere special to welcome Serena into the family. Not that Rupak had announced any plans to marry her, but on all the sitcoms white families embrace their children's girlfriends and boyfriends, and he didn't want Serena to feel uncomfortable. It would be so wonderful to go back to Delhi, Gurgaon in particular, with pictures of Rupak and his blond-haired, blue-eyed "friend." One white special friend would surely trump Johnny's dozens of Indian girls. He would show the pictures to Mr. Chopra and shake his head and say, "What can one do? He's just so modern. No Indian women for him. He has such an international mind."

They had sent Rupak to the United States to expand his horizons, and if that included an American special friend, so be it. It would help him get a green card too.

Mrs. Jha nervously adjusted her dupatta as she stepped out of the taxi on the Ithaca

Commons. They were going to Maggie's, an American restaurant where, Mr. Jha had read online, they served some special steak that was cut from cows that were raised on farms in Japan where they were fed beer and grass so they were always drunk and happy. And, he had read out earlier, when they were slaughtered, it was done from behind by sticking a knife into their necks so they wouldn't realize what's coming and wouldn't feel fear. "That way their bodies don't tense up and the meat is extra soft. It costs thirty dollars an ounce! An ounce! Those Japanese really know what they're doing. I bet our Indian cows would enjoy beer and grass," Mr. Jha said, trying to figure out a way to keep a receipt of the meal to show the neighbors. That might prove impossible, he decided. He would have to work it into conversation.

"I really wish we were going to Moosewood," Mrs. Jha said. "Anil, it's the most famous vegetarian restaurant in the world."

"Bindu, you can get vegetarian food on every street corner in India. Maggie's will be a different experience. And I'm sure Rupak's . . . friend . . . will enjoy it."

Mrs. Jha was nervous about meeting Rupak's friend. Would Serena call her Bindu? Americans all behaved with such familiarity. And what would Serena think of her outfit? Tonight Mrs. Jha was wearing a black kurta and black salwar, with a red dupatta draped around her shoulders. Fortunately Ithaca was much more relaxed than New York. In New York, Mrs. Jha constantly wondered how women managed to walk in stilettos on cobblestones. She could not even wear wedge heels. It was strange that she had such a different idea of what it meant to be a woman. For her, life had been about raising a family. There was no mystery, there were no secrets. She had never thought about her clothes or her body and apart from the occasional pedicure, she did not pay much attention to how anything looked below the neck. Maybe it was time to change. Look at Shobha De, after all. She's old but still wears sleeveless blouses and sometimes even skirts. Maybe tomorrow Mrs. Jha would buy herself a long skirt. And when she got back to Delhi, she vowed to take longer walks in the evening and maybe even start yoga. Forget Shobha De, Mrs. Jha thought, just look at Mrs. Ray. Maybe someday Rupak would have a church wedding, and she did not want to be the frumpy one in flat shoes while Serena's mother wore some fitted, sleeveless dress and high heels.

Mr. Jha looked around for his son's special friend. He hoped she would be beautiful. He liked the idea of having a blond exotic woman calling him Dad. Although it had sounded nice to hear Rupak say "Papa" earlier. They had come a long way from Mayur Palli. If only the Chopras could see them now.

"There she is!" Rupak said. "Serena! Serena! Over here."

And they all turned to see Serena walking toward them dressed, like Mrs. Jha, in black leggings, a kurta, and a dupatta. Serena adjusted her dupatta and wondered if she looked appropriate for the evening.

"Isn't this restaurant lovely? Anil, I'm glad you booked it. I feel like I'm in Paris," Mrs. Jha said.

Mrs. Jha looked around the restaurant and then over to her son and Serena. She smiled. Serena was Indian. With an unusual name and a degree in theater, but Indian nevertheless. Rupak had his choice of all the women in America and he had chosen an Indian woman who was dressed similarly to his mother.

"I like it," Serena said. "I had never been here before because I always wonder if the price will be worth it at places like this, you know? Like, can the food really be that much better?"

"You aren't paying just for the food," Mr. Jha said. How had his son managed to find a woman who was so similar to his own mother? Of all the women in America, he had to pick this one, whom nobody in Delhi would look at twice. He could easily have met and charmed a beautiful young blond woman whom all of Mayur Palli and Gurgaon would sit up and notice, but instead he had found a younger version of Mrs. Jha.

"I agree with you, Serena," Mrs. Jha said. "I can never understand such expensive restaurants."

"Can we not ruin the dinner by talking about the prices?" Rupak said. He was only half listening because he was busy imagining what it would have been like to have Elizabeth sitting at the table instead of Serena.

"You're right," Mrs. Jha said. "Let's order. Should we get some appetizers?"

"You can order appetizers. I'm just going to order a main course," Mr. Jha said.

"Should we get snails?" Rupak said. "Ma, have you tried snails?"

"Like garden snails?" Mrs. Jha said.

"You'll like them," Serena said. "Let's get

one order. Aunty, do you eat chicken stomach?"

"I love chicken stomach," Mrs. Jha said.

"Snails are kind of similar in their consistency," Serena said. "Let's try some — make this even more of an evening in Paris."

"Have you even been to Paris?" Mr. Jha asked.

"Well, no, but," Serena said.

"Well," Mr. Jha said.

"Anil, what's wrong with you?" Mrs. Jha said. "Are you tired? We walked a lot in New York. And we hardly took any time to get over the jet lag so it's all catching up with us."

"We went to Tiffany's," Mr. Jha said. "Have you ever been to Tiffany's?"

"No," Serena said. "Did you go to any museums?"

"We went to the MoMA shop in Soho," Mr. Jha said.

Serena looked toward Rupak, but he looked down at the menu.

"I'm going to order a whiskey," Mr. Jha said. "A Lagavulin 16. Bindu, we should take a bottle of good whiskey back for our neighbors. Rupak, you will enjoy meeting them. They have a son about your age."

"Do you find the people in Gurgaon really

different from what you're used to?" Serena asked.

"We're still adjusting," Mrs. Jha said.

"Not at all. The people of Gurgaon are people like us," Mr. Jha said. "They're very sophisticated. Rupak, Mr. Chopra has a Jaguar."

Serena again made eyes toward Rupak and smiled as if they shared a secret. Rupak didn't return the smile. Instead he said, "What does the son do?"

"He's an aspiring poet," Mrs. Jha said.

"In Gurgaon? And his parents are okay with that?" Rupak said.

"His parents are probably proud because it means he doesn't earn any money," Serena said. "All these rich Delhi kids pretend they're in the arts. It's like the wives of Bollywood stars calling themselves interior designers. Next thing you know, his father will be funding a literary magazine."

"But weren't you saying nobody in India funds the arts?" Rupak asked. "Isn't them funding it, even if it's for their son, better than nothing?"

After the dishes of the main course had been cleared away, Mrs. Jha asked Rupak how his classes were going this semester and instead of telling her he was at risk of failing, he said they were going fine and then quickly said, "By the way, you know Serena is Mrs. Gupta's niece."

"Which Mrs. Gupta?" Mr. Jha said. He hadn't spoken much through the meal.

"From Mayur Palli. Our neighbors," Rupak said.

"Oh, how wonderful!" Mrs. Jha said. "You're basically family already! Should we order dessert? And I feel like a cup of chamomile tea."

"What? You never order tea at restaurants. Since when are you willing to pay five dollars for something you can make for free in Rupak's apartment?" Mr. Jha said. And then added to Rupak, "Your mother brought a box of tea bags from India so she wouldn't have to buy tea out. But now you want dessert?"

"That's different. I brought the tea bags because we both like having a cup of tea first thing in the morning in the hotel in New York, and going out to buy it every day is a waste. But tonight is different. We're at a restaurant, and we've just met Serena. I'm going to order some tea."

"Look how special you are, Serena," Mr. Jha said.

Serena laughed.

"Oh, I understand. My mother is the same

336

way," she said. "I like it."

Mrs. Jha smiled. What a lovely young woman, she thought. She would fit right into their world in Delhi.

"Rupak, your father and I will take a taxi home. You should drop Serena home safely," Mrs. Jha said. "Take your time. We'll have a cup of tea and go to sleep if we get tired."

Was his mother implying that he could stay out late with a woman and do the things young men and women do and she wouldn't wait up? This was his mother's way of giving approval, Rupak knew.

"Oh no, that's okay," Screna said. "Ithaca is completely safe. Rupak, you should go with your parents."

"Okay, then," Mr. Jha said. "It was lovely meeting you, Serena."

"Anil," Mrs. Jha said. "Stop that. Rupak will be a gentleman. Serena, it was wonderful meeting you. This is such a quick trip, but hopefully we'll see you back in Delhi soon? Come have dinner with us when you're in town."

"Sure, Aunty, I'll do that. It was nice meeting you."

"I like your mother," Serena said in the taxi.

Rupak nodded. This felt like a veiled insult

toward his father.

"What are you going to do with them for the rest of the time they're here?"

Rupak shrugged.

"Not much. I have to go to class and they're leaving on Wednesday."

"I would suggest you take them to the Johnson Art Museum, but I get the feeling your father doesn't really like museums," Serena said with a small laugh. "He's sweet."

"There's no need to be condescending. He's not just sweet; he also created one of the most successful Indian startups," Rupak said, defending his father in a way he had never done before.

"I wasn't being condescending," Serena said. "He is sweet. And I admire the fact that he's achieved what he's achieved. It must be weird to suddenly get money like that overnight. For all of you."

On the one hand, Rupak was happy to have an opening to be able to talk about it, but on the other hand, he refused to believe that calling an adult "sweet" was not condescending, so he wasn't sure how much he wanted to open up to Serena. Nobody ever had much sympathy for the woes of being suddenly wealthy.

"I don't live at home anymore, so it

doesn't really affect me," he said.

"Well, it allows you to go to grad school without going into debt."

"That's true," Rupak said. "And I'm grateful for that. Are you doing anything exciting this week?"

"What do you think you're going to do when you finish? I noticed you avoid all your parents' questions about the future. I mean, I get it — I'm trying to do theater and as supportive as my parents are, they don't really understand. But I guess even though they may not understand, I know what I'm trying to do," Serena said. "Do your parents even know how much you want to do film?"

"Please stop," Rupak interrupted her. "Please don't continue asking the same questions my mother was asking. I don't need another mother."

Serena turned to face him, the passing lights making her dark eyes look darker. Rupak turned away and looked out the window.

"You're touchy," she said. "I wasn't asking anything out of the ordinary."

"You just sound like my mother," Rupak repeated.

"Rupak, you realize this is more because you don't have an answer to the simple question of what you want to do next in life. Stop projecting this onto me."

"Now you sound like a therapist," Rupak said.

"And you sound like an asshole," Serena said.

"Hey, I'm sorry," Rupak said. "It's just stressful having parents visit, you know."

"I've got a regular week ahead," Serena said. "Pretty busy."

"I could come up to Cornell for dinner after my parents leave on Wednesday."

"I'll get off at this corner on the right," Serena said to the taxi driver. "And then you can take this same taxi home. Text me about Wednesday — I might have to help stage manage a show. Like I said, it's a pretty busy week."

"Okay," Rupak said. "I'll keep Wednesday free, though."

"See you later," Serena said, stepping out of the car. "I hope your parents enjoy the rest of their stay."

As the taxi pulled away from her apartment, Rupak sent Elizabeth a text message that said, *What are you doing tonight?* but she didn't reply.

When he got home his father had already gone to sleep, but his mother was sitting on the couch in the living room, drinking a cup of tea and watching television. She smiled up at him when he entered.

"She's lovely," Mrs. Jha said.

Rupak nodded and went into the bathroom and closed the door. Mrs. Jha sat on the sofa and worried that Serena was too good for her son.

TWENTY-ONE

A week after they got back to Delhi, in Gurgaon, after dinner, Mrs. Jha was sitting in the living room at her husband's laptop humming to herself while researching exercise machines for the home. She was considering ordering one of those small stepping machines. Mr. Jha meanwhile, was fidgeting on the sofa. He was suffering from dreadful jet lag and was still falling asleep by nine p.m. every evening.

"These crystals are so uncomfortable to lie down on," he said, turning sideways to try to minimize the poking.

"Would you use a stair stepper as well?" Mrs. Jha said. "If we keep it near the television, we can use it while watching the news in the evenings."

"Now why are you so interested in fitness all of a sudden? For years you've done nothing, but now you want to buy a stair stepper?"

"You're the one who was encouraging me to wear skirts and be more Westernized. And you were the one who wanted to join a gym. Why not put all your tracksuits to some use? You're just being grumpy now because you're sleepy. Go upstairs and go to bed if you're so tired. Although I don't know how you will ever get over your jet lag at this rate," Mrs. Jha said. "I wish we had stayed in New York for longer."

"You're the one who insisted you wanted to be back in Delhi well in time for Diwali," Mr. Jha said. "And I don't think we should encourage Rupak to pursue things with Serena. She's not suitable."

"What are you talking about? She's perfect. She's exactly the kind of wife we would have picked for him," Mrs. Jha said.

"Hardly. She's related to the Guptas, which means she knows all about our money, and I bet she's just trying to get her hands on it. I don't trust those Guptas one bit."

Mrs. Jha ignored her husband and was reading the reviews for one of the stair steppers. A Mrs. Sonia Prasad from Pune had written, *Good for exercise and handles provide an excellent place to dry clothes in rainy season.*

"I should speak to the Chopras and see if

they have an exercise machine at home," Mrs. Jha said. "I was thinking we should invite them over for dinner soon. Maybe next Sunday night?"

"No need to appear so eager. We'll see them when we see them," Mr. Jha said.

Ever since Mr. Jha had met Serena and returned from America, he had been avoiding Mr. Chopra. How would he explain Rupak's MBA and Indian girlfriend while Johnny continued to drive around in his new car and bring home an assortment of young girls every night? Mr. Jha often heard the loud bass coming from Johnny's car. And he would see other cars parked along the road outside their gates and young boys and girls with cigarettes and strange hats and multicolored hair going in and out of the Chopras' home. How could Mr. Jha admit that while Johnny was living this life of luxury, paid for by his father, Rupak was busy studying and preparing to have a regular income while dating a woman who looked like a younger version of his own mother?

"We've been back for a week and you haven't even gone to say hello to the neighbors. What happened? I thought you and Mr. Chopra were on your way to becoming best friends," Mrs. Jha said.

"I have been busy. And tired. This jet lag is getting me down."

"If you just force yourself to stay awake one day, you will get over it. Why don't you sit up? Or why don't we go out for a walk to wake up? Maybe we can even see if the Chopras are home and say hello?" Mrs. Jha said.

You could smell winter in the air, more clearly here in Gurgaon than you ever could in Mayur Palli, and it was Mrs. Jha's favorite time of year. If she was completely quiet, she was certain she could hear the crackle of burning wood coming from the street where thc guards huddled around the flames for warmth at this time of night.

"Or we can even pull the car out and go to the market for some hot gulab jamuns," Mrs. Jha said.

Mr. Jha turned to look at her, but one of the crystals caught on his ear. He jerked upright, now feeling more awake than he wished to be.

"Stupid crystals," he said.

What was wrong with his wife? Now she wanted to go out in the cold for dessert? And she wanted to drop in and see the Chopras after she was the one who had been so reluctant about leaving Mayur Palli in the first place? And his son, who Mr. Jha knew for a fact once had a small cutout picture of Pamela Anderson in her red bathing suit that he kept in this bedside drawer, had settled on a plain girl from Delhi. All Mr. Jha wanted to do was sleep.

But, as if the gods were finally listening — although maybe they had been listening for a while because despite everything else going wrong, this morning Mr. Jha's Mercedes hit an auto-rickshaw on the main road and only the auto-rickshaw got dented while his Mercedes did not even suffer a scratch — the phone rang and Mr. Jha got up from the sofa and went to the dining room to answer.

"Papa," Rupak said, "I have some bad news. I'm really sorry."

Rupak had been kicked out of his MBA program. On top of near-failing grades, he had stupidly been caught buying marijuana.

"Marijuana?" Mr. Jha asked his son. Was that the really dangerous one or was that the one that was on the way to being legalized, Mr. Jha wondered.

"Yeah, it's going to be legal soon anyway. And I was buying such a small amount. And only in order to help myself focus — I study better with marijuana. It's just that they have this zero-tolerance policy, so I can't stay here anymore. Look, I promise I'll come back to India and fix everything. Maybe even see if I can get into IIM to finish my degree. I promise I won't let you and Ma down. I'm really so sorry," Rupak said.

Mr. Jha walked with the cordless phone to the cabinet in the dining room and poured himself an Old Monk. Let Mr. Chopra call it swill. Mr. Jha was now the father of an expelled child, a failure, a financial burden who would need money that he, Mr. Jha, could provide. Plenty of money. Mr. Jha could confidently drink whatever he wanted. He dropped three ice cubes into his glass, swirled the dark, sweet rum around, and said, "No, no. Business school is clearly not meant for you. Serena must be very disappointed in you. But don't worry — you will meet someone else. You are too young to be settling down anyway."

"No, Dad, please. Papa, I'm so sorry. I can finish the degree in India. I promise. I'll get a job at a bank. Or maybe consulting. I know how embarrassing this is for you. I'll fix it — I won't let you down."

"Rupak, calm down. You come back to India. You wanted to be a filmmaker, no? Done. I will produce your first film. You focus on that. And don't weigh that Serena girl down. It's best you call things off."

". . . Filmmaking? That was a while ago. I don't want to do that anymore. I promise."

"You will try to be a filmmaker. If it works, good. If it doesn't, *chalo,* we'll see then."

Mr. Jha went back to where his wife was sitting and said, "Maybe you're right. Maybe the only way to get over jet lag is by going out for some hot gulab jamuns. I'll get the car ready. Oh, and Rupak will be back next week."

"Are you going to come back?" Serena asked on the phone.

"Can we discuss this in person, please?" Rupak said. He pulled out an open shoebox that had been lying under his bed since he had moved to Ithaca. There were pictures — pictures of his life in Mayur Palli, pictures of the life he kept separate from his life here, pictures of a life he now had to return to.

"Rupak, I'm not sure there's that much to say, right? I mean you have to leave. For buying pot. I'm sorry, I don't really know how to react to that," Serena said.

"But you and all your friends smoke pot too," Rupak said.

"Sure, but we aren't stupid enough to get arrested for buying it. And we all kind of know what we're trying to do in life at this point. You have no idea."

"Okay, but I'll be in India. You said you wanted to move back," Rupak said. He looked at a framed picture of himself in his school uniform, leaning back against his father's cream-colored Fiat, the first car Rupak had ever known. His mother had this picture framed when he was leaving, and one copy of it remained on her bedside table in Delhi and one was with him in Ithaca. How was he going to face his mother? Even though he was supposed to be packing, Rupak took the picture and walked out to the living room to place it on the shelf.

"Please just see me once," he said. The only way to face his mother would be with Serena still in the picture. He placed the picture on an empty shelf and looked around the room. His room was bare and not just because he was packing. If someone came into his apartment, they would have no sense of who he was, he thought. The only hint of something personal, something deliberate was one framed postcard, not even a poster, advertising a Fellini retrospective at the Museum of Modern Art. He hadn't even attended the exhibition; he had picked up the postcard from a table at a coffee shop downtown. If he really wanted to be a filmmaker, why hadn't he gone to New York for the weekend and seen the exhibition, he wondered.

"I just get the feeling we don't have the same goals in life," Serena said. "I don't have the big safety net that you have. I actually want to work. I don't want to just fuck around. I don't know if you thought we were going to have some kind of happily ever after, but, Rupak, we just don't have enough in common. You can't try to force yourself to be with me for the sake of your parents. I'm not from the world that gets impressed by fancy restaurants and jewelry from Tiffany's."

"Neither am I," Rupak said.

"Well, that's not really true, is it? I met your family. I don't mean that to be rude. I just mean that we come from different worlds and that's fine. We're friends. And we'll stay friends."

Rupak wanted to slam the phone down, but he looked at his picture again. "Can you imagine this little boy is off to America to study?" his mother had said to all the neighbors of Mayur Palli when they got the news that he had been accepted to Ithaca College. His father had invited everyone over to celebrate and his mother had passed this picture around, beaming. "To our future," his father had toasted, and Rupak had smiled, and his mother had put her hand on his shoulder and squeezed.

"Please just meet me for a cup of coffee," he said in a quieter voice.

"Rupak," Serena said, and paused. "You're going to be in Delhi, right? I'll be there for Christmas. I'll see you then."

"Okay, what if I see you and just say good-bye? You don't have to react. We don't have to discuss anything."

"You're leaving the country while the rest of us are studying for midterms. There's no way to not react."

Fine, Rupak decided. He couldn't ask for more. He didn't want to ask for more.

Twenty-Two

The next morning, Mr. Jha found Mrs. Jha sitting alone quietly on the front porch.

"Did you order the exercise machine?" he asked.

"No," Mrs. Jha said. She continued looking out toward their front yard. There was nothing to see. No sights, no sounds. Nothing at all to link with.

"Good," Mr. Jha said. "Now with Rupak coming back, an LRC membership makes even more sense. The whole family can use it. And Bindu, you were right — my jet lag has lifted completely. I feel wonderful. I'm off to the market. Do you need anything?"

Mrs. Jha continued staring into the distance.

Mr. Jha got in the car and went to buy some bottles of champagne. Moët had recently introduced a sparking pink wine — a sparkling rosé, if you will — to India, and Mr. Jha picked up three bottles and came home and put them in the freezer to chill faster. When he got home, Mrs. Jha was up in the bedroom lying on the bed, still staring into the distance. Two hours later, when he went to check on the bottles, he saw that one of them had exploded and left a pink syrup all over the freezer, so he removed the other two and put them down in the fridge. He would tell Mrs. Jha about the exploded one later — no point making her even grumpier than she already was; he was considerate like that.

In the evening, he went out to his driveway and sat near the gate with one of the cold bottles of Moët and two champagne flutes. He sat waiting for the sound of Mr. Chopra's car coming down the road. He could hear Balwinder pottering around outside their gate, listening to the latest Bollywood song on his phone.

At about twenty minutes past eight, he heard the creak of Mr. Chopra's gate being pushed open and the crunch of gravel as the Jaguar went into the driveway. Holding the bottle of champagne and the glasses, Mr. Jha rushed past Balwinder and said, "Mr. Chopra, we are celebrating! A glass of champagne for you! Rupak is coming back to India."

"Lovely," Mr. Chopra said, stepping out

of his car. "For Diwali? Or have you found him a good Indian bride?"

Mr. Jha laughed while twisting the thin gold wire around the edge of the champagne bottle.

"No, no, no," he said, turning the fat brown cork in the neck, paying no attention to where it was pointing or how much he had shaken it up in his enthusiastic run over to Mr. Chopra's driveway. "Nothing useful like that. He's taking a break from his MBA program. Coming back."

At that, the cork popped and flew up and out of the bottle and landed at the base of the hedge shaped like a duck, and white fizzy bubbles spilled over the sides of the dark green bottle.

"I'm so happy he'll be home soon. To that, we must raise a toast," Mr. Jha said, and handed a glass to Mr. Chopra. "Both our sons will be home. We must introduce them soon. I have told Rupak a lot about you. Anyway, you must drop in for a drink and meet him when he arrives."

"Indeed," Mr. Chopra said. "This is very good news for you. Rupak will find a job here, then? Half an MBA means job prospects will be good."

"Sadly, no. Now he wants to be a film-maker. Idiotic dreams. As if there's any money in filmmaking," Mr. Jha said, emptying his glass of champagne.

"Well, well," Mr. Chopra said. "Filmmaking these days can be very lucrative. Good for him. Much better than poetry, I tell you. Now that is a field with no money. Johnny should learn from Rupak. He gives absolutely no thought to the future."

"Yes, maybe. But Rupak has little talent, so it is likely that he will fail completely," Mr. Jha said.

Both the men laughed heartily.

"I'm not feeling too well," Mrs. Jha said before dinner. "Will you manage dinner yourself? I think I'm just going to have a slice of toast and read in bed."

"Are you feeling unwell? Should I sleep in the guest room? No sense both of us falling ill," Mr. Jha said.

"I'm not falling ill, Anil. I'm worried. And you should be too," Mrs. Jha said. "About our son. And his life."

"Bindu, these things happen," Mr. Jha said. "What's done is done. Now we will simply figure out the best way forward."

"What if you had never sold your website, Anil?" Mrs. Jha said.

"What are you talking about? What if we still lived in Mayur Palli with the neighbors interfering in our lives and bathrooms that are too hot in the summer and too cold in the winter? That's what you're talking about? What if we lived with seepage on our walls and electricity outages every other day? What if you still had to use a kitchen in which you felt suffocated by the smell of haldi and chili? What if we lived with no full-length mirrors? Why stop there? Let's go back to the days before we could even afford air conditioners, let alone business class travel to America."

"That's enough; I'm going upstairs," Mrs. Jha said.

"We have an upstairs to go to," Mr. Jha said.

She went up the stairs to the bedroom and shut the door. She sat on the edge of the bed and picked the cordless phone up off the bedside table to call Mrs. Ray.

"Bindu?" Mrs. Ray said. "How nice to hear from you. Oh, Bindu, I'm so glad you called. I've been meaning to call you but I just haven't had time. I just got home — it's nearly eleven! Imagine. I had gone to a dance recital with Upen. Bindu, he's wonderful."

Mrs. Jha pictured Mrs. Ray sitting in her living room, talking on the phone. If her curtains were open, the light from the neighboring apartments would be visible. Not here in Gurgaon, though — the windows were wide open and nothing was visible. She interrupted Mrs. Ray and said, "Reema. Do you mind if I interrupt you? Just for one second. It's about Rupak."

Mrs. Jha had to say the words to make them feel more real. She needed someone other than her husband to know. So it all came tumbling out to Mrs. Ray — about Rupak, about Serena, about their trip to America, and about her husband's strange behavior. She needed to tell someone she was lonely and that living in this huge house made her feel smaller than she ever had in Mayur Palli.

"I just don't know who he is anymore," Mrs. Jha said. "I'm worried he doesn't even know who he is. I want him to stand for something."

"He's figuring that out, Reema," Mrs. Ray said when Mrs. Jha stopped. "And he's made a mistake. And you will forgive him and you will love him and you will support him because you have him and you have Anil and even if they drive you up the wall, you have them. You don't have to forgive him right away — for now you just have to figure out how to interact with him. The rest will follow."

"You're right. I know you're right," Mrs. Jha said. "Tell me good things instead — tell me more about Upen."

"No, that can wait, but Bindu, it's connected in a way. Upen has made me realize how nice it is to have people around. I thought I was fine alone, and I was, but it's nice to have someone. And you have that. Even when it gets difficult."

"You sound like you've been reading self-help books," Mrs. Jha said with a smile. It was nice talking to Mrs. Ray, but clearly they were in different mental states at the moment.

"I could write a self-help book right now," Mrs. Ray said. "But you know it'll be fine — he's a wonderful boy. I'm surprised by this as well, Bindu, but you've all been going through such a change. Things will settle."

Mrs. Jha nodded and thanked Mrs. Ray for calming her down even though she wasn't feeling any calmer.

Downstairs, after he had eaten and Mrs. Jha was still upstairs, still hardly speaking, Mr. Jha gingerly sat on the sofa with a cup of tea and stared up at the crystal chandelier. The house was silent. He had to admit that Mrs. Jha was correct. It was too silent.

You could not hear traffic, you could not hear the clanking of dishes from neighbors' kitchens, you could not even hear your own wife upstairs. He listened for Mrs. Jha. Nothing. In Mayur Palli, Shatrugan would walk around every night lazily hitting his stick on the ground to keep away thieves and stray dogs. From midnight to five a.m., Mr. Jha used to sleep deeply knowing that life was right outside his window. In Gurgaon, life was far away. He would try desperately to listen for sounds of Balwinder, but even he could hardly be heard late at night. Even the big malls on MG Road were kept secure by computers and cameras instead of humans. This was his world now. It was much too easy to think.

He snapped back into attention when he heard a loud rapping on his front door. Who would be knocking this late at night, he wondered? This was exactly why they needed a guard. He looked through the peephole and saw Mr. Chopra standing and waving a piece of paper around. He opened the door.

"Is everything okay?" Mr. Jha said. "It's nearing eleven o'clock."

"Oh, Anil, what to tell you. I came over to have a good laugh with you because you will understand this. My son is so useless, I just don't know what to do. Listen to this poem he has written.

> I have heard the pigeons of Defence
> Colony
> Make their faint thunder, and the garden
> bees

"What is this nonsense he is writing? About pigeons? Dirty birds. You know they are called the rats of the skies? Here, listen, Johnny goes on:

> Hum in the neem tree flowers; and put
> away
> The unavailable — sorry, what does this
> say? — unavailing

"He must mean unavailable. In any case, it goes on and on like this — utterly meaningless. He calls this poetry. It doesn't even make any sense."

Mr. Chopra dropped the piece of paper onto Mr. Jha's coffee table, laughed heartily, and took a sip of Mr. Jha's tea.

"See? I'm telling you, my Johnny has no talent. I found this on his desk. Of course now he's out partying and God knows what time he will come home."

"That poem is not so bad, Mr. Chopra,"

Mr. Jha said.

"Nonsense. He is useless. Unlike Rupak. I hope he can talk some sense into Johnny. Filmmaking is a good industry."

"Oh, it is," Mr. Jha said. "For talented people. But Rupak has no talent. Only dreams. What can one do?"

Both the men laughed, each trying to be slightly louder than the other.

"You know," Mr. Jha said. "That poem is quite good. I have a friend who works with Penguin Books. Maybe I can set up a meeting with him and Johnny. I think Johnny could be a real success. I'm telling you his poetry reminds me of something. Some poet. Johnny can go far. Writers get a lot of respect these days."

"This poem? No, no. It is too bad. Johnny has no talent. Maybe he would if he didn't waste his time with all those pretty young girls all day. I really think he should be more like Rupak — studious, hardworking. Not writing garbage about pigeons," Mr. Chopra said.

"No, no. Please don't encourage him to be like Rupak. He is too bad. Who takes a break in the middle of his MBA? Your son should focus on his poetry and talent. At least he is trying to make something of his life."

Mr. Chopra finished Mr. Jha's tea, put the cup down on the table, and said, "Well, I should get going. But my wife wanted me to ask Mrs. Jha if she would like to go shopping with her sometime. Maybe buy some new saris. Let her know. I can send one of our cars."

With that, Mr. Chopra picked up Johnny's poem and was gone. He was hurrying down Mr. Jha's driveway toward his own home. He rushed through the Sistine Chapel–inspired dome and into his study. He turned on his laptop and typed in the first line of Johnny's poem and was amazed to find that the whole poem had already been written by someone named William Butler Yeats. Johnny had plagiarized! Well, not completely — he had made the poem about Delhi. The original said something about the pigeons of Seven Woods, wherever that might be, and Johnny had made it about Defence Colony so really he was quite intelligent but it was still plagiarism. Mr. Chopra called Mr. Jha immediately.

"Oh, Anil. You were correct," Mr. Chopra said, laughing. "Johnny's poetry does sound like something you've heard before! That good-for-nothing son of mine has plagiarized the whole poem. Some fellow named William Yeats has written this. I should have known. Johnny is not intelligent enough to write so beautifully about a subject so dirty. It takes talent to make pigeons sound beautiful and romantic and Johnny has no talent. Thank God we can take care of him."

Mr. Jha had no response. It was his own fault. He should never have said anything about Johnny's poetry reminding him of something. He should have just quietly worked hard to help get Johnny a meeting with the people at Penguin.

TWENTY-THREE

"You fool," Elizabeth said as she walked in the door. "Why would you buy weed in a public parking lot in the middle of the day? You should have just waited until I could get you some. I haven't heard from you in nearly two months, and then this is the text I get?"

Rupak was putting his books into a large brown box.

"Do you want any of this stuff? My TV, my microwave? Speakers, the toaster — you can take whatever you want from here."

"I might take your juicer," Elizabeth said. She walked around his living room, which was full of boxes, piles of books and clothes, and open suitcases with things spilling out. She sat down on the floor near the window.

"You're really leaving."

Rupak placed a pile of management textbooks into a box and nodded.

"Do you want a cup of coffee?" he said.

"Or a beer or something?"

"Are you okay?" Elizabeth asked.

"I think I also have half a bottle of wine."

"Sure, I'll have a glass of wine," Elizabeth said.

Rupak went to the fridge and split the remaining wine between two coffee cups. He used to own two wineglasses but he had taken those, along with two other boxes of kitchenware, to the Goodwill shop the previous day. When he came back to the living room, Elizabeth was standing up near his almost-empty shelf and looking at the framed picture of him in his school uniform. He handed her the cup of wine.

"We used to be poor," Rupak said. "Well, not poor but not rich. That picture is of me in my uniform from my first day of school. My father was so excited that I was going to go to a rich kids' school."

He sat down on the floor across the room from her and leaned against the wall.

"I had the opposite. We used to be rich. Actually rich-rich," Elizabeth said. "Can I have this picture?"

"You were?"

"Well, not like we're poor now. But yeah, my father made some bad investments, I guess. I don't really know details. I just know that we changed neighborhoods and homes when I was in the seventh grade and nobody was really allowed to talk about it," Elizabeth said.

"I never knew that about you."

"I think there's a lot we didn't know about each other. I certainly didn't know you looked so handsome in your uniform. Anyway, I don't talk about it because I know how spoiled it sounds — it's not like we were ever homeless. It took some adjusting but I don't feel scarred, you know. The only thing that stands out in my mind is when I overheard my parents fighting one night about whether to keep giving ten percent of their income to the church. My father was really adamant about it, but my mother thought we could use that money more. I could hear the whole fight — it started there and then it just spiraled. My father eventually stormed out and said he was going to spend the night in his office."

"Who won? Did they keep giving money?" Rupak asked.

"Yes. My father won. He always does."

"Mine tends to too," Rupak said.

They both fell silent for a while. Rupak looked around his apartment. He was going to miss it. He was going to miss Ithaca, he was going to miss America, and he was going to miss Elizabeth. He had just assumed he was going to have a life here, but now it seemed impossible. He had an Indian passport, which meant the only way he could live here was either by studying or getting a job that would sponsor his visa, and he knew that the latter was next to impossible these days anyway, and would be completely impossible without a proper degree. Or he could get married to an American.

"Why didn't you ever tell them about me?" Elizabeth broke the silence.

Rupak leaned his head back against the wall.

"Because I'm an idiot," Rupak said, and got up and went to the kitchen. He opened the fridge. There was a single Corona. On top of the fridge was a bottle of Maker's Mark that was not yet empty. He took both and went back to the living room and sat down next to Elizabeth on the floor. He opened the Corona and placed it on the floor in between them and poured Maker's Mark into both of their empty cups.

"Because I was a fucking idiot, Elizabeth. And I'm sorry. I am so sorry. I just hope I hurt myself more than I hurt you," Rupak said.

Elizabeth took a sip.

"That's an easy way to avoid feeling bad,

isn't it?" Elizabeth said. "I have to say it helps, though. I don't feel angry toward you anymore. I guess I'm being petty too."

"I'm going to try to find a way back," Rupak said. "Don't be surprised if I show up on your doorstep in Florida to fight to get you back, okay?"

"That's a nice sentiment, Rupak, but I wouldn't bother. I'm not saying that angrily, I promise. I just — I'm not one for dramatic gestures."

Elizabeth moved the bottle of beer and leaned her weight against his. He pressed his face to the top of her head. He wondered why he had never bothered asking her much about her life before. He had been so swept up in the idea of her because of what she looked like that he hadn't bothered with any of the details — he just filled in the gaps himself and created the perfect American sitcom character. In the perfect American sitcom, they would sleep together tonight. And when he woke up in the morning, she would be gone, the sun streaming down on the pillow she had used. And perhaps there would be a note left on his table. But there was none of that.

They kissed. They kissed for about an hour, but all their clothes stayed on. He tried once to reach under her shirt, but she pulled back and he let it be. Just kissing her was nice; he hadn't realized that before. And he didn't have the energy to try anything more tonight.

TWENTY-FOUR

"Why don't we meet out somewhere for dinner?" Mrs. Ray said. She was standing in front of her bathroom mirror combing her hair and smiling to herself. She put the comb down on the edge of the sink and scraped at a small stain of dried toothpaste on the mirror with her thumbnail.

"We've already been all over Delhi. It'll be nicer to eat at home. I want to see where you live," Upen said. "I'll come around eight. You don't have to cook. I can bring food, or we can order in?"

"No, of course not," Mrs. Ray said. He was right — since their day at Dilli Haat, they had been out for two more dinners, one midafternoon session of drinks in Hauz Khas Village, and a bharatanatyam dance performance. Each time he had asked to come over, and each time she had come up with an excuse not to let him. "I'd love to cook for you. I just — well, I haven't

370

entertained in a while."

"I'm sure you make a wonderful host," Upen said. "Tell me what I can bring, and I'll come at eight."

"You don't need to bring anything. I'll see you this evening."

Mrs. Ray put the phone down, grateful for once that Ganga was still in Siliguri, with still no concrete plans to return anytime soon. She did not want Ganga fluttering around and interfering when she was enjoying her evening with Upen. At first her home felt empty without Ganga, but she found she soon got used to it. Even though she had often been lonely, she realized that she had really never been alone her whole life. She had always been scared of being alone, but, and she knew she was probably thinking this way because of Upen, being alone was proving to be quite easy.

She had hardly even entered her kitchen while Ganga was here, but now she was planning to use some of her savings to have the kitchen redone. If the Jhas could move to Gurgaon, she could get a new refrigerator and microwave put in. Mrs. Ray was tired of falling into the role of widow that others were placing on her.

In any case, she could worry about all that later. For now, she had to worry about only one thing — Upen. He was coming over at eight and Shatrugan downstairs was quite a gossip. He did it in a harmless way, thinking he was just being a part of all their lives here, but he still did it. And Mrs. Ray knew that if Upen stopped at the front gate and asked how to reach her apartment, Shatrugan would ask him a dozen questions and then repeat the information to everyone. She pulled a shawl over her shoulders and went downstairs to talk to him. She found him sitting on his haunches near the main gate flipping through a tattered copy of *Stardust* magazine. He was wearing sandals despite the chill in the air.

"Shatrugan, come tomorrow morning and see me — I have an old pair of Mr. Ray's shoes that I'll give you. It's too cold for sandals."

"Madam, you are too kind. It was not nice of Ganga to leave you. These days, maids have no sense of duty. I will be here guarding all of you till the day I die."

"Shatrugan, my accountant will be coming around eight this evening. You make sure you let him in and show him where my apartment is. And don't start chatting his ear off."

"Madam, your accountant makes house calls on a Sunday?" Shatrugan asked. "That is very decent of him. Madam, you know last week a woman died in the Leela Housing Complex? Her husband is still living, I have heard."

"So?" Mrs. Ray asked.

"Just letting you know, madam," Shatrugan said, wobbling his head from side to side.

"Just please let my accountant in when he comes," Mrs. Ray said, and walked back up to her apartment.

Back at home, Mrs. Ray tied her hair into a bun and went to her cupboard and took out a gray silk sari and black blouse with long sleeves. She changed into the sari and looked in the full-length mirror that was attached to the back of her bedroom door. This was silly, she thought. Why was she putting on such a formal outfit for tonight? The whole point of having dinner at home was to be more casual. She undraped the sari and stood for a moment in front of her mirror in just her petticoat and blouse. She tugged at the sides of her stomach and pulled it back. Her skin was getting a little loose in parts but she was not fat. Even though she was home alone, Mrs. Ray closed and locked her bedroom door and removed her blouse. She wore a cream-colored bra. A dull cream-colored bra that had three hooks at the back and, despite looking industrial, allowed her breasts to sag and fall on two sides of her chest. She had no time today, but tomorrow she would go to a mall and buy some new bras. She was older now but not dead, and underwear these days was made to let women like her be sexual. She did not have to change into a thong and a push-up bra, but something with a bit of underwire would not hurt.

Mrs. Ray tugged at the string of her petticoat and allowed it to fall in a puddle at her feet. Yes, her thighs had some cellulite and her knees looked crumpled, but her legs were not so bad. Yoga had given her thighs a hint of a vertical line of muscle, and her body was strong. She did not look like a Bollywood star, but she also did not look like someone who had to spend her days in oversized nighties ignoring her body. Mrs. Ray pulled her jeans back on and put on a black sweater and a pair of small gold earrings. She went to her cupboard and found her brown wedge-heeled sandals and stepped into them. She dabbed perfume on her wrists and two coats of lipstick on her lips. She picked up her black eyeliner and lined her lower lids. She blinked in the mirror. She picked up the eyeliner again and lined her upper lids, lifting the line at the edges to create a slight cat-eye effect that she had not tried since her college days.

The doorbell rang at eight fifteen. Thank God Upen wasn't the kind to show up at eight when invited for eight. Mrs. Ray walked through the living room to the front door and stopped to see the candles. How could she possibly have thought candles were a good idea? How embarrassing. She stooped to blow out the seven candles that she had lit across the room. A faint smell of smoke wafted through the air as the wicks smoldered. He would know she had candles lit earlier. The doorbell rang again and Mrs. Ray quickly waved her sofa cushions in the air to make the smoke disappear. She pushed the candles behind books and lamps and walked to open the door. Upen was there holding a bouquet with four orchids in one hand and a bottle of wine in the other.

"I hope you have a long vase," Upen said, handing Mrs. Ray the flowers. "Or we will just have to drink four bottles of wine and place one flower in each bottle."

She smiled and took the flowers from him — Shatrugan would be very suspicious of her accountant. Maybe she could have left the candles lit after all.

"Come in. Please sit. Make yourself at

home. Shoes on or off is up to you — I don't have any strict rules here," Mrs. Ray said. "Would you like a glass of wine? Should I open this bottle? Or I can open the wine I have in the fridge, but it's only Indian wine, I'm afraid. It's hard to get imported wines in this neighborhood. I also have other drinks though — vodka, whiskey, gin. I can make you a gin and tonic if you prefer."

She was talking too much. She hadn't, she realized, had a drink with a man in this home since her husband had died. The only other men who even entered were workers — electricians, carpenters, plumbers — and Mr. Jha a few times, but always with Mrs. Jha, and always only for a cup of tea. No other men had entered her home in the past few years.

"Reema," Upen said, laughing. "You seem tense."

"No, no. Oh no. Let me just get us our drinks. Did you say wine? I'll get wine. Oh no. Please — don't come to the kitchen," she said as he moved toward her. She didn't want him to see her kitchen. Her kitchen was messy, countertops stained and sticky, the walls in need of painting. "Please just sit. I'll bring us drinks."

Upen grabbed her elbow and pulled her

toward him. Her body tensed and tightened.

"Wine is fine," he said. "But first let me do this because otherwise I'll keep thinking about it until I do it and then we'll both end up as awkward and tense as you are. So let's get it over with and then we can enjoy the rest of the evening together."

And he kissed her. He put both his hands on her shoulders and pulled her in and kissed her. She felt his beard, his skin, his lips and even, she inhaled sharply, a hint of his tongue. Her body remained tense; her arms hung by her side. She wished she could bring herself to reach up and touch him, to let him know she liked this, but she couldn't move. He released her, let go of her shoulders, and stepped back.

"Was that okay?" he asked.

Mrs. Ray smiled and nodded.

"It was okay. No. It was more than okay. Thank you. For, you know, getting that over with," Mrs. Ray said, smiling, calmer now. Her hands moved up to touch her own face, which felt hot.

"Try to participate next time," Upen said, laughing. "We'll practice. But for now, the wine."

They drank the first bottle of wine before they even sat for dinner, and they talked without a break, without a single awkward pause. Mrs. Ray couldn't get the kiss out of her mind, but Upen seemed unaffected. He talked again of travel — his recent trip alone to Vietnam. Vietnam. She had just assumed she would never again leave India, but sitting here, listening to him talk, she was no longer so sure. After all, the Jhas, older than her, had just been to New York. Did she have to assume the doors to the world were closed for her?

"There's so much of the world to see, Reema," Upen said, and rested his hand against her thigh. "Japan. Have you been to Japan? I want to go there next. For the cherry blossoms."

"Japan?" Mrs. Ray said. Of course she hadn't been to Japan.

"And Cambodia. Of course all the usual places like Europe and Brazil and Argentina, but recently I've been excited about exploring more of Asia," Upen said, the tension of his hand increasing and decreasing against her leg. "The world is just so endlessly fascinating."

She would travel, Mrs. Ray decided. She would start small — maybe take a trip to Jaipur. And she would try to see the world as fascinating, she promised herself.

"What about you?" Upen said. "What's on your bucket list?"

"Bucket list?"

"You know — list of things to do or see before you die," Upen said.

"I've never heard that term before. Where does it come from?"

"I'm not too sure. I believe 'kicking the bucket' used to be a term for dying, but I'm not sure where that came from."

"I doubt it was Indian. You say 'kicking the bucket' and I just think of moving the bucket aside when I'm finished with my bath; I don't think of death."

What was on her bucket list? Being in Mayur Palli day in and day out with nothing new was like being dead before dying. This kind of widowhood wasn't that different from throwing herself on her husband's funeral pyre. No, she was being dramatic, she told herself. It was the wine. She would give some thought to her bucket list. Right now, the only thing she could think of was that she wanted to kiss Upen again before she died. Mrs. Ray opened another bottle of wine as they sat down to eat.

"What keeps you here?" Upen asked halfway through the meal.

"Here, as in?"

"Here. Delhi, East Delhi. What keeps you here? Why don't you move?"

"And go where? Start over how? This city,

this country, doesn't make it easy for single women. You know that. It's changing — the next generation will have it easier, thank God. But where would I go? I don't know anything else."

"Come to Chandigarh," Upen said.

Mrs. Ray laughed. She wiped her hands on the paper napkin and poured the last of the second bottle of wine into Upen's glass. How had they finished two bottles already? She was going to have a headache in the morning. And, say what you will, a meal without a nonvegetarian dish just didn't feel like a full meal, so the alcohol was having even more of an effect.

"I'm serious. Come with me. No, more than that. Marry me. Marry me and then come with me to Chandigarh," Upen said.

"You've had too much wine. We both have."

"That's probably true," Upen said.

"Should I put on some coffee?" Mrs. Ray asked.

"But let's discuss this anyway. Even if it's because of the wine. Let's discuss it when we aren't thinking straight so I can convince you — and myself. Don't worry, I'm not completely insane. I hear how crazy this idea is. And I'm not sure either, but let's just talk. And then we can revisit it tomorrow morning over breakfast. With coffee."

So he was planning to spend the night, Mrs. Ray thought.

"You ask someone to marry you after kissing her just once?" she said, smiling and shaking her head. She stood and picked up both of their plates and walked toward the kitchen. She was still smiling to herself as she dropped the plates into the sink and ran water over them. She stopped for a moment and imagined having a home with him, picking out bedsheets, agreeing on a brand of soap, and deciding which pictures to frame for the wall. She pictured sitting on a balcony and having a glass of wine with dinner and discussing buying brighter bedside lamps so they could read in bed at night together. She imagined offering him dessert every night, not just tonight.

"Would you like —" she was shouting out to the living room when she turned and saw Upen standing in the doorway of the kitchen, bringing her the dishes from the dining table.

"How many times did you kiss your husband before you decided to marry him?" he asked.

"You don't need to help with the dishes. Just sit. I've got some dessert," she said, taking the bowls from him at the door and edging him back out.

"How many times?"

She smiled at him. "Zero."

"Exactly," Upen said, walking back to the dining room. "And you had a perfectly happy marriage. Bring some more wine. I think we have reason to celebrate tonight."

Mrs. Ray returned to the dining room with another bottle of wine and a bowl of four gulab jamuns.

"Do you prefer your gulab jamuns hot or cold?" she asked.

"Either way, Reema. But what do you think? Should we do it? They say you're only young once, but you're also only middle-aged once. We should take advantage. Why leave all the fun, impulsive things to the youth? Look at it this way: at our age . . . well, you're younger than me so let's say at our stage, there's less left to lose. Everyone else talks about us anyway. Your guard downstairs asked me if I was your accountant."

Mrs. Ray laughed.

"That may have been my fault," she said.

"We discussed this — the fact that arranged marriages have worked so well for years and years and years," Upen said. "What's the difference here? We know each other better than either of us knew our spouses before we married them. We just no longer have parents to set us up. But that shouldn't stand in the way of companionship."

"But your wife had an affair," Mrs. Ray said.

"So? We were happy for quite a while. And then we weren't anymore. That had nothing to do with the marriage being arranged or love."

"You're funny," Mrs. Ray said.

"I'm being serious," Upen said, no longer laughing. "The next generation gets to fall in love. Our generation had our love planned for us. But we're stuck in the middle. What was arranged for us fell through and we can hardly go online looking for a fellow widow or divorcé — India doesn't have those websites as far as I know, at least not yet. Hopefully they will in the future — I still think you should start a website for widows to find new love; after shaadi.com, maybe? But until enough people start to think it's socially acceptable, what are the rest of us supposed to do? We're too young to give up, don't you think? And it isn't just that — God, that sounds awful. I don't mean to say we're each other's last resort. I mean I like you — I really like you. And you like me. And we should be together all the time."

Mrs. Ray handed him a bowl with a gulab jamun and one scoop of vanilla ice cream and took one bowl for herself. Upen put the bowl down on the table without touching the food and said, "I'm being completely serious. Spend the rest of your life with me."

Mrs. Ray sat down on the sofa and put her bowl of dessert down on the coffee table.

"And if it doesn't work, we get . . . divorced?"

"What happened to all your romance talk? Who mentions divorce in the middle of a proposal?" Upen said with a laugh, and sat down next to her. "Well, let's hope it doesn't come to that, but yes, if it doesn't work, we get divorced."

"But, divorce . . . ," Mrs. Ray trailed off.

"What? Yes, divorce. It's no longer the end of the world, you know. I've survived a divorce before. We'll be gentle with each other; we're too old to be petty. But we won't get divorced! I'm trying to ask you to marry me; stop talking about divorce!"

He pulled Mrs. Ray closer to him on the sofa.

"I'm trying to think of a reason to say no, but I can't seem to come up with any," she said, smiling. What she wanted was to say yes. What she wanted was to throw her arms around him with happiness. What she wanted was to feel this way forever. Was it possible? Was it allowed? Who made the rules once your parents died and your husband died and your only friend moved away and the rest of the world seemed to forget about you? Could she just say yes and choose to be happy? Was it really that simple?

"Then say yes."

"As simple as that?"

"As simple as that," Upen said.

"But not a big wedding. That would be embarrassing."

"A court wedding."

"Maybe followed by a small dinner with our friends," Mrs. Ray added.

"Why not?" Upen said.

"Why not," Mrs. Ray said, and picked up her dessert bowl. Then she put it back down and leaned over and kissed Upen on the mouth.

TWENTY-FIVE

Mrs. Jha had hardly been able to make eye contact with Rupak since he had arrived at two a.m. She had not even been able to go downstairs to see him even though she was wide awake when she heard the taxi pull up outside.

"You sleep," Mr. Jha had said. "Tomorrow will be a long day. I will open the gate and let Rupak in and make sure he is okay."

Under any other circumstances, she would have refused. In fact, she would have insisted on being at the airport to greet him. But tonight, she did not know how to face him. When her husband went downstairs, Mrs. Jha got up and looked out the window. The taxi pulled into their driveway and Rupak got out, looking less sloppy than he had been of late. He was wearing dark jeans and a long-sleeved shirt with actual buttons. His hair was cut neatly and his face was clean-shaven. He had made an effort because he knew he had failed them, Mrs. Jha thought. Her son knew he was a disappointment. She saw Mr. Jha patting him on his back while laughing, and she felt grateful to her husband for being nice to Rupak. She wanted to go downstairs and hold him and hug him and tell him that it was going to be okay and they would help him overcome this and whatever other problems he had, but she also wanted to slap him across the face and tell him that she had raised him better than this. She had not raised him to do drugs. But she did not say any of that. Instead she went back to bed and pretended to be asleep when Mr. Jha came back in.

In the morning, Rupak and Mr. Jha were both fast asleep and Mrs. Jha was grateful for the silence in the house. She was starting to get used to the quiet mornings and the sound of birds. In Mayur Palli, she had not realized how much she missed the quiet. There, mornings were filled with sounds of people living lives — dishes clanking in kitchens punctuated by the hissing of pressure cookers, neighbors paying milkmen, maids gossiping in hallways, cleaners listening to loud Bollywood music while washing the cars parked downstairs. In Gurgaon, all she heard in the mornings was the distant rumble of a truck on the main road. Mrs.

Jha made a cup of tea and sat with it and the cordless phone on a cane chair on the small marble patio in front of the front door. She was about to call Mrs. Ray to find out how things were going with her and Upen when Rupak came out and joined her on the porch. She hung up the phone while it was ringing.

"Papa seems pretty excited about me meeting the neighbors. Do you need me to do anything before they come over?"

"No, nothing. You settle in. I'm sure you're tired. You relax. I'll see to everything," Mrs. Jha said in a rush. She was startled by the phone ringing in her hand.

"Hello?"

"Bindu? Did you call just now?" Mrs. Ray said. "Is he home? Is everything okay?"

"I did, but I'm just a bit tied up now. I'll give you a call back later tonight or tomorrow morning."

"Okay, call soon. I have some good news to share," Mrs. Ray said.

"Maybe I'll come to Mayur Palli next weekend and see you. I miss it," Mrs. Jha said. She looked over at Rupak sitting on the cane chair, looking like an adult.

"Is that Reema Aunty? Tell her I say hello," Rupak said.

"So we'll speak soon," Mrs. Jha said, and

put down the phone.

"She was in a rush but we'll invite her over soon. I better go see what your father wants for breakfast," Mrs. Jha said, and got up, picked up the newspaper, empty cup, and cordless phone and went back into the house.

Drugs. That had never been her world. Even when she was young, she was never rebellious. She knew that when she was in college, many people in Delhi were experimenting with drugs, but she had never gone near any of it. What was she supposed to say to him? Was she supposed to ignore it? Was she supposed to act happy that he was home?

"I really wish we were having a quiet family dinner tonight," Mrs. Jha said to Mr. Jha in their bedroom. The windows were large, nearly floor to ceiling, but outside all you could see was darkness. They hardly ever bothered pulling the curtains shut in Gurgaon. Mrs. Jha wondered what they would look like to someone standing on the street. Yellow lighting, a bed with more pillows than two people would ever use, and a normal, well-to-do middle-aged couple getting ready for an evening with friends. Mr. Jha held his skinny tie from New York up against his collar. He was wearing brown slacks and a darker brown collared shirt.

"You're the one who says it's too lonely and quiet here. It's only the Chopras and I told them to just drop in for a quick drink, say hello. Is a tie too much? It's probably too much. Why don't you wear a skirt tonight?"

"We need to talk to Rupak. I don't know how to speak to him anymore."

Mr. Jha laughed and shook his head.

"Marijuana. They call it four twenty," he said. "There's some debate over how that became the popular term for it."

"Drugs," Mrs. Jha said, and sat down on the edge of their bed. "What did we do wrong?" She ran her hand along the off-white duvet and smoothed it down.

"Speaking of skirts, do you think we need to get a bed skirt?" Mr. Jha asked, looking at where his wife was sitting at the edge of the bed.

They had a coir mattress on a wooden frame, the bottom part of which had drawers that could be pulled out to provide storage space for their extra linens. Why would they want to put a bed skirt on that, and when had her husband learned what a bed skirt was?

"You know what? I'm going to change.

This looks too formal. Like you said, it's basically a family dinner tonight," Mr. Jha said.

"That isn't what I said."

"I'll put on my tracksuit. Casual but still fashionable. As if maybe I've just been to the gym. Oh, Bindu, we simply must remember to speak to the Chopras tonight about joining the LRC. I want to start using the gym."

Mr. Jha went into the master bathroom and left the door half open so he could change into his tracksuit while still talking to his wife. They had installed two sinks and two mirrors in the bathroom because Mr. Jha had once seen that in a movie and he liked the idea of it, but Mrs. Jha never used the bathroom at the same time as him.

"You've never been to a gym in your life," Mrs. Jha said. "If you want to start exercising, come for evening walks with me."

"Nobody walks here, Bindu. We'll make people nervous."

"That's exactly why it's pleasant to walk here — the roads are nice and empty. We don't have to watch for rickshaws and cars and cows. Nobody walks on the empty roads here, but the roads around Mayur Palli just get more and more crowded. I don't understand it."

Mr. Jha came out and stood in front of the mirror admiring his tracksuit.

"Perfect," he said. "But I think I need to get the elastic in the waist loosened a bit. I seem to be gaining weight. Have you noticed, Bindu, that men usually put their pants either above their paunch or below their paunch? But Mr. Chopra wears his pants smack through the middle of his paunch. What confidence that man has."

"Anil, listen to me. Tomorrow we need to have a serious talk with Rupak. Tonight you've left me no choice so we have to have the neighbors here, but only one drink and then I want them to leave, okay?"

"And the soup," Mr. Jha said. He had insisted that it was rude to send the guests away without at least a small snack, so he had made Mrs. Jha prepare six bowls of mulligatawny soup. He had heard on *MasterChef Australia* that soup was the in thing to serve these days. "I've heard cold soups are particularly in fashion, so see if you can put it in the fridge for some time before the neighbors arrive."

"I'm not serving anyone cold soup," Mrs. Jha said. "I don't care what the fashion is in Australia or America, but in India, serving someone cold soup is rude."

Despite everything, Mrs. Jha was relieved

in a way. She wasn't ready to speak to Rupak yet. Mr. Jha was still standing and looking at himself in the mirror, playing with the waistband of his tracksuit.

"I'll leave the shirt tucked in and the jacket unzipped," he said.

He patted his face, pulled back his jowls, and sucked in his cheeks. "You know there's a new type of facelift you can do that specifically makes you look good on Skype and FaceTime. What a world we live in." He lifted his chin and looked down his nose. "The best plastic surgeon in Delhi is a Mr. Trehan who also lives in Gurgaon, you know."

The doorbell rang. He looked at his watch and said, "Who comes at the exact time? Bindu, can you go and answer the door? And where are my white sneakers?"

He bent down and peeked under the bed. His dark brown leather Woodlands shoes were lying there but not his sneakers. He pulled out the leather shoes and looked at them.

"Look at how scuffed these are. I shouldn't have returned that shoe polisher. We could have just kept it upstairs where nobody would have seen it," Mr. Jha said.

"What shoe polisher?" Mrs. Jha asked.

"Bindu, please just go and open the door.

I need to find my sneakers," Mr. Jha said, and walked into the closet to search for his shoes.

Mrs. Jha patted some baby powder on her nose, checked the pleats of her sari in the mirror, and headed down the stairs to greet the guests.

"Hurry up, please," she said. "I don't want to be the one to explain why Rupak is visiting again so soon."

"I already told them he's in town," Mr. Jha said, emerging from the closet with his white sneakers in hand.

"What?" Mrs. Jha said. "What did you say to them?"

"Nothing, Bindu. Nothing much. I just bumped into Dinesh and told him that Rupak had decided to take some time off from his program. I didn't say anything more than that."

"Please don't tell them anything more. We can imply that he's going back next semester. I don't want the Chopras being so involved in our lives. Now hurry up."

Mrs. Jha walked out of the room toward the steps. Rupak heard her footsteps from his bedroom, which was the guest room. There was nothing of his in this room; his parents had clearly not expected him to ever live here. His things were in suitcases and boxes that were hidden away around the house. Most of the furniture in this house was new, and if he were brought to this room, blindfolded, he would never have known that it belonged to his parents. One of the walls was fully mirrored; their Mayur Palli home didn't have even a single full-length mirror, let alone a mirror wall in every room. Rupak waited until he could no longer hear his mother. He was glad his parents had invited the neighbors over tonight. While his father seemed only happy to have him home, his mother seemed to be avoiding eye contact with him. He knew his parents were not the type to discuss things explicitly, but how could he seamlessly return to life at home after what had happened? Surely it was going to be brought up. And the longer it took to bring up, the more it made Rupak uncomfortable.

What was he supposed to do next? Was he supposed to enroll in an MBA in India? Was he really supposed to pursue a career in film? And in the meantime, was he supposed to settle into living at home and get back in touch with his old friends and develop a life here in Delhi? Was he supposed to date? Was he supposed to let his parents set him up as an apology for what he was putting them through? As usual, he did not feel like he could make any decisions on his own, but he also did not know how to talk to his parents right now. Which was exactly why he needed a drink, but he decided it was best not to have anything to drink tonight. His parents would think he was not taking the situation seriously if he sat and sipped whiskey with the neighbors all evening.

Rupak pulled a cream-colored sweater over his dark blue collared shirt that was tucked into a pair of jeans. He was wearing clean brown leather shoes, and he had shaved. He ran his hand through his hair and went downstairs to meet the neighbors.

His father, in a tracksuit, was coming out of his bedroom at the same time.

"Ah it's nice to have you at home, Rupak," Mr. Jha said. "But why so stiff? It's just a casual drink with the neighbors tonight. You don't have to be dressed so formally."

Rupak looked down at his outfit.

"I'm just wearing jeans and a sweater, Papa," he said.

"You don't need to, you know. You can wear shorts and a T-shirt," Mr. Jha said. "Or a tracksuit. Would you like to borrow one? I bought three."

"I'm fine in this. It's getting cold anyway,"

Rupak said.

"It is. It really is. You know what we need? Central heating. Have you noticed that no homes in Delhi have that yet? Everyone still just has those small room heaters that you have to turn on when you enter a room and then you spend half the evening huddled as close to it as possible. Although, come to think of it, I haven't been in the Chopras' home since it started getting cold. I wonder if they have central heating. We'll get it anyway. It's important these days. Thank God for global warming. Although, in Delhi, it really should be called global cooling," Mr. Jha said with a laugh. "Oh, Rupak, it's good to have you home."

"Papa, what have you told the neighbors?" Rupak said.

"I was telling your mother about how in Korean homes, you can turn on appliances from your phone. So I suppose the other option would be to get the room heaters but to hook them up to our phones so we could put them on an hour or two before entering the room to make it nice and warm. That could be an alternative to central heating, if your mother insists. But then I would insist on getting a heater in the bathroom also, and I don't know how safe that would be."

"Anil, Rupak, what are you both doing standing up there? Come downstairs. The guests are here," Mrs. Jha said, looking up from the base of the stairs.

"Yes, we are coming. We were just discussing central heating. Rupak also agrees that it's a good idea. I'm going to look into it tomorrow," Mr. Jha said. "Global warming, you see."

"No, I didn't say," Rupak said, but he couldn't finish his defense to his mother because his father was booming, "Dinesh! Mrs. Chopra! Welcome, welcome. Make yourself at home. How wonderful to see you. Johnny, hello. How nice that you could come too. Sit, sit. Wonderful that we can have both sons home as well. This is Rupak."

"Ah, the prodigal son returns. Or is it prodigy? Prodigal? What's the word I'm looking for?" Mr. Chopra said, looking around the room. Everyone shrugged. "In any case, welcome home, Rupak. It's nice to finally meet you. Here, we brought along a bottle of white wine for you from" — Mr. Chopra squinted at the bottle — "Italy. A bottle of white wine from Italy. It's not quite cold enough for now, I'm afraid."

"Thank you so much, Uncle," Rupak said politely. "I'll put it in the fridge. Please sit."

"Careful there," Mr. Chopra said to his wife. "Do not sit on those small pieces of glass."

"Crystals," Mr. Jha said. "Swarovski crystals. And they are perfectly safe to sit on."

"Right," Mr. Chopra said.

"I like how they glint," Mrs. Chopra said.

Mr. Jha smiled. "I like that also. I ordered it from Japan. I'd be happy to give you the details if you'd like."

"So what are we drinking to welcome Rupak home?" Mr. Chopra said.

"Right this way. All the drinks are set out here," Mrs. Jha said. Even though it was just the neighbors, Mr. Jha had insisted on setting up a bar of sorts on the side table. He had put out all their spirits, glasses, and even a stainless steel ice bucket with tongs that she didn't remember ever having bought.

"And there's red and white wine if you prefer. The red wine will just have to be decanted first," Mr. Jha said, smiling and pointing to a crystal decanter.

"What is that?" Mrs. Jha whispered.

"I bought it from Amazon. I had to have it rush delivered but thank God, it arrived this morning," Mr. Jha whispered back.

"I wouldn't mind some white wine," Mrs.

Chopra said.

"You know what? I'll start with some white wine as well," Mr. Chopra said. "To toast. And then we can move on to the real liquor."

"Excellent idea," Mr. Jha said.

"We could have the one you brought with ice if it isn't quite cold enough yet," Mrs. Jha suggested, thinking the guests might appreciate that. So she was surprised when Mr. Chopra laughed and her husband joined in laughing even more loudly.

"Oh, Bindu, we can't ruin the wine they brought with ice," Mr. Jha said, shaking his head at Mr. Chopra. "I'll get a different chilled bottle."

Mr. Jha turned to walk toward the kitchen and glared at his wife along the way. In the kitchen, he opened the fridge and took a deep breath. No, he would not be defeated today. Everything was going well — his son was back, halfway through his MBA, which meant that he did not need to earn money, so even if his wife had suggested putting ice cubes in the wine, it was clear that they were wealthy. He reached for the bottle of wine and noticed that the soup was not in the fridge. He looked around and spotted a large glass bowl with the mulligatawny soup on the marble countertop. Soup looked a lot like daal, he thought. He put the large bowl of soup in the fridge and took out the wine.

When he returned to the living room with the bottle, Mr. Chopra was looking around the room and saying, "Big houses take longer to decorate. It will all come together soon."

"Are you planning to put in carpeting?" Mrs. Chopra asked.

"Perhaps," Mrs. Jha said. "Although I quite like the marble floors. It feels nice and cool in the summers."

"Yes, but carpeting feels nice and warm in the winters. It's difficult to decide," Mrs. Chopra said. "Global warming has made interior decorating more difficult."

"Do let us know if we can help with anything," Mr. Chopra said. "We have worked with some of the best contractors in the area. They're more expensive here than in other parts of Delhi, but I say when you're paying for quality, it's worth it. Pay less, get less, isn't that so? I still think you should consider getting some artwork done like we have in our foyer."

"That is true," Mrs. Chopra said. "It really changes the feel of the home to have original art. Did Dinesh tell you that the artists can also do Bollywood re-creations? That's what

I want to get done in the upstairs hall. Maybe a still from some old film. *Dhoom* — the first one. And now is the time to do it, really. The Singhs who live at the end of the lane — they got their living room wall done just hardly a year or so before their daughter had a child. Practically the week the child started walking, he took a colored marker and destroyed the painting. Can you imagine? I've heard the Singhs haven't spoken to their daughter in over a year now. The artist refused to just clean up the area that was ruined — he said that isn't how art works. You can't blame him. So they had to pay the full amount again."

"Hard to say who is to blame. That's why I, personally, think the painting works best on the ceiling," Mr. Chopra said. "The Singhs should have thought it through. You don't leave the Mona Lisa lying unprotected on the floor when there is a toddler running around."

"Perhaps you're right," Mrs. Chopra said, taking a sip from her glass.

"Well, I was hoping at some point to get a full bookshelf made along that wall," Mrs. Jha said. That was really the only decorating thing left on her list.

"If your books are causing a space problem, you should invest in a Kindle. There's no reason to fill up the house with books these days," Mr. Chopra said.

"He is correct," Mrs. Chopra said. "I download everything onto my iPad. You can even get full magazine subscriptions. All the film magazines — can you imagine? But I just love the feel of magazines in my hand, so I still get hard copies of those. I can't resist. And I love those folded pages with the perfume samples — say what you will, you can't get that on an iPad."

"I like books," Johnny said to Mrs. Jha. She smiled at him.

"Drinks! Here's the white wine we have. It's from Chile and it's nice and cold," Mr. Jha said.

"You know, I'm glad Chile has started manufacturing wine," Mr. Chopra said. "Those wines are so much cheaper to get in India. Italian wines or French wines cost an arm and a leg here. Does it taste decent?"

Mr. Jha put the bottle down on the counter with more force than he had expected, his limbs suddenly heavy.

"I'll have a whiskey, if you don't mind," Johnny said. He moved to the counter and poured himself about four fingers' worth from the bottle of Black Label. He dropped two ice cubes into the glass and returned to the sofa.

Mr. Chopra said, "Look at that. Look at how much he drinks. He has no sense of the value of money. Rupak, you must speak to Johnny. You heard about the plagiarizing."

Johnny looked at his father, raised his glass, smiled mischievously, and drank.

"Well, Mr. Chopra," Mr. Jha said. "Look on the bright side. At least he is plagiarizing from a talented poet. He has taste. And that is the first step for success. Mark my words. And writing can be very lucrative these days. It is a good decision. Secure. Wine for everyone else?"

"I'll just have a plain soda, Papa, thanks. I'll get it myself," Rupak said. His mother smiled at him. Mr. Jha was silent. His family was so uncooperative. He was worried he would never completely win.

"Did you hear that, Johnny?" Mr. Chopra said, laughing and shaking his head. "Rupak, I want to know more about your filmmaking plans. I want you to talk to Johnny. He should learn some sense of responsibility from you. Look at you working hard. You know that you can't rely on your parents' money forever."

"Filmmaking is more of a hobby for him," Mrs. Jha added. How did Mr. Chopra know about Rupak's interest in film?

"You know how young people are these days," Mr. Jha said. "Not a care in the world — they think hobbies can be real careers. What can we do? It's our fault really, for having spoiled them so much. Anyway, what can we do but support him?"

"You shouldn't worry; you won't have to support him," Mr. Chopra said. "Filmmaking is where all the money is these days. Your son is your own retirement plan, Anil! Just look at all those Bollywood people — they're buying up homes in Dubai left and right. Very good decision, Rupak."

"No, my mother's right, it's more of a hobby. I'm probably going to finish my degree in India itself. The Indian Institute of Management has a good program and I like living here," Rupak said. "There are so many opportunities. America just hasn't been the same since the recession."

"It will be best to focus on filmmaking now. It is a risky career but I think it will be good to try. Rupak, I have been thinking I will invest in your first film. Of course saying 'invest' means there will be returns, so maybe that's the wrong word. Indian Institute of Management is a very good idea, but let's be realistic, they won't accept you," Mr. Jha said.

"Anil!" Mrs. Jha said. "Why don't I serve

the soup?"

"He was kicked out of graduate school in America, so even completing in India is not really an option now," Mr. Jha continued.

Mrs. Jha got up and walked over to Mr. Jha and took his wineglass from him. She stayed standing next to her husband, avoiding going to the kitchen in case he gave away more information to the neighbors. She looked at him and didn't recognize him, his eyes large and wild, darting around the room from person to person. A small V-shape of sweat had formed on the white T-shirt he was wearing under his tracksuit.

"Well, no harm," Mr. Chopra said. "There are other options. You can join a company and work your way up. Even Bill Gates was a dropout. There are many paths to success these days."

"Oh, unlikely," Mr. Jha said. "Very, very unlikely."

"Don't despair," Mr. Chopra said. "I'd be happy to put you in touch with some people. What are you interested in? Banking? Consulting? We know lots of people. Half the board members of HSBC are members of the LRC. I will set up some introductions. Take advantage of the neighbors. Let us help."

"That won't work!" Mr. Jha said, more

loudly than before. "Don't you hear me? He was kicked out. We wouldn't want to embarrass you by asking for your help. There's no hope. I will be taking care of him forever. Forever. Thank God I've earned enough for the next generation. And maybe the one after that as well. But who will marry Rupak?" Mr. Jha slapped his thigh and faked a loud laugh. He took his glasses off and used the sleeve of his tracksuit to wipe the sweat off his face. "Wine! Who wants more wine? Where's my glass?"

Mrs. Jha put her hand on his shoulder. The rest of the room went silent. Even Mr. Chopra had no words left to offer. Mrs. Chopra fidgeted slightly — a crystal was poking her right thigh.

"We should head home," she said after a few more uncomfortable moments that felt like long minutes. "Rupak, you must be tired."

"Not before the soup!" Mr. Jha said. "There's chilled soup."

Mr. Chopra put his wineglass, still half full, down on the coffee table.

"What happened? Don't you like that wine?" Mr. Jha said. "It's good wine."

"It is," Mr. Chopra said. Everyone wanted to get up, but nobody moved. "You just poured a bit too much for me. I'm not much of a wine drinker. And my wife is right, we really should get going."

Mr. Jha nodded absentmindedly and continued, "Drugs. He was kicked out for drugs. Expelled. For drugs."

"Anil," Mrs. Jha said. "That's enough."

"Papa," Rupak started.

"He had to leave the university and the country," Mr. Jha said, shaking his head now but also smiling.

"You know what? I'm starting to get worried that I left the oven on," Mrs. Chopra said. "I really should go home and check on it. You know how maids are — they're probably watching television in the back and won't even notice until the whole house burns down around them."

"Of course," Mrs. Jha said. "We can continue this some other —"

"I'll go!" Mr. Jha said, and jumped up. "I'll go and check the stove. Bindu, serve the soup. You can't leave before the soup. It's chilled soup. Like they serve on *MasterChef.* I'll just dart over and check your stove and be back in two minutes flat. Meanwhile, you start with the soup. How convenient to live next to each other, isn't it? No reason to go home early. Let the neighbors help, like you said, Dinesh. Take advantage of the neighbors."

With that, Mr. Jha rushed out his front door into the dark night before anybody could stop him.

"Good evening, good evening, Balwinder. No need to get up. I'll let myself in. Stay where you are. I'm just doing a quick favor for Mrs. Chopra and then I'll be gone," Mr. Jha said. "And Balwinder, please tell your agency to send a guard for us to interview. Tomorrow. We can do it tomorrow. I want a guard."

The cobblestones on the Chopras' driveway crunched under his white sneakers, which were looking bright in the moonlight. He entered the foyer of the Chopras' home and looked up at the mural on the ceiling. He walked through the quiet living room toward the kitchen at the back — the ground floor of their home was designed almost exactly the same as the Jhas' home. He could hear the television on in the back room. Everything in this home felt expensive. He took his sneakers and socks off and let his feet sink into the thick carpet in the living room. He stroked the smooth head of the Buddha bust as he walked past it. He stopped and kneeled and touched his hot cheek against the cool stone.

He continued past the dining room to the

kitchen. The home was perfect, not a thing out of place yet not a trace of the maids, except for the faint sounds of the television from the back. But the kitchen, their kitchen wasn't as nice. A wooden stepladder leaned against the wall, a cobweb thick under one of the steps. Under it, on a yellowed newspaper, lay a rusted paint can and a hardened paintbrush. He looked at the kitchen counter and noticed a round metal spice box, the kind every home in Mayur Palli had and he was certain no house in Gurgaon had. The fridge handle was sticky. The faucet dripped. Mr. Jha leaned against the fridge and steadied his breathing, tied it to the sound of the drip — breathe in for two drips, out for two. He should hurry. If he didn't go back home, one of them would come looking for him. The stove wasn't on; he knew it wouldn't be. Mr. Jha walked back out to the dining room, then the living room.

He stopped to put on his socks and sneakers. The light from the foyer trickled into the living room. He had one sock on but he left the remaining sock and shoes on the floor in the living room and walked into the foyer and looked up at the Sistine Chapel. The painting was ugly, the lines too harsh, and the colors too basic.

410

He walked back through the living room and dining room to the kitchen and kneeled by the paint can. He used the wooden tip of the paintbrush handle to wedge the lid open. The paint was yellow. Mr. Jha dipped the hardened bristles into the paint, stood, and picked up the stepladder. He didn't like spiders. He was, in fact, quite scared of spiders and under any other circumstances, he would have first used something to clean the cobweb off before touching the ladder, but he had no time tonight. He took the ladder and paintbrush back out to the foyer, a series of yellow paint drops marking his path behind him. The leg of the ladder bumped a shelf in the living room on the way, and a small glass figurine of a butterfly tumbled to the ground and shattered. Mr. Jha stopped. He leaned the ladder against the wall and used his socked foot to kick the broken pieces under the shelf. He picked the ladder up and continued to the foyer.

He placed it down and looked up, the paintbrush now hanging limply from his hand, paint pooling under it, where he stood. The ceiling was domed here and he could see that the top would be difficult to reach. They say you aren't supposed to climb to the top platform of a stepladder.

But then they say a lot of things, Mr. Jha reasoned with himself. They say every generation should be more successful than the previous one, but they had clearly never lived in Gurgaon. He climbed up the ladder as it creaked under his weight. Slowly he reached the top, one foot still socked, one still bare. He stood upright. With his left hand he held the light that hung about a foot down from the ceiling and steadied himself. With the paintbrush in his right hand, he reached toward the sky, toward the center of the mural. He would need to perch higher on his toes. The ladder shifted slightly and Mr. Jha tightened his grasp around the metal rod of the light. With the brush, he reached up and pulled a small yellow streak against the painting. He needed a bit more height. A drop of yellow paint dripped onto his forehead and blended with his sweat. Mr. Jha shook his head to stop it from falling into his eye. He reached higher as he heard behind him, "Papa? Papa? What are you doing?"

Mr. Jha turned to look and saw his son standing in the doorway. As he turned, the ladder creaked and swayed and gave way below him. Rupak reacted immediately. When he was growing up, his father had always taught him that if someone was

412

about to fall from a ladder or a chair or a stool, you had to rush to grab the person, not the ladder or chair or stool. The person — it was the person who needed protecting. Rupak remembered standing guard as his father climbed on stools and chairs in Mayur Palli to change lightbulbs or fix the time on clocks. He had always stood there nervously, unsure he was big enough to save his father from a fall. But his father never fell. Rupak thought of that as he rushed to his father. Mr. Jha fell into his son's arms. Rupak fell to the ground. His father, with one sock on, fell on him. The paintbrush fell on the floor beside them. The wooden ladder fell on them both. A small spider scrambled off the ladder and down Mr. Jha's pant leg.

Mrs. Jha came to the door, followed by Mr. and Mrs. Chopra and Johnny, to see what was taking her husband so long. Balwinder came running up behind them and said in Hindi, "He's gone mad?"

Everyone else remained where they were. Rupak could feel his father breathing heavily on top of him. He thought he felt him trembling and he wanted to put his arms around his father. There was a click and Rupak looked toward the door and saw Balwinder putting his phone away, having taken

413

a picture.

"Balwinder, get out," Mr. Chopra said. "I should never have bought you a phone with a camera."

"I . . ." Mr. Jha stuttered. "I was . . ."

Mrs. Jha wanted to go to him but she didn't move.

"Papa . . ." Rupak started, unsure how to go on. "Papa has been to the Sistine Chapel. He loves it. And he was trying to correct one of the . . ." Rupak looked up at the ceiling. There wasn't any yellow anywhere. "Rays of sunshine? There's some more sun right in the middle of the original."

"What? There's no sunlight . . ." Mrs. Chopra said.

"He's right," Mrs. Jha said. "The sun. Anil has always been such a fan of the Sistine Chapel. And he's such a perfectionist, you know. That's why he's so successful, but sometimes it goes too far."

Rupak got up and helped his father up. They left the ladder and the paintbrush on the ground. Rupak guided his father to the door, where his mother took over, putting her arm through her husband's and leading him out. Rupak looked into the living room, found his father's shoes and second sock, and picked them up.

"It was very nice meeting you tonight," he

said to the Chopras, then followed his parents out into the darkness.

TWENTY-SIX

"She's too old to be getting married," Mr. Jha said. It was Saturday afternoon and he was lying on the sofa, a crystal poking him in the back, blankly flipping channels. A flannel blanket was wrapped around his legs. He had been avoiding discussing Mrs. Ray's wedding celebration ever since she had announced it three weeks ago.

"It's a mockery of the whole institution," he continued. He changed the channel again from the news about an unexpected winter downpour in Bangalore to a channel that played Bollywood songs on a loop. "There's nothing good on television these days."

"Stop wasting time watching television every evening. You need to get out," Mrs. Jha said. She was sitting on the chair near him, putting an extra hook on her blouse because, much to her pleasure, she seemed to have lost a bit of weight since returning from New York. "And there's no such thing as too old to be getting married. We should be happy for her. I'm sad that she's moving to Chandigarh, but it's very exciting for her. Reema deserves this."

"They've only known each other for a few months," Mr. Jha said. "Besides, it's too cold to even go outside. I wouldn't be surprised if it starts to snow in Delhi one of these years."

He adjusted his blanket.

"They call these 'throws' in America, Bindu," he said. "You're meant to just casually throw it on the sofa, not kccp it neatly folded away in the closet."

"We had only met twice before we got married, Anil. These things don't matter. In many ways online dating is similar to arranged marriage. I think gradually people are returning to that way of doing things."

"There's an app now that lets you find someone according to distance — so you can say you want to find a person within only a one-kilometer radius and bam, you can marry your neighbor," Mr. Jha said.

"I don't think those programs are for marriage," Mrs. Jha said. "Tonight will do us good. All three of us just need an evening out. Reema has asked Rupak to film the whole reception. He's saying he's going to

417

edit it and make it into a video to give them. The dinner starts at eight p.m. If we leave at seven forty-five, that should give us enough time. Although I'm not quite sure how parking works."

"How will it take only fifteen minutes to get there? Where is it? If it's outdoors, I don't think we should go. It's too cold in Delhi this time of year," Mr. Jha said. "I don't want to get sick. I don't want you to get sick."

"It's at the LRC," Mrs. Jha said. "Maybe we can even look into a membership while we're there. Surely that'll cheer you up."

"The LRC? Where every single person from this neighborhood will be? Interfering in everyone's business? Rupak really wants to go?"

"He's already gone. He wanted to set up his equipment; he rented everything from a shop in INA Market — he said he didn't want to buy new equipment until he could prove he was good at it. He'll meet us there." Mrs. Jha stood up and picked up her blouse and her sewing kit. "And he invited Serena along as well, so he's picking her up. She's in town for the holidays and I think it'll be nice for all of us to see her."

"He's seeing Serena again? Bindu, doesn't it worry you that she would put up with him after what he did?"

It was true that Mrs. Jha was surprised that Serena was coming — from everything Rupak had said about her after their Ithaca trip, she got the distinct feeling that Rupak and Serena didn't actually get along. She hoped Rupak wasn't forcing things just because he felt he ought to. As upset as Mrs. Jha was about his actions in Ithaca, she didn't want him to live his life with some false sense of duty. She wanted him to be happy. But she was glad Serena would be there, because having an outsider in the midst always makes things easier. Knowing they could not discuss any private family matters took the pressure off needing to discuss private family matters.

"Anil, this isn't about Rupak, or you, or me. This is about Reema and Upen. And we are going. Get up, get ready, and plan to leave the house at seven forty-five," Mrs. Jha said. "And put the blanket away when you get up. It makes the living room look messy."

"I'm not at all happy about this," Mr. Jha said. "And it's called a throw, not a blanket."

They were both silent for some time.

"Bindu," Mr. Jha said.

She looked over at him. He had taken his glasses off and was rubbing his eyes.

"Bindu. Do you think if we asked the Ramaswamys to leave early, they would? I could return the rent they've paid so far."

Mrs. Jha said nothing. She wanted to go over to him, but her body felt too heavy.

After picking up his equipment from INA Market, Rupak drove to Khan Market to get Serena. He wasn't feeling particularly excited about seeing her, but he was grateful that she had agreed to come tonight. His parents were making a real effort to forgive him and resume some sort of normalcy, so he still felt he owed them Serena even though it was Elizabeth he couldn't stop thinking about.

Rupak was fiddling with the radio tuner, trying to find a channel that played anything other than Bollywood hits or the news, when Serena approached the car and knocked on the window. She was holding a cup of take-out coffee from Café Turtle, and her hair was loose and more wavy because of the humidity, and she was wearing a bindi on her forehead that made her dark kohl-lined eyes somehow look even bigger. She smiled at him as he unlocked the doors. When she got in, he noticed that she was wearing an off-white salwar kameez with a green and gold dupatta draped like a scarf around her neck, and was carrying a cloth bag. She certainly looked beautiful but her clothes were completely inappropriate for the LRC. He had assumed she would be wearing jeans and heels like she always wore in Ithaca.

"You look nice," Rupak said, hoping she would respond with an explanation for why she was dressed like this.

"Thank you. I love being back in my Indian clothes," Serena said.

"It's strange seeing you in Delhi."

"I can't believe we're going to the famous LRC. I never thought I'd set foot in there," Serena said, as if she could read his mind.

"Do you know much about it?"

"I know that they frown upon Indian clothes. On Indians anyway. I'm sure they'd be thrilled if a white hippie showed up wearing a shabby kurta. Right?"

Rupak didn't answer. He was irritated that she was trying to turn dinner into a statement of some sort.

"How are all your friends in Ithaca? Is everyone back in Delhi for the holidays?" he said.

At the Moti Bagh intersection, on the pavement, a young girl sat in a torn salwar kameez, two sizes too large, her face dirty and her hair matted. She was watching over a toddler who sat between her legs, naked with dried snot on his face. A man with one arm moved from car to car selling strings of fresh jasmine flowers wrapped in newspaper.

"Uncle! Uncle!" Serena called out to him, and turned to Rupak and said, "I've seen him on this corner for years. I wonder if he'll remember me."

The man came over.

"How are you, Uncle?" Serena said in Hindi.

"Thirty rupees for a bunch, fifty for two," the man said, not responding in the slightest to Serena's attempted familiarity.

"The price has gone up," Serena turned and said to Rupak. "Just one, please. You're looking well, Uncle."

The light changed to green and cars were honking from behind them and circling around to get past them.

"Madam, please hurry," the man said, looking over his shoulder toward the impatient cars behind them.

"Membership card, sir," the guard at the LRC said to Mr. Jha.

"We aren't members," Mr. Jha said. He looked down the tree-lined driveway of the LRC and tried to imagine himself being a member here, coming in his gym clothes for a hit of tennis or a few swings of golf. Were those the right terms? Or was it a swing of tennis and a hit of golf?

"Yet." Mrs. Jha undid her seat belt and leaned across from the passenger seat. "Jhas. We're here for the wedding dinner for Reema . . . Ray? Chopra? Did she change her name? Maybe it's under Upen Chopra?"

"Do widows change their names back to their maiden name after the husband dies?" Mr. Jha asked his wife.

"Mr. Anil Kumar Jha?" the guard said, holding up a sheet of paper with a list of names on it.

Mr. Jha nodded. Mrs. Jha sat back upright in her seat. The guard handed Mr. Jha a red plastic card and said, "Sir, please keep this carefully to return at the exit gate. For security purposes. Your party is in the back lawns called Peacock Haven. You can give your car to the valet at the main entrance at the end of this driveway."

"He didn't check our ID. I could have just nodded and not actually been Anil Kumar Jha," Mr. Jha said as he drove slowly, very slowly down the driveway. "I really don't think I should be here, Bindu."

Mrs. Jha put her hand on her husband's hand on the gear.

"It will be a nice evening," she said. "And if you hate it, we'll leave. Okay?"

Mr. Jha nodded. They had arrived at the end of the driveway, where the valet drivers were waiting in black pants and white tucked-in shirts. The entrance was large and regal with dim lighting and five-foot-tall vases with purple bougainvilleas spilling out. The awning was fitted with heat lamps and Mr. and Mrs. Jha stepped out of their car into the outdoor warmth in the middle of the Delhi cold. Mrs. Jha looked up at the warm yellow glow above.

"This feels even less like Delhi than the rest of Gurgaon. Do you want to get one of those for our front entrance too?" she said with a laugh.

Mr. Jha said nothing and handed the car keys to the valet driver.

"Where's the Peacock Haven?" Mrs. Jha asked the valet. "We're here for the wedding reception."

"That's the back lawn. It's quite a walk so you can just take one of our rickshaws," the valet said, and whistled toward the row of three-wheeled auto-rickshaws that was parked to the right of the main entrance. They looked almost like the regular rickety auto-rickshaws of Delhi except that each one was brightly painted in a different style.

"We have to take a rickshaw from here?" Mr. Jha asked.

"Yes, sir," the valet said. "They are solar powered and each rickshaw has been hand-painted by a contemporary artist from Delhi."

A rickshaw with a Technicolor painting of the Taj Mahal on it pulled up, driven by a man wearing a crisp white kurta pajama with a red turban perched on his head. Mr. Jha had spent most of his life avoiding getting in auto-rickshaws, but now he was stepping from his Mercedes into one. He got into the rickshaw behind his wife as the valet driver took his Mercedes away to the parking spot.

"What a lovely idea. Too many people avoid rickshaws these days. This is nice," she said.

"Seems a little gimmicky," Mr. Jha said. It was bad enough that the local trains were getting popular, but now rickshaws?

"Will you please try to enjoy yourself today?"

"I'm just surprised that you like this," Mr. Jha said. "I thought you hated everything about Gurgaon."

"I never said I hated Gurgaon. It's just very different from what we're used to, that's all."

"You don't want a guard, you didn't want me to join the LRC, you want Rupak to keep studying, you don't wear diamonds. It's understandable that I'm surprised that you like these rickshaws. Isn't this the equivalent of when that Hollywood actress wore a bindi and you got annoyed about it being culturally inappropriate?"

"That's different. And in any case, wanting Rupak to keep studying has nothing to do with Gurgaon. I want our son to be like you — I want him to work hard and earn his success. And as for the LRC, I admit that I'm surprised. So far it seems quite tastefully done. I may have been wrong about it."

Mrs. Jha just wanted him to enjoy this world again. It had been a difficult few weeks. It had been a difficult year but they had to move on. They had to be happy.

"Peacock Haven," the rickshaw driver said.

Mr. and Mrs. Jha stepped out of the rickshaw and walked toward the large lawn. Big round bouquets of multicolored flowers dangled down from the trees on strings made of more fresh flowers. The lawn was dotted with metal heat lamps that gave off a hazy glow. A DJ console was set up at the back and a Frank Sinatra song played loudly. There were several stations set up for food — kebabs, pastas, pizza, a taco and burrito station, one section for Chinese food — vegetarian and nonvegetarian, one table just for Burmese khausuey, and a whole different section for desserts from all around the world. At all four corners of the lawn, there were bars set up and even from the entrance Mr. Jha could see that it was all imported top-shelf liquor and wine.

"Who are all these people?" Mr. Jha whispered to his wife.

"Just regular club members," Mrs. Jha said. "Reema said they do this every Saturday night at the LRC. And members are allowed to invite guests. They haven't set this up just for their reception. They just added us and the Guptas as guests."

"This is a regular Saturday night here?" Mr. Jha asked. He looked around at the people dressed in Delhi's Saturday best. There were women in tight bandage dresses with high heels that were digging into the grass every time they stood still. Some wore expensive designer saris with embroidered shawls or heavy furs over their shoulders. The men mostly wore suits, some with fashionable black coats that came all the way down to their ankles. A few wore turtlenecks under their blazers. It was easier to fit in, in the winter, Mr. Jha thought. He was also wearing a plain black suit with a blue button-down shirt and a black tie. And his wife, even though she was once again wearing one of her monochromatic sari-blouse combinations, had a dark red cardigan and a darker red shawl covering her shoulders that added a warmth to her face and made her look beautiful even though you could hardly even tell she had diamond earrings on, they were so small.

"Not quite the monthly Mayur Palli meetings, is it?" Mrs. Jha said. "Come on. Let's go find the happy couple."

As they walked across the lawn, Mr. Chopra saw them and boomed, "Jha! There you are! Where have you vanished?"

Getting a drink, he mouthed to Mr. Chopra, and pointed toward the bar. "Quick," he whispered to his wife. "Move quickly before he comes up to us."

"You're going to have to talk to him. Reema just married his brother."

"Later. We'll do that later. Let's get a drink first."

"Anil," Mrs. Jha said. But then she stopped. What was there to say? Nothing had been said after the last time they had seen the Chopras, and nothing could be said now.

"Come," she said. "Let's go to the bar.

Isn't it nice that nobody here knows us?"

As they walked toward the bar, a couple about the same age as them stopped and looked at them walking. Mrs. Jha smiled, trying to be friendly. They needed more friends in this neighborhood. But then the wife leaned forward and whispered to her husband, who looked at them more carefully, and then they both turned away. Mrs. Jha noticed her husband look at them and then look down at the ground for the rest of the walk to the bar.

Two young boys who looked about fifteen came up and asked the bartender for two glasses of vodka.

"My father will kill me," one of them said.

"That's why we're getting vodka. He'll think it's water," the other one said.

The bartender looked around, unsure what to do.

"I don't think we're supposed to serve you alcohol," he said quietly.

"There's no rules here," one of the boys said. "My father's on the board of the club and he won't be happy to hear I was denied something."

The waiter put out two glasses and filled them to the brim with ice.

"No, no, no," said the same boy. "I don't just want a glass of ice with a thimble of vodka, man. Just give us like four or five cubes of ice and fill the rest up with vodka."

The waiter did as the fifteen-year-old demanded, and the two boys took their glasses and walked away.

"Black Label, on the rocks," Mr. Jha said to the bartender, who was wearing a tie that was similar to his, equally narrow. "Make it a double."

"And I'll have a Limca, please. No ice," Mrs. Jha said.

"Bindu!" Mrs. Ray said, rushing toward the bar toward the Jhas. She was wearing a gold chiffon sari and, despite the chill in the air, no shawl or sweater. Her hair was pulled into a low chignon and Mrs. Jha marveled at how beautiful her friend looked.

"I feel like a twenty-year-old," Mrs. Ray laughed. "I'm wearing sindoor. I haven't bothered putting on sindoor since the day I got married last time."

She pointed at the part in her hair, where a stroke of red vermillion marked her as a married woman. Mrs. Jha had also stopped wearing sindoor nearly thirty years ago. It had seemed dated and sexist to her, but now it suddenly looked like a symbol of rebellion, or, at least, love and commitment.

"Congratulations," Mrs. Jha said. She

stepped forward and pulled Mrs. Ray into a hug.

"Life is so strange," Mrs. Ray said. "Is this all absurd?"

"It's a little odd," Mr. Jha said, sipping his whiskey. "But congratulations. You look lovely."

Mrs. Jha smiled at her husband.

"You do look lovely. And odd is wonderful. And this club is much nicer than I had expected," Mrs. Jha said.

"It really is. I'm glad Upen insisted on doing the dinner here," Mrs. Ray said. "But don't fill up on the snacks. Just have a few drinks, and then we've made reservations at the Chinese restaurant at the main clubhouse for dinner — just us and the Chopras."

"Aren't the Guptas coming as well?" Mrs. Jha said. "It's been so long since we've seen them."

"They were going to," Mrs. Ray said. "I spoke first to Mr. Gupta on the phone and he was so nice and sounded happy for me and said they would come. Then this morning he called me and said something urgent had come up and they wouldn't be able to make it. Not everyone is as excited about my wedding, I suppose."

"Mrs. Gupta must have refused to attend," Mrs. Jha said. "Anyway, never mind. All that doesn't matter now."

"It hasn't been easy in Mayur Palli, Bindu. But Shatrugan cried when I told him — said something about me deserving love. It was quite sweet but he needs to stop watching all those Hindi soap operas. And Mr. and Mrs. De sent over a box of Bengali sandesh."

"So just the Chopras and us?" Mr. Jha asked, taking a large sip of his whiskey.

"And the two sons. After Rupak has finished all his hard work. Bindu, Anil — that son of yours has made us as proud as we all expected. He's such a professional. Who is that young woman with him? I didn't know he had a special friend."

"She's just a friend from Ithaca," Mr. Jha said. "Nothing important. Where is he?"

"He's off filming shots around the club to add to the footage," Mrs. Ray said. "And you heard that he wouldn't accept any payment either? He's a wonderful boy. I think it's good that he's come back to India — we need more young men like him."

"We do," Mrs. Jha said. "Reverse brain drain — it's time to bring the talent home."

"Exactly," Mrs. Ray said. "For whatever reason it may be, it's a good thing he's here now. It'll be nice for you two as well. Now

432

let me go find Upen and bring him over to say hello."

With that, Mrs. Ray walked back toward the center of the lawn to look for her husband.

"What did she mean by that?" Mr. Jha said, putting his empty glass down on the bar. "Does she know? Does everyone know? What does everyone know?"

He looked around the lawn to see if anyone was looking at him.

"It doesn't matter. What matters is, like she said, that Rupak is here and he's still as intelligent and wonderful as he was before this fiasco," Mrs. Jha said. "Do you want another drink? I think I'll try a glass of wine, or champagne. Anil, the last time we drank champagne was in New York. Gosh, that feels like a lifetime ago, doesn't it?"

She turned to the bartender and said, "Do you have any champagne?"

"No, madam, sorry. But will a white wine spritzer do?" the bartender asked.

"You know what? I'll try that, yes. And another Black Label on the rocks for my husband. Just a single, please."

Mrs. Ray came back holding Upen's hand. Mrs. Jha looked away, not used to such physical displays of affection.

"Anil, Bindu, I'm so glad you came tonight," Upen said with a smile. "Well, this is all thanks to you after all."

"Congratulations, Upen," Mrs. Jha said. Next to her Mr. Jha nodded, looking straight at Upen's large hand wrapped around Mrs. Ray's. If he tried to hold his wife's hand, she would think he'd lost his balance, he thought.

"I hope you don't mind that I'm stealing your friend away to Chandigarh for a little while," Upen said. "She's nervous about leaving Delhi, but I think she'll enjoy Chandigarh."

"New beginnings can be difficult but nice," Mrs. Jha said. "We're still adjusting to Gurgaon."

"I've heard," Upen said. "I mean, I haven't heard anything specific. I haven't heard anything. I just mean yes, yes, you are right. New beginnings can indeed be difficult but nice. You will have to plan a trip to Chandigarh soon."

"Why don't you two finish your drink and then make your way to the main restaurant?" Mrs. Ray said. "We'll see if we can round up everyone else."

"Do Upen and Mrs. Ray know?" Mr. Jha asked his wife after Mrs. Ray and Upen walked away. "Bindu, I'm too tired to be here tonight. Please can we go home?

Reema will understand. We can celebrate with them later, privately."

Mrs. Jha was tired as well. She was tired of fighting and pretending everything was okay. The Chopras must have told Upen, who must have told Mrs. Ray, who must be thinking of her friend with such pity.

"Fine," she said. "Let's just go. I'm tired as well. I'll just finish my drink and then we can leave."

As Mr. and Mrs. Jha stood in silence finishing their drinks and looking out at the crowd, three women approached the bar, all looking to be in their midforties, with plumped-up lips and wavy thick hair. One was wearing a tight purple kurta with a slit up the leg, and wide black patiala pants underneath, with wedge-heeled boots and a leather jacket on top. Another was wearing a dark blue dress that she kept having to pull down and adjust over her thighs. She was wearing a brown fur coat to keep warm and she was slim but her knees looked crumpled. And the third was wearing a flowing long patterned kaftan-style dress with multi-colored flowers on it with an open, ankle-length white sweater that reached to the ground.

The Jhas stepped to the side with their drinks and watched this cluster of women.

435

Two of them ordered Grey Goose and soda and one ordered a glass of sangria, with extra rum.

"I hear he's going back to Chandigarh," one of them said. "Can you imagine wearing sindoor in your part at that age? It's embarrassing. Not to mention that cheap-looking gold sari she has on."

"Don't worry, it won't last," another one said.

"I'm not worried. I'm not interested in him," the first one said. "I was just telling you what I heard."

The third, the one in the long dress who had ordered the sangria and already seemed quite drunk, ignored the other two and said, "Have either of you spent much time in the Maldives? Rakesh wants to go and I'm worried I'll be dreadfully bored."

"You will, darling. There's nothing to do there. You're not going to want to go diving and there's absolutely no shopping. Go to Mallorca, it's much better."

"Take a skiing vacation. That's what we did last year, and it's so cozy to sit in the log cabins all bundled up with some mulled wine."

"That's not a bad idea," the first one said. "I hardly get to wear my heavy winter clothes in Delhi."

"We just got back from New York," Mrs. Jha interjected.

The three women looked at her and did not respond for a moment. They looked behind her at Mr. Jha and then back at each other. One of them finally said, "Well, New York is always an option. It never loses its charm."

Mrs. Jha was relieved that they had not laughed in her face.

"It was lovely," she continued.

"We saw the musical *Cats*," Mr. Jha added, also pleased that these women were talking to them.

"I've seen *Cats*," the one in the long dress said. "I saw three Broadway shows when I was there last time, can you believe it? Oh, you're right. I do miss New York. Maybe it's best to go back there again. I haven't been in almost a year. It's a wonderful idea."

"Absolutely," Mr. Jha said. "Always a good excuse to go to Tiffany's."

The three women laughed and nodded in agreement and sipped their drinks.

Rupak, with his camera draped around his shoulder, came to his parents.

"Where's Serena?" Mrs. Jha asked.

"In the bathroom. Reema Aunty told me you were here already," he said. "I'm enjoying shooting this — it's a strange part of the city. I probably shouldn't have invited her tonight when I'm trying to work."

"Oh, are you a photographer?" one of the women cooed at him while touching his upper arm. Mrs. Jha looked alarmed. She had never seen women, especially older women, treating her son like this. Rupak looked toward his parents. Mrs. Jha pretended not to notice, and Rupak, convinced that she hadn't, looked back at the woman, smiled, and said, "Film. I want to make films. Here, say hello. It's a wedding video."

Rupak lifted the camera up and pointed it at the woman, who laughed and tossed her hair over her shoulder and said, "Men with cameras are always charming."

Mrs. Jha wanted to pull Rupak back by the arm and hold him close to her, but she resisted.

"I haven't seen you here before," the woman in the short dress and fur jacket said. "Are you members of the club?"

"We only just moved to Gurgaon," Mrs. Jha said.

"But we are hoping to join the club. We thought we would check it out," Mr. Jha added.

"Well, I hope you do, director sir," the woman in the short dress said to Rupak, and the other two laughed. Mr. Jha also laughed along. Look at Rupak charming everyone. His son, his genes. He looked over at his wife, who was not laughing.

Mr. and Mrs. Chopra came to the bar to find the Jhas. Mrs. Chopra was wearing yet another heavy sari with gems stitched into it. Her jewelry sparkled and she was carrying a small Birkin bag. Mrs. Jha had heard that you had to put your name on a waitlist to get a Birkin bag in India.

"Anil, where have you been?" Mr. Chopra said, slapping Mr. Jha on the back. "You've all but vanished."

"We've been around. Just a bit busy," Mr. Jha said.

Serena approached the group then, and nobody reacted except for Mrs. Jha, who noted that Serena was dressed rather casually for the evening — had Rupak not told her that it was a formal event? Never mind. Mrs. Jha gave her a hug.

"Rupak, you have an assistant already?" Mr. Chopra said, his hand still on Mr. Jha's shoulder. "Good to see all of you here tonight."

Who would say that, Mr. Jha wondered nervously. Why had they even come tonight? It had seemed until now that everyone in Gurgaon lived in their own big homes and paid no attention to the neighbors, but suddenly this felt exactly like Mayur Palli. Worse. At least there the neighbors liked each other despite the gossip. At least there Mr. and Mrs. De would still send a box of sweets to Mrs. Ray even though she had accused him of stealing her yoga pants.

"Seema, Pinky, Delilah, have you met our new neighbors?" Mr. Chopra said to the three women standing next to them.

"Neighbors?" the one in the short dress said.

"You mean the . . . ," the one in the kurta trailed off.

Seema, Pinky, Delilah? Those were really their names, Mrs. Jha thought. Who had their parents been? With a name like Delilah, of course you would be wearing a long kaftan dress and ankle-length white flowing cardigan on a Saturday night. With a name like Delilah, you would never be wearing a neatly ironed sari.

"The Jhas. Mr. and Mrs. Anil Jha. And their son, Rupak," Mr. Chopra finished.

"Oh . . . ," the one in the dress said. "The Jhas."

"Oh my God," the one in the kurta said. "Yes, you're the . . . my driver . . . my guard . . ." She tried to stop herself from laughing. She turned her face into her shoulder to muffle the sound. The woman

440

in the dress tugged it down and sipped from her glass, smirking into it while looking the Jhas up and down.

"What? What happened?" Delilah said. "And I've finished my sangria already. It was mostly ice anyway. Why are you two laughing?"

"Nothing," the one in the kurta said, still stifling laughter. "We aren't laughing. Nothing. We'll tell you later. And that drink was not mostly ice. You're drunk."

"What will you tell me later?" Delilah said, while motioning to the bartender to get her another drink. "What about your driver and guard?"

"Shh, forget it," the one in the kurta said. "These are the Jhas. Mr. and Mrs. Jha. The new neighbors."

"The Jhas? The Chopras' new neighbor!" The woman in the kaftan dress spun away from the bar and slurred loudly. "The one who fell off the ladder. Who your guard told your driver about? The ones from East Delhi!"

The woman in the kaftan dress laughed with less discretion than her two friends, staring straight at Mr. Jha, who wasn't breathing. Next to him his wife had moved a few inches away without even realizing, and Rupak had quietly lowered his camera.

"That's right," Mr. Chopra said, putting his hand again on Mr. Jha's shoulder. "Our new neighbors. Mr. Jha here is the one you must have heard fell off a ladder while trying to fix a part of the painting on our foyer ceiling. He's been to Italy and has seen the real Sistine Chapel, you see. What a wonderful new neighbor to have. Have you ladies been to Italy?"

"Apparently there's some sunlight in the middle of the painting," Mrs. Chopra added confidently.

Rupak looked surprised. Everyone looked a little surprised.

"It's true," Rupak said. "And yes, you really should visit Italy. It's beautiful."

"It really is," Mrs. Jha added. "Forget New York. If you haven't been to Italy, that's where you must go."

"You must," Mr. Chopra said. "Come along, then. We must get going. Let's go find the happy couple and head to dinner. You ladies enjoy your evening."

The Chopras turned and walked away toward the main dining hall. A few steps behind, Mrs. Jha took her husband's glass from his hand and put it and her wineglass down on the bar, smiled and said good-bye to the three women, grabbed her husband by the elbow, and led him after the Chopras.

Rupak glanced at the women one last time, then turned his camera on his parents walking away.

"What was that all about?" Serena asked. "Your father was painting their ceiling?"

"Nothing, don't worry about it," Rupak said, starting to walk through the crowd with his camera on.

"Is this whole night like an audition for your parents to become members of this club?"

Rupak ignored her and kept walking until he had reached the far edge of the lawn, where there were only staff members entering and exiting with platters of appetizers. One of the waiters came out with a platter of what looked like miniature tacos.

"Desi tacos, madam?" he said to Serena. "They're pulled pork vindaloo wrapped in mini dosas."

"How is that a taco?" Serena said, picking one up and biting into it. She turned to Rupak. "Why can't they just call it what it is?"

"What is it?" Rupak said.

"Pulled pork vindaloo wrapped in a mini dosa, like he said."

"That doesn't have quite the same ring to it as a desi taco, Serena," Rupak said.

Serena put the second bite into her mouth and said, "It's really good, though. I'll give them that."

Rupak didn't answer and kept filming instead. He wondered where Elizabeth was right now. Probably in Florida on vacation. If she were here with him today, this would all be so different. It would all be fun, despite everything working hard to make it not fun.

"Why did you wear that outfit today?" he said to Serena.

"What do you mean?"

"You know what I mean. I told you where we were going. You knew what the LRC is like. Why did you wear that outfit?"

"Am I supposed to wear a tight skirt or something? This is India. I'm wearing Indian clothes. I think it's ridiculous that everyone here thinks wearing short dresses makes you trendy."

"Come on, Serena. You're hardly the type to wear a sari every day. I know you prefer jeans. I've met your friends. What is this Mother India thing all of a sudden?"

"Did you invite me here just to fight with me?" Serena said. "I don't even know why I agreed to come today. I guess I was hoping that somehow you'd be different. But I'm seeing you here in India and I'm realizing you're just another rich kid coasting along on Daddy's money. Are you even embarrassed that you got kicked out of grad school? This is going to be your life now? I can't believe your family is the type to want to try to join a club like this."

"You've done nothing but complain the whole time we've been here," Rupak said. "What do you want? Do you want everyone here to donate all their money and never travel again and never enjoy themselves? There are people a lot poorer than you and I don't see you giving up your life in America and moving into a slum. Is your life the exact boundary of what's acceptable? Anything more becomes crass, but you having a two hundred rupee cup of coffee at Khan Market is fine? I bet someone who couldn't afford that could also be pretty quick to pretend to look down on it."

"Why did you invite me tonight? Not just tonight, but why did you invite me to meet your parents in Ithaca? For their sake? Do I tick off some box on a checklist of things you have to give them in exchange for their money? MBA, Indian woman, what else have you promised them?"

Rupak switched off his camera and let it rest around his neck. He turned to face Serena and looked straight into her eyes.

"Yes," he said. "That's exactly why I invited you."

"What?" Serena said.

"You're completely right," Rupak said. "And I'm actually glad you said it out loud because I need to hear someone else say it so I can process how ridiculous it is, how ridiculous I've been. I've been an idiot. I lost someone I'm in love with and I'm about to lose a good friend."

"You were in love with me?" Serena asked.

"No. I was in love with someone else," Rupak said. "And I was a coward. And I'm being a coward again now. And I have to stop. Mrs. Ray is a widow who is having a love marriage. My father came out today to face the people he embarrassed himself in front of a month ago. And I invited you only to try to make my parents happy. You are completely right."

"I'm going to go," Serena said. "You need to get your life together. I hope you and your family find whatever it is you're all looking for."

"I think we have," Rupak said. For the first time since his father had come home from work and said, "Rupak, Bindu, don't get too excited yet, this is early stages but I got a very interesting phone call today," Rupak felt safe again. That night, Mr. and Mrs. Jha had drunk Old Monk and laughed together until two a.m. and Rupak had felt a strange sense of doom that now he would never get out of his family's shadow. And tonight, standing in a shadowed corner of the lawns of the LRC, he finally felt a hint of that doom lifting.

"I'm sorry, Serena," he said, and walked toward the Chinese restaurant to find his family.

TWENTY-SEVEN

Rupak entered the dining hall and sat down next to his mother.

"Where did Serena go?" his mother asked.

"She left," he said. "Ma, I've made a huge mistake."

All around them the restaurant buzzed with other families and conversation and the clink of cutlery against plates. Waiters in Chinese-inspired silk red shirts and plain black trousers wove in and out of the tables with trays full of food or empty bowls and plates. Paintings of red dragons covered the walls, and the lights were shaped like lanterns that hung from the ceiling. The theme of dark wood and red accents gave the whole restaurant a warm glow.

"I'm in love with a woman in America. An American woman," Rupak said. "Her name is Elizabeth and she's from Florida and I think you'd really like her, but I also think I may never see her again."

Rupak braced himself to see his mother's disappointment, her sadness, her alienation. But instead she patted his hand and said, "Never say never. It's impossible to predict the future. You tell me about her when we get home. And your father will be very happy to hear about this."

"Ma, she's American. White American."

Mrs. Jha nodded.

"We can send her a ticket to come and visit you. Like I said, never say never."

"What makes Indian Chinese food so tasty?" Mrs. Ray said, across the table.

"MSG. Exactly what makes it so unhealthy," Upen said.

"Everything that is tasty is bad for you, Upen," Mr. Chopra said. "But tonight we are celebrating. Friends, neighbors, good food, and new beginnings. All the MSG in the world can't stop this."

"It's bad enough you refused to eat meat even tonight," Mrs. Chopra added. "Mrs. Ray, you must make him relax more."

Mrs. Ray smiled at her and said, "Chopra. You can call me Mrs. Chopra now. Well, you should just call me Reema, but it's Reema Chopra."

"You changed your name?" Mrs. Jha asked.

Mrs. Ray nodded.

"I'm not modern enough to not take my husband's name. And I figured Ray wasn't my maiden name anyway. Who knows? There's no rules for all this."

"I like it," Rupak said. "Reema Chopra. You're a brand-new person. I should record some of this. After the meal — after the party, after the celebrations — that's where real life is, right?"

"Thank you for doing this, Rupak," Upen said. "You're good at it. You have a good eye. It's lucky for us that you're back in India."

"Thank you," Rupak said. "Here, let me show you the shot I got of the rickshaws at the entrance."

From the other side of the table, Mr. Jha watched his son get up and walk over to Upen with his camera. Two seats away, Johnny was sitting and playing with his phone. He was dressed in a tight collared T-shirt with the collar sticking up and his hair was falling across half his face. He had played with his phone all evening and hardly spoken to anyone else. He was like a bored teenager, and Mr. Jha admitted to himself that he was grateful that Rupak was different.

"Johnny, put your phone away and look at what Rupak is showing us," Mr. Chopra said, shaking his head. "Useless fellow. Learn something."

The table was peppered with empty bowls left with the lone strand of noodle or purple sliver of onion. The bowl that held the chicken Manchurian was coated with the orange film of the batter. Soy sauce and gravy drops marked the white tablecloth. Why did Indian Chinese restaurants always use white tablecloths, Mr. Jha wondered. They must have to bleach them with every wash. Unless the more expensive restaurants used brand-new tablecloths every day. Could that be? There was a spoonful of fried rice left in one of the bowls, but everyone seemed to be finished eating. The rice was right next to him and Mr. Jha was tempted to take it, but he stopped himself. He had had the right amount of food tonight. Too often at the end of a dinner party, he felt full and bloated and didn't sleep well at night, but tonight he could tell he had eaten just the perfect amount.

Wasting food was the ultimate sin when he was a child. "Waste not, want not," his aunt always used to say, and when he lived in their home he would force himself to finish every last morsel on his plate even if his stomach protested and he felt on the brink of vomiting. What did "waste not, want not" even mean, Mr. Jha now wondered. He had never questioned it when he was young, but now, instead of making sure all the food was finished, he was not finishing all the food even though he still wasn't stuffed. Had Mr. Chopra noticed, he wondered? The fried rice was closer to Mr. Jha's side of the table, but he hoped Mr. Chopra had noticed. No. Mr. Jha stopped himself. What Mr. Chopra thought didn't matter; what mattered was that his family was here, and his friends were here, and the restaurant was nice, and the food was satisfying, and everyone seemed content.

"Dessert," Mrs. Chopra said, opening the menu that the waiter had just handed her. "Let's order some dessert. They do a wonderful crème caramel here."

"That isn't very Chinese," Upen said. "But I could have one. Reema?"

"I don't usually have dessert," Mrs. Ray said. "But it's a celebration tonight, isn't it? I'll have a scoop of ice cream. The green tea one sounds quite good. Bindu? Anil? Dessert?"

Mrs. Jha looked at her husband, sitting to her left, who had hardly spoken during dinner. She usually knew exactly what he was thinking about, but tonight she wasn't sure. She wanted to tell him it would all be okay, that their son would find his way and they would help him. She wanted to talk to him about how nice it was that Mrs. Ray was now Mrs. Chopra but she was still Mrs. Ray to them. She wanted to tell him to look around the table at their friends, their neighbors, and their life. She wanted to tell him she was glad he hadn't finished the fried rice because she knows he sleeps poorly and has bad dreams when he overeats and she wanted to tell him that she was happy tonight. But that was all too much to say, so instead she said, "The crème caramel does sound good. Anil, should we share one?"

"Let's share one," Mr. Jha said. "We'll have one crème caramel with two spoons."

Mr. Jha leaned back and put his right arm on the backrest of his wife's chair, his thumb lightly touching her shoulder. Mrs. Jha gave his right knee a quick squeeze with her left hand and then put her hand on the table where everyone could see it clearly. This was their life now.

ACKNOWLEDGMENTS

My agent, Adam Eaglin.

And everyone else at the Elyse Cheney Agency. In particular, Elyse Cheney and Alex Jacobs.

My editor, Hilary Teeman.

And everyone else at Crown Publishing and Penguin Random House. In particular, Jillian Buckley, Rachel Rokicki, Molly Stern, Annsley Rosner, Kayleigh George, Terry Deal, Amy J. Schneider, Ruth Liebmann, Lara Phan, Beth Koehler, Kim Shannon, Elina Nudelman, Sarah Grimm, Kevin Callahan, and Alaina Waagner.

Alexandra Pringle and Faiza Khan.

And everyone else at Bloomsbury Publishing.

The Columbia University MFA in creative writing. In particular, Gary Shteyngart, David Ebershoff, Alan Ziegler, Binnie Kirshenbaum, Donald Antrim, Heidi Julavits, John Freeman, Bill Wadsworth, Clarence

Coo, Carlo Cattaneo Adorno, Alexandra Watson, Crystal Kim, and Olivia Ciacci.

Jon Elek, Kevin Cotter, Alice Lawson, Diya Kar Hazra, Karan Mahajan, Millie Hoskins, Rosalie Swedlin, Doreen Wilcox Little, Richard Gold, Jaclyn Danielak, Himanjali Sankar, Madeleine Feeny, Joe Thomas, Janet Aspey, Sumika Rajput, and Smit Zaveri.

The Vermont Studio Center.

My expanding family, which now includes Basus, Malwades, and McClearys.

My grandmother, Mai. And the memory of Appa, Mani, and Dadai.

Karna Basu, Shabnam Faruki, and Avaaz Austen Basu.

My parents, Kaushik and Alaka Basu, thank you for a home filled with laughter and books.

And for everything, my deepest gratitude to my husband, Mikey McCleary.

ABOUT THE AUTHOR

Diksha Basu is a writer and an occasional actor. Originally from New Delhi, India, she holds a BA in economics from Cornell University and an MFA in creative writing from Columbia University and now divides her time between New York City and Mumbai.

The employees of Thorndike Press hope you have enjoyed this Large Print book. All our Thorndike, Wheeler, and Kennebec Large Print titles are designed for easy reading, and all our books are made to last. Other Thorndike Press Large Print books are available at your library, through selected bookstores, or directly from us.

For information about titles, please call:
(800) 223-1244

or visit our website at:
gale.com/thorndike

To share your comments, please write:
Publisher
Thorndike Press
10 Water St., Suite 310
Waterville, ME 04901